★ IBPA Benjamin Franklin Awards: Best New Voice Children's/ Young Adult, Silver Medal

★ Readers Favorite Awards Children Preteen: Silver Medal Winner

"This fast-moving adventure—the beginning of a trilogy— is sure to appease mythology fans who are outgrowing Percy Jackson's antics and looking for darker, weightier storytelling. VERDICT: A great choice for middle school collections."

—*School Library Journal*

"Percy Jackson meets Norse mythology in this captivating and unique adventure."

—*Foreword Reviews* (4 stars out of 5)

"*The Red Sun: Legends of Orkney* by Alane Adams is a book that will take children on a roller coaster ride of adventure and fantasy where whimsical and menacing creatures and witches will enthrall readers."

—*Readers' Favorite* (5 stars out of 5)

"This novel may appeal to young readers who have enjoyed other 'chosen one' fantasy stories: It moves along at a speedy clip, and preteens will likely identify with Sam's anger and frustration with the world . . . it's a high fantasy tale that maintains a quick pace..."

—*Kirkus Reviews*

"*The Red Sun* is a roller coaster ride of adventure, Norse mythology, magic and mayhem. Between Sam facing awesome villains in the magical realm of Orkney to teachers turning into lizards, I had the best time doing the voiceover for the audiobook. Don't miss out on this terrific story!"

—Karan Brar, actor on Disney's *Jessie* and *Bunk'd*

# THE RAVEN GOD

The Legends of Orkney Series

Book 3

## ALANE ADAMS

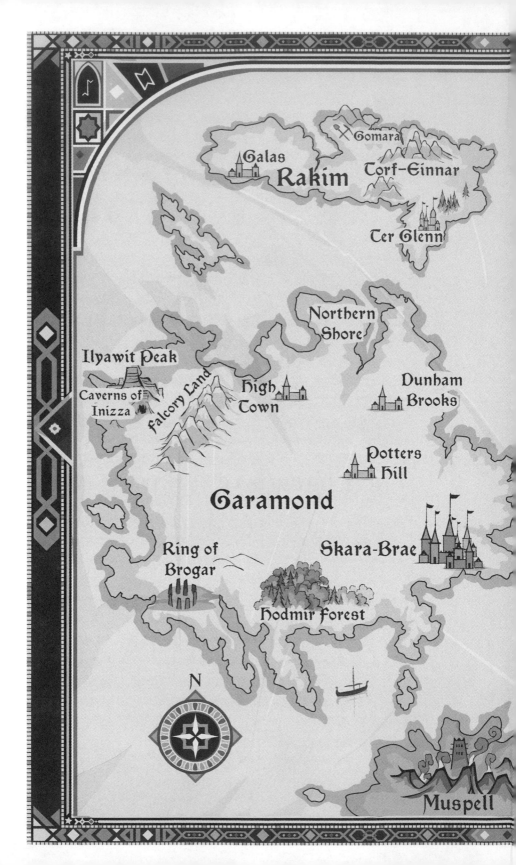

Asgard

Pantros

Jadewick

Tarkana Fortress

Balfour Island

Orkney

Published by SparkPress, a BookSparks imprint,
A division of SparkPoint Studio, LLC
Tempe, Arizona, USA, 85281
www.gosparkpress.com

Published 2017
Printed in the United States of America
ISBN: 978-1-943006-36-6 (pbk)
ISBN: 978-1-943006-37-3 (e-bk)
Library of Congress Control Number: 2017939148

Cover design © Jonathan Stroh
Illustrations by Jonathan Stroh
Interior design by Tabitha Lahr

For Henry, who finally discovered reading is fun!

# ANCIENT DAYS

❦

## Valhalla

*Hall of the Gods*

# Prologue

The haggard old woman knocked on the door to Frigga's chambers. The Annual Festival of Games was in full swing, with every god and goddess of Asgard crowding Valhalla with their boisterous shouts and boasts of greatness. The smell of roasting meat and sour ale filled the air in the stone hallway. Frigga, wife to Odin, called wearily for her to enter. The serving woman came in, carrying a bowl of steaming water in shaky hands.

"Put it on the table," Frigga commanded. Fiery red hair was coiled up on top of her head. There were fine lines etched around her eyes, but she was still a great beauty. She tightened the sash on the silken robe wrapped tightly about her regal form as she sat herself at her vanity. "These festivals tire me so. Thank you. You may leave."

The old woman hesitated, twisting gnarled hands together. "Your children are so beautiful, my lady. I saw them at the festival today. Thor, Hod, and that Baldur." Her words were tinged with awe.

Frigga glowed as she dipped a cloth in the water and dabbed at her face. "Yes, I am rather proud of them all."

The old servant crept closer. "I hear Baldur is invincible. Surely that cannot be!"

Frigga smiled, staring at her reflection in her mirror. "Yes, it is true. Not a living thing in any of the nine realms may harm Baldur."

"My word, not a living thing?" the servant crowed. "That is something! Not even the mushrooms?"

"Of course not," Frigga snapped, dabbing harder at her face. "Mushrooms can be quite poisonous."

"And the wild beasts with claws and fangs?"

Frigga picked up a brush, flicking it through her hair as she dismissed the comment. "Baldur is immune to them all. From the fish in the sea to the serpents in the grass to the deadly berries and hemlock on the vine."

The old woman clapped her hands with glee. "By the gods, so there is nothing that can harm the boy?"

The queen hesitated, then threw her brush down. "Nothing of consequence. Truth be told, I have not yet spoken to the mistletoe. But there is no danger in mistletoe. Leave me now, woman."

The servant backed away and shut the door. Outside in the hallway, her shoulders shook with laughter as her arms thickened and legs grew sturdier until Loki, God of Mischief, had shifted into his natural form.

"Let the games begin," he cackled softly.

The next morning, as the gods and goddesses assembled for the daily games, Loki huddled in the shadows watching and listening as Odin sat on his throne beside his beloved wife Frigga and patted her hand.

"We have done well, my love. Look at how our son is so loved." For everyone in the great hall found Baldur, son of Odin and Frigga, to be kind and strong and worthy. "But I am troubled by his dreams. He tells me he has foreseen his own death. Such a vision must be heeded."

Frigga just smiled serenely. "Fear not, husband. I have taken care of the matter."

Odin frowned. "What do you mean? What have you done, woman?"

She gave a small shrug of her shoulder. "I went to every living creature in all the nine realms and received a promise that none would harm our son."

Odin stared at her in disbelief then guffawed with laughter. "Truly, wife, you astound me."

She just smiled, her eyes glowing with pride as she watched the festival.

Odin clapped his hands. "Hear me, gods and goddesses of Asgard. I declare Baldur to be invincible. Let us see any one try and harm him. I will grant the challenger ten pieces of gold the size of my fist for a single scratch."

Baldur flashed his father a grin and planted his hands on his hips. "Aye, father, I welcome the challenge."

Up first was Baldur's big brother, Thor. The blond giant threw his mighty hammer, but the spinning weapon stopped an inch from Baldur's face and returned to Thor's hand, refusing to harm Baldur.

After Thor, the gods and goddesses lined up, each tossing their powers at the bold figure, who didn't even flinch at the barbs and weapons thrown at his head.

"This is boring," Loki muttered to himself. "Let's liven things up. Make them interesting." Moving through the crowd, he searched out Hod, Odin's youngest offspring. Hod stood in the corner, nursing a glass of mead, looking quite downcast.

"Dear boy, why so glum?" Loki said, slapping him on the back.

Hod's sightless eyes stared blankly at him. "Have you forgotten I'm blind? If I could see, I would get a lick in on my brother." Hod grinned wryly. "Odin knows he's tormented me enough over the years, always pinching me and running off. I wouldn't mind leaving my mark."

"No fear, my boy, Loki is here to help. Here," Loki pressed a thin branch in Hod's hands. "Follow me, and when I say swing, swing as hard as you can."

Hod laughed. "This switch will not do much to the mighty Baldur." But he grinned and put a hand on Loki's shoulder. "Still, I shall have fun. Lead on."

Loki made his way through the crowds, leading Hod until they stood just behind the golden-haired warrior.

"Baldur, turn around," Hod shouted.

The handsome Baldur turned with a grin as Loki faded back into the crowd. "What is it, little brother?"

"Just wanted to get my lick in," Hod said, and then as Loki called out "now!" he swung the branch at Baldur.

The warrior held up a hand, easily blocking the sprig of mistletoe.

There were roars of laughter. Hod joined in, not minding the teasing.

But Baldur stood frozen, staring at the tiny thorn embedded in his palm.

"What is it, brother?" Hod asked, cocking his head as his keen ears picked up on Baldur's moan of distress. "Do you not find this funny?"

"I . . . I feel weak," Baldur said, and he stumbled, falling to his knees.

Hod reached for his brother, grasping his shoulders. "Baldur, what is it?"

"I can't breathe," Baldur gasped, and then he collapsed.

Frigga pushed her way through the crowds. "What is it? What has happened?"

"Mother! I am sorry!" Hod cried. "I meant only to have some fun. I hit him with just this sprig."

He held up the mistletoe branch.

Frigga gasped, paling. "No! Hod, how could you?"

"What have I done?" The poor blind boy looked stricken.

And then Odin was there, laying a hand on Baldur's forehead. "Baldur, enough of this nonsense, you aren't even wounded."

But Baldur lay still. Vacant eyes stared up at the frescoed ceiling.

"He's dead," Odin whispered, shock etched into his brow.

"Who did this?" Frigga cried, grabbing Hod by the shoulders. "Who gave you that branch?"

"It was Loki. He meant only for me to have some fun."

"LOKI!" Odin leapt to his feet, his eyes blazing fire. "Come out, you sniveling worm."

Loki scurried away, but a battalion of Valkyrie wrestled him to the ground. They hauled him forward, kicking and screaming, "It's not my fault!" he shouted. "I was just having a bit of fun. How was I to know a tiny thorn would cause such harm?"

But Frigga pointed a finger over Baldur's still form. "It was you," she hissed. "You evil shape-shifter. You came into my chambers last night. That serving woman was the only one I told of the mistletoe."

Loki's guilt was written all over his face.

Odin's glare was cold enough to freeze even Loki's hard heart. "You killed my beloved son. For that, you will die." He drew the mighty sword at his side, the Sword of Tyrfing, and raised it over his head. He was about to bring it down on Loki when his wife shouted at him.

"Stop!"

Odin froze, the sword clutched over his head.

Frigga sobbed as she held Baldur to her chest. "Death will be too easy and quick for one as evil as Loki. He must be punished. Lock him up for eternity in the darkness of the underworld. Let him be tormented every day with the dripping of water on his chains. Let his children also be punished. Banish them to the farthest reaches of Asgard."

"No!" Loki screeched. "My children don't deserve such punishment."

"Your children are monsters," Frigga announced. "A menace on the world."

Odin slowly lowered his sword. "Wife, you are wise. It shall be as you say. The Valkyries will escort Loki to Sinmara's underworld and chain him there. I will see to securing Loki's horrible offspring myself. Frey, you will contain his wife, Angerboda, lest her wrath bring down the walls of Valhalla."

Frey, the sprightly God of the Elves, nodded, his round eyes full of sadness as he studied Baldur's still form. "I will take her to the black dwarves of Gomara. They will encase her in ice and bury her deep in their mines."

Odin looked at Loki, hatred and pain etched into his face. "I never want to see or hear from this traitor or any of his family members ever again. I curse him for eternity. Should he ever come in contact with mistletoe, let it bring him unending pain, but not death."

Loki wrestled against the tight grip of Thor and Tyr. "You will regret this, brother," he snarled. "One day, I will make you pay. You will lose the things you value the most, the same as you have made me lose those I love."

# ISLE OF MUSSPELL

## The Eighth Realm of Odin

*Present–Day Orkney*

# Chapter 1

The raven's wings beat the air with a fury and strength that belied its size. In its beak, it carried a tattered black triangle of skin. The ear of a once-mighty beast. A bolt of lightning split the sky, singeing the wing of the bird and knocking it spinning before it regained its speed. Next to it, a figure appeared, a falcon with golden eyes and sharp claws that reached for it, grabbing at the black bird with its talons. The raven tucked its wings, dropping like a stone. In a flash, the falcon was after it, letting out a high-pitched screech. Another winged being joined in the chase, a white swan bearing a gilded breastplate and a helmet of shining gold.

The two birds pinned the raven between them, flying in tandem and closing in on it. The falcon clawed at the scrap of skin, trying to snatch it. The raven tucked its beak, determinedly holding on. The sky shimmered ahead.

Not far now.

The swan butted the raven, trying to knock it off its path, but the raven struggled on. And then the air grew still as the raven broke through the shimmering veil. The air felt stuffed with cotton, all noise blotted out. The falcon let out a sharp cry of anguish as the raven released the tattered scrap of skin, letting it fall into the raging water of the seas below.

The swan tried to snatch it, but a sudden sharp breeze carried it out of reach, and the piece of flesh fluttered down into the water. A bright light lit up the sky for a moment, and then a puff of wind swept across the waves, wiping away the veil of cotton, bringing with it the smell of sulfur. In the distance, the skies were revealed a fiery red, lit up by the perpetual rumblings of the volcanoes that marked that land and heated the air.

The swan and the falcon chased after the raven with increased fury. Desperate to escape, the raven pecked at the eye of the swan, drawing blood and forcing it to move off. As the swan tumbled blindly, the falcon veered off, aiding the swan to a spire of rock jutting out of the depths of the ocean.

The raven continued on, not looking back, keeping its eyes on the growing red city in front of it.

The swan landed hard on the stone, transforming into a woman with flaxen hair tied into a thick braid. Around her wrists, she wore golden cuffs that matched her shining breastplate and helmet. An ornately carved sword hung at her side. The falcon shed its cloak of feathers and became a woman with ginger-red hair liberally laced with gray. On her head sat a crown of finest gold. Kneeling by the injured woman, she cradled her head in her arms.

"Dear Geela, are you all right?"

"Fine, my queen. The Valkyrie are made of iron." Climbing to her feet, Geela held a hand to her bleeding eye and asked, "Do you think we stopped him?"

Frigga, queen of the gods, wife to Odin, watched the fluttering black shape of the raven make its way toward the city of their enemy.

"No, Geela. I'm afraid we failed. When Odin's flesh

touched the sea, the veil protecting Orkney was torn." She sighed, and it was as if the world sighed with her. The waves rose and crashed against the rock, and a wail echoed from the depths of the ocean as the creatures of the deep joined her in her despair.

"What will Surt do when he finds out Odin is dead?" Geela asked, her blue eyes clouded with fear.

Surt ruled over the fire giants of the South in Musspell, the Eighth Realm of Odin. Since the dawn of time, the giants and the gods had warred over mankind. Odin had always been mankind's protector, and Surt had always stood ready to destroy them.

Frigga stared at the distant island of smoking volcanoes and replied, "He will go to war. Return to Valhalla and wait for me. There is something I must attend to."

Circling above the spires of the stone fortress, the raven settled on a window ledge, spent and out of breath. Its heart hammered in its chest, but it was a black heart, devoid of human emotion.

As the raven regained its strength, it reshaped its form. Wings lengthened out into arms. The bird's feet thickened and grew, sprouting knees and toes. Its beak flattened out and broadened into a face that broke into a smile as he looked down at his human shape.

Spitting out a black feather, Loki, God of Mischief, jumped down lightly. His feet were bare. Stocky legs stuck out through the tattered pants he had worn for centuries while chained to the rock in Odin's underground prison. Loki stood in a long open-air hallway marked by archways that led to a pair of double wooden doors reinforced with bars of steel.

The red sky outside was lit up by plumes of shooting lava. Heat emanated from the stone walls. Under his feet, a stinging burn rose up from the deep chasms of molten rock flowing underneath the floors. Skipping along to the barred entrance, Loki grabbed hold of the handles and ripped the doors off their hinges, hurling them to the side before springing into the chambers of the great lord of the South, Surt.

More than two dozen of the fire giants were assembled at a long table at the base of a throne. As one, they leapt to their feet, letting out angry roars, drawing swords, and surrounding Loki in a flurry of red flesh and muscled anger.

Pushing the tip of one sword away from his face, Loki called loudly, "Would you kill your guest before he delivered the best news of the century?"

"Let him through." The deep rumbly voice of Surt came from across the vast room.

Loki ducked between the legs of the warriors and made his way to the throne where Surt held court. The warlord had thick red skin, bumpy like that of an alligator, and a flat broad face. His nose was pierced with a gold ring. A thick black ponytail sprouted from the top of his head and was tied in a long braid down his back. His eyes were yellow, slanted upward slightly, and filled with curiosity and simmering rage. A pair of female she-giants lolled against him, stroking his arm. His stained fingernails were filed into razor-sharp points.

Loki was not a tall creature, but being near the giants made him appear like a waif. Climbing up onto a chair, Loki bowed at the waist.

"Greetings, my brother."

Surt snorted with laughter. "Brother, you say? I killed my brothers and threw their headless corpses into the fires of Musspell."

The volcanoes of the Eighth Realm spewed lava every day of the year. The hardened residents lived under clouds of ash that darkened the sky and searing heat that choked the life out of any living plants.

Loki grinned, undeterred by the raucous laughter of the giant men who crowded in closer. The points of their swords pricked his back.

He hadn't broken out of that underworld to be skewered by this lot—not before he'd regained everything he'd lost.

"Really, Surt, is all this sword rattling necessary? There is only one of me, and I'm quite harmless. Might we share a leg of lamb and drink to the glory of your victory?"

Surt's yellow eyes narrowed into slits. "I know who you are, Loki, God of Mischief. You cause only trouble. What victory do you speak of?"

Loki grabbed a helmet and pounded it once with his fist, flattening the metal so he could sit on it. Reaching across the table, he helped himself to a roasted leg of meat. As he was about to bite into it, Surt drew a blade and skewered the lamb in place in front of Loki.

"I asked you a question, mischief-maker. What victory?"

A slow grin raised his cheeks. "Why, your victory over mankind. The war you have wanted to wage since you drew your first squalling breath."

"Mankind is protected by that fool Odin. We have already had our Ragnarok, the war between the gods and the giants. No one came away a winner."

Loki leaned forward, pulling Surt's knife out and holding it up to the light. "But what if Odin were dead?" He looked Surt in the eye. "Would you go to war then?"

Surt stared at Loki, searching his eyes. The giant slammed his meaty palms on the table. "What proof do you bring me of this?"

Loki bit into the leg of lamb and waved it at Surt. "Can you not smell the sweetness of grass and fresh air in the wind? The veil has been taken down; you know, the one

Odin put in place to keep you lot here in this miserable pit of lava."

Surt drew back, waving Loki away. "Bah, you are full of lies and nonsense. I would know if the veil had been torn. Odin cannot be dead. The gods continue on like the sun. It sets and disappears from sight and then it rises again. Odin is not gone." He shook his head, folding his thick arms. "It is not possible."

Loki gnawed the meat down to the bone, licked his fingers, and tossed the skeletal piece back on the table, letting out a satisfied belch. "Suit yourself, my giant high lord. But don't blame me if you're late to the party."

The fire giant's eyes narrowed. "What do you mean?"

"I mean, with or without you, I am going to war. Orkney is ripe for the picking. No one's running the place. I say it's time for a change at the top."

"You're up to something. I can smell your lies."

Loki grinned. "Here's the truth: Odin took my wife and kids from me. I intend to get them back."

Surt leapt out of his chair, drawing a broad sword from his back—the flaming Sword of Bal. A blast of glowing fire shot from the blade as he wielded it over Loki's head. "Those evil spawn?" he roared. "I will split you in half before I let that happen."

Loki reached up and pinched Surt's cheeks. "Okay, gotta run, good talking to you." Then he shifted into his raven form, slipping through Surt's fingers and flapping his wings to take to the air. A twisting blade of fire from Surt's sword singed his tail feathers, but he flew higher and higher, up through the chimney and into the night sky.

As Loki flew through the ash and embers of the Musspell volcanoes, he couldn't stifle a grin. His beak opened wide. Finally, after centuries of waiting and plotting, his plan for revenge was in motion.

# Chapter 2

Gilded sunlight pierced the branches of the forest, spreading a dappled pattern on the mossy ground, but Sam had no time to enjoy the summer day. He was too busy running for his life. Bushes whipped at him as sweat poured down his face.

"Keep up," Keely chided at his side as she leapt fluidly over a log. "They're closing in."

Sam increased the pace, sending a blast of witchfire at a branch, bringing it down behind them to slow their pursuers. "They've got Leo and Howie," he huffed.

"We can save them," Keely said. "Just stay close."

Easier said than done. Now that Keely was part Eifalian, she could run like a deer. Her steps were light-footed and sure as she dodged low branches and tumbled rocks. Her bow was slung over her shoulder along with a quiver of arrows. Her white hair was a blur as she ran. Sam's heart pounded, his breath labored, but he grimly kept pace.

Shouts behind them let him know they'd been seen. The crashing of brush warned of their pursuers closing in. The low-pitched howl of a Shun Kara made the hair on the back of Sam's neck rise. With a slight turn of his head he saw the large black wolf loping off to the side, hemming them in. Its tongue lolled out of its mouth, exposing bone-rending fangs.

"I can see water," Keely said. Through the trees, Sam caught the blue shimmer of the lake.

"You're sure Howie and Leo are there?" he managed between breaths.

"Yes, I sense them." Keely's legs stretched even longer.

Sam had learned not to argue with Keely's new Eifalian senses. She was uncannily right.

Then he saw them.

The two boys were tied to a tree. Leo shouted a warning, but Sam was in too big of a hurry to save his friends. He broke into the clearing and took two more steps before a vine snapped up, tripping his feet and sending him flying.

Keely nimbly dodged the trap, but a blast of witchfire ripped a hole in the ground in front of her and she lost her footing. She fell facedown, sliding to a stop next to Sam. They sat up, spitting out bits of grass and mud to look up into the grinning faces of Perrin and Mavery.

"Gotcha," Mavery crowed.

Jey jumped out of the brush. "My trap worked!"

The Shun Kara placed a large paw on Sam's chest with a rumbling growl.

Perrin gave a sharp whistle, calling her pet to her. "Damarius. Come."

"Yeah, get lost, dog-breath," Sam said, shoving the shaggy head away. The oversized wolf trotted back to Perrin's side, and she ran her knuckles over his ears.

"No fair," Howie said as Leo untied them from the tree. "They were just about to free us."

"Sorry, losers, we win," Jey said smugly. "Never thought I'd like teaming up with a pair of witches, but these two aren't half bad."

He high-fived the little witchling. Perrin folded her arms and smirked.

Sam watched as Leo tackled Jey into the lake. Howie climbed on a rock and jumped in with an awkward cannonball. They splashed about in the shallows, taunting the rest until Keely shed her boots and waded in to her knees. Mavery went in, dress and all, floating lazily.

Only Perrin held back, leaning against a tree, Damarius at her feet. The Shun Kara had belonged to her mother. After her death, it had become her constant shadow.

Sam grinned. It was good to see them having fun. It had been a long time coming.

In the days following the defeat of the Volgrim witches, life had been filled with the task of rebuilding Orkney. Keely, Leo, and Howie didn't talk about going back to Pilot Rock, which was just as well because Sam's mom had shaken her head with a frown when asked if it was possible. Portals were tricky things, she explained. They opened when Orkney needed its heroes and disappeared when she was done with them. Skara Brae was home for now.

Howie and Keely made the best of it. Keely worked on her newly gained Eifalian magic, and Howie trained with the Orkadian Guard as Captain Teren's squire. Even Perrin was slowly warming up to being part of their circle of friends.

Only Leo seemed troubled, nagged by something he couldn't remember about his time in the underworld. He had confided in Sam that he had failed in his role as the Sacrifice, but, for the life of him, he couldn't remember how.

Guilt prickled Sam's skin. His friends were trapped here because he had killed Odin. That was the problem. While Sam had been locked in a battle with his darker side, he'd let Catriona influence him to take the deadliest of actions. With a single plunge of his enchanted blade, Odin, the mighty god who held the very essence of life in him, was gone.

Above the clearing, a falcon let out a piercing shriek. Covering his eyes from the bright sun, Sam tried to spot it in the cloudless sky. It was probably Lingas. The annoying bird was always following them. A dark blob circled overhead.

*Hmm, that's too large to be Howie's iolar*, Sam thought. Curious to see what the bird of prey was after, he watched as it dropped like a bullet out of the sky. It was aiming straight for him.

Stunned, Sam didn't have time to move before talons raked at his face, clawing to get at him.

"Hey, get off me. What's your problem?" Flinging his hands out, he shouted, "*Testera ventimus*," and blew the falcon back, tumbling it against a tree with a sharp wind.

The bird hit the trunk and slumped to the ground, and then it shimmered before turning into the shape of a woman. She was old, but regal. Once-red hair was liberally streaked with gray. Her head was topped by a crown of gold. She wore a gown of heavy white silk tied at the waist with a golden cord.

Perrin swiftly moved to Sam's side, Damarius snarling and crouched, ready to pounce at her signal. The others splashed out of the water to form a semicircle.

"What do you want?" Sam demanded.

The woman drew herself up tall as she strode three steps forward to stand in front of Sam, planting large hands on her ample hips before stating in a voice thick with contempt, "I am the goddess Frigga, witch-boy. Wife of Odin. You killed my husband. For that you will die."

The queen of the gods drew a golden dagger from her side. The hasp was encrusted with fiery jewels. The long, pointed blade glinted in the sunlight as she advanced on him. "I intend to carve your heart out and then mount it on a stake outside my window so that every day the crows might feed on it and I might remember the vengeance I executed on his behalf."

"Over my dead body," Perrin said, stepping in front of Sam. Damarius snapped at the air as she drew a ball of witchfire over her hand.

"Mine, too," Mavery hissed, holding a matching ball of witchfire.

"And mine," Keely said, notching an arrow in her bow.

"Mine," Jey said, flashing his hunting knife.

"Mine as well." Leo stood at Jey's side, his own blade in hand.

"What they said," Howie added, curling his hands into fists.

Sam held a hand out to quiet his friends. "Look, I'm sorry. If I could take it back I would. I loved Odin."

Frigga grabbed him by the shirt, placing the knife to his throat, ignoring the others as she spat out, "And yet you betrayed him."

Guilt lanced his heart as if she had stuck him with the knife. His shoulders sagged. "I know. I would do anything to undo it. I still can't believe he's really gone." He raised his eyes to hers, not flinching as he said, "So go ahead. End my life. I won't blame you."

"Sam!" Keely punched his arm. "Don't be ridiculous. Odin was a god. He should have stopped you."

"Yeah," Perrin added, stepping closer to the queen. "Why didn't he do anything about that enchanted blade?"

Frigga ignored them. She pressed the blade harder against Sam's throat, and he waited for her to remove his head. Part of him wanted her to, just to get rid of this guilt he carried.

Her brows drew together as she studied him. And then slowly she lowered her blade. "You humans are curious beings. You profess your guilt, but I see no malice in you."

Frigga sheathed her dagger and crossed her arms. Her golden eyes flashed with sparks of amber. "You said you would do anything to bring my husband back. Did you mean that? Or are they just words?"

Sam nodded. "I meant it. I would do anything."

The queen stared at each of them, weighing them, and then she came to a decision. "Very well. You will have a chance at redemption. There is little time, and you will likely perish, but there may yet be a way to bring Odin back."

Hope surged in Sam. "How? Tell me what to do."

Frigga paced the clearing, one hand to her chin as she said, "What's left of Odin's soul will be in the underworld. I would go myself, but entry by the gods is forbidden. But you, witch-boy, you can get into that dark place and find him."

Howie slapped Sam on the shoulder. "Count me in. I've wanted to go to that dump since Leo said it was such a hunky-dory place."

"Yeah, we've had a run-in with Sinmara before," Sam said with an excited grin. "The entrance to Nifelheim is on the island of Pantros. If Odin's there, we'll get him back."

His confidence faltered at her harsh laughter.

"You think a fool like Sinmara can hold someone as powerful as Odin?" Frigga looked down her nose at Sam and his friends. "Nifelheim is a playground compared to Helheim."

"Where?" Sam asked.

"Helheim. The underworld of the gods. It's overseen by Helva, the Goddess of Death." She spat the name out like it was poison.

Frigga resumed her pacing. "Helva won't risk keeping my husband's soul in her catacombs. She will send it into the void, and Odin will be lost forever." She whirled on them, raising her dagger over her head as she announced, "Hear me, Son of Odin. Bring my husband home to Valhalla before the rising of the new moon, or you and all your friends will face judgment in front of the Gods' High Council."

Shock made Sam weak in the knees. "Valhalla? Where's that?"

Frigga glared at him. "Asgard, you fool. Do you know nothing of the gods?"

Sam's temper rose. "I know Asgard was destroyed when Odin died."

Frigga snorted, waving one hand. "Asgard is like a house with many rooms. That island was just one piece of it, Odin's private retreat. The gods reside in the golden city of Valhalla. You must cross the Bifrost bridge to reach it. Only those worthy can pass the gatekeeper."

"How do we find that?" Keely asked.

Frigga wrapped her cloak around her. "Look to the sky. When you see a rainbow that doesn't fade with daylight, head toward it and hope that the gatekeeper, Hemidall, doesn't kill you." She shimmered as her form began to shift back into a falcon.

Sam stepped forward, pleading, "Frigga, please tell us where to start. How do we find Helva?"

"You are a Son of Odin. Find a way or face your execution. All of you." With a flash of light, she became the winged bird again. She sprang with taloned feet into the air, grazing Sam's face with her beak, leaving a long, thin cut that stung.

They watched in awe as the falcon gained in altitude. Sam strained his eyes so as not to lose sight of the majestic bird. Frigga was flying to the west. If she was heading back to Valhalla, it would give them a direction. It was all they had to go on.

"Well, I must say this is a lot of trouble to be in, even for you." Perrin raised one dark eyebrow at him. Damarius woofed softly, looking at her like he agreed Sam was nuts. "Find Odin in some dark underworld or face the judgment of the gods? Bravo, brother. How do you always find yourself in so much trouble?"

"Just a gift I have. So, what do you guys think?"

"I think when you fail to save Odin, Frigga's going to skewer our guts," Jey said bluntly.

Keely elbowed the Falcory. "I think she's given us a plan," she said quietly. "A way to go forward. There must be hope if she has asked you to bring Odin back."

Sam rubbed his hands together. "Right. Finding Valhalla should be a piece of cake compared to finding Helheim. Any idea where to start?" He looked at Perrin. She had the most experience with Orkney magic.

She shook her head. "Sorry, my mother never mentioned it."

Keely nibbled on one finger as she thought it over. "I could find Mimir and drink from his well? It worked last time when I cut off my hair to see Sam's fate."

"No one knows how to find Mimir unless he wants to be found," Sam said. "It could take weeks to locate him. There has to be another way."

"I know how to find Helva," a voice piped up. They turned to see Mavery twirling her skirts as she danced in a circle. "Jasper told me a story about the Goddess of Death once. But I don't think you're gonna like it.

Perrin looked at Sam. "Who's Jasper?"

"An old sea captain that plucked this pest out of the ocean. He's a Son of Aegir, the sea god. Spill it, imp; don't keep us waiting."

They sat down on the ground and waited for Mavery to tell the story. She hopped from foot to foot as she chewed her lower lip, remembering.

"In the days of the gods, Loki, God of Mischief, had three children with his wife, Angerboda. One day, Loki played a trick on Odin's son Baldur to prove he wasn't invincible, and Baldur died. Odin was so mad he banished Loki and his family forever. His oldest son, Fenrir, is a giant wolf with claws that can rip a man in half with one swipe. Odin sent

Fenrir to Groll, a rock in the middle of the ocean, and tied him up with a chain that couldn't be broken no matter how hard Fenrir pulled. But his brother was even worse."

"Who was his brother?" Keely asked.

Mavery's eyes shone as she waved her hands in the air. "Jormungand, the biggest, horriblest sea monster you ever saw. A snake as long as the world and as wide as the ocean. Teeth like needles and red eyes you can see from a mile away. He's locked up in an underwater prison with bars so thick he can't gnaw through them. Fenrir holds the key to unlocking his cell in the collar around his neck."

"Why would anyone want to open it and let him out?" Leo asked.

"Because Jormungand has the only map to Helva's underworld. It's scratched into the wall in the back of his cell."

"Great," Sam said. "And what's Helva, a two-headed wild beast with fangs and claws?"

"Worse, Helva is half-corpse, half-human, and completely evil." Mavery curtsied as her story ended. "So, who's up for an adventure?"

Before any of them could answer, a blood-curdling screech sounded overhead. Sam looked up as a giant winged creature flew past, larger than an Omera and shimmering with red and orange scales. Its head was square and feline, with long white teeth curving down over its jaw, like a saber-toothed tiger. On its back sat a massive man, his skin a similar red. A long black ponytail sprouted from the top of his head. His chest was strapped with leather coverings and a breastplate of studded metal with sharp points. He drew back on a large bow and unleashed a flaming arrow at them. Sam rolled aside as the fiery shaft struck the ground next to him.

# Chapter 3

News of the attack spread quickly. Captain Teren greeted them at the gates as Howie gingerly carried the still-flaming arrow inside. The stalwart Orkadian soldier looked frightened. His face was pale under his sheaf of thick blond hair. "High Council chambers, now," Teren ordered. The gate was closed and sealed firmly behind them.

They crowded into the meeting room. Perrin had to order Damarius to stay outside three times. The Shun Kara hated being parted from her, but his fearsome size tended to intimidate even the most battle-worn Orkadians.

Inside the meeting room, Orkadian banners hung from the wall made of red silk with the white heron emblazoned on the front. A pair of chandeliers held burning candles that cast a warm glow over the room.

Sam's mom, Abigail, sat at the head of the table claiming her place as Chief High Council. The pesky dwarf, Rego, sat on her left rubbing his whiskered chin worriedly. To Abigail's right sat Leyes, the newly appointed Eifalian representative. With Gael now king, his young cousin had taken his place on the council. Leyes had long white hair he left loose, and he wore the aqua green robes favored by the Eifalians.

Next to him sat Beo. A row of dangling iolar feathers hung from his ear lobes. The Falcory's face looked grim as he eyed the still-flaming arrow Howie carried into the room.

"Quickly, put it on the table," Abigail said.

Howie set it down and she leaned forward, murmuring a spell. With a wave of her hand, the arrow finally went out. It lay there, glowing red and smoldering.

"Anyone care to explain the meaning of this?" she asked.

"Only one army has fire like this," Beo said. He sniffed at the smell of sulfur rising from the ashes. "The Eldjotnar. An army of fire giants to the south. Their arrows are dipped in the molten lava of Musspell. Surt is said to own a flaming sword named Bal. With it he could burn an entire village and hardly trouble himself."

There were gasps and groans from around the room.

"Who are they?" Sam whispered to Perrin.

"The fire giants are ruled by the warrior god, Surt," she whispered in his ear. "They are the enemy of mankind. Odin's protection kept them at bay, but somebody killed him," she pointed out.

Sam ignored her dig, gulping back his fear as Captain Teren said, "We have always known that Surt was a threat, but he has never made a move against us before. Why now?"

Leyes waved a hand, releasing a cloud of fog across the table. "Captain, surely the veil has been torn?"

They watched as an image of a long-ago Odin appeared, standing on the shores of Orkney and sealing off their world from the fiery mountains of the South.

Abigail sighed heavily. "You think Odin's passing has made it possible for Surt to advance?"

Leyes nodded over steepled fingers. "So it would seem."

Rego snorted, jumping up on his stubby legs. "Then we stop him. I'll take our best men and ride out to meet his army."

Beo laughed harshly. "Dwarf, you speak a death sentence

for those men. The fire giants are fiercer than any warrior alive. It would take a hundred times the forces we have at hand to defeat them, and, even then, I'm not sure we would win."

"What do we do, then? Wait until they march on Skara Brae and burn it to the ground?" Rego thundered. "I say we fight."

"Take heed, Rego," Abigail murmured. "We must not act in haste. We do not have the power to defeat Surt. Today was just a survey party. They will need to amass their weapons and move them into position. We have time yet to plan."

"What are you thinking, my lady?" Captain Teren asked.

"We will need powerful magic to fight them. Perhaps if I speak with Hestera, convince her to join with us. A coven of witches will do much toward balancing the power."

Teren drummed his fingers on the table. "Even if every last witch joined us, it wouldn't be enough to defeat Surt—"

Before he could finish the sentence, the door to the chambers banged open. A hunched man shuffled in wearing a hooded cloak. A cold wind blew in with him, snuffing out most of the candles.

The room went silent.

Captain Teren rose, one hand to his sword. "Excuse us, sir, this is a private meeting."

The man ignored him, hobbling forward in the dim light until he was at the head of the table. Then with a flourish he threw back the hood and grinned at them.

"Isn't this a lovely sight," he said.

Sam frowned. For some reason, his skin crawled with dread. The man was stocky, not too tall, with a broad face and a wide grin. Bushy eyebrows made him look almost feral, and his deep-set eyes glittered with a potent evil.

Abigail rose, sniffing at the air. "Who are you? I sense powerful magic."

The intruder raised innocent hands. "Who, me? I was just looking for the kitchens. I always did like the kidney pies here."

Leo shoved past Sam. "I know you. You're the one that hit me on the head with that rock in the underworld."

The man's eyes narrowed into slits of evil. Then he grinned, spreading his hands. "You caught me. Loki's the name; mischief's my game. Hear me, oh, wise council of Orkney. Enjoy your last days of peace. Surt's army of angry fire giants will soon be marching down your throats."

"You did this," Abigail breathed. "You went to Surt." She raised her hand, and a blue ball of witchfire sprang up, but before she could throw it he snapped his fingers and the fire sputtered out.

"Take a seat, deary." Abigail was slammed into her seat with some invisible force.

Magic boiled under Sam's skin. He was ready to blast this mischief-maker into the next world, but his mother silently shook her head at him.

Loki strutted around the table. "I might have stirred the pot, but Surt would have figured it out soon enough." He scanned the room, eyeing the banners and the shields mounted on the walls. "I just wanted to see the old place one last time before he burns it to the ground."

He stopped in front of Sam, who had to ask, "Why are you doing this?"

Loki leaned in and sniffed Sam's scent, and then his eyes lit up. "You're the Son of Odin that took his life. I should give you a medal. Why, you ask? Do you know what Odin did to me? What he did to my wife and children?"

"Your children are horrible beasts," Keely said fiercely. "They deserve to be chained up."

Loki flung his hand out, and, with a snap of his fingers, Keely went flying backward. She crashed into the wall with a thud. "My children will rule this world on the ashes of your bones."

Leo and Jey rushed to Keely's side to help her up. She looked shaken but unhurt.

"You've been warned," Loki continued, pointing a finger at all of them. "Now that your precious Odin is dead, you don't have a prayer. Surt will burn your cities and cut you down like paper dolls."

There was shocked silence, and then Captain Teren stepped forward. "Surt will not defeat us. We have friends. Allies. They will join us. We stand united."

Loki laughed bitterly. "United? There's a joke. The witches hate you. The Balfins are all but destroyed. The Falcory, well, don't get me started; they're weak, clinging to their old ways. The Vanir need only the slightest push to unleash their bloodthirst for war on the Eifalians. Who does that leave? You lot. Well, sorry, you don't scare me. And, speaking of those frosty Vanir, it's time they were reminded of their hatred for the Eifalians. Ta-ta!"

As a group of Orkadian soldiers burst into the room, closely followed by Damarius howling with rage, Loki transformed into a raven, scattering feathers everywhere before he flew up the chimney.

Sam was the first to speak in the silence. "Did you hear that? Loki's going to trick the Vanir into starting a war with the Eifalians."

Perrin looped her arms around Damarius as Keely limped back to the table. "The Vanir will keep to their treaty. I know their king, Joran. He is an honorable man."

But Leyes slammed two hands down on the table, shouting, "The Vanir have no honor! Look how they executed our king because of a thousand-year-old hatred." He stood abruptly. "I must warn my people. I will leave for Torf-Einnar immediately. I'm sorry I cannot stay and help in this fight."

"What if I go to Rakim and talk to Joran?" Keely said. "I know he'll listen to me."

There was silence as the council digested that, and then Leo stepped forward. "Keely's right," he said. "She has the best chance of reaching the king of the Vanir. I'll go with her," he added, his voice thick with guilt. "This is my fault. I freed Loki."

Jey jumped into it. "If Leo's going, I'm going. Keely will need a lot of protecting."

Abigail shook her head. "Thank you, Jey, but I think your father might need you here. Beo, what say you?"

The dangling feathers in Beo's ears swayed as he shook his head. "The frost giants have always stood in brotherhood with the fire giants. Between them they can take Orkney apart. If the girl believes she can convince the Vanir to join with us, I'm for it. Until then, our biggest threat is Surt's army of boercats, the flying red beasts he rides on. I have an idea. There is an ancient mountain of stone to the east of the Falcory lands, the Caverns of Inizza. They are said to be the birthplace of the ancient Safyre Omeras."

Abigail's hand fluttered to her throat. "Surely those horrid beasts are long dead?"

"Not dead. Sleeping. Catriona awoke one in her battle with your son. In recent days, we have seen signs, strange burn marks on the stones, and our hunting grounds have been disturbed. There are whispers in the sands that when the beast was called, its mate was also awoken."

"It might give us an edge," Abigail said quietly, looking to Teren. "One we desperately need."

The captain slowly nodded his agreement. He looked tired, weary to the bone, and Sam couldn't blame him. He had just led the Orkadian army through a difficult battle with the witches, and now this.

"Let me go with you, father," Jey said eagerly. "I will help you find this Safyre Omera and bring it to heel like a dog."

Beo shook his head, his dark eyes unflinching. "Hunting this beast will be the most dangerous thing the Falcory have undertaken. You will stay here in Skara Brae and await my return. That is my final word."

Jey scowled and folded his arms.

Teren stood. "Then we're agreed. There is no time to waste. The tides will be in our favor this afternoon to sail to Rakim. Galatin, you will escort Keely and Leo on their journey."

The young Orkadian soldier nodded. Galatin had traveled with Keely to the North once before. "Aye, Teren, I know my way around there. Didn't lose my head last time." He winked at Keely.

Abigail also rose. "My friends, once again we face an enemy greater than any we have faced before. We must stand together, or we will lose. May Odin's fortunes smile upon you on your journeys."

# Chapter 4

As the room emptied, Sam grabbed Keely's arm and pulled her aside. "I'm going after Odin. He's the only one who can fix this. Don't say anything to my mom or she'll have me locked in the dungeon."

"Just be careful. Helva is one of Loki's offspring. I don't need Eifalian senses to tell me there's something strange going on here."

Sam nodded. A prickly premonition ran up his spine that this was going to end badly.

At midday, they stood on the dock preparing to say goodbye. Sam had sent out a call to an Omera to fly his mother to Balfour Island. It hadn't taken long for one to circle overhead.

The Orkadians eyed the jet-black creature warily as it perched on a piling, sunning itself in the sun. The scratch of its talons across the wood made everyone keep a safe distance. Even the rustle of its wings was enough to make Teren go pale. Only Sam had greeted it with a hug and a long nose rub.

Howie looped his arms around Keely. "I wish I could go with you, but the captain would be lost without me."

Jey jostled him aside, sweeping her into a hug. "Are you sure you don't want me to come? A Falcory brave at your side would be much smarter than this lowly Umatilla."

Keely rolled her eyes as Jey slapped Leo hard on the back. "May the winds be behind you so Keely doesn't smell how bad you stink."

Abigail came over to wrap Sam in a warm embrace. "Stay out of trouble," she said sternly.

Sam grinned innocently. "Who, me?"

Her eyes narrowed. "You're hiding something. What is it?"

Trust his mother's witch instincts to see right through him. He looked down, scuffing at the wooden plank, and then crossed his fingers behind his back, hoping a half-truth would help. "I'm just, you know, a little jealous Leo's going, and I'm stuck here."

His mom rolled her eyes. "Teenagers." But it did the trick. She climbed up on top of the Omera. As it launched into the air, she called out to Rego, "Keep watch over him. He's up to something."

"Aye, my lady, he usually is." Rego came up behind Sam and gripped his shoulder tight enough to make him wince. "Wanna tell me what it is, lad? Or should I just wait for you to get into hot water before I wring your neck?"

Sam plucked Rego's hand off and stepped back, shrugging innocently. "No idea what you're talking about."

They made their way up from the docks into the square in front of the Great Hall. The marketplace bustled with carts. Sam's stomach rumbled at the smell of roasted meat kabobs. He could do with a snack before he hatched his plan to rescue Odin. A shimmer of green caught his eye. A small figure dragging its knuckles on the ground scurried under a cart.

Rego started listing all of Sam's chores, but Sam hardly

heard him, too busy puzzling out what he'd just seen. Because it had looked an awful lot like Fetch, Odin's little green servant who had annoyed Sam on Asgard when he'd first met Odin.

Sam elbowed Howie. "Distract Rego. There's someone I need to see. Meet me in the stables after supper."

Howie grabbed Rego's arm and said the one thing sure to get the dwarf's attention. "Hey, I'm worried about Lingas. She didn't want to go hunting this morning. She hasn't eaten all day."

"Not hungry? She might be sick. Why didn't you tell me?" The dwarf scurried away to the barn where Lingas had her perch. Howie flashed Sam a thumbs-up as Sam shoved his way forward, moving between the carts and searching for the flash of green. The scamp had rolled under a cart selling pickled vegetables and dried gourds. Sam peered under the wheels, drawing a glare from the woman tending the cart.

"Did you steal my pickle jar?" she blustered, her face red.

"No, ma'am, I'm just looking for a friend."

She shooed him away, flapping her apron at him. Behind her, a flash of green caught his eye, moving toward a side alley.

Sam pushed his way through the crowd and burst out into the narrow alley. An empty jar lay on the ground in a pool of spilled pickle juice. At the end, he made out the outline of Fetch's forlorn shape dragging itself around the corner.

"Fetch, wait up!" he called, breaking into a run.

He turned the corner and . . . tripped over the spindly green leg that was sticking out. Sam went flying, scuffing his palms on the rough stones. Winded, he caught his breath before rolling over and looking up into the large almond-shaped eyes of Fetch.

For once the furry green pest wasn't laughing at Sam's folly. The creature's normally placid face was drawn into a scowl. From behind him, the bushy red head of the squirrel Ratatosk appeared.

"Traitor!" the squirrel barked. "How could you hurt the boss?" Ratatosk ran up Sam's leg all the way to his shoulder and started pounding on Sam's head with his little fists.

"Hey, knock it off!" Sam grabbed the squirrel by the nape of its neck and held it away a safe distance.

Odin's minions glared at Sam like he was a—well, a murderous traitor.

"I ought to chew your ears off," Ratatosk threatened, shaking a tiny fist at him. "The boss was your friend."

Great, like he didn't feel bad enough, he had a squirrel rubbing his face in the biggest mistake of his life. "I know, I'm sorry. What are you guys doing here?" Sam carefully set the squirrel on the ground.

Fetch stepped forward, but Ratatosk jumped in front of the green creature. "Don't give it to him," the squirrel said. "I don't trust him."

Sam's pulse quickened. "Give me what?"

Fetch cleared his throat, pushing the squirrel to the side. "A gift have I, to deliver to you, in the case of . . . upon . . . that is . . . rather . . . as has happened . . . the demise," his voice broke a bit as he went on, "of his Highest." He fumbled with something in his furred hands, but Ratatosk was a blur and snatched the tiny object from him.

"How can you trust him after what he did to the boss?" the squirrel demanded.

"Easy, Ratatosk," Fetch said softly, prying the little wooden object away. "Trust him or not, Odin's orders must be obeyed."

He handed Sam a tiny wooden ship that fit in the palm of his hand. It was beautiful, carved with fine details, complete with rigging and a rudder.

"Did you carve this?" Sam asked, holding it up to his eye so he could look into the little cabin. He ran a finger over the smooth face of the sails.

Fetch blinked guiltily. "I, er, borrowed it from someone. Odin said if anything were to happen to him, we were to help. I believe this will assist you in your journey. We must be getting back now." He began backing away.

"Hey, not so fast!" Sam said. "What do I do with this?"

Fetch continued to move away, ears drooping as he nervously twisted his fingers. "This is Skidbladnir. It will take you where you need to go. Please," his voice broke, "bring him back." Then Fetch turned the corner with the squirrel still shaking its fist in disgust at him. Sam ran after them, but the pair had disappeared.

Sam was left holding the boat, rubbing the polished wood with a frown.

# Chapter 5

Loki flew north, ignoring his fatigue and reveling in his freedom. After eons locked in a dank underground prison, he savored the sun on his face, the wind under his wings, blood coursing through his veins. In his raven form, he could travel faster and pass unseen by most.

The frost giants to the north, brothers to Surt and his kind, would not fall into alliance with the fire giants so easily. They had grown soft over the centuries. They would need to be properly motivated, reminded of their hatred of their Eifalian neighbors to the south. When Loki was done with his plan for revenge, Odin's precious Orkney would be nothing but rubble.

Circling above the Vanirian kingdom of Rakim, Loki searched out their capital city. Galas was built into the sea-wall and surrounded by a high stone wall, though few would be foolish enough to attack the bloodthirsty Vanir. Purple banners flapped in the breeze. The day was sunny, but the northern air carried a bite.

Loki landed on the rooftop of the palace. Preening his feathers, he shook them out, shrinking down in size and changing colors to a brilliant blue. He chirped once, testing his new voice, then fluttered down to a window where the sound of children's laughter escaped. Alighting on the ledge, he trilled sweetly, getting the attention of the two children playing inside.

"Papa, look, it's a mockingbird," the older child, a boy of about eight, said.

Loki chirped, bobbing his head at the boy who ran to the window. His father, king of the Vanir and a giant of a man, Joran, came up behind him and put his hand on the boy's shoulder.

"Be careful, Kaleb, the bird may bite."

The boy looked up at his father with shining eyes. "Don't be silly, Papa. Birds can't bite."

Kaleb put his finger out, and Loki hopped onto it to the delight of the boy. Loki tilted his head back and sang a little song. The young girl crept closer, slipping her hand in her father's.

"Can we keep him?" she asked shyly, reaching up to touch the bird. Loki ruffled out his feathers, rubbing his head along her finger.

Joran laughed. "Sweet Madilyn, would you tame a lion and take away his roar? If you cage a bird, you take away its song. Birds must be left to fly free. If it chooses to return, it honors you with its company."

Reluctantly Kaleb held up his finger, and Loki took flight, smiling slyly as he flew off. Soon the boy would follow him wherever he chose.

The next day, Loki sat in a tree above where the children were having a picnic under the watchful eye of a nanny. He trilled a merry song.

The boy's brown head came up. He dropped the ball he was playing with and walked over to the tree.

"Hello, little bird," Kaleb called up.

Loki hopped down to a lower branch and let the boy

stroke his feathers. He reached for Loki, but Loki took flight, landing on a tree farther down the path.

Kaleb ran after him. His nanny called out, minding him not to wander off, but she was distracted with the girl.

Loki flitted from tree to tree, calling to the boy, letting him get close before taking flight. Before long, they were deep into the forest. The brush grew thicker, the sounds of the palace muffled by the dense woods and the thick moss that hung from the branches. Trees towered overhead on massive ironwood trunks. Finally, Kaleb stopped and turned around, realizing he was surrounded by endless forest.

"Nanna?" he called, standing still and cocking his head to listen. Loki flew behind a tree and let himself shift into human form.

Coming around the trunk, he appeared dressed in a heavy gray cloak. The hood was pulled over his head, hiding his face.

"Nanna, there you are," the boy said with relief, running toward the cloaked figure.

Loki held out his hand, gripping the boy's fingers and silently leading him away.

"I followed the bird, Nanna, did you see? It called to me." The boy babbled on, telling Loki all about his inane thoughts. "I had a brother once. He got lost in the snow. I won't get lost, will I, Nanna?" Joran's son stopped and looked up at him.

"Nanna, why don't you speak? You're so quiet." His voice sounded hesitant. A thick snowflake landed on his cheek, quickly melting. Looking up, the boy eyed the sky through the trees. Gray clouds had moved in, and snow drifted down in large clumps. The temperature dropped the same time the boy shivered.

He tugged on Loki's arm. "Please, Nanna, say something. I'm scared."

Loki threw his hood back, revealing himself.

Kaleb drew back in fear.

"You—you're not my Nanna. Who are you?"

"I am Leyes of the Eifalians, and I am going to kill you," Loki said. He had made his hair appear long and white and his oversized eyes the aqua blue of the young Eifalian delegate.

The boy didn't cower. Befitting the son of a king, he kicked Loki hard in the shin and then turned and ran, darting like a deer through the trees. Loki let him go, nursing his bruise, and then laughed loud and long, letting himself transform back into his own physical form.

Fear coiled in Joran's gut, clawing at his heart, leaving him sick to his stomach. He couldn't lose his son. Not again. It was like déjà vu, the sense of horror when the nanny had come running into the council meeting and burst into tears. He had nearly killed the frantic woman on the spot for taking her eyes off Kaleb.

His wife, Reesa, had calmed him, quietly reminding him that finding Kaleb was more important. Joran had his entire army searching the woods. The faint footprints had been quickly covered by the thin layer of falling snow. They spread out, calling the boy's name, walking shoulder to shoulder so as not to miss a tree or hollow the boy might have hidden in.

His firstborn son, Jorri, had been lost in a storm. The memory filled him with such torment he nearly cried out. A shout from one of his men had him crashing through the woods. There, in a clearing, stood Kaleb, out of breath, tears streaming down his cheeks. He ran and threw his arms around Joran's legs.

"I'm sorry, Papa. I followed the bird."

"It's okay, Kaleb." Relief flooded Joran. He lifted his son, holding him close. Taking the horn from his side, he let out three loud blasts to let his wife know the boy was safe.

He cupped his hand to his son's cheek. "Don't ever scare me like that again. How did you come to follow a bird so far?"

"It was so pretty. And then when I was scared, my Nanna was there, only she wasn't Nanna, and when I asked her who she was, she took off her hood and her hair was white."

Joran turned to stone as his men pushed in closer. Every man knew what that meant.

Eifalians.

"What did she say?" he asked quietly, not wanting to scare the boy.

"She wasn't a she," Kaleb corrected. "He said his name was Leyes of the 'falians and that he was going to kill me."

Angry murmurs and rumbles came from Joran's men. The Eifalians had been their sworn enemies, ever since the dawn of Orkney when they had been brought into the Ninth Realm and made their home to the south of Rakim and named it Torf-Einnar.

The only thing that kept them from going to war was a blood treaty signed generations ago. This treaty had been broken once in the last year, when the Eifalian king, Einolach, had followed a young girl and her companions into Rakim. Einolach had sacrificed himself to restore the treaty. Were the Eifalians getting their due back?

"I kicked him hard, like this." Kaleb showed Joran how he kicked the man. "And then I ran. Did I do good, Papa?"

Joran smiled, his eyes moist with tears as he brushed the boy's hair from his face. "Yes, my son, you did very well. You will make a great warrior someday."

Looking over his son's head at his men, he jerked his chin at the woods. They spread out. He didn't expect them to find the filthy Eifalian, but if he was still in the area, they would catch him.

And tear him in half.

# Chapter 6

The stables were quiet as Sam made his way up the ladder to the loft. He had spent the afternoon dodging Rego and his long list of chores, and puzzling over the strange little carving Fetch had given him. Perrin and Mavery perched on a bale of hay. Damarius lay sprawled, paws in the air as he scratched his back on the rough boards. Jey slouched against a post. Howie swung his legs from atop a stack of crates, chewing on a piece of straw. Lingas sat on her perch, eyes closed as she snored softly.

"What's the plan?" Jey said, straightening. "Whatever it is, I'm in," he added, rolling his shoulders to flex his muscles.

"Me too," Howie said, jumping down to stand next to Jey. "Look, I get that we're not powerful witches," he waggled his fingers. "But we aren't going to just sit around and let you have all the fun. We're going with you after this Helva zombie."

Sam hesitated, knowing his next words were going to disappoint his best friend. "You can't come."

Howie's face fell. "Why not? Sam, you're not leaving me behind again. We need an epic adventure together!"

"We're coming, like it or not," Jey added, his cheeks flushed with anger.

"Look, I'd love for you both to come," Sam said, taking a step away to run his hand through his hair. "Believe me, I've thought about it all day, but Captain Teren needs Howie here. If Skara Brae falls, everything falls."

Howie slumped, but he nodded. "I get it. I am the Great Protector after all."

"Why do I have to stay?" Jey asked angrily. "I am a Falcory warrior. I can fight my way into the underworld better than anyone."

Sam stared Jey down. "Because I'm not leaving Howie alone. Not again." Sam held the boy's gaze until, finally, the Falcory slouched back, muttering how unfair it was.

"One problem: the imp doesn't know where Groll is," Perrin said.

"It's a big rock in the middle of the ocean with a giant wolf chained to it. How hard could it be to find?" Sam joked.

"And we need a boat," Perrin added, "which we don't have."

Sam took the tiny wood carving out of his pocket and fingered it absently.

Mavery jumped to her feet, nearly knocking Perrin over as she lunged for the little boat. "Where did you get that?" she cried excitedly as Sam held it out of her reach.

"Back off, little witch, it's mine. I ran into Fetch in the marketplace. He said it was a gift from Odin. It's fragile, so don't touch."

Mavery hopped up and down, reaching for it. "It's not fragile. Give it to me."

Perrin unfolded her legs and stood, her brow pinched into a frown. "Let me see that."

She took the boat from Sam and held it up to an oil lamp, then brought it to her face, inhaling its scent deeply. She held it out to him. "This boat has magic."

Sam took it, turning it over in his hands before handing it over to Mavery. "Okay, what is it?"

The girl cradled it on her palm, looking at it with wide eyes and something close to awe. "Mighty Skidbladnir," she whispered, "mightiest of ships, large enough to hold the gods, small enough to fit in the palm of my hand, take me where I might go, over land, over sea and in the air, like a swift-moving cloud." She climbed up on the bale of hay and threw the chute doors open, exposing the bright moon to her face. She held the ship over her head and cried out, "Skidbladnir, I command you to take us to Groll."

For a moment, Sam almost believed she was telling the truth. But the seconds ticked off, and nothing happened.

"It's just a toy," Jey scoffed.

Sam was about to agree when the ship vibrated on her palm, spinning in a circle slowly at first, then faster and faster until it was a blur.

The ship lifted off her palm and rose into the night sky. It spun, creating a cloud around it. The cloud grew thick, white, and puffy, engulfing the ship as it grew larger and larger. There was a loud pop, and then the cloud thinned, revealing a full-scale ship complete with riggings, masts, and crisp sails. The sails flapped in the light wind as it floated in place, waiting.

Mavery clapped her hands and chuckled with glee. Sam had seen a lot of strange things since he'd come through that stonefire to Orkney, but this was a whole new level of magic.

"Cool beans," Howie whispered.

Perrin arched an eyebrow. "I guess we have our ship."

Mavery grabbed on to the rope ladder that hung down and scrambled up like a monkey.

They had no provisions, no idea of their destination, but

it didn't seem they were being given a choice. The ship rattled its timbers like it was eager to take off.

"You ready?" he turned to ask Perrin, but she was kneeling by Damarius.

She buried her face in his fur. "I'm sorry, mutt. You can't come with me."

The Shun Kara's eyes glistened with outrage as it howled. She grabbed its snout, pinching it closed.

"Quiet, fool, do you want all of Skara Brae to hear us?"

The wolf sat on its haunches and raised one paw, silently pleading with her.

Perrin's eyes misted, but she shook her head, rubbing his ears. "You're a knucklehead. A ship is no place for a wolf. This one," she pointed at Howie, "will watch over you."

Howie paled. "Me? Last time I got close to a Shun Kara, it tried to eat me."

The witch glared at him, and Howie sighed. "Okay, fine. Just tell him not to bite the hand that feeds him."

Perrin straightened, pointing her finger at Howie until the wolf slowly moved to sit by him. She didn't give the Shun Kara another look as she stiffly climbed the ladder, but Sam could see it cost her.

Howie slapped Sam on the shoulders. "Ditching me again. Some best friend you are."

"I know. You should really replace me." Sam saluted him with a grin, then stepped off and put his feet on the rungs. Immediately the ship began sailing through the night, making him sway on the rope ladder. He looked down over the towers of Skara Brae as the ship climbed into the sky.

He wanted to whoop with joy but thought better of rousing the sentries. They might think it was Surt launching an attack and shoot them down. He settled for punching his fist in the air and then began climbing the ladder.

As he vaulted over the rail and dropped onto the deck,

the ship swayed slightly. They were headed west. He grabbed on to the rail and moved his way across the deck.

The ship was like a giant schooner. The three tiny masts had grown as thick as telephone poles and towered high in the sky. The sails snapped sharply as they found a stiff breeze. Mavery's face was plastered with a silly grin as she sat on the back of the captain's perch, her feet on the wheel as she steered.

Sam explored, admiring the details, from the brass fittings down to the neatly coiled ropes. He lifted a hatch, and light spilled out from below. He dropped down and found bunks fitted with soft beddings and a galley. Perrin was in there, rooting through the cupboards.

She looked at Sam in awe. "I've been around magic my whole life, but never have I seen anything like this."

Sam opened the pantry door. Provisions were stocked to the brim. Dried meats, jars of preserves, spices. Another cupboard revealed bins of fresh vegetables and fruits.

"How?" Sam asked, but Perrin just shrugged.

Grabbing a red apple to snack on, Sam followed Perrin up to the deck.

They were several hundred feet off the ground. The night was clear, and the moon shone down, half full. They had left the island of Garamond behind and were headed out to sea. The boat drifted lower until it settled down onto the water. Foamy white waves rolled them forward.

Sam sat down next to Perrin and bit into the fruit. It was as sweet and crisp as any he'd ever had. "How did my little ship turn into this?" he asked, waving his apple at the sturdy vessel that carried them.

"Skidbladnir is not a little ship," Mavery said from the helm. "Jasper told me all about it. It was his favorite story. It was made by the black dwarves of Gomara for the god Frey. He wanted a ship that could fit into his pocket, to take him places."

"That's some magic," Sam said, looking up at the riggings. "And it flies?"

"It can go anywhere. And it always finds wind," Mavery said eagerly.

"And you're sure it's taking us to Groll?" Perrin asked.

In answer, the ship rattled, shaking its timbers. Sam grinned, looking around. "You offended it."

The sleek ship cut through the water, hardly rolling to the side as the waves swelled. They were moving fast, faster than the light wind would account for.

Perrin jumped up and went to the rail. She held her face up to the moonlight. After a long moment, she turned back toward Sam. "Something feels wrong."

"Wrong?" Sam went over to the railing and leaned against it, folding his arms. "How so?"

She shook her head, running her fingers lightly over the rail. "I don't know. It just seems a little convenient. We needed a ship, you got one, and here we are."

"Odin must have known something bad might happen that day," Sam laughed, still excited about the wonder of it. "Maybe this is his backup plan. He is a god, after all."

"Well, then I'm wrong," Perrin snapped. She waved her hands in the air. "This is not going to end in disaster, and you'll be a hero. Happy?" She shoved past him and went down below.

Sam shook his head. Sometimes girls made no sense to him. "Did you catch that?" he asked Mavery.

The little witch just shrugged. "Maybe she's scared of Fenrir. He is a giant wolf that will probably tear us to pieces and use our bones to pick his teeth."

Sam glared at her. "Really? That's a big help. I feel soooo much better."

Mavery just grinned and spun the wheel with her feet.

"What good does steering do? I thought the boat had a mind of its own," Sam grumbled, slumping against the railing.

"Every ship needs a captain," Mavery answered cryptically, like she knew more than Sam.

That irritated him, and he was already teed off. He got up and shoved her off the perch harder than he intended, making her land on the deck with a thump. "Then move it. Because no way you're captain of my ship."

Mavery picked herself up and stuck her tongue out at him, then yawned widely. "Fine, be a big jerk, I'm tired anyway." She skipped over to the hatch and disappeared down below.

Sam mentally kicked himself. A bed sounded really good right about now. The ship had its own course. What did he need to stick around for?

He took his hands off the wheel, and immediately it spun wildly, tilting the hull sharply to the left. Snapping his hands back on the wheel, Sam righted the course and the ship smoothed, moving forward again. The imp was right, which was annoying: the ship needed a captain. Sam hunkered in for a long night, wondering if Fenrir was really as big as Mavery said he was.

# Chapter 7

Beyla, servant to Frey, God of the Elves, lifted her skirts and began to run, her broad feet pounding on the stone floor as she crossed the hall to the vaulted temple where the assembled gods and goddesses were seated in a circle of thrones.

Behind the high gods, the Valkyrie stood watch in their gilded armor and golden breastplates. Queen Frigga sat on the highest throne, as befitted Odin's wife. On her right sat Iduna, the gentle Goddess of Youth. To her left, her son Bragi, God of Poetry and Mirth, stroked his lyre softly. Beyla sought out the eye of her master. She flushed with embarrassment as all turned to stare at her abrupt intrusion.

Geela drew her sword and stood in front of her, barring her way.

"What business do you have here, woman?" she demanded.

"Let her pass," Frey said, rising from his seat to peer at her. "Dear Beyla, what brings you running? Has something come to pass?"

Beyla curtsied at him, then at Frigga and the rest of the gods. "Yes, your godship, something terrible has happened."

"What is it, woman?" Frigga demanded irritably. "We are in the midst of an important conversation."

"It's gone. Gone, your lordship."

"What's gone?" Frey asked, coming to her side and gently taking her arm. "No harm will come to you; speak freely."

She flushed with shame. "Your little ship, sire, the one you keep next to your bed."

"Skidbladnir?" His hand flew to cover his shocked gasp.

The gods murmured and rustled about in their seats. Geela frowned. How could someone steal from the gods here in Valhalla? It was unheard of.

"I went in to clean, like I always do," Beyla said, twisting her apron between her rough hands. "Dusting the table and the dresser and the odd trinkets you have. And that's when I noticed the ship was gone. I looked under the bed and in every corner, but there's no sign of it."

Tyr, the one-handed Son of Odin and God of War, leapt to his feet. "It must be the work of Loki. No other has the power to enter this world and steal from us."

"We must find him, bind him, and unwind him," the poet Bragi said, striking a harsh chord on his lyre.

"Cut him to pieces and bury the parts in the four corners of the earth," Thor added, gripping his mighty hammer.

Frigga rammed the staff she held into the ground. "Silence! Loki has not been anywhere near Valhalla. I would smell his evil stench in these halls."

A woman with pale milky eyes stood. Vor, Goddess of Wisdom, moved into the circle and waved her arm. "Let us see where Skidbladnir is." The floor beneath her was solid stone, but the moment she stepped on it, the gray stones disappeared and became a scenery of clouds. The servant, Beyla, fainted cold. Geela snapped her fingers, and two Valkyrie hauled her away.

The clouds parted and shifted to show a night sky shining

on the sea. Far below, a ship could be seen sailing across the ocean. The view zoomed closer, and the gods leaned in, giving a collective gasp as they recognized who was at the helm.

Tyr shouted, jumping to his feet. "It is that witch-boy. The one who killed Father. I will go after him and cut his thieving murdering heart out."

Frigga seemed unconcerned. "Calm yourself, Tyr. I have no idea how the boy came into possession of Skidbladnir, but, I assure you, he will be punished for his crimes."

Vor turned to face the goddess. "Your highness, surely the boy is not to blame for Odin's demise. He was bespelled under the power of the Volgrim witches. He did not understand what he did."

"That is no excuse," Frigga thundered. "He took Odin's life with that cursed blade of Rubicus. He must be made to pay. I have sent him into the underworld to face Helva. If Odin is there, and the boy can free him, then he will be redeemed. If he fails, Helva will see that he suffers for eternity."

Several of the gods thumped their feet in agreement, but Vor held her hand up for silence.

"Would Odin have let a mere boy end his reign after thousands of years? Have none of you questioned how this boy could get close enough to cause harm to Odin? Perhaps he is nothing more than a pawn in Odin's great plan."

The gods began shouting and arguing, but Vor waved her hand, and the image disappeared, returning to solid stone. "You are wise, Frigga, and compassionate. Sam is a Son of Odin, a descendent of Baldur, your most precious son. He has a good heart. He has chosen the right path."

"Too late!" Frigga thundered. "Odin trusted him, just like he trusted Loki. Loki was blood brother to my husband, and look how he betrayed him. He killed my dear Baldur, and for that he was cursed to an eternity of suffering, which only ended with this boy's friend interfering."

Vor turned in a circle to address the gods' council. "All know the story of Loki, the lost boy Odin found one day and brought back here. They formed a bond, a brotherhood forged in a blood oath they shared. None know why Odin took Loki in. Only Odin. Yes, Loki is trouble. Full of mischief." She turned to face the queen. "And, yes, he was at fault for Baldur's death. But who set apart Baldur with such power to be immune from death? Who challenged the fates that one might be so much more blessed than any other?"

"You dare criticize me?" Frigga demanded, her face a mottled red.

Vor demurred. "No, my queen, I seek only to remind you that giving Baldur such invincibility was a challenge to someone like Loki. He has been punished greatly for his bad deed."

"I will never forgive Loki for taking my son," Frigga said bitterly. "And this Barconian boy is no different. Mischief, you call it? Destruction and chaos, say I. Since Loki was released, the veil sealing off the Eighth Realm from us is torn. Even now, our greatest enemy, Surt, gathers his army of fire giants to invade Orkney and destroy the very people Odin spent his lifetime protecting. If Surt succeeds, what will stop that red monster from coming here?"

The assembled group gasped.

Frigga left her throne to stand in the center of the circle next to Vor, turning to look at each god as she spoke. "You all know the Ninth Realm is like a house with many rooms. When Surt enters Orkney, he will be worming his way into our home like vermin. If he is not stopped, we will have no choice but to destroy Orkney."

"No!" Vor said, her hand going to her throat. "Odin would never allow it."

"Odin is lost to us. Destroying Orkney will be the only way to protect Valhalla," Frigga said coldly.

"If there is a chance to bring Odin back, we should help

the boy, not condemn him to certain death," Vor argued. "Alone, he will surely perish. Send a battalion of Valkyrie to assist him."

Frigga glared at Vor, and then her face fell as the lines deepened around her eyes. "In my heart, I know Odin is gone. He has been lost before, but I could always feel him here," she laid a hand on her chest. "But now it is like an empty vessel. I did the boy a mercy sending him to Helva rather than face this court." She sat up straighter. "But you are wise, Vor." She turned to Geela. "You will go after the boy and assist him on his quest. If he gives you any reason to doubt his purpose, end his life."

The Valkyrie bowed low, but before she could move away, Frigga rose.

"We must come to a decision," she said to the council of gods. "If it appears Orkney will fall to Surt, we destroy it. Are we in agreement?"

The gods and goddesses hesitated, and then, as one, they raised their right hands, signaling yes—all except for Vor.

Geela returned to her simple quarters and prepared her armor. A soft knock sounded at the door, and a pale figure entered. Vor stood in the doorway.

Geela always felt awkward around the pale woman, as if the wise goddess could read her thoughts, see into her soul.

"Come in, my lady Vor. What can I do for you?" Geela asked steadily, biting back her nerves.

"Beware, Geela, for you are being sent on a perilous mission."

"The boy is dangerous?" Geela asked, blood zinging at the thought of a challenge.

Vor frowned, shaking her head. "The boy is no danger to you, but the journey will be hard. You must ensure no harm comes to the boy."

It was Geela's turn to frown, pulling her arm away. "I take orders from my queen, Frigga, and only my queen."

"The queen does not understand what is at stake," Vor said with a fierceness Geela had never before heard from the gentle goddess. "Grief blinds her to the truth, or she would see what I do."

"And what is that?" Geela said.

"That the boy is being used for some purpose. That he is in extreme danger." Vor moved away, then paused at the door, adding, "Hear me, Geela, he must complete his tasks, no matter how contrary they seem. He must complete them."

# Chapter 8

Sometime between the moon dipping low in the sky and the sun rising, Sam fell asleep with his hands on the wheel, slumped over the top, drooling like a baby. A spray of salt water woke him in time to see a large wave rolling over the front of the ship. He held on as the sluice of water nearly swept him off his feet. The placid ocean had turned into an angry roiling sea. Oddly, the winds were calm, and the day was sunny and clear. It was as if a storm raged under the surface.

"What's going on?" Perrin shouted. She gripped the railing as water lashed the boat.

"I don't know," Sam shouted back. "Get Mavery up here." Another wave crashed over the bow, pouring into the holds.

As Mavery joined them on deck, Perrin pointed at the horizon. "What is that?"

They looked in horror at the oncoming wave. It rolled across the ocean like a freight train, growing bigger with every second. The ship surged forward, sucked in by the receding water as the rogue wave rose up, curling into a white foamy lip at the top.

"Hold on!" Sam shouted, steering Skidbladnir across the wave.

The sturdy ship steadily climbed the face of it. With any luck, they could make it over the top to the other side before the wave broke on them. The ship tilted as the lip curled over. Water began raining down on them as they sailed into the curve of the wave. It closed in over them, curling ever more sharply until the water simply collapsed on top of the ship.

Sam was flushed overboard by the crushing wall of water. He grasped at a rope but missed, and then he was underwater, choking in the cold salty sea. A sharp undertow dragged him down, rolling and tumbling in the wave's aftermath. He held his breath, fighting to stay upright.

Kicking his legs, he swam with the current, edging outward until he broke through the surface. The water had returned to calmness, the surface flat and undisturbed. The sun continued to shine. There was no sign of Perrin or Mavery. He shouted for them, but the seas were empty. A tiny blob floated by.

Skidbladnir.

It had shrunk back to fit into the palm of his hand. Snagging the carving, he tucked it into the pouch he wore around his neck. Sam paddled, searching for a heading. A dark spot on the horizon offered the only hope. Maybe a slice of land. Setting out with long strokes, Sam held on to the hope that Mavery and Perrin would find their own way.

After endless strokes, his feet brushed something solid. He could stand. Wiping the sea from his eyes, he looked around in wonder.

The island lay before him. A strip of white sandy beach was broken by a gurgling stream of crystal-clear water. Sam bent down and drank deeply.

When he could drink no more, he began exploring. The island was pretty barren, flat with a rocky interior that blocked any view to the other side. Was this just a spit of land in the sea? Or had he found Groll, the island rock that held Fenrir the wolf?

And where were the girls? Sam began walking down the beach, shouting for his friends. "Mavery? Perrin?"

Waves crashed on the sand, throwing up white foam. Sam kept calling, but it was like the wind just laughed at him, carrying the words away and dropping them into the vast sea. As Sam clambered over some rocks, he broke out onto a sandy beach. It looked familiar. There was the stream with his footprints in the sand. He had come full circle. The island was barely longer than a football field and not even as wide. There was nothing moving on it besides Sam. No wolf, no Perrin, no Mavery. Kicking the sand in disgust, Sam sat down, grabbing his knees, and stared out at the water. What was he supposed to do now?

He reached for his pouch, thinking about the ship. Maybe he could get it to restart. Pulling it out, he rubbed off the sand and held it up.

"Hey, Skidbladnir, mighty old ship. Do me a solid and make yourself big again so I can get off this island and get back to finding Fenrir and the girls."

He waited, feeling foolish but determined. The ship didn't budge, didn't vibrate, didn't move at all. "Come on, Skid, old buddy, you did it before for Mavery. I'm the captain of the ship; I order you to take me off this rotten island."

He held the ship high, hoping, but nothing happened. Setting it onto the sand, Sam stepped back and conjured up his magic.

"*Fein kinter*," he said, rubbing his hands and then drawing them through the air, calling on his magic. "*Fein kinter, enorma, sentera, sentera, acai*!" He sent a blast of energy at the ship. The sand puffed around it, but the ship stubbornly remained the size of a chicken egg.

"Aarrgh!" Sam said, wanting to throw it into the sea.

The sun was starting to set. It looked like he was stuck on the island for the night. If he wanted some warmth, he would have to gather some firewood and see if there was anything to eat on this deserted sliver of land.

Heading inland, he clambered over rocks until he reached the center of the island and the highest point. Standing on a boulder, he could see end to end, side to side. The only slice of greenery was a small stand of three scraggly trees just below.

The trees weren't like any Sam had ever seen. Their limbs were graceful and narrow, with long, thin leaves that had a silvery-gray coloring. Scrambling down, he picked up what few twigs and dead branches he could find. He would have to break some off the trees if he wanted to make a fire. He reached up and tested a branch then stopped.

Was that a moan?

He tugged on the branch again, bending it backward so he could break it loose, and this time he was certain the tree moaned. Before he could process the thought, the branch sprang out of his hands, flinging him onto his backside.

The three trees drew closer together and advanced on him, as if they weren't rooted into the ground at all but were living things that wanted to attack him. They waved their branches at him, long leaves rattling. Shrill moans split the air.

Covering his ears, Sam called out to them, "Stop it! I'm sorry I tried to take your branch; I thought you were just a tree."

"Who are you?" the leaves whispered at him.

"I am Sam, Sam Barconian, Lord of the Ninth Realm, Son of Odin, Son of Catriona," Sam added, just to make sure he covered all his bases.

The trees rattled and shook as they whispered furtively.

"We can't show ourselves."

"He's dangerous."

"I've seen his path."

"Torturous."

"Frightening."

"Awful."

"Hey," Sam interrupted them, dusting himself off and rising, "if you're talking about me, I'm not awful or frightening. I'm just a kid who found himself making all kinds of mistakes before he figured out who he was. But I'm on the right path; you don't have to be afraid of me."

The trees stopped chattering and remained still. Sam drew closer, warily studying them. It took a moment, but then he made out faces in the tree trunks. A set of eyes he thought were knots blinked at him. The curling bark formed into mouths drawn back in fear.

"It's okay," he said gently, holding his hands out to show he wasn't armed. "I just want to know how to get off this island."

They turned their trunks to one another and whispered among themselves. Sam waited, crossing his fingers they would help him.

"Turn around," one of them said. "Don't look at us."

Sam obliged, turning his back, hoping they wouldn't try to choke him with their branches when he did.

"You may look now," a voice said, and this time it didn't sound raspy. It sounded female and, well, kind of pretty.

Sam turned slowly, and his jaw fell open. Three beautiful women stood dressed in simple gowns of thin gauzy material, long silvery hair falling past their shoulders to their waists. Their hair was braided with green leaves and white flowers. They looked identical, only different ages. One appeared to be the age of Sam's mom, one was his age, and the other was somewhere in between.

"Who are you?" Sam asked, stepping into the circle where they stood.

"We are the Norns," the oldest one said. "I am Urd, Goddess of the Past."

The middle one said, "I am Verdoni, Goddess of the Present."

And the one his age giggled and then said shyly, "I'm Skald, Goddess of the Future."

"What is a Norn?" Sam asked.

"The Norns decide the fate of every human in all the nine realms," Urd answered. "We see their fates and spin them in our looms at night when we take our human form."

Behind the figures, in the shelter of the rock cairn, stood three looms, giant golden machines that held white shining thread. Stacks of fabric were piled next to the machines with words written on them that Sam couldn't make out.

Frowning, Sam shook his head. "No, our fates are not determined for us; we make our own fate."

The young one, Skald, giggled again, and Verdoni elbowed her. "You are right, Son of Odin, but the fate you make is as predictable as the sun rising. So is it your making, or is it ours?"

The eldest, Urd, waved her hand, creating a foggy image that floated in front of Sam. It was him, riding with the witches into battle, his face twisted in rage. "Did you not choose the path of darkness, Son of Catriona, the moment it was offered you?"

Sam recoiled from the image. He brushed the fog away. "Yes, but Catriona bewitched me, drugged me with a potent spell. I had no choice."

"There is always a choice," Urd chided. "We knew your choice. We saw it before you did, wove it into the threads."

Sam glared at them. "Fine, you know everything. Where am I going, then?"

It was Skald's turn to smile. "You are going to your doom." The youngest Norn held up a scrap of fabric. "It is written right here. The wolf Fenrir will tear you to pieces with his teeth, and that will be the end of your story."

Every drop of blood drained out of Sam's body. He stared at the tree spirits, not believing their words. "I can't die," he whispered, as real fear set in. "I have to save everyone—that's my job. I have to bring Odin back. I can't die!" he shouted at them, pushing forward and grabbing Skald by her arm. "You're wrong. Do it again."

He snatched the fabric from her hands and tore it in half. As he did, his soul felt as if it were ripped apart. He screamed in agony, falling to his knees. It felt as if a knife had been planted in his chest. He couldn't breathe, couldn't speak, couldn't feel his arms or legs. He fell forward onto the ground.

Around him, the whispers of the Norns teased his ears and then faded. Slowly the feeling came back in his arms. He pushed himself upright, and the pain eased. He could take in a shallow breath, and the dizziness behind his eyes cleared up.

When he sat up, the Norns were gone. The trees were solid and unmoving again. Gray leaves shimmered in the fading light. He looked around. The island was changing. Water rose as the tide came in, erasing the sandy beach and swirling around his ankles.

"What does this mean?" he said to the trees.

Their branches hung limply, not even stirring in the breeze.

"Answer me. Did I change my fate?" he shouted.

The water rose higher, engulfing the trees and then swallowing the island in one large gulp, leaving him floundering back in the cold sea.

# Chapter 9

Sam flailed his arms as he gagged on seawater. His boots weighed him down. It was so much work to fight all the time, to hold his head up, to not be buried in the shame of the past, of the anger, of everyone he'd ever hurt. The list was long, after all. He sank lower in the water as the weight of it pulled on him. The Norns had reminded him of his failings. He could hear Catriona whispering in his ear, calling him her son.

*Kalifus.*

How he had welcomed those words when he'd been under her spell. How he'd craved to hear them. Now they repelled him, filled him with disgust. But, still, they called him like a spider that had taken up nest in his ear. He clutched the pouch around his neck. Odin couldn't help him, but maybe another could.

"Vor, I need your help. You have always been there in my time of need. Please, help me bring Odin back. I can't fail. I have to make things right."

He waited, hoping for a sign the Goddess of Wisdom had heard him. He sank lower as nothing happened. It was no use. There was no help coming. Just as his head was about to go under, something bumped him. A dark shape. He twisted, fearing what he would find. A pair of dorsal fins cut through the water, swimming in a circle around him, butting him with smooth gray snouts.

Dolphins!

A burst of hope ran through him. He grabbed on to a fin with each hand. They took off, jerking him forward as they swam, tails thrusting them like jets. Sam held on, keeping his head up as water rushed past.

It didn't take long for a dark landmass to take shape, a sharp outcrop of rock rising from the ocean. The dolphins slowed and then peeled away to each side, forcing Sam to let go. He floated, kicking his feet as he surveyed the island.

Craggy and unapproachable, the island held no palm trees or any sign of green. He struck out for it, worried the waves were going to smash him against the rocks but seeing no other option.

As he got closer, his fear grew. Something was moving on the island, something large and black.

Was this Groll? The island prison of Fenrir? The wolf the Norns had said was going to tear him apart?

Sam paused, holding himself still. Every bone in his body told him to swim the other way, no matter how far. And then a familiar scream rang out.

Mavery.

A flash of green light splashed across the rocks. Perrin must be there, too. And then came the long low notes of a wolf howling. It echoed over the water, as if it was calling Sam personally: *Come on in, witch-boy. Let me have a nibble or two.*

Panic rose up, choking him with fear as he recalled the fate the Norns had predicted. Mavery screamed again, and Sam moved, kicking his legs as he chopped the water with his arms. Waves crashed against the rocks in a spray of white foam that threatened to smash him to pieces.

He wasn't that lucky. As Sam got closer, he noticed an inlet between the rocks. If he struck out hard, he could slide through the channel and land on a smooth slab. It was also conveniently out of sight of the giant creature he had glimpsed between mouthfuls of seawater.

Pulling himself up, Sam took a moment to catch his breath. If he was going to be mauled to death, he might as well give it his best. He wrung out his clothes and dumped the water out of his boots. There was no mystery as to where the girls were. He could hear Mavery scream and Perrin shouting out and sending blasts of green energy. The wolf let out intermittent howls and snarls that made the hair on the back of Sam's neck stand up.

Finding no other excuse to delay his fate, Sam began climbing over the rocks toward the sounds. He came out on top of a flat rock. Below him, Fenrir came into sight. He made Damarius look like a puppy.

The giant wolf was every bit as fearsome as Sam had expected. He was the size of a two-story house, with paws like a Mack truck. His pelt was a wiry gray fur with patches of black. He pawed at the ground, drawing boulders and scraping up dust. Piles of bones were scattered on the rocky plain, the remnants of seals and whales that had drifted too close.

Sam sized up the situation. The girls were trapped against a rock wall. The wolf lunged at them, snapping and snarling, but he couldn't quite reach them. He strained against a long silver leash too thin to hold back the fearsome power of such a creature. Then Sam remembered: it was bespelled with magic.

Around the wolf's neck, a silver key dangled from his collar—the key to the chamber of that deadly sea serpent, Jormungand—the chamber that held the map to Helva's underworld, where Odin was being held. Or so Sam hoped.

Sam drew in a deep breath and let it out slowly, drawing courage into his bones. He might die today. He might get eaten by the wolf, but not before he'd saved the girls, and not before he'd gotten the key so that they could carry on the mission without him.

That much he could do.

"All right, then, Baron," he said aloud to himself, "let's get this show on the road. Here, wolfie, wolfie," he called out, using his magic to catapult himself across the craggy rock and land in a tumble at the wolf's feet. Sam looked up at the beast, seeing the razor-sharp talons, the thickly matted fur, the feral eyes.

As Sam called, the wolf turned, baring his lips into a snarl as he snapped at Sam. Thrusting his hands out, Sam let his magic flow and lifted the closest rock, flinging it at the wolf's head as he dove to the side, avoiding the snap of his jaws. The rock landed, striking the beast in the brow and causing him to yelp. A thin trail of blood ran into his eye. Fenrir stalked forward warily, taking his time, as if he knew Sam couldn't leave this island alive.

Sam sidestepped, inching closer to the girls, but Fenrir moved to cut him off.

"Sam, watch out!" Perrin shouted as the wolf crouched low. "You're in range."

No kidding. Sam had already scoped out how far the wolf could go.

He was the bait.

He readied himself as the wolf coiled into a crouch. "When he comes at me, you run behind him and get Mavery to safety," he called.

"Get back, Baron, you fool!" But Perrin's shout was lost as the wolf howled and sprang forward. Fenrir flew through the air with lethal speed, paws outstretched, teeth drawn into a snarl as he lunged at Sam.

Sam held himself still, fighting the fear and urge to flee until the last second, when he hoped for a miracle.

The wolf's fetid breath blew on his face as he shouted, "*Fein kinter, temporalis!*"

And then he waited to see if he was wolf food.

A blast of arctic chill filled his bones, like he'd been injected with frozen Jell-O. A sharp wind buffeted his face, and then there was sudden stillness. Opening his eyes, he looked around. He was fifty feet away from the wolf's jaws.

He'd done it! The transportation spell witches used to disappear and reappear somewhere else. He had never mastered it until now.

Desperation was a good motivator.

The wolf looked confused, wagging his head from side to side, searching for Sam. Perrin and Mavery climbed the rocks a safe distance above the wolf. Sam nodded at them, drawing his hands in a circle as the girls did the same. As one, they released a blast of witchfire, sending green balls of fire at Fenrir.

The wolf yelped in pain and flipped over onto his back to rub out the fire in his fur. Sam sent another blast as he ran in closer, dropping into a slide and then reaching up to grab the dangling key.

Fenrir snapped at Sam, nearly snatching him up in his jaws. Sam got under his chin, grabbed on to the collar, and hung on as the wolf rolled onto his feet. Fenrir was working his jaw up and down, trying to bite him, but Sam dangled under his chin, out of reach. He could smell the wolf's stinking breath as he brought a paw up to try and claw him away. Perrin moved in, sending boulders flying at the beast as Mavery added her own smaller rocks to distract him.

Sam had his hands on the key, but it wouldn't come loose. It was attached to the chain that went around the beast's neck that kept him bound to the rock. To release the key, he would have to break the chain.

Before Sam could think through all the reasons not to, he conjured up a spell in his mind. Dangling by one arm, he called on all of his strength. "In the name of Odin, you will yield to my hand!" he shouted, and he blasted the links with a bolt of energy from his palm.

The chain glowed a fluorescent orange color, sending off a thin trail of smoke before it shattered in an explosion of sparks. The whole length of it began disintegrating into a pile of hot metal chunks.

Sam dropped as the chain broke apart, hitting the ground with a bruising thump. The key landed next to him, tinkling and clanging on the granite.

The beast had his chance. Sam was winded, flat on his back. Using that much magic had drained him. He couldn't move, let alone run.

*This is it, then; the Norns spoke the truth. I'm wolf food.*

Fenrir came closer, prowling forward to sniff at him. Sam held himself still, refusing to cower or show fear. Let the beast eat him. Mavery and Perrin were shouting and screaming, but Fenrir ignored them. The wolf sniffed Sam from head to toe. Sam waited for Fenrir to snatch him up, but the wolf hesitated, as if he wasn't sure.

Then he howled in Sam's face, baring his teeth and spraying him with foul spittle. "You freed me, Son of Magic," he growled, surprising Sam with his ability to speak. "For that I owe you a debt." Then the beast launched in the air, springing over Sam's head to land with a loud splash in the ocean. He swam away with fearsomely strong strokes.

Sam lay flat, heart racing in his chest as he came to grips with two facts. One, he was still alive, which meant the Norns were wrong. And two, he had just released Fenrir from his chains. That had to be bad.

Then Perrin and Mavery were at his side, helping him up.

"Are you crazy?" Perrin shouted at him. "Or do you just have a death wish?"

Mavery flung her arms around him, squeezing him tightly. "I knew you'd come," she said, her face pressed against Sam's waist.

He grinned wryly, patting her back as he looked at Perrin. "Hey, I saved your life, didn't I?"

"But you let Fenrir go!" she shouted, practically beside herself. "Do you realize what you've done?"

Sam pried Mavery off and picked up the key and showed it to her. "What I've done is found the key to the cave of Jormungand the serpent! The key that is going to get Odin back. Once he's back, it won't matter what I've done; he'll fix everything."

"You think Odin is going to fix this?" She pointed at the wolf's dark head bobbing in the water.

Actually, Sam wasn't sure at all. He looked down at the thick silver key and gripped it tighter. "I'm fine; thanks for asking. And, no, I don't know, but there's not much I can do about it now. So if you're done yelling at me, I say let's get off this island before Fenrir finds out there isn't any land for a hundred miles and comes back."

"But we lost Skidbladnir," Mavery said, her smile drooping. "When we got washed overboard."

"You mean this lousy piece of wood?" Sam pulled it out from the pouch around his neck and tossed it to her. "I can't get it to do diddly-squat for me. Maybe you'll have better luck."

Mavery's eyes lit up as she snatched the carving out of the air and cradled it reverently. "Oh, mighty Skidbladnir, ship of the gods, I knew you wouldn't desert us in our time of need. Help us find Jormungand; take us across the sea to his underwater cave. Help us so that we might help Odin be restored."

She held it up. Her eyes shone as if she had absolute faith in the ship's ability to transform. An annoyed Perrin wouldn't look at Sam.

"Please, Skidbladnir, I know the way is hard and the journey long, but you can do it. I believe in you, and so does Sam."

The little witch elbowed Sam. Personally, he didn't know what he believed anymore, but he nodded. "Yup, I believe in you, old Skid, buddy. Would love to be your captain again. It was so much fun last time."

Mavery reached back and threw the ship as far as she could into the water. It bobbed there, floating. Sam had visions of it just sinking, but then a cloud of smoke swirled around it, and the carving began to grow.

In a blink, it was there in full sail. Sam shook his head and followed Perrin and Mavery up the gangplank that rested on top of the rocks. As they stepped onto the deck, Skidbladnir lifted anchor and the wind puffed out its sails, sending it lurching forward.

Mavery took over the helm while Sam approached Perrin. She had her back to him, staring out across the sea.

"That was a pretty gnarly talking wolf," he joked.

Waves of anger bounced off her skin, and she remained silent, her lips pursed tightly together.

"What's the deal? Why are you so mad? It's not like I had a choice."

She whirled on him, giving him a hard shove. "You always have a choice, and you always choose something that makes everything worse."

The Norns had said the same thing.

Sam's hackles rose. Perrin didn't understand how hard it was for him to adjust to being a witch and a Son of Odin. She had grown up knowing who she was, and he was just figuring it out. "I couldn't let that wolf eat you."

"So you just let him go? What if he eats an entire village? What if he kills innocent people? What then, Baron? Not your fault?" She shoved him again. "Not your fault people get hurt around you?"

"Hey!" he shouted back at her. "At least I'm doing something. All you do is stand around and point out my mistakes."

"Somebody has to because you don't ever bother to think about the consequences."

"What do you mean?"

"We just released Fenrir the wolf, a beast so terrible he was chained for eternity to that rock, and now he's free, swimming across the ocean to who knows where. And we're heading to an underwater sea monster, and maybe we're going to free him, too. Doesn't that seem a bit odd that in order to rescue Odin, we have to let go every bad thing he fought to contain?"

Sam sat down on the deck, holding his head in his hands. It was all so confusing. "Maybe. I don't know. I don't know!" he shouted, looking up at her. "Maybe you're right." The enormity of it hit him. The wolf and his vicious fangs loose on the world. "Crud, what am I doing?"

Perrin slumped next to him, sighing. "Probably the best you can."

She leaned her head on his shoulder as the ship cut through the seas, sending a spray of water into the sun and creating a cascade of colors.

Sam's stomach chilled, like he'd swallowed a block of ice. Because he felt it now, that feeling that it was all wrong, that he'd just made the biggest mistake of his life, and he was about to make another.

And even knowing that, he didn't have a better plan.

# Chapter 10

The sleek ship carrying Keely and Leo was small and cramped with only basic bunks and a tiny galley for cooking, but it was fast. The second morning after they departed, Keely stood in the prow, letting the water spray her. Dolphins kept pace with them, gliding along with their silvery bodies. They made her feel hopeful, as if the world had not yet turned against them.

Life was so different now. Good golly, she had magic! How crazy was that? She looked down at her hands, wondering at the energy that flowed in her veins. Her encounter with Mimir had left her with a touch of Eifalian blood. She reached a hand up to her silvery white hair. It was cool to be able to do things. Like, she could sense when someone was lying. Howie was the easiest. His aura fairly burned with shame when he denied passing gas or taking the last serving of jookberry pie.

In a leather satchel, she carried the pink healing crystal she had acquired in Ter Glenn and the small phoralite shell that lit up at night. The shell had given her courage in the darkness more times than she could count. Orkney had become her second home, in a way, more home than Pilot Rock had ever been—at least since her mom had died.

A wave of regret washed over her as she thought of her dad and what he must be going through. Even though she'd asked the god Ymir to let him know she was okay, the great creator probably had far bigger things to worry about than whether or not a foolish girl had sent a message to her father.

Keely leaned back and let the sun warm her face. It would get colder soon. They had passed the eastern shores of Garamond at dawn and would soon reach Rakim, the icy island to the north. Memories of her last visit haunted her. If only she had done something different, somehow stopped King Einolach from sacrificing himself. A tear slid down her cheek at the memory.

Leo joined her. That boy moved silent as a cat. "Why so sad?" he asked, wiping the tear away with his thumb. "You're thinking of the king," he guessed. "It's not your fault, you know. You couldn't have seen what would happen."

Keely shrugged, wrapping her arms tightly around her chest. "You don't look so hot yourself. You've been quiet since we left."

Tension coiled under his skin like a live wire, and then he exploded. "I should have never let Loki go! I should have just stayed in the underworld. I was the Sacrifice, and I failed." He pounded his fist on the railing.

"Hey, stop it." Keely gripped his arm, yanking him around to face her. "Don't you dare say that. We all have a lot to bear. Sam killed Odin, someone he loved and respected. I let a king die, let him lose his head in front of me. You let Loki out of his prison. We can't fall apart because we made mistakes; we have to go forward together, or we will never beat this."

Leo didn't look convinced, but before Keely could go on, Galatin called out, "Land ahead."

Keely looked to her left and gasped as the forbidding cliffs of

Rakim jutted from the sea. Snow frosted the distant mountains that divided Rakim from the Eifalian kingdom of Torf-Einnar. The Vanirian capital city, Galas, perched on the cliffs, warning off invaders with its high ramparts. The long trail leading up to the gates brought back memories of her last visit.

Galatin eased the boat into the channel. The air was crisp, and a light snow had recently fallen. Keely was grateful for the fur coat and comfortable deerskin boots she wore.

The docks were surprisingly deserted. A few ships bobbed, but the walkways were empty, as if everyone had left.

"Was it this quiet last time?" Leo asked as Galatin led them up the hill.

Keely shook her head, uneasy. They couldn't be too late. They just couldn't.

Leo took her hand and squeezed it. "Don't worry; everything is going to be fine."

Keely very much wanted to believe that, but as they crested the top, winded and out of breath, she gasped. The Vanirian army that had taken up ranks in the large arena, filling the barracks and the stands, was gone.

They stood looking down at the empty practice grounds.

"Maybe they're out on a training mission," Leo said.

"All of them?" Keely asked. "No, we're too late. Loki's beat us to it."

"Not all of them." Galatin nodded at an approaching rider. It was a Vanirian soldier, an older one, by the looks of it. Gray hair came past his shoulders, but he sat up ramrod straight on his horse. Vanirian horses were as big as Clydesdales, with well-muscled legs to hold their oversized riders.

He stopped in front of them and eyed them from atop his mount. "I know you," he pointed to Keely. "You are the Eifalian girl. You should not have returned here." He looked back over his shoulder to see if anyone else was coming. "Leave now, or I cannot guarantee your safety."

Keely stepped forward, putting her hand on his horse. "Please, where is Joran? The king is a friend to us. He mustn't go to war with the Eifalians."

"Joran is no friend of yours, child," he said bitterly, pulling his horse sharply away. "And it's the Eifalians that have declared war on us. They will pay for their treachery."

Behind him, the sound of more horses clattering over the bridge had him turning away. "I warned you. You should have left when you had the chance."

A group of Vanirian soldiers rode up in a swarm, their faces angry masks. Keely was confused. They grabbed the visitors roughly, jostling them and shoving them. "I don't understand," she cried. "Why are you acting this way?"

"Keely!" Leo shouted. He reached for her, but a frost giant twisted her arms behind her back. When Leo struck out at one, the giant simply swatted him away and lofted him over his shoulder. Galatin drew his sword, then lowered it. He was surrounded by three of them.

Another horse rode up, pushing its way forward. A woman's voice called out, "What is going on here?"

Keely recognized the regal figure. It was the queen, Joran's wife. Keely wriggled free from the slackened grasp of the frost giant. "Your Highness, why have you gone to war against the Eifalians?"

The queen's eyes flicked over her, then widened in recognition. "Come, this is better said inside the walls of the keep. I promise you no harm will come to you." She snapped out orders to her men. Leo was set down, and the giants sheathed their weapons.

As they entered the main plaza, the streets were mostly empty. A few women and children hurried along. Except for the group that had ridden out to harass them, everyone left was either old, young, or female.

Keely's anxiety grew with every step. What had Loki

done to make Joran break their treaty with the Eifalians? And was it too late to stop him?

They were shown into a large salon with comfortable chairs and colorful throw rugs. Galatin stood guard at the door. Leo slumped down in a chair that was so big his feet barely reached the ground.

Everything inside the palace was sized for a frost giant. The broad sofa covered in velvety brocade would seat eight men comfortably. The ceilings were painted with a fresco of bare-chested frost giants locked in an ancient battle against some fearsome winged beasts.

Keely walked to the open window, drawn by the noises outside. In the garden, two kids were laughing and playing. She smiled, seeing the mischievous glint in the boy's eyes as he teased his little sister with a ball he kept just out of reach. These must be Joran's children. They had his chin and their mother's coloring.

The door opened, and they all turned, bowing as the queen entered. She was tall and big-boned but still graceful.

"Please, sit; you have had a long journey."

Keely perched on a seat to her right. "Your Highness—" she began, but the queen cut her off.

"Call me Reesa. We are not so formal here."

"Reesa, I'm Keely. These are my friends Leo and Galatin."

Reesa's slim eyebrow arched high as she looked at the soldier. "As I recall, last time you were here, you nearly lost your head."

Galatin bowed. "I hope to keep it this time as well. The Vanir proved steadfast friends to Orkney in our time of greatest need."

"But at what price?" Reesa probed. "We lost many men that day to those awful Balfin creatures."

Galatin stepped forward. "And for that we are deeply sorry. I have no wish to be rude, but time is of the essence.

What have the Eifalians done to deserve your ire? Surely it is a time for healing."

The queen's face grew dark, and her eyes went to the window, where the children could still be heard playing. "You remember the son that I lost?" she said quietly, turning to face Keely.

Keely nodded. "Yes. When I was with Ymir, he gave me a flute that belonged to him."

Reesa reached to her throat and drew out the small carving. It hung on a long silver chain around her neck. "My son, Jorri, was my life. When he was lost, I thought my life would end. But then I was blessed with another son, Kaleb, and then a daughter, Madilyn." Her eyes fluttered closed as she gripped the flute. "They brought me back to life and gave me reason to live again. Joran, too, became filled with joy and smiled once more. But then that man came and threatened us." Her eyes snapped open, and Keely could read the fierceness there.

"What man?" Keely asked.

"Leyes." Reesa said his name like it was poison.

# Chapter 11

Keely and Leo exchanged puzzled looks. "Surely you don't mean Leyes of the Eifalians?" Leo said. "He is the gentlest of souls. What trouble could he have caused you?"

"Trouble?" The queen rose out of her chair and began pacing. "He tried to kill my son. Lured him away from his nanny and then took him through the woods. The boy was nearly lost in the snow. We searched for him for hours. It was only by luck that we found him before . . . before he froze to death." Her voice choked up. "I could not have survived losing another child. Joran was beside himself. Kaleb told us of the man who dressed as a woman and tricked him into following him."

"And you're sure that man was Leyes?" Galatin asked. "When was this?"

"Three days ago. He had the white hair of the Eifalians and gave his name as such."

"My lady"—Galatin drew closer and bowed—"I swear to you, on my honor, that man was not Leyes."

She held herself very still as she faced him. "How can you be so sure?"

"Because three days ago he was in Skara Brae meeting with the High Council to discuss the pending invasion of Surt's army."

"Surt?" Now it was her turn to look puzzled. "The fire giants are banished to Musspell. They have not ventured into Orkney in a thousand years."

"Not while Odin was alive," Galatin said.

Her face dawned with realization. "Of course. Odin made sure Surt and his kind never troubled mankind. But you offer no proof. It might not have been Leyes, but there is no doubt he was Eifalian. My son's description was very vivid. He described his eyes, his face, his hair."

"May we speak with him?" Keely asked. "Maybe there is an explanation, some way to make sense of this."

The queen hesitated, then nodded. "Yes, I will bring him in."

She went to the window and called out. The boy came bounding in, his face flushed red from running about in the cold. He was almost as big as Keely, but his face had the rounded features of a young child. He gave his mother a hug, looping his arms around her waist, looking suddenly shy as he saw the four of them.

He said something to her in their language, but she chided him.

"Speak English, Kaleb. Say hello."

"Hello," he said shyly before looking up at the queen and whispering loudly, "Who are they, Mama?"

She took his hand and led him over to the sofa where they were seated. She pulled him up on her lap so that he faced Keely and Leo. "They are friends. They would like to talk to you about what happened."

"You mean that day?" He looked frightened.

She nodded, brushing the hair off his forehead. "You must be brave and tell them everything, starting with the moment you wandered off."

"It was the bird, Mama, the mockingbird. It came to our window and hopped on my finger. Papa said we couldn't keep it. Then the next day, it was in a tree, but every time I went to touch it, it flew off. I followed it, but it disappeared, and I was all alone. I called out to Nanna, and then she was there."

"What do you mean, there?" Keely asked.

"She came around a tree and took my hand and led me away. I thought we were coming home, but she wouldn't speak, and then I got scared."

Keely turned sharply toward Leo. "Are you thinking what I'm thinking?"

He nodded, his eyes gaunt with guilt.

"What?" Reesa commanded. "Tell me."

"The bird wasn't a bird," Keely said confidently.

"And that man wasn't Leyes," Leo added.

"Then who was it?" Reesa looked from one to the other.

They said the name together. "Loki."

She frowned, puzzled. "Loki, the mischief-maker? But he's been banished to the underworld for a millennium."

"He tricked me into releasing him," Leo explained.

"Loki can shape-shift," Keely added. "He can take the form of any animal or person, but he is especially fond of birds."

"But why?" Reesa asked. "Why harm my son?"

"Don't you see?" Keely said, sitting forward. "He didn't want to hurt Kaleb; he just wanted you to think that the Eifalians did, so you would go after them. Loki is out to start a war. He's punishing everyone in Orkney for what Odin did to him."

Reesa's frown grew deeper. "If what you say is true, then my husband is about to slaughter an innocent kingdom."

"My lady, is it too late to stop them, call them back?" Galatin asked. "We can send word to him."

"None he will listen to. Unless he hears it from my own lips, he won't withdraw. He is too proud, and he has lost too much."

"Then we must go after him. How long before his men reach Ter Glenn?"

"They left a day ago. Three days more, I would guess."

"Is there any way to get there ahead of them?" Keely asked. "What if we sailed?"

"No. The tides are against you. It would take too long. Your only chance would be to take a coastal route. It is more direct, but the way is narrow and open, which is why Joran went over the mountain pass. I can draw you a map to follow. You might catch them before they arrive, but it will be close."

Keely frowned. "You're not coming with us?"

The queen shook her head. "I am sorry; I cannot leave my children. They are unprotected here. We have only a few of my private guards who are bound to remain at my side and some old men too feeble to go to battle. They would be left with no one to protect them."

"I can stay," Galatin offered. "I would protect them with my life."

The queen caught her knuckle between her teeth, warring emotions on her face. After a long moment, she sighed. She bent down to look Kaleb in the eye. "I must go, my son. That means you are in charge of the kingdom."

His eyes grew large. "What should I do?"

"Be brave, be wise, be kind. Take care of your people. This man will guard you with his life."

The boy looked up at Galatin with a pinched look on his face, then whispered loudly, "But he's so small."

Everyone laughed because Galatin was a large man to any but a frost giant.

Galatin bowed to the boy. "I might be small to you, young prince, but my sword is big enough to carve up any beast."

"I take lessons in sword fighting," the boy boasted. "Will you teach me?"

Galatin tapped his sword to his forehead, "Your wish is my command." Over the boy's head, he nodded at the queen. "He will be safe, Your Highness. I swear it on my life."

In a matter of an hour, they were suited up on horses with provisions to last them the journey. They were traveling light, with only a few weapons and bedrolls. The horses were fresh. Reesa had six of her men with her, burly frost giants with bare chests crossed with leather straps that held their fearsome blades.

The sun was high in the sky, but the day was cold. A light frost covered the ground. Exhilaration soared through Keely as she held on to the broad waist of a Vanirian soldier. Everything would be okay. They just had to get to Ter Glenn before Joran. The Vanirian king would listen to reason. She would make him see he was making a huge mistake.

# Chapter 12

In the days of the ancient gods, Surt had walked among many of the greatest. From Odin to Frey to even that lowest of imps, Loki. In those years, he had always been treated as a stepchild, a second son, someone to be ignored. Impugned. Someone who had no voice. Now that time had changed. No longer would he be silent. No longer would he be shuttled to the outer regions of Musspell, where not a single blade of grass dared show its sprout.

The fiery-red skies over Musspell were dotted with Surt's army of flying beasts. They were known as boercats, giant saber-toothed animals with leathery wings that spanned two of his men. They belched fire that could incinerate entire armies. Red and yellow scales covered muscled legs that could run down their victims, and the set of jutting fangs that curved out from their jaws could rip flesh apart.

The patrols he had sent to every corner of Orkney were returning. Soon he would have his proof the veil that had kept him prisoner all these years was down. Proof Odin was truly gone. Then Surt would not hesitate to crush every living creature in this world, and any world beyond.

A crowd of troops had gathered in the wide square below him. Musspell was made of plain stone buildings carved out of the volcanic rock from the many slaves who toiled for him. Slave or soldier; those were the only two choices in life. Fight or work. Male or female, it didn't matter. There were no roles assigned based on gender, only what was clawed for. It had taken centuries to unite this kingdom under his leadership. Rebellions still sprouted in the outer regions where the fire giants battled for control with each other, bloody battles where no one emerged a winner. Surt encouraged it because it kept his soldiers hungry and battle-ready.

Surveying his legions below, the lord of the fire giants swelled with pride. They were chanting his name so that it rose like an ugly song from them, beating their chests with iron-wrapped fists and stomping their boots.

So what if it had taken centuries? Finally, the moment of victory was at hand. He would have liked to have been the one to crush the life out of Odin, but he didn't let that bother him. Odin's end was a thing of the past. The future was what mattered.

Stepping out into sight, Surt raised his hand for silence.

A hush fell over the battle-hardened soldiers.

"Brothers and sisters, how long have we waited for this day? For how many centuries have we been under Odin's thumb?"

The crowd roared with anger. Somewhere below, a burning effigy of Odin was raised.

"We stand on the edge of victory. As we make our final preparations for our journey across the sea, know this: One day, the fire giants will rule all of Orkney. Every living creature will bow to our strength. We will not be defeated. We will not be stopped. Victory will be ours!"

Surt's voice rose as he spoke until he was shouting the last words. Cheers erupted, and the warriors began pounding their spears into the ground so that the earth shook with their rage.

Surt waved and backed away, heading back into his council chambers.

Throwing his helmet onto the table, he grabbed a chalice and gulped down the contents, wiping his mouth with the back of his hand. Three of his generals stood before him. "What news do you bring me?" he asked. "Did you find the proof? Is Odin really dead? What are their armaments like?"

The soldier on the end, Lukas, an ugly beast of a giant with a face like a bull, stepped forward and laid a green swath of grass on the table. "The mischief-maker told the truth. The veil is down. We surveyed the western coastline. Odin's dead and gone. You could smell it in the wind. Not an ounce of his magic remains." He stepped back. Surt nodded at him, fingering the velvety grass in awe. How many centuries since he had touched greenery like this?

Bellac, a vicious female with two black ponytails sprouting from the top of her otherwise-bald pate, swaggered forward. A twisted scar marred her left cheek. Surt had given her that in a combat trial, and Bellac had proudly refused to stitch it up. Her teeth were capped in metal, and they glinted in the light as she growled out her report. "We flew the eastern coastline, lord. Burned seven Falcory villages to the ground. No sign of resistance or weapons, sire. They are feeble and weak."

Surt nodded, excitement growing as he continued on to Arek, his second-in-command. "You have studied their strongholds?"

Arek was smaller than the others but just as brutal. Surt had once seen him wrestle a feral boercat to the ground, placing the animal in a chokehold until it collapsed.

Arek spread out on the table a map that showed the isles of Orkney. The general put a finger on the island marked Garamond. "Once we take their capital city of Skara Brae, we will shatter their hold on the realm." He moved his finger to a smaller island. "The witches on Balfour Island will not come to Orkney's aid so soon after they were defeated." He moved his finger north. "Rakim is ruled by our brothers, the Vanir."

Surt's eyes narrowed. "What makes you think they will remember us?"

"They have no love of mankind. If we have to remind them of our bond, we will do so."

Bellac snarled. "Let me show those frost giants what my love feels like." She pounded one metal-clad fist into the other.

Surt waved a hand. "Let us hope our alliance holds. What of the Eifalians?"

Arek laughed. "Their magic is weak. Their only skill is to read auras and fire arrows."

Even Surt laughed. Arrows could hardly penetrate their thick skin.

"Ready the men. We leave in the morning. We'll make land here." He stabbed his finger on a point just east of Skara Brae. "Lukas and Bellac will lead the ground troops. Destroy everything in your path as you move toward the capital. Take no prisoners."

His two generals snarled with delight.

"Arek and I will lead the aerial assault from the boercats."

Arek bowed. "Orkney will be ours before the moon wanes."

# Chapter 13

Howie sat on the rampart, swinging his legs and whistling to keep himself awake. Sentry duty could get pretty boring, but a squire had to pay his dues. Fact is, he couldn't even remember the days he had passed his time playing video games and watching movies. Heck, he could hardly remember his last name, let alone his parents or his nine brothers and sisters.

"Vogelstein," he whispered to himself. "Howard Ronald Vogelstein."

Sometimes saying his name helped remind him who he was. A kid from Pilot Rock, Oregon, who loved Chuggies burgers and scary movies.

He had promised Sam to stick close to Skara Brae and play the role of Protector, but he was antsy, wishing he were off on a grand adventure like his friends. Not to mention that Rego and Teren had nearly chewed his ear off when they had discovered that Sam and that pair of witches had disappeared. He had told more lies than Pinocchio.

"Hey."

A slender figure dropped down next to him. It was Selina, the girl who had taught him everything he knew about holding a sword. Dabs of flour dotted her face from her work in the kitchens. She elbowed him and slipped a crunchy fresh roll in his hands.

"Anything out there?" she said, swinging her legs alongside his.

He shook his head, tearing a chunk of the thick bread with his teeth. "Not even a stray rathos." He tossed a piece to Lingas. The bird caught it out of the air and then ate it daintily. Damarius didn't even raise his head from his paws. The Shun Kara had barely eaten or taken interest in anything since Perrin had left him behind.

Selina searched the area. "Where's Jey? I swear that boy flirts with me more every day."

Howie smiled. "Jey's all right. Once you get used to him." He suddenly sat up straighter.

"What is it?" she asked.

He pointed at the horizon. A small cloud of dust moved quickly across the fields. It was a rider, bent low over the front of his horse and whipping it as if it were being chased by a pack of wolves. He squinted. It looked like a Falcory. Maybe Beo was back.

Howie ran to the railing and whistled, calling down to the gatekeeper, "Rider, coming in fast. Open the gates."

Howie clambered down the stairs with Selina and Damarius a step behind. Something about the rider told Howie it was not good news. The gatekeeper had just raised the gate as the horse broke into the square. Howie held up his hands, waving at the animal to stop. It reared up, nearly unseating its rider.

"Whoa, there, nice and easy." He grabbed the reins and calmed the horse. It was streaked with sweat and gray foam. Its flanks quivered, and its chest heaved, eyes wild with fear.

The rider was a Falcory in his early twenties. Howie didn't recognize him. He collapsed as Howie helped him down. When Howie pulled his hands back, a sticky dampness clung to them.

Blood.

Two guards helped Howie carry the wounded man up the stairs into the Great Hall. Howie sent a serving boy for the physician as Captain Teren entered the room.

"What's going on, Howie?"

"A Falcory arrived," Howie said, lifting up the leather jerkin the man wore to reveal an ugly hole where someone had speared him. "Looks like he ran into one of Surt's men."

Teren kneeled, frowning. "This is one of Beo's men."

Then Jey was there, shoving Howie aside as he dropped down by the man's side. "Turoq! What has happened? Where is my father?"

Turoq's eyes fluttered open. He grasped at Jey's shirt. "Your father led us into the Caverns of Inizza. But it all went wrong. That fire-breathing she-monster knocked down a rockfall with its tail, trapping them inside. A few of us got out and went for help, and then the red devils in the sky arrived."

Teren turned white as a sheet. "Surt's army has reached that far into Orkney?" he whispered. "How many?" He gripped the man's arm. "How many were there?"

"A dozen or so. They were on the backs of wild beasts." He choked down some water Teren fed him. "They rode them like flying demons, shooting flames and launching spears that could kill a man from the sky. Then they burned our huts to ash and left."

"You were brave to come and warn us. We will send help as soon as we can. I'm afraid it could be awhile." Teren stood as the physician arrived. "I must meet with the council. Howie, with me." The captain moved quickly away, barking orders out. The physician had Turoq taken to his infirmary, leaving the two boys alone.

Jey looked like he had been sucker punched. Howie touched his arm, but he pulled away.

"My father's not dead," he said, his face gray.

Howie had his doubts, but he didn't argue. "I'm sure he's fine. Teren will send help as soon as he can." He started to follow Teren when Jey's words stopped him.

"No. Someone has to rescue him. Now. I'm leaving."

Howie turned around, shaking his head. "Bad idea, amigo. You can't go up against that Safyre monster alone."

Jey's eyes were desperate. For once the cocky kid was at a loss.

"Then come with me."

Howie stared at him as all the reasons he shouldn't ran through his head. Skara Brae was doomed if they didn't come up with a way to slow that army of Surt's. The idea that had been running around in the back of his head popped up. It was a wild idea, but it was better than nothing. And if it bought them some time, maybe he and Jey could play at being hero.

He nodded, clasping Jey's shoulder. "I'm in. You gather some supplies and horses while I tell the captain how to hold off Surt until we get back."

Howie slipped into the High Council chambers. Teren sat around the table with his best remaining men, the red-headed Heppner on Teren's left and the wiry Speria on his right. Rego was giving an earful to Teren.

"There's no way we can stop Surt with what we've got. Maybe we need to be thinking of our options."

"What do you mean, dwarf? What other choice is there than fighting?" Teren demanded.

Rego shrugged, stroking his beard thoughtfully. "There's surrender," he said bluntly.

Speria jumped up, slamming his hand on the table. "We're Orkadian soldiers, sworn to defend this land from any and all who threaten it."

"That's right," Heppner added, shoving his chair back to join him. "We've stood a thousand years against all intruders. I reckon we can handle a few ugly fire giants."

Rego's face was red as he shouted back, "You think I like the idea? We have no weapons that can take down those boercats. They'll burn us from the sky, drive us out, and then come in force by land and tear down the walls of the castle. Surrender may be the only option if we are to survive."

"You mean be their slaves?" Speria said incredulously. "No chance. I'd rather die in battle than settle for that." The others murmured their agreement.

"What of the people?" Rego said quietly. "What of their wishes? Do we give them no choice?"

The two men stared each other down. Teren aged in front of Howie, but his face remained resolute. "I am responsible for making that decision for them. We have to figure out a way to hold off Surt until we get reinforcements. Now, does anyone have any ideas?"

There was silence all around.

Howie slouched down from his perch on the windowsill. "Yeah, I've got one."

Teren eyed him hesitantly, then waved him closer. "All right, squire, tell us, what magic can you conjure up to save us?"

"Well, it's not magic; more like a big fake-out." He waggled his hands in front of his face mysteriously.

"He's wasting our time," Speria scoffed, but Teren held his hand up for silence.

"Let the boy speak. Odin chose him as Protector once before. Go ahead," he nodded encouragingly to Howie.

Howie put his palms on the table and leaned in, eyeing the group. "Okay, so there was this ancient guy—he was emperor of China once upon a time. This bad guy wanted him and everyone that lived there dead. Dude didn't have much of an army, so he came up with this idea. He had his men create a fake army. They made a ton of soldiers out of clay and put them out on the battlefield. They stood them up in battalions with real shields and swords. Then they set smoke-pots so the field was blurred, so you couldn't really see. He ran some of his men among them so there were people moving about and shouting to each other, so that anyone looking would think it was an army of soldiers."

The men around the table looked skeptical.

Howie ignored their looks and continued. "When the warlord arrived to attack, he saw a battlefield filled with men. He wasn't expecting that kind of resistance, and he turned around and left. The people were saved."

Howie waited to see if they would burst out laughing, but there was a long stretch of silence broken only when Speria grunted, looking at Heppner, "Is that the dumbest idea you ever heard?"

Heppner nodded. "Yup. Even dumber than that time he called up an army of the dead."

Speria looked back thoughtfully at Howie. "Course, that turned out all right, now, didn't it?"

Teren drummed his fingers on the table. "Even if we were desperate enough to consider it, we don't have clay around here."

"That's the brilliant part," Howie said. "We're gonna make an army of dummy soldiers."

Rego snorted. "The boy has lost his mind."

"No, hear me out," Howie said. "We got stacks of old armor piled up in the basement of the armory. Plus all the Balfin ape-men armor we recovered. We stand it up out in the cornfields. With enough smoke and mirrors, Surt won't know what to make of it."

Speria scowled. "Surt's not going to believe it for long. He'll find out our army is a bunch of empty tin suits and then laugh himself silly as he burns us all to the ground."

"But that's the point, right?" Howie defended his little battle plan. "To get him to hold back long enough for the big guns to arrive. Sam is out there doing something. I know my friend; he's going to fix this. Maybe we just have to trust in that and hope that Mrs. Abigail brings back a pack of witches, and Keely and Leo ride in with an army of frost giants in tow."

The men looked around the table at each other. Teren drummed his fingers. Speria rubbed at the scruff on his face. Heppner tilted his chair back, shaking his head side to side.

Speria finally spoke up. "The boy's got a point. We have enough rusted armor to outfit a legion."

Heppner's chair hit the ground with a thump as he glared at his comrade. Then he sighed, "We're short on helmets, but I suppose that lazy blacksmith can make us some more."

Teren studied the group seated at the table, his shoulders squaring. "I say we give the boy's plan a shot. Unless someone has a better idea?"

There was silence. Rego twitched his whiskers side to side, then stood up. "I say we have as much chance of surviving this as a pig on Christmas. So what are we waiting for?"

Teren stood. "Speria, you lead a group down to the fields and begin assembling the dummy soldiers. Use all the old shields and armor you can find. Make them look real as you can. Heppner, to the blacksmith. I want helmets, shields, swords, whatever he can hammer out. From now on, everyone works on Howie's plan."

The two soldiers nodded and left.

The room emptied. Howie watched them leave, unable to shake the nagging feeling that Rego was right and Surt would probably burn them to the ground with one puff of his boercat.

# Chapter 14

Valkyrie warriors had few limitations. They never tired; they were able to fly for hours in the form of the swan and transform instantly into warrior mode and do battle. Their swan form displayed the golden shield and helmet of their armor, their swords tucked under their wings, ready to access at a thought.

As Geela crossed the great waters that stretched between the Orkney islands, she wondered if it had been a mistake to join with the gods. She was tired, deep down in her soul. She had served for close to two centuries now, never questioning the orders, never doubting her mission, never once asking if this was what she wanted.

A maiden when the goddess Frigga had found her, she had been fighting off a rival landlord after her father had died and her mother had taken ill. Her younger brother, Emmet, had gone to get help. The lord thought she was easy prey for his ruffians and had tried to take over their lands, but she had drawn a sword and battled for their rights. She had been pinned down, having taken out over a dozen of his men, but their numbers were too many.

And then Frigga had been there, blasting her horn and swooping down from the sky to pluck Geela out of their grasp before they ran her through. She had fought it at first, wanting to go back to her family, but Frigga had shown her how empty that life was. The men had taken the land, and, even if Geela had stayed, there was rot in the vines that plagued the farm for years. She only wished she'd been able to say goodbye to her mother and to find out how Emmet had fared.

Frigga had done her a favor, Geela knew, ignoring the salty tear that leaked from her swan eye. A big favor. One of the raiders would have taken her as his wife and forced her to be his servant. She was far better off as a golden warrior of the Valkyrie, but sometimes her human-self asserted its contrariness.

Like now.

She felt sorry for the boy. Vor had always been kind to Geela, honest to a fault, and had seen her struggle with accepting life with the Valkyrie. Vor had often offered kind words of encouragement. Geela trusted Vor in ways that Frigga couldn't understand, even though her loyalty lay with her queen. Vor's words of caution weighed on her.

Movement in the water caught her eye. Something large, like a small island, but mobile. Geela veered sharply to her left and soared lower over the ocean, enjoying the spray from the whitecaps.

The wet smell of feral wolf reached her at the same time the waves parted and revealed a mass of fur and gnashing teeth pawing through the water. Geela reared back, her wings flaring out as she squawked in surprise.

It couldn't be.

Fenrir? The giant wolf Odin had banished to Groll? The beast was swimming freely in the ocean, but how was this possible?

She gritted her teeth. The boy. Of course. Was this part of his plan or Loki's? Geela didn't have time to puzzle it out. The distant shores of Garamond were within reach. Fenrir could not be allowed to make land.

A beast like Fenrir would devour, destroy, and ravage anything he came in contact with. She soared toward the paddling wolf, transforming from her swan form to warrior. She gripped her gleaming sword between two hands. He wasn't aware of her presence. She still had the element of surprise. If she could come up behind him, she might land a lucky blow to his skull.

But Fenrir must have sensed her because his ears pricked up and he turned, snapping at her as she landed on his back and aimed for a spot behind his ear. She missed, tumbling forward, and hit the surface of the water, skipping across it as she regrouped.

The water frothed as the wolf paddled furiously, swiping at her with his paw. She brought her sword up, thrusting it into the tender part of his pad.

Fenrir yowled. She hauled herself up by grabbing clumps of his fur and ran up to his shoulder, diving to reach the soft vulnerable spot under his neck so she could sever his artery.

She got her blade up, but the wolf swung his jaw hard to the side and knocked her in the head. The solid bone acted like a hammer and jarred her helmet so hard that stars danced behind her eyes. She was flung backward into the water. A cloak of darkness settled over her as her body went limp.

It must have been some time later when warm rays of sunlight licked at her face, bathing her with golden warmth and energizing her blood. Geela sat up with a gasp, coughing and spitting up water. She was on a ship, sailing across the water, fast and low.

Skidbladnir.

Her hand rested on the deck. Magic flowed in the boards

under her fingers. Somehow, she'd found her way onto the very ship she had been searching for. Wiping her mouth, she staggered to her feet, reaching for her sword.

There it was, strapped to her waist securely. She touched her head. The golden helmet she wore was missing. Her breastplate was in place, but she felt exposed without her gleaming headpiece.

Voices and the sound of laughter rang out from the back of the ship. Still dizzy, she stepped carefully so as not to faint and headed for the sounds.

They were children, three of them. The boy she recognized as the Son of Odin, and two girls, one only a waif. She sniffed. Witches. Her lip curled. She hated witches. She had forgotten the boy was one of them. *What does Vor see in him?* she wondered as she prowled forward, sword in front of her.

They seemed unaware of her presence, laughing among themselves and chattering like monkeys. The small girl wore Geela's helmet, prancing around in it like it was part of a costume. They had no weapons other than daggers strapped to their sides. The older girl kept one hand on the wheel. Did they not realize the great injustice they had done, releasing Fenrir? The savage beast would devour entire villages, and these children acted as if they hadn't a care in the world.

Enraged, Geela leapt forward, intending to land in the middle of them and scare them, but as she leapt, a funny thing happened. The trio split apart seamlessly and bent the air so that she was pushed to the side, landing hard against the rigging. Her sword was ripped out of her hands by some strange pull, and she was on her back like a turtle, helpless to move as she gasped air into her lungs.

They stood over her, green eyes narrowed, taking wary stances. She had seriously underestimated them. They had been aware of her every move. Not knowing who she was or if she could be trusted, they had waited to see how she would act, and, like a fool, she had attacked them. She dragged in a long gulp of air and held her hands up in an act of surrender.

"Peace, I come in peace. I'm sorry." She sat up slowly so they wouldn't blast her with the balls of green energy that hovered over their hands. She got to her feet. "I am Geela of the Valkyrie. I am commanded by Queen Frigga to assist you in finding Odin. How did I come onto this ship?"

The trio exchanged a look that told her they were as surprised as she was.

"The ship kind of has a mind of its own," the boy said. "It swung around. Almost knocked us overboard and headed your way."

"Why did you release Fenrir?" Geela asked, casually kneeling to collect her sword. Frigga had ordered her to end the boy's life if he posed a threat.

The boy looked pained. "I had to, to get the key."

"What key?"

The little one butted in. "Don't tell her, Sam; she just wants to trick us into turning around." The brat still wore Geela's helmet.

Geela swung her sword in a blaze of gold light and placed it against the neck of the third witch, who had stood silently by, keeping her hand on the wheel. The girl didn't flinch. "Tell me why you wanted the key," Geela said evenly, her eyes never leaving the girl's.

The girl didn't answer, but her eyes told Geela that she was conflicted about this journey of theirs.

"Can we put our weapons down?" Sam said, lowering his hands and extinguishing the green light. "It sounds like we're on the same side. We needed the key around Fenrir's neck in order to get into Jormungand's cell."

Geela gasped. Were these children insane? Or working

for Loki? "Why in Odin's name would you seek out that evil creature?"

Sam ran a hand through his hair. "Frigga sent us to find Odin in Helva's underworld, but she didn't think to give us a map."

Perrin firmly pushed the sword away from her neck before she said, "There's one scratched in the back of Jormungand's cell. Sam didn't mean to free Fenrir; it just happened. That's usually how it goes with him. My name's Perrin. You obviously know who Sam is, and the imp is Mavery."

The little one silently handed over the helmet.

Geela sheathed her sword, tucking her helmet under her arm. She was still puzzled by the events. "And now you are headed to Jormungand's lair? To find this map?"

The witch-boy grinned at her. "Yup. Unless you have a better idea?"

Geela did not. She had heard of the treacherous underground tunnels that led to Helva's underworld entrance. A map would save valuable time.

"Is Odin really dead?"

The question had come from Sam, but all three witches stared at her, awaiting her answer.

Geela met his eyes. "I don't know. Death does not follow the same rules for the gods. They live on in a cycle that never ends."

His eyes flickered with frustration. "What's different about this time? Why doesn't he just come back?"

She shook her head. "I don't know, but something has changed. Odin has never been gone this long."

Perrin asked bluntly, "Do you think we're too late?"

Geela sighed as she made her decision, knowing Frigga would not approve. "I think we have to find Jormungand and see if this map really exists."

# Chapter 15

Skidbladnir cut through the water as if there were a strong wind at its back. The striped sails billowed out, but Sam could swear there wasn't so much as a breeze stirring the heat of the day. As he sat at the wheel, the sun was in his eyes and the skin on his face burned with the afternoon rays.

Cupping his hand, he searched the horizon. The sea was flat and blue. There was no sign of land, not even a shore bird in sight. Perrin was teaching Mavery some new magic spells at the front of the boat, drawing their hands through the air and sending out small bursts of crackling energy. Sam wanted to join them. It looked a lot more fun than having his hands clamped to the wheel, but it was his turn to steer.

Letting out a sigh, he wondered for the hundredth time if they were doing the right thing. He wished more than anything that he could warn his friends back in Skara Brae to be on the lookout for Fenrir. How were they supposed to fight a giant wolf anyway? Was there a weapon big enough to bring the canine beast to its knees?

Horrible thoughts filled his head, images of Fenrir pouncing on villages and swallowing them whole. Sam's hands were slick with sweat as he gripped the wheel, fighting the urge to turn around before he made everything worse. Because that was definitely his specialty: taking a situation and making it go from bad to plain end-of-the-world we're-all-going-to-die awful.

A noise came from overhead. That Valkyrie, Geela, was up in the riggings in the small crow's nest. She slid down the ropes, landing lightly on the deck next to him.

"Did you see anything?" he asked.

She shook her head. "We seem to be in the middle of nowhere. Jormungand's lair is deep underwater. Just how do you expect to find it?"

"I found Groll, didn't I?" he reminded her. "Ol' Skidbladnir's taking us somewhere."

"But you don't know where or how long it will take? Even now Surt marches on your cities. His men may have breached the walls of Skara Brae. Fenrir could have reached land by now."

Sam exploded at the Valkyrie. "Enough! You think I don't see that every time I close my eyes? I want to vomit at the thought of what that wolf could be doing. I can't eat; I can't sleep. This is the craziest, dumbest, riskiest idea I have ever had, but guess what? I don't know what else to do. The only way I can fix things is to bring Odin back. If we don't bring him back, it won't matter that Fenrir is loose. Surt will wipe out everything, so you know what? Keep quiet unless you have something useful to say."

"We're here," she said quietly.

"Yeah, right."

"Look." She pointed over his head.

Behind him, a spout of water rose out of the sea, shooting a hundred feet in the sky. A vortex began swirling around the spout, creating a whirlpool of foamy white water. Sam squinted, not sure if he was seeing clearly. Sea animals of all kinds were swept up into the jet stream. Their silvery dark bodies flashed through the column of blue water. The boat turned toward it, drawn in by the pull of the current.

"Oh, no you don't, not again," Sam said, steering the ship away. Perrin and Mavery raced to the back.

"What is that?" Mavery asked in awe.

"That's the serpent's feeding tube," Geela shouted as the sound of the water churning grew louder. Skidbladnir barreled straight for the funnel of water.

"Turn the ship!" Perrin shouted at Sam.

"I'm trying," Sam shouted back in frustration, "but it's not listening." He tugged on the wheel with all his strength. Perrin joined in, adding her hands to the slick wood, but the ship stubbornly held course for the spout.

"Use your magic, Sam," Perrin said calmly, looking into his eyes. "Transport yourself out of here. It's not too late for you."

He stared at her, feeling the deck tilt as the spray from the funnel rained down. He saw her fear and her concern for him, and, somehow, that gave him the courage to smile. "I'm not leaving you. We've just found Jormungand."

Geela pulled them apart. "The ship won't enter the funnel. We need to be prepared when it transforms back."

The roaring column of water was directly overhead. They stood, holding hands, the four of them lined up. As the ship's prow pierced the column, Skidbladnir shuddered, and then, with a violent shake and a shimmy, the ship simply vanished, dropping them straight into the icy water.

Sam held on to Perrin's hand, and Geela grabbed Mavery as the seas frothed and whirled them around, spinning them higher up in the air.

He lost his grip on Perrin when something rough and scaly bumped into him. He found himself staring into the eyes of a shark with rows of sharp teeth. It was swept away before it could latch on to him. Furiously kicking, Sam swam to the edge of the column. He got his hand out, then his head, and he was gasping in fresh air when the column abruptly stopped rotating.

It was as if someone had reversed the suction. The water imploded on itself. Sam fell, sucked downward like an elevator that had lost its brakes. Pressure built in his ears as the world went dark and cold water pressed in. Fish swam by, brushing him with their slimy scales. Then a rush of bubbles tickled his face, and he bumped up against a rock.

A dark opening yawned—an entrance to a cave. He grabbed for the lip of rock, but the pull was too strong, and his fingers slipped off. He was sucked into a narrow tunnel.

The water stopped pouring in, and the current slowed. Sam turned, pulling his arms through the water to escape, but a large rock moved into place, sealing him in. Swimming side to side, he found only solid stone. Pounding his hands on it, he screamed in frustration, letting the air bubble out of him. Black spots sprang up behind his eyes. His chest burned with the need to breathe.

Then the current dragged him forward as the tunnel drained. The water level dropped quickly. Sam's head broke the surface, bumping up against the rock ceiling. He dragged in air that was moist and damp and smelled of rotted seaweed. It was the sweetest air he'd ever tasted.

Spinning around, he searched for the others. No one surfaced.

"Perrin!" he shouted. "Mavery!"

Wiping the seawater from his eyes, he swam forward, searching the cavern. A dim glow came from the water—some kind of plankton, he guessed. He could just make out the dim outline of the cave. The water drained toward the far end. He let himself be carried with the current until his feet touched bottom and he was able to stand.

He called out every few moments for his friends. They had to be here.

"Perrin?" His voice echoed off the walls. Something cold and bony grasped his ankle and yanked him under. His shout of surprise was muffled by a mouthful of seawater. He pried it off, thinking it was Jormungand, but he found himself staring into Perrin's green eyes.

He stood up, dripping mad. "What the heck, Perrin? You scared the pants off me." Then he grabbed her and hugged her quickly. "But where's the imp? Tell me you know where she is."

Her face clouded. "Sorry, Sam, I haven't seen her. But you know Mavery. She's probably torturing Jormungand as we speak."

"Is no one worried about me?"

The quiet voice of Geela came from behind them. Sam and Perrin turned together and gasped. She stood on a ledge that ran along the side of the tunnel. In her arms, she held Mavery. The witchling looked a little green but held her thumb up to Sam.

The water was down to Sam's waist. He began wading to the side when the suction increased and dragged him back. It was like getting swept up in the outgoing tide at the beach. He reached for Perrin, who was just behind him, but he missed as the current jerked her away.

"Sam!"

"Hold on." He waded toward her, but he was knocked off his feet by a large turtle. He caught sight of Geela running along the ledge. A yawning black hole at the end of the tunnel made him paddle harder for safety.

Geela reached down and grabbed his collar, hauling him up to the ledge.

"Get Perrin," he said, coughing out water.

But Geela was already racing toward the dark head bobbing in the water.

Perrin clung to the lip of the opening, gripping the rock with white fingers.

Mavery knocked him on the shoulder. "Do something!" she cried.

Sam stood up, shaking himself to clear his head. "*Fereza, fereza, nae movio*," he shouted, and he pushed forward with his hand.

At once, the water stopped moving, frozen in place. The Valkyrie grasped Perrin's wrist and hauled her up. Sam dropped his hand, and the current resumed its relentless surge. The rest of the tunnel emptied out into the gaping black hole. It could only lead to one place.

The sea serpent's pen.

As the last bit of water drained away, it revealed a slick stone chute. The sea creatures that remained began flopping, gasping for water, sliding forward until they were swept over the edge.

"This is amazing," Mavery said, an awed look on her face. "There's even fresh air."

"Not bad for a sea serpent. He's figured out a way to keep himself alive while he's locked up down here," Perrin said between chattering teeth.

An earsplitting screech rent the air. Mavery covered her ears. Fear coiled Sam's stomach into knots. They stared at the gaping hole where the serpent could be heard thrashing around. Feeding.

Geela spoke after the dwindling echo faded. "I will scout ahead and see what the layout is. The rest of you stay here."

Sam shook his head. "That's not how it works. We don't split up the team, right, imp?"

Mavery smiled up at him and shook her head. Sam and the girls turned and began climbing over the slippery rock to a trail that disappeared into the black hole, leaving Geela to stare after them.

# Chapter 16

Geela gripped her sword in damp hands as she trailed behind the boy and his two companions. They had some sort of ball of light that lit their way. She was worried. More than worried. She was terrified about what they would encounter and was completely unsure if it was the right thing to do. Geela had never strayed from her mission before, and this was clearly not what Frigga had commanded her to do.

If the queen mother of the gods knew she was on her way to see Loki's ill-begotten child, Jormungand, and possibly free him in the process, Frigga would strip Geela of her right to wear the golden crest of the Valkyrie.

There were times Geela regretted, with every cell in her body, the day she'd left her simple farm behind and joined the ranks of the gods, but it had seemed like such an honor, and she'd fit into the role like she'd been born to it. Now she wasn't so sure she had the wisdom to decide her path and the strength to carry it out.

Odin was in trouble, maybe even gone this time. But what if he could be brought back? And if so, did she bear the burden of making it happen, even if it meant terrible things were unleashed? Already the witch-boy had released Fenrir, the fiercest, most destructive flesh-eating beast in the Nine Realms. And now she was helping them get to Jormungand. What if the sea monster escaped as well? What then? All for a map that might not exist, to an underworld where Odin might not even be.

Dread filled Geela's veins with every step forward they took. Worst of all, the children didn't seem to realize the seriousness of what they attempted. Sam laughed at something Perrin said, his voice echoing in the cold, damp tunnel. The beast would surely hear them and be waiting for them. The boy needed to learn caution.

Frustrated, Geela lunged forward and swept Sam's legs out from behind, dropping him to the ground. She pinned him with her sword across his neck as she hissed, "This isn't a game, child; we are about to face the most dangerous creature in this world. Jormungand can strike you with his forked tongue from twenty feet away. We may all be dead in a few minutes, and you laugh as if it is nothing."

Sam stared up at her, silent.

The young waif giggled, holding her hand over her mouth.

Geela whirled her head to the side. "You think this is funny?"

Perrin stepped forward, shoving the younger girl behind her. "No, we don't think it's funny. It's just not the first time we've been in a bad situation, and sometimes laughing makes us not think about the fact that were probably going to die. Plus, you're holding a fish."

Geela frowned, looking down. In her hands was a long, slimy eel-like fish. Where was her golden sword? At that moment, the fish started wiggling. She released it, stepping back in shock as Sam grinned at her and sat up.

Confused and angry, she said, "What kind of magic is that? Where is my sword?"

"Relax." Sam reached behind her and pulled the gleaming blade from her belt. "It's right here."

Geela shook her head, snatching her sword. "I should have never come here. I should have brought you all straight to Frigga. This is wrong. We need to turn around now."

The youngest one rolled her eyes, while the boy just folded his arms and said, "We're not turning back. If you want to leave, leave. We don't need you."

Perrin elbowed him. "Of course we need her; don't be an idiot." She turned toward Geela. "But we understand if you have to go. You know, if Odin really is trapped, then we're his only hope of getting out. If he's not brought back, then Surt is going to destroy our world. Are the gods going to stop him? Is Frigga going to bring an army to fight him off?"

Geela lowered her sword. They might be kids, but they weren't foolish. They stood in front of her, resolved and resolute, even knowing that they were facing imminent death.

"They don't have the power," she said slowly. "The gods can't interfere with mankind. Odin alone had the knowledge of their ways."

"Then we're Orkney's only chance," Perrin continued. "The gods aren't going to save us. We need Odin. And we're the only ones who can find him."

They were right. If Odin was trapped, they were the only ones who could help him. If he wasn't, none of it would matter much to the kingdom of men once Surt burned it to the ground. Or Frigga destroyed it. Geela kept that last piece of information to herself.

"Okay," she said, sheathing her sword. "We'll do it your way."

Sam eyed the stiff back of the Valkyrie as she marched ahead of them. Part of him resented her bossiness, but the other part, the intelligent part, recognized her usefulness. Geela radiated power. And wisdom. Something he sorely lacked.

They continued until a dim circle of light appeared ahead—an opening with thick iron bars. The trail turned to the left. Creeping forward, they peered through the bars. They were looking down into Jormungand's prison, a large underground cavern with rough-hewn walls and a vaulted ceiling that rose two stories. Long stalactites with sharp pointed ends hung down like jagged teeth. A circular pool of water was barricaded by more iron bars that stretched from floor to ceiling

The water roiled and bubbled in a frenzy of feeding. Sam searched for a glimpse of the creature, but he must have been drifting under the surface, devouring his latest catch. After a bit, the water calmed. Sam could make out a dark shape slithering underneath.

He gripped the bars, standing on his tiptoes to peer down for a better look when suddenly the serpent reared upward, rising fifty feet in the air. Vicious jaws snapped at the bars, sending Sam sprawling backward. Mavery screamed, ducking her head.

A set of red eyes glared at them over a long green snout. It was capped with a set of flared nostrils over a row of spiny teeth. The serpent's body was covered in thick emerald scales. He let out a roar that rattled his iron cage. A forked tongue slithered through the bars, seeking prey to snag. Sam could feel the spray of his foul breath as he shrugged off Jormungand's grasping tongue. The sea serpent battered himself against the iron bars. Then he dropped back into the water, circling around.

They risked another glance. A fat padlock hung from the gate below.

"There it is," Geela whispered.

Yeah. There it was. Fat lot of good it was going to do them. The lock was blackened with age and rusted over. Barnacles crusted the keyhole. Even if the key he'd taken from Fenrir fit, it was so rusted that it probably wouldn't open. Not without some effort. And if he spent any time fiddling with it, Jormungand was sure to devour him.

Sam looked at Geela. "Any ideas?"

The Valkyrie stared intently at the lock, her golden brow furrowed. "None that guarantee I survive." A cheeky grin brightened her face. "Finally, some real action. Be ready when I give the sign."

Before Sam could blink, she was gone, her sword held before her as she picked her way down a narrow trail carved into the side of the wall, just wide enough for one person.

"What is she doing?" Perrin hissed.

"I think she's the bait. You and Mavery help distract Jormungand while I get the lock open and find the map."

"Where do you suppose it is?"

They studied the beast's lair. A rock shelf ran behind the pool under an overhang, marked with the worn indentation where Jormungand rested.

"There." Sam pointed to the back wall. He could just make out a set of markings in the recesses of the overhang. "If I can get through the gate, I'll be able to read it."

"Why don't you transport yourself the way you did with Fenrir?" Mavery asked.

Sam flushed. "I'm not exactly sure how I did it. I can't control it yet. I might end up inside its jaws."

"Look at her," Perrin interrupted. "Is she crazy?"

Geela had climbed down and stood outside the cage. She began to run along the edge, clinking the bars with her sword as she shouted, "Jormungand, you ugly sea monster, come meet your destiny!"

The water bubbled and turned frothy. Geela came to the end, where the bars met the stone wall. She waited, holding her sword out while she waved at Sam to move with her other hand.

"Go on, then," Perrin urged, giving Sam a shove. "We'll stay here and give you cover."

Sam began running down the trail, hoping he didn't slip and break an ankle.

The beast rose out of the water and towered over Geela. Glowering eyes like hot coals stared fiercely down at her. His forked tongue slithered out of his mouth, striking at Geela through the bars.

Sam paused, transfixed by the sight of Geela pressed back against the wall. For a second, he thought she was going to be snatched up, but she ducked and rolled under the beast's tongue and came up on the other side, driving him back with pointed jabs of her sword.

Relieved, Sam hurried to the gate. The lock hung rusted and dull. He pulled the key from the pouch, but his hands shook so badly he dropped it. Bending to pick it up, he came face-to-face with the creature as he rose out of the water in front of him. Jormungand lunged forward, gnashing at the bars so hard the whole place shook.

Perrin sent a bolt of green witchfire that bounced off his scaly head. Jormungand bawled and pulled back. Sam snatched up the key and shoved it into the lock, twisting it. The key didn't budge. There was too much rust. As Jormungand circled back, he bumped up against the gate, shaking the bars of his cage and rattling Sam.

"Watch out, witch-boy," Geela called.

Then she did an amazing thing. As she ran along the bars, she transformed herself into a swan, a beautiful white bird with a helmet of gold and matching breastplate.

She slipped through the bars and flew straight up into the

red eye of the beast. Geela's swan form clawed and pecked at his eye, her sharp beak making Jormungand yowl with pain. The sea serpent snapped at her, chasing the nimble bird around his pen, one eye oozing a sticky green blood.

"Come on, come on," Sam muttered, jiggling the key. Stepping back, he sent a blast of magic at the lock.

Nothing.

He pulled on it, tugging with all his might. Frustrated, he let it drop. He needed something more.

Closing his eyes, he centered himself. Sam imagined the key in the lock, the key that he needed to bring Odin back.

*Father Odin*, he said as he quieted his mind, *help me help you, help me open this lock.*

The chamber went silent. All Sam could hear was the beating of his heart. When he felt certain, he stepped forward, put his hand on the key, and turned it.

With a click, the lock fell apart, shattering into pieces onto the ground, and the door swung open. Sam took two steps into the pen and then stumbled back as Jormungand roared out of the water, launching his long body toward him, screeching like a foghorn.

Pushing his hands out, Sam called on his witch magic. He sent up a spray of water, blinding the creature and sending him backward until Jormungand hit the back wall.

Geela landed on the ledge, transforming back into her human form. "Go. I'll take care of this beast."

Sam ran, careful not to slip into the roiling pool. He bent low under the overhang. The back side of the lair was empty, except for scattered bones.

On the far wall, he found the map. He ran his fingers over it, tracing the lines etched into the stone.

It reminded him of a subway map with lines connecting to circles running in every direction. There were symbols and markings, like ancient hieroglyphs at each stop. Before he could make sense of it, a raspy tongue wrapped around his ankles and swept him off his feet.

Jormungand dragged him across the ledge toward the water. He shouted for help, struggling to get free as he bounced over the rocks. Then Geela was there, stabbing her golden sword downward into Jormungand's fleshy appendage. The serpent screamed in pain, releasing Sam and thrashing about in the pool.

Overhead, the cavern rumbled and shook as the giant beast hit the bars hard enough to shake the floor. A stalactite fell from the ceiling and dropped into the water. The beast cried out again, whipping around in a circle in the water, and another spiked column fell, knocking Geela to the ground.

"This place is coming apart," Geela said, pushing off the debris. "You must hurry and read the map."

Sam turned back toward the map, but Mavery's scream spun him around. The girls were huddled against the wall as one by one the bars fell into the water.

Jormungand surged upward, snapping his jaws at them. Geela was still struggling to free herself. Drawing the dagger at his side, Sam launched himself into the air onto the back of the creature. His jagged spikes were sharp, but Sam grabbed hold, scrambling up toward Jormungand's head.

Sam reached the spot behind the serpent's small slitted ears and plunged the dagger down into his skull.

Dumb idea.

He should have aimed for a soft spot. The blade snapped in two as it penetrated the flesh and hit solid bone. Jormungand shook himself like a wet dog, flinging Sam off.

He went sailing in the air and tumbled on the ledge. The serpent turned back to the girls. He reared his head back, opening his spiny-tooth-filled mouth wide, preparing to snatch them up. Perrin shielded Mavery, a ball of green witchfire in her hands, but it wouldn't be enough to stop him from eating them both.

Desperate, Sam blasted a stalactite with witchfire, knocking it loose, and then, using all his magic, he brought it down with as much force as he had. The pointed rock pierced the beast's snout, skewering his jaw shut. Jormungand collapsed sideways, tumbling down to the ledge, half his body submerged. Blood-streaked bubbles foamed at his mouth as he gasped for air.

There was no time to celebrate. Perrin and Mavery made it safely down as more stalactites fell from the ceiling.

"We have to get out of here!" Geela shouted, limping because of a deep gash in her knee.

"How?" Perrin asked. "The way we came in is blocked."

"We'll find another way," Geela said, herding them under the overhang as another rock crashed down. Sam turned to stare at the map, trying to make sense of it.

"We have to leave," Geela said.

"But I can't read it."

"It doesn't matter." Geela pulled at him, but he resisted.

"It does matter!" he shouted at her. "I have to bring Odin back, and I need to be able to read this map."

"We need to be looking for a way out of here, or we'll all be dead."

"Then look while I try to decipher it."

He yanked his arm free and turned back to the map. It was a maze. A dark mansion scratched at the far right was the end. That must be where Helva was.

He started at the beginning and traced a route. The maze began with two possible paths, each marked by a different symbol, one an open eye, the other a closed eye. He traced the line of the closed eye, but it ran into a dead end. He went back and ran his finger along the open-eye line. It ended in a junction with three more possible paths marked by different glyphs.

The walls of the serpent's prison shook with an ominous rumble as more stalactites fell. Sam began to sweat. Time was running out.

The second set of glyphs looked like symbols from Rego's rune stones: a funny looking *F*, a three-pronged *Y*, and a large *X*. He traced the large *X*, but it quickly dead-ended. He tried the funny *F* next. Its path crossed the three-pronged *Y* and ended. The three-pronged *Y* had to be right.

He kept going, tracing and retracing and putting the correct symbols in his memory. There was a series of familiar celestial objects: lightning bolt, sun, crescent moon, and star. Which was it? His fingers flew over the lines as he traced his way to one dead end, and then another. Finally, he reached a row of animals: ox, horse, rabbit, snake, and raven. *Aargh! There were too many.*

Sweat rolled down his temples as he struggled to trace the paths. He'd eliminated three of them when the overhang split with a loud crack, and spider-vein cracks spread across the wall, shooting out in every direction.

"No!" Sam tried to hold the map in place as the wall crumbled in his hands. "I'm not done!" he shouted.

He frantically searched for the last set of symbols on the map, but the rock wall shattered, crumbling to the ground, exposing an opening behind it. Sam dropped to his knees sifting through the rocks to put the pieces back together.

Someone grabbed him by the collar and threw him forward into the safety of the tunnel. Geela pushed Perrin and Mavery in behind Sam as the cavern collapsed behind them in a crush of tumbling debris. Geela was struck on the head with a falling rock as she joined them.

From inside the tunnel, the rumbling sound of the walls collapsing around Jormungand's holding pen echoed. The Valkyrie kept pushing them along the tunnel. Too soon they came to the end. A solid rock wall greeted them.

The girls sat down, out of breath. Geela staggered, blood streaming down the side of her face. Sam grabbed her arm as her knees went out, and she sank to the ground.

Behind them, a whisper of wind touched his face.

"What's that?" Mavery asked, noticing it as well.

"Shh, listen," Sam hissed. Had the serpent followed somehow?

No, not the serpent.

Worse.

Water.

Rushing toward them.

"Come on," he said, calling Perrin and Mavery to him. "We have to break through this."

The three witches stood in front of the wall and began blasting it with an emerald blaze of witchfire. The rock wall appeared impenetrable. The wall of water rushed closer, growing louder. The breeze blew harder. The sea had come in and would bury them down here forever.

Sam let his fury build in him, not willing to give in. He wasn't finished yet. Not by a long shot.

"*Nemaste, nemaste, kin teali.*" He pushed with every cell in his body, letting his magic flow through his fingers out toward the rock. It exploded in a burst of gray shards. Half expecting the sea to come racing at them from the other direction, Sam grabbed Geela's arm as he leapt forward. Perrin took Mavery's hand, and the four of them tumbled through the opening onto a polished marble floor, leaping ahead of the wave that crested behind them.

They looked up at a sea of beautiful men and women staring at them in shock. From a coral throne, a man rose, wearing a crown of seashells. He carried a staff that looked like a large whalebone. He pointed the staff at the hole in the wall as the wave rolled in. Blue fire shot out, hit the water, and sent it backward. With a dazzling burst of light, the rocks regrouped and sealed up the hole.

Sam turned to find the owner of the staff looking down at him. His eyes blazed with a blue fire that speared Sam in place. The man was old, his beard thin and pointed. He had knobby hands that gripped the staff he pointed toward Sam, as if he were about to sizzle Sam next.

"Hey, sorry, we didn't mean to intrude," Sam began, but Mavery moved in front of him, planting her hands on her hips.

"Hey, don't you hurt my friend. Jasper said the sea god is the god of mirth and friendship."

The blaze in the sea god's eyes died down, and a smile crinkled his face, deepening the lines as he knelt to Mavery's level.

"So I am. I'm Aegir. And who might you be?"

"I'm Mavery, and this here"—she jerked her thumb at Sam—"this is Sam. He's a Son of Odin, and, you know, that whole red sun thing was him," she whispered.

The sea god raised a thick eyebrow. "So it was. But it turned out okay in the end, didn't it?"

She shrugged. "Well, it did until a witch turned him into Sam-the-crazy-guy, and he killed Odin."

There was silence in the room as every merman and mermaid conversation came to a halt. Aegir straightened himself. Sam waited for the blue fire to cinder him into ashes. Aegir stared at him for several long seconds.

"I see," he said at last. "And why were you in Jormungand's chamber? The serpent was banished to an eternity of isolation."

"Not anymore," Sam said, risking getting to his feet. "He's dead. And we're on our way to Helva's underworld to bring Odin back."

There were gasps from the assembled crowd. Even Aegir looked surprised at Sam's words, though he said nothing.

Behind Sam, Perrin spoke softly. "We need to get help for Geela. She's not waking up."

The Valkyrie lay unconscious on the coral floor. Before Sam could move, Aegir waved a hand, and a swarm of attendants lifted her limp body and carried her off. Perrin took Mavery by the hand and tugged her away to follow Geela.

"We will speak more of this later," Aegir said. "For now, rest, relax, and enjoy the company of my lovely daughters."

A row of giggling girls in varying heights stood behind Aegir. There were too many to count, at least eight or nine. They looked at Sam like he was fish bait.

"Hi." Sam smiled weakly as they swarmed around him and carried him forward into the room.

# Chapter 17

In his raven form, few people noticed Loki lurking about. A raven was far too common a creature. Ruffling out his feathers, Loki scanned the busy streets of Ter Glenn. The Eifalian capital city bustled with shoppers. Carriages rambled up and down the cobblestone streets. The peace-loving Eifalians were oblivious to the threat marching downward toward them from the north, a wave of frost giants so fierce and angry that even Loki quaked at their massive forces.

The thought of bringing the wrath of the Vanir down on the heads of the Eifalians made him quiver with joy. The two races had been bitter enemies for centuries. War was inevitable. How delightful to be the one to light the fuse.

Loki studied the fair-skinned, long-limbed people that milled about in the streets. Everyone had a kind word for his or her neighbor, politely stepping aside to let another pass.

His heart hardened as he remembered how Frey, God of the Elves, and from whom the Eifalians had descended, had taken his lovely wife, Angerboda, and encased her in a crypt of ice deep in the mines of Gomara under the watch of the black dwarves. No, the Eifalians would pay for Frey's part in this. Let the god suffer as Loki had suffered these centuries with only the dead for company.

Letting out a harsh caw, Loki launched himself out of the tree and flew up into the sky. Let them enjoy their day. Soon enough the Vanir would arrive and wipe them out of existence.

Loki headed north. It was time to pay a visit to Gomara. Angerboda awaited.

He flew fast, not stopping for several hours. He passed several roving bands of black dwarves—probably out searching for new slaves for their mines.

His sharp raven vision caught a flurry of movement along the coastal trail. He wheeled around, making a lazy circle above the party.

The Vanirian queen. Riding hard. Trying to intercept her husband? But why? Dropping lower, Loki cawed harshly.

A pair of familiar kids traveled with her. The same meddling children Odin had used as his guardians.

Loki landed in the high limb of a tree and morphed back into human form, holding on to the branch for balance as they passed below. Rage flowed through his veins, making his head pound with fury. The queen would try to stop her husband.

Loki made a clicking sound. "Now, that will not do, my lady. Not at all." He cupped a hand to his mouth and sent out a shrill caw. At once, birds lifted from the branches of every tree, black birds, dark as night. Ravens. They heard his call and came swarming, circling above him as he cawed out his instructions.

After two days of hard riding, Keely had no feeling left in her lower limbs. Their small party followed a thin rocky trail along the coastline. They had stopped for snatches of rest to water the horses and sleep for a few hours. In the evenings, after supper, Leo showed her how to whittle arrows. He preferred wood from the small birch saplings they passed and quills from the wing feathers of iolars, but Keely had been playing with a special arrow. One she hoped would kill its target.

Late in the afternoon on the third day, Reesa raised her hand to signal a halt. "We will stop here," she announced.

Keely sank to the ground, collapsing on a patch of frost-covered grass while the queen's men set up a tent for the queen for privacy. Leo started a small fire and began boiling water. The air had a sharp bite to it even though the sun shone down; it was cold enough that Keely's nose was red. She cradled numb fingers around the steaming cup of tea Leo passed her.

"Do you think we'll get there in time?" Keely asked.

Leo shrugged, warming his hands over the fire. "It will be close. The horses are tired. We can't push them this hard for much longer."

A strange sound made the hairs on the back of Keely's neck stand up.

Leo lifted his head sharply and looked at the woods. "Did you hear that?"

"Yes. It sounded like the call of a raven, only different."

Keely's Eifalian senses were buzzing with danger. Something about that call had been off. Wrong. Electricity crackled in the crisp air. Keely stood, searching for any signs. The cry came again, and this time it was echoed by others.

Hundreds.

The queen and her men stopped talking and turned to face the woods.

And then the attack began.

Swarms of ravens spiraled out of the trees and attacked

them with beaks and claws. These birds were not normal. Their eyes glowed red, their beaks were hooked, and their talons were razor sharp as they descended on their small group.

The frost giants roared in rage, swinging their broad swords at the swarming birds. Three of them formed a shield around their queen, pushing her down and covering her while the other three battled the flock. They knocked some down with their shields, but more birds appeared, covering the sky like a swelling black cloud. In the center was a large raven, cawing loudly.

Loki.

Keely ignored the swarming birds. "Keep them off me," she shouted to Leo. He grabbed a shield and swatted at them. The birds pecked his arms and face, but he kept them away from Keely. She drew her bow and calmly nocked the special arrow she had made. She hadn't explained to anyone why she had carved it, and even now she didn't know if it would work. She took a breath to steady her aim, following the bobbing and weaving black bird as it danced in the sky, urging the other ravens to attack.

With a silent prayer, Keely released the arrow. It flew straight and true for the large raven. At the last second her target spied the danger and flared its wings to spiral away. The shot, aimed for its heart, just missed, but it embedded under its wing.

The bird spiraled into the woods, shifting and transforming into a familiar stocky figure with only its raven's wings remaining. Whatever spell Loki had held over the ravens was broken, and they began to move off, flitting through the trees as the frost giants chased them with shields and swords.

Keely went weak in the knees. Several of Reesa's guards had suffered serious injuries to their faces and arms, pecked mercilessly by the ravens.

One of their horses was dead, having plunged off the shoreline cliff to the rocky beach below. Two more had bolted.

Reesa was bleeding from a deep gouge on her arm. Keely knelt by her side, pulling out her healing crystal.

"Tend to my men first," she said, her voice hoarse with pain.

But the frost giants refused any care until their queen was seen to.

"Stay here," Leo said. "I'm going after him."

Keely nodded, already passing the crystal over Reesa's arm. "Be careful. He's wounded, but he's still dangerous."

Leo ducked under thick undergrowth. He had been reading tracks since he was old enough to go with his father on hunting trips. Finally, he had a chance to undo the damage he had done. If he could find Loki, he would find a way to stop him. Leo gently touched the broken stems of bushes and eyed the impressions in the ground. This was where Loki had crash-landed.

The God of Mischief would be bleeding from the arrow Keely had shot.

There. A drop of blood on the leaf. Loki had gone in that direction.

Leo moved swiftly, enjoying being out in the woods. It had been too long. He had too many memories of being trapped in darkness and death in the underworld. Leo trotted easily while following the trail of blood, and then, abruptly, the trail stopped.

He turned in a circle, going back to the last drop of blood and carefully tracking his way forward. There were no more signs, no footsteps, no broken stems. He circled again until he was certain. Loki had vanished.

The hair on the back of his neck prickled. The birds had gone silent in the trees. He turned slowly, keeping his breathing steady. His hand went to the knife at his belt.

A spry muscular man stood behind him, a wide grin plastered on his face. He held a small boulder over his head with one hand. The other hung limp at his side.

"Surprise," Loki chortled, and then he threw the rock at Leo's head.

Leo was ready this time, his reflexes primed to react. He dodged the rock. It scraped his shoulder, bruising him, but he stayed on his feet. He lunged for Loki's throat with both hands, but the spry goat leapt up into the low branches of a tree and crouched on his haunches, staring down at Leo.

"You're faster but not any smarter," he said wickedly, and then he dropped down and landed on Leo, taking him to the ground. Leo fought him off, but Loki put his good arm around Leo's neck and tightened the grip, cutting off Leo's air.

Leo pried futilely at his arm. Loki was stronger than he looked. With a last-ditch effort, he punched the god in his wounded shoulder.

Bingo.

Loki howled with pain and rolled off. Leo leapt to his feet, his knife drawn. The two faced off.

"Keely's arrow hurt you," Leo said. "How is that possible? You are a god."

"Your little friend must have run into a mistletoe bush," Loki said, swiping at his shoulder and staring at the blood on his hand in awe. Then he wiped it off on his trousers like it was nothing. "Another thing I can thank Odin for besides centuries of imprisonment. I'm going to enjoy making her feel pain, boy. Revenge is sweetest when it's dished out in spades."

Leo danced on the balls of his feet, watching for an opening. Loki had his own knife out. It looked like it was made of carved obsidian. He slashed clumsily at the boy, feigning ineptitude. Leo didn't fall for it, holding back, and Loki grinned wider.

"Come on; show me what you've got. I'm in a bit of a hurry, and I've decided you're going to help me."

"I'll never help you," Leo said, lunging with the knife for Loki's heart, but the god of mischief was faster than he expected and he simply jumped in the air, pulling his knees up and leaping over Leo's head to land behind him.

Before Leo could turn around, something sharp pierced his back. There was a wrenching twist, a snap, then unending pain. He reached behind him, seeking the source, finding the cold hilt of Loki's knife.

He pulled it out, dropping to his knees as coldness flooded his veins. He looked up to see his own face grinning down at him. Leo tried to make sense of his twin, and then it hit him.

Loki had shape-shifted into Leo.

*Keely is in danger*, his brain screamed, but a funny numbness had taken over his limbs.

"Oh, I think you'll help me, like it or not," Loki said, pushing Leo over with one finger.

Keely had been tying off wounds and using her healing crystal for an hour when Leo finally emerged from the woods. He clutched at his shoulder as he limped into their campground.

"Leo, are you okay?" She put her arms around his shoulders and helped him to the campfire.

"Yes. Loki put a knife in me," he grunted out, visibly in pain. There was a small crimson patch at his collarbone. "Then he got away."

"Let me see."

"No!" He pulled away. "I already tended to it. It's just a shallow cut."

Keely frowned. Something was wrong, but she couldn't put her finger on it. Her Eifalian senses were sending up warning flares. Before she could question him further, the queen cut in.

"We must ride now," she said. Her men looked uneasily at the trees as a raven let out a caw. "If we don't, we will be too late. And that mischief-maker might return."

# Chapter 18

Their remaining horses quickly lathered up as they raced toward Ter Glenn. Their breaths came in labored *chuffs* in their chests. The rocky terrain followed the coastline, green trees lining one side and then dropping off to the sea on the other.

Keely was sure every bone in her body had been jarred loose. Her backside ached, her head hurt, and her teeth had been jolted out of their roots. Then as they came around a sharp bend, the breath went out of her. Black smoke rose from the distant spires of Ter Glenn. Reesa drew up her horse sharply.

"Oh no," Keely breathed.

"Maybe it's not as bad as it looks," Reesa said. But her words were hollow. Rolling plumes of smoke stained the sky, blotting out the crisp blue promise of the day.

If only they hadn't been delayed.

The streets of Ter Glenn were deserted as they made their way into the city. A haze of smoke filled the air, stinging Keely's eyes. Windows were broken out of shops, goods strewn into the sidewalks. A horse pulling an empty carriage raced down the street, hooves clattering on the cobblestones as it flew past them.

"Where is everyone?" Keely asked.

The queen answered through tight lips. "Joran has them corralled."

Keely's heart clenched. "What does that mean?"

"It means he will execute them one by one and then destroy the city."

Horror made her gasp. "What about the women and children?"

Reesa shook her head. "There is no mercy during war."

"That's horrible," Keely said, rethinking her image of the man who had been almost kind to her.

A shrill horn blast pierced the air. Reesa kicked her horse sharply, and they clipped along an alley toward the sound. As they made their way around a wrecked storefront, they came to a wide-open park of green grass.

A sea of Eifalians dressed in white robes sat cross-legged, heads tilted back slightly as they murmured a low chant.

"They're combining their auras," Keely said, feeling the tingling sensation of hundreds of Eifalians sending out tranquil blue waves. "They're trying to calm the Vanir."

It wasn't working. The frost giants taunted the enclosed Eifalians, shouting threats at them. Thankfully, it didn't look like anyone had been harmed.

Yet.

"Can you stop them?" Keely asked Reesa, but before the queen could answer, Joran appeared in the crowd.

The king held a double-headed ax, which he swung in a broad stroke over his head. Before him, a man kneeled, his head held down on a solid block of wood by another frost giant.

Gael!

Keely gasped. The new Eifalian king didn't struggle, but she could feel his fear, his tight grip on his composure. Their eyes met across the square. He silently pleaded with her to stop this. She opened her mouth to scream. She would not allow another king to die, but, before she could cry out, a voice rang out.

"Stop!"

Reesa's voice rang in the chilly air.

Joran flinched, and the ax he was bringing down swung to the side and thankfully missed Gael's neck, embedding in the dirt. A wall of frost giants raised swords, protecting their king.

At the sight of his wife, Joran's face flashed with surprise. "Reesa?" He stepped forward, thrusting his men aside to reach her. "The children, are they okay?"

"Yes, Joran. They're fine." She dropped down from her horse to face him. "You must stop this."

Keely slid down to stand beside her, but Joran's eyes were locked on his wife's. "I cannot. The Eifalians threatened our son."

Reesa remained calm. "The Eifalians had nothing to do with it. It was Loki. He was toying with us."

Joran snorted with laughter. "Loki? That mischief-maker has been long dead. What nonsense is this?"

"It's not nonsense," Keely said. "My friend Leo freed him from the underworld." Speaking of Leo, where was he? He should be here, at her side.

"I listened to you once," Joran said. "It cost me many good men."

"Listen to her again," Reesa said. "The Eifalians have done us no harm. It was Loki who led our son astray and then pretended to be one of them. They are innocent."

His face clouded with anger. "No! I don't believe you. You heard our son. It was an Eifalian that took him. This girl has talked nonsense to you."

One of his men pressed a double-bladed ax in his hands,

and he raised it over Gael's head. The Eifalian king was gagged, his head held in place by two large frost giants.

"I am not so easily swayed, husband."

"We must avenge our treaty," he growled.

"No." She laid a hand on his arm. "We must rebuild a new world."

Keely could sense that Joran wasn't going to back down. The warrior in him needed revenge. This was going to be worse than the day King Einolach died. Keely couldn't let that happen.

She stepped forward. "Joran, these people are not your enemy. But if blood must be spilled, take mine."

Joran gripped the ax, frowning at her as if he was confused. "You would give your life for these people? You are not even of this world. Why do you care so much?"

"Because they're my friends. I may not have been born here, but I'm here now. King Einolach sacrificed his life for honor—would you take another life to keep your stupid pride intact?"

Joran switched his attention to his wife. "My love, you are certain of this treachery? Loki is behind this?"

"Yes," she answered, clasping her hands around his death grip on the ax and forcing him to lower it. "I would swear it on the life of our children."

He held her gaze a long moment. Then he gritted his jaw and nodded. Throwing the ax to the side, he spoke. "People of Ter Glenn, we have grieved you. We will make amends."

The seated Eifalians stirred.

"We will withdraw from your city and offer our help to rebuild what we have destroyed."

Keely rushed forward, taking Gael's arm and lifting him, loosening his bonds. A small body hurtled toward her, tackling her.

Theo. Gael's orphaned nephew.

"You came." He hugged her tight. His face was streaked with dirt and blood from a scratch over his eye.

She patted his back. "Of course we came, Theo. Everything's going to be okay now."

Gael held his hand out to Joran. "The Eifalians have long sought peace with our neighbors to the north. We cannot erase the past, but we can write a future where we are no longer enemies."

The two kings stood face-to-face and clasped arms, at once so different and alike. One was tall and gigantic, the other frail-looking and pale in comparison, but both had the same regal bearing.

A mewling voice interrupted the peaceful moment.

"No, no, no, this is not how it's supposed to go!"

A man stood up in the center of the park and threw back his hood, revealing a chiseled face and angry sneer. He had long white hair, but Keely recognized something ancient in that cold gaze.

Loki.

He drew a bow from his robe and nocked an arrow. "These Vanirian filth have defiled our city! They killed our king! Slaughtered him like livestock. We must fight!" He let loose the arrow as the Vanir stood in shock.

Keely was the first to react, flinging herself at the queen and shoving her to the side. But Loki had aimed for Joran. The arrow flew past her head, straight for the Vanirian king. In a blur of green, Gael was there, his body shielding the frost giant's.

The arrow struck with a thud, and the plaza froze.

Joran's guards were the first to fight back, lashing out at the Eifalians that rushed forward to assist Gael. Joran shouted to his men to stay calm, but the bloodthirsty giants had seen firsthand the Eifalians attack their king.

They took up their swords and attacked the passive

Eifalians. Then from the trees surrounding the field, a contingent of hidden Eifalian warriors appeared, flinging back their robes and unleashing a flurry of arrows at the Vanir.

Keely tried to keep an eye on the bow-wielding culprit, but he was lost in the crowd of teeming Eifalians. Arrows soared through the air. As they were about to land on the Vanir, Gael nodded at her from where he lay with the arrow still embedded in his shoulder.

*You can do it*, he mouthed.

His message was clear.

She had to stop this.

She closed her eyes and felt Gael sending her his powerful aura. Magic surged in her veins, and she felt so light she wondered if she were floating.

She thought of King Einolach and his needless sacrifice, and she let the fury of it whip the power coiling in her until she felt it ready to explode, and then she unleashed it.

"ENOUGH!"

Her voice was like a boom of thunder. A ring of blinding light rippled over the heads of the battling enemies, incinerating the arrows in the air to ash. Power hummed in Keely like white fire. "No one here is going to die! Not today."

All eyes turned to her. At least they had stopped fighting each other.

"I saw an Eifalian shoot an arrow at me," Joran growled.

"The Eifalian king saved your life!" Keely shouted, as power still burned through her veins. "Do you really think he would do that if he wanted you dead? It was Loki. He can shape-shift into anyone he wants to be."

Joran glared at her, then lifted the horn at his side and gave it two loud blasts. "Find the one that started this!" he shouted.

The frost giants began searching the crowds, but Keely knew Loki was long gone.

Joran whirled on her. "Why would Loki come after my son? The frost giants have no fight with the ancient gods."

"Loki wanted you to go to war with the Eifalians. To distract you," Keely said.

"From what?"

"From the real fight," Reesa said. "The fire giants of the South have been awakened. With the death of Odin, his protection has ended. Loki has convinced Surt to go to war with mankind."

Joran's eyes grew cold. "I am not the protector of mankind. Once already I have sent my men to battle on your behalf. What part do we have in this?"

"But you promised you would come if we needed you!" Keely cried. "We can't fight them alone. They're too strong. We need your army."

"The Eldjotnar are our brothers," he said, striding back and forth. "We have no quarrel with them. We cannot be involved in this."

"Then I pity you," Reesa said.

Joran stopped in shock. "Pity? By the gods, why would you pity me? My wife? You can't be serious." He laughed, but it sounded hollow.

The queen gave him a long look and then turned her back and walked away, head high.

"Reesa, where are you going?" he called after her haughty figure.

"I must get back to my children and decide what I am going to do next." She mounted her horse, giving Joran one last searing look before turning it sharply with a swift kick. Her men swiftly followed without a backward glance at their king.

Tears stung Keely's eyes as she watched the queen ride away. Why was nothing ever easy in Orkney? Shock was setting in, the aftereffect of using that much magic. Gael had almost overloaded her, but at least it had worked.

As Gael was carried away on a stretcher, Joran's men began loading up their gear on their horses. In minutes, the field would be empty of men, and there would be no evidence a slaughter had been narrowly avoided.

Leyes strode over to her, his robes flowing behind him. "Aren't you a surprise!" He grasped Keely by the shoulders. "You channeled our energy like nothing I've ever seen."

"It was Gael, he helped me," Keely said.

Leyes tilted his forehead to hers in the way of the Eifalians. "You stopped a great bloodshed. You should be proud."

He straightened, waving a hand at the port. "Come, there is a small vessel headed for Skara Brae. You and your companion must be on it. We will gather our fleet and join you in three days' time. Deliver that message to Captain Teren."

Keely should have been pleased by his words, but, without the Vanir's support, her mission felt like a failure. Surt was still coming, and they wouldn't be able to stop his army, not even with the help of every able-bodied Eifalian.

Tiredness crept over her. She could do with a full night's sleep before dealing with Orkney's problems. But where was Leo? She hadn't seen him since the battle had begun. She turned to search for him, determined to give him a piece of her mind for deserting her. Then he was there, hurrying toward her.

She bit back the words at the look on his face. Something was wrong with him. Very wrong. His caramel skin was white with rage, like he alone was to blame for their failed mission.

When she had him alone on the ship she would corner him and find out just what his problem was.

Loki meekly followed that arrogant Eifalian, Leyes, down to the docks, twitching at the unfamiliar form he wore. His fingers itched to toss the man's pale body into the sea, but he held back. His plan had unraveled, but all was not lost. The fire giants would still tear Orkney to pieces, and, when they finished with Skara Brae, they would move north and do the job the frost giants refused to do.

In the meantime, Angerboda was waiting.

The ship the Eifalian led them to was nothing more than a fishing trawler, a small rickety vessel manned by a sea captain with fewer teeth than a six-month-old baby. Leyes apologized, claiming all the Eifalian warships were tied up preparing for the coming battle.

Leyes gave the ship's captain a small bag of coins, and the old seaman tugged on his cap. Moments later, they pushed off, and the sailor hauled up the sails to catch the afternoon breeze.

"Why don't you take a nap," Loki said to Keely, keeping up his appearance as her little friend. "You look like you could use the rest. I'll keep watch with the captain."

"I am bushed," she said with a yawn. "But when I'm done, we need to talk, okay?"

Loki just smiled, patting her arm until she went below. Then he rubbed his hands and went to find the captain. The decrepit sailor hunched over the wheel. Loki tapped him on the shoulder.

The old man turned around, and Loki lifted him by the scruff of his shirt. "Sorry, mate. No room for two captains." Before the sailor could call out, Loki tossed him overboard to bob in the sea, a confused look on his face as the ship swiftly moved on.

Dusting his hands off, Loki checked the sails. The ship looked sturdy enough. There was only the matter of the girl. She was extra baggage. His shoulder throbbed from that dratted mistletoe arrow she had fired on him.

He considered going down below and hauling her up

to swim with the fishes, but she had been impressive back in the square, channeling all that Eifalian energy. His mind ticked over to an idea brewing. She could be put to good use before he got rid of her.

Loki reached around his neck and pulled out a locket on a thick silver chain. He breathed on it, polishing it with his shirt. Pinching the clasp, he let it pop open. Inside was painted the face of a beautiful woman, hair long and black, skin white as milk, eyes like chips of ice. Angerboda, his beloved wife. Taken from him on that day they'd thrown him into the underworld of lost souls and chained him to the stone.

He spun the wheel to catch the wind. "I'm coming for you, my love," he promised her image. "I'm coming very soon. And nothing will stop me from reuniting with you and our children."

Keely woke from a long nap, stretching her arms over her head. It was the first time she had slept soundly in days. Water lapped at the sides of the boat, and the gentle rocking motion let her know they were moving swiftly. With luck, they would be back in Skara Brae by the end of the day tomorrow.

She plucked at her blanket. Would they make it in time? She thought of Sam and what he must be going through. She sent up a silent prayer that he would find Odin and bring him back.

Stumbling out of the bunk, she hauled her boots on and popped the hatch open. Morning sunlight made her blink. She must have slept all night. Her stomach rumbled with hunger. Poor Leo had been left to keep watch alone with the captain.

She frowned as she scanned the open deck. Where was Leo? Not below deck and not above. Just the figure of the captain wrapped in a blanket huddled over the wheel.

Her frown deepened as she saw they were following the shoreline. They should be on the open sea heading for the southern coast of Garamond, but this green tree line and distant ice-covered peaks reminded her of the coastline of Torf-Einnar.

Something was wrong.

She made her way to the back. "Have you seen Leo?" The words died in her mouth as the captain threw his blanket off to reveal Loki's evil grinning face.

"You," she breathed. "How did you get on board?"

He shrugged. "I might have impersonated your little friend."

Of course. How could she have been so stupid! Leo had been acting so weird because he wasn't Leo. Keely frantically searched for a weapon, but all she could find was a hooked fishing knife for gutting fish. She snatched it up and held it to Loki's throat. "Tell me where Leo is, or I'll take your head off."

With a jerk of his chin, the knife flew out of her hand into the sea. "Your friend is dead. And you will be shortly if you don't sit down and be quiet."

Keely's knees buckled under her. "Dead?"

*No.*

*No, no, no.*

Leo couldn't be dead. Brave and wonderful Leo. "You can't mean it?"

"Oh, I mean it. I put the knife in his back myself," Loki said cheerfully.

Keely began beating on him with her fists. "How could you? You're as evil as they come. You will never know what it is to have friends or love or be loved."

"Nonsense," Loki chortled. "I have a wife and three children that love me as much as the moon loves the stars." He turned just in time to catch her by the wrist.

"Just kill me and get it over with," she sobbed at him.

Loki pointed a finger at her. "This is all your fault. If you hadn't shot me with that mistletoe arrow, I would have been out of your hair, so you have no one to blame but yourself."

The words struck her like a knife. As much as she knew it was his fault, she was also to blame for Leo's death. "You tricked the Vanir into almost slaughtering the Eifalians. All of Orkney is threatened because you told Surt about Odin's death. Even now he marches on Skara Brae, and the Vanir were our only hope of defeating him."

Loki's eyes burned with triumph. "And what a glorious day that will be when Skara Brae burns."

"Why are you so full of hate? What did Odin ever do to you?"

He snorted. "Like you would understand."

"Try me." She sat down. Maybe talking would help her come to grips with the sadness that swamped her.

He ignored her for several seconds, and then his nose wrinkled. "Fine. What do you want to know?"

"Start with why you killed Baldur."

A flash of pain crossed his face so fast she almost missed it. He sneered, "Because he was a pompous god, so full of himself."

"You're lying," she said, using her keen senses to sift through his words. "You didn't mean to kill him, did you?" she said slowly, testing the words. They felt surprisingly right.

He inhaled sharply. "Everyone says I did."

Keely nibbled on a fingernail as she thought through what she knew. "Baldur was immune to everything but mistletoe. You knew that, but . . ." A light went off. "You didn't know it would kill him, did you?"

A muscle in his cheek was ticking furiously, and then Loki exploded at her. "It was mistletoe! What harm could it do? I thought there would be a good laugh and that would be that."

Keely sat back, stunned. "So it was an accident. You didn't know. And yet Odin punished you for it."

"My brother," he spat out the word like it tasted foul, "sent me away for eternity, and banished my family."

"You just need to explain what happened. Tell Frigga you're sorry."

"I will never apologize! Never, never, never!" he shouted, jumping up and down. "Now get down to the galley and make us some food. If you don't make yourself useful, maybe I will just toss you overboard, and you can join the captain in swimming back to shore."

Keely went below with a frown on her face as she puzzled over Loki's words.

# Chapter 19

"Are we there yet?" Howie asked for the tenth time that morning. He stood up in his stirrups, stretching his cramped legs. His backside was going to have blisters by the end of the day. It made him miss the bus he used to take to school, even with its hard-backed seats and flying spitballs. At least it didn't take three days to get anywhere.

Jey sighed. "Are you always this annoying? I told you, when we see the red tip of Ilyawit Peak, we turn to the right. We will see a large black hole in the side of a mountain. That is the entrance to the Caverns of Inizza. They were sealed off for centuries until that witch Catriona called up the Safyre."

The ever-superior Falcory boy rode bareback atop a brown-and-white pinto horse like he had been born on it.

Howie's horse was thick around the middle, with one eye cockeyed to the left and a tongue that lolled out of its mouth, but it was the best Jey could steal. Howie had named her Sunny because he was trying to look on the bright side. All they had to do was save Beo, then fly back to Skara Brae on the back of the Safyre Omera, and Captain Teren would forget all about the fact that Howie had abandoned his post.

They had been riding day and night for almost two days, with only a few hours of sleep snatched between midnight and dawn. Lingas dug her claws into his shoulder, reminding him the iolar hadn't eaten yet today.

Damarius, or Big D, as Howie had taken to calling the animal, trotted just behind Sunny like a dark shadow. Howie was a regular animal whisperer. He had tried shooing the wolf, yelling at him to stay in Skara Brae; he even tried tying him up, only to have the beast snap his tether with one swipe of its jaws.

Finally, pressed for time, Howie had given in, reminding the shaggy animal that if he missed a meal, it was on him, and that he couldn't eat Howie, or his horse, or whatever it was Shun Kara wolves ate.

Right now, they had bigger problems than a missed meal. Water was in short supply. Their trek across the desert had been hot and tiring. Damarius panted with thirst. Empty skins of water hung off Howie's horse. He tilted one to his lips, shaking out the last few drops.

They had started with four each. Jey had managed to scrounge up a pair under some rocks in the middle of the desert, but they were down to their last waterskin.

Eager to pass the time and not dwell on his guilt, his thirst, or his sore bum, Howie asked, "How do you know so much about the place if you've never been there?"

"My father tells me stories of the past. The old ones told us that when Catriona and her cronies were put into those stones at the Ring of Brogar, the Safyre Omeras went to sleep in hopes that one day Catriona might return to them."

Howie clucked his tongue. "Sounds like a long nap. Oh, snap, Ilyawit Peak."

"Stop asking me how long—"

"No, look," Howie pointed over Jey's shoulder. "The red-tipped peak."

Jey's eyes lit up. "Ilyawit. That's where Leo and I faced the she-she-kana. He would have been toast if I hadn't saved him," he boasted.

Howie snorted. "The way Leo tells it, you almost came out the back end of that thing."

Jey tossed him a glare, and then he smiled. "When Leo tells the story, the she-she-kana was as big as the moon. Come on, if we ride hard, we can make the entrance to the caverns by dusk."

He dug his heels in the flanks of his horse, and the animal took off. Howie watched, whistling in admiration as the Falcory boy hung low over the side of the horse, urging it on as he whispered in its ear.

"Come on, girl." He kicked Sunny in the side. "Giddyap." Lingas launched herself in the air and took wing. Big D ran ahead, silvery black fur blown back as he raced.

Before they got within spitting distance of the cavern entrance, Howie could feel a chill washing over the desert air. Like they were about to step into an icebox. The smell coming out of there was like three-day-old roadkill.

Sunny pulled her ears back, tossing him a wild look over her shoulder as if to ask if he was crazy. Even Damarius raised a lip in a snarl, prancing foot to foot as he studied the opening.

Lingas settled on a mesquite branch, fluttering her wings as she skreaked loudly. The message was clear: this was a bad idea.

"Yeah, I got it, guys," Howie said. "None of you like this place."

The black hole was big enough to drive a bus through. Tumbled rocks littered the ground, like the Safyre had punched its way through, disintegrating solid rock into rubble. Howie tried not to think about how strong those beasts were.

Jey tied his horse to some scrub. It immediately began chewing on the branches.

Howie slid off his horse, hanging on to the saddle until enough blood flowed back to his legs that he could stand.

"Are we really going in there?" he asked.

Jey was already moving toward the entrance. "My father's in there."

Howie tied Sunny to a branch. It would do no good telling Damarius to stay, but Lingas would be in the way.

He slipped a small leather hood over the iolar's head. "Sorry, Lingas; I can't be worrying about you in there. You stay here and take a nice nap." Howie scurried after Jey as Lingas let out a high-pitched complaint.

"So what's the plan?" Howie asked.

"We rescue my father; then we tame the beast."

"I know, but what if the big, fire-breathing Safyre doesn't like us coming in there?"

"Then she will feel my blade in her heart," Jey said, drawing out the knife strapped to his thigh. The hilt was carved from yellowed bone, and the six-inch blade looked lethal. "This belonged to my father. He gave it to me on my twelfth birthday." He slashed the air with it. "I will do what I must."

Howie hopped in front of Jey. "You know, you remind me a lot of Leo. He's all about brave talk but short on making plans. We've both seen a Safyre Omera before. The one Catriona rode was as big as a house."

"If you are scared, stay here," Jey said, shoving past him to march toward the cave.

"Hey!"

Howie grabbed him and spun him back around. "Of course I'm scared. If you're not, you're just . . . well, lying or stupid. Before we go running in there, we need a plan. Like, how are we going to see? It looks pitch black inside."

Damarius growled low in his throat at Howie's side, glaring at Jey as if, for once, the stubborn beast agreed.

Grudgingly the Falcory boy gave it thought. "We could make torches. There is sap in the green mesquite. I have my flint with me. If we wrap the ends with some cloth, they will burn a long time."

Howie rubbed his hands. "Good, we have light. Now what say we carve a few spears while we're at it so I don't go in there empty-handed? If the Safyre attacks, I want to give it a good poke in the eye before it incinerates me."

Jey stared at him for a long moment. "You are not what I expected."

Howie grinned. "I know. I get that a lot. Come on, lets whittle some sticks and get moving; I'd like to be back in Skara Brae before Surt burns it to the ground."

An hour later, Howie trailed behind Jey, one hand resting on Big D's square head as they entered into the towering cavern of the Safyre Omera. The Shun Kara tolerated his touch for once, as if he, too, were unnerved by the smell of sulfur and burnt flesh that hung in the air.

Jey's torch sent shadows looming across the stone floor. Scattered bones littered the area, a warning to the unwary who entered. Jey leaned the torch against the wall and cupped his hands to his mouth, shouting, "Father? Where are you?"

Howie smacked him on the arm. "Are you crazy?" he hissed. "Are you trying to get us killed?"

"No, I'm trying to find my father," Jey hissed back.

"Well, if the Mrs. Safyre finds us first, that's bad news. So zip it."

The cavern narrowed into a tunnel that headed deeper underground. With every step, the air grew colder, and goosebumps were crawling all over Howie's skin. A distant screech made him jump.

"What was that?" he asked. The hackles on the Shun Kara were stiff under his fingers.

"We're getting closer."

Jey walked faster. The rocky floor was uneven. Sharp stalactites hung down. One almost knocked Howie out as he eased around it.

And then they emerged into a giant cavern. It was impossible to see how tall it was. Jey's torch couldn't pierce the deep shadows, but it was at least five stories high. Tunnels shot off in every direction. A rockfall scattered boulders across the floor, leaving a fresh scar in the rock wall, paler than the rest.

Jey ran toward it, and Howie scurried to keep up. Jey dropped the torch and began frantically feeling the rocks. "Father!" he called loudly. "Can you hear me?'

They listened but heard nothing.

"Here, let me try," Howie said. He picked up a rock and banged it against one of the rocks three times.

They stood back and waited. A moment later, there was an echoing bang. Three of them.

"Dad!" Jey shouted. "We're coming. Hang on."

They began pulling rocks away, but with every stone they took away, two more rolled down. It was backbreaking work. Damarius stood guard as they pried away rock after rock. Howie lit their second torch as the first one burned out. After another hour, they managed to make a small opening. Howie held up the torch as Jey peered in.

"Father?" he called.

"Jey, is that you?" The voice filtering through was weak, but it was Beo.

"You're alive!" Jey shouted.

Howie could just make out glittering black eyes as Beo glared through the small opening. "Jey, what are you doing here? I told you not to come."

"I had to. We're going to get you out of there." Jey began pulling on more rocks, but his father stopped him.

"No. I want you to leave right now. The rocks are too unstable. The whole wall could come down."

"I'm not leaving without you. Who's with you?"

"I have five men. This tunnel leads to a dead end. There is a stream. We've been able to survive with the water and provisions we have, but it is too dangerous for you here. The Safyre attacked us and brought down the rockfall."

"Don't worry, father. I can do this," Jey said. He began pulling more rocks away, but another tumble of rocks came down.

As they dodged the falling rock, Damarius growled, rising to his feet to stare at one of the tunnels.

Howie paused, listening. He heard it. A chuffing noise, like deep breathing. A flicker in the shadows made him go cold. "Uh, Jey, I think—"

"Quiet, Howie; we're not leaving until we free my father and his men," Jey said.

"Jey, you'd better have a look."

Damarius howled a warning as the flickering shadow took shape. Howie made out a long snout with pointed ears.

"Run!" Howie shouted.

# Chapter 20

Howie barely had time to shout the warning before the female Safyre stepped into full view. Even though he had seen the one Catriona had ridden, he hadn't been this close. Damarius was going crazy, hopping side to side, barking with a ferocious warning to the intruder.

The ancient beast was spectacular, glistening black like it was coated in slick tar. It spread its wings, showing off its strength as Howie counted a dozen sharpened talons at the tip of each wing bone. Purple streaks tinged its wings. It reminded Howie of a T. rex, and it had a mouth full of teeth to prove it. Behind it, a lethal barbed tail flickered as its fiery red eyes lasered in on them.

Jey drew his knife. "Come and get me, old one. I will cut your heart out and eat it for my breakfast."

The Safyre belched a ball of fire that filled the cavern with rolling flames. Howie tackled Jey and dove behind some rocks with the boy as the flames washed over them. Damarius yelped and followed them into cover.

After the flames passed, the walls lit up hidden crystals, casting a bright glow across the cavern.

"That is cool," Howie said even as he wondered how they were going to survive this. He picked up his spear, realizing how ridiculously small it was against this giant. "We should make a run for it." He eyed the nearest exit, but the Safyre moved its bulky body in front, hunkering down as it raised one lip in a snarl.

"Jey, be careful," his father shouted through the small opening. "Try to wear it down."

"Wear it down," Howie repeated, thinking fast. He had watched a rodeo once on TV where the rodeo clown had distracted the bull from the rider until it was too pooped to give chase.

Time to rodeo up.

Howie ran out into the open, waving his hands wildly to draw its attention.

"Look at me, you big ugly beast. Try to catch me, ooga, ooga, ooga." He waggled his hands in the air and then scurried away as the Safyre whirled on him and sent a blazing path of fire at him. "Your turn, Jey!" he shouted, diving behind tumbled rocks and patting out the singed parts of his pants.

"Go ahead, try to fry me," Jey said, moving out behind the Safyre and dancing side to side on his feet. "You're nothing but an oversized rathos with bad breath." The Safyre screeched in rage as it whirled around and chased him down.

Howie grinned. Jey was a fast learner.

As the boy dove for cover, Howie was up. Damarius caught on to the game. He followed Howie, snapping and growling as Howie waved his arms in the center of the arena. "You're so ugly your husband chose to be frozen rather than look at your ugly face one more minute."

It was like the Safyre understood his words, because she grew completely still. There was silence in the cavern. All Howie could hear was the loud beating of his own heart. Then the oversized Omera slowly turned her head and growled low in her throat, a low rumbling like a lawn mower on idle. Her eyes were burning embers of coal as she glared at him.

"Oh, beans," Howie said. He started to run, but the Safyre was faster.

She blazed a trail straight for him and Big D. The Shun Kara was fast as the wind as it raced for cover, but Howie moved slow as a snail. The Safyre sprung into the air, flapping powerful wings as she easily closed the distance.

Howie dodged to the side, but the trail of fire followed him. He could feel the burn, the smoke at the edge of his clothes. This was it. The Safyre was going to incinerate him. Blisters started to form on the back of his neck as he pounded his feet.

A loud squeal echoed in the chamber. The Safyre nearly stumbled over its own feet as it skidded to a stop, whirling around, snapping its flaming snout shut.

Howie stopped to see what was happening.

Three more Safyre Omeras had entered the cavern. They were junior versions of the flame-belching monster in front of him. Hatchlings, Howie guessed. Two of them took flight and began laying down skimpy trails of fire, but the third one couldn't lift its right wing. It tried, then squawked forlornly.

Out of the shadows, Jey pounced, wrapping his arms around the neck of the injured Safyre. In an instant, he had it in an armlock. His knife was pressed to its throat.

The mama Safyre screamed, belching flames at the ceiling, whipping around to fly directly at Jey. But she couldn't very well incinerate him, not while he was holding her youngling. She flared off at the last second and settled with a loud thump in front of him, screaming her rage.

Her two other younglings settled behind her, hissing and snarling and burping out small bolts of fire.

Before he could ask himself if it was a good idea, Howie ran into the center of the cavern to stand in front of the large beast. "Hold on, just hold on; he's not going to hurt your baby. Are you, Jey?"

At his side, Damarius appeared, butting up against Howie's legs like a dark shadow. Howie couldn't lie; the Shun Kara's warm strength gave him courage when his knees were wobbly as pixie sticks.

Jey kept his arm firmly locked around the Omera so it couldn't burn him with the belches of fire it spit out. "Why not?"

"Because that would make the mama Safyre very angry," Howie said. He held his hands out as she roared fire over his head, singeing his hair, but not incinerating him. She was holding back.

This could work.

"Look," he said to the Safyre, "you look like a smart lady. We just need some help, and it looks like you do, too. Your baby has an injured wing. What if I could fix it?"

She growled low in her throat, but she settled her body lower.

"Let it go," Howie called to Jey.

"No! It's our only leverage."

"Someone's got to make the first step. We can trust her; just, don't hurt it."

Jey hesitated. Howie didn't think he would do it. He held his breath, and then slowly Jey lowered the knife. The Safyre waddled over to its mother. The three younglings nestled under her wings as she squared off against the boys.

Now was the moment Howie would find out whether or not he was right, or they were burnt toast.

Howie took a step closer, keeping his eyes on her, his hands in front of him. "Now, just let me look at that wing. I promise not to hurt it, okay?" He ordered Damarius to stay back as he moved closer, not trusting the feral animal to stay calm next to this powerful beast.

Damarius sat on his haunches, clearly unhappy, but he obeyed.

The Safyre growled low in her throat, but she raised one wing up. Howie stepped under it. He could feel the heat coming from her body, smell the scent of her last meal—rotten meat of some kind—and the sulfur from her fire.

The young Omera looked at him with curious black eyes. It wasn't afraid. Howie touched its nose. He had seen Omeras before. Sam rode them all the time. Maybe this wouldn't be so bad.

He put his hand on the injured wing. The skin was like leather, smooth and warm. He lifted it, and the young Safyre snapped at him, sending a small blaze of fire. Howie pulled his hand back, blowing on his singed fingers.

The mother snarled at her baby, and it whimpered and then lifted its wing. Howie saw the problem. There was a wooden shaft lodged under the wing, the remnants of a spear. Which meant the pointed tip was lodged inside.

"Jey, I need your knife."

"You're crazy. I'm not coming near that beast," Jey said, standing back, arms folded. He looked a little pale.

"I thought Falcory warriors weren't afraid of anything," Howie joked. "Come on, I need another set of hands. It has a spear stuck in its side. If I pull, it's going to make it worse. I need to cut it out."

Slowly and carefully Jey stepped under the shadow of the giant Safyre and stood next to Howie. The Falcory boy was shaking as he held out his knife. "Here, do what you need to."

"Hold up its wing."

Jey looked green, like he'd rather be anywhere else. Then he gingerly put his hands on the wing as the young Safyre looked trustingly at him.

The youngling whimpered as Howie cut into the leathery flesh. "Almost got it," he said softly.

It squealed loudly as Howie pulled the spear tip out. Green blood sprayed his face, and he almost gagged. The mother looked alarmed, snarling as she whirled her head around. Howie managed to rip a piece of his shirttail off and made a bandage, stuffing it into the small hole. After a minute, the green blood slowed.

The young Safyre sighed and lay down, resting its head on its front talons, and it went to sleep.

Howie turned to Jey, bowing. "See, I told you—"

But Jey grabbed him. "Howie, what is she doing?" The mama Safyre was stalking over to the section of fallen rock. "She's going to kill my father."

But Howie had the first good feeling he'd had in days. "No, I don't think so."

The Safyre battered her head at the rock. More rock tumbled, but she was like a bulldozer, pushing and tossing rocks with her teeth and creating a big dust storm. When she was done, there was a large opening. As the dust settled, Beo stood, flanked by his remaining men.

# Chapter 21

S am tried to remember what he had been so upset about. Here in Aegir's undersea palace, there were no worries, no pressure. No one getting in your face telling you to do more, work harder, stop being such a failure.

Aegir took Sam under his wing, shepherding him around and showing him all the benefits of being a sea king. It was hard to fathom that they were deep under the sea in the lavish castle of pink coral walls and floors of polished mother of pearl. Light shone down from crystal chandeliers that were lit with a phosphorescent glow.

Aegir had an appetite for entertaining. Mermaids and mermen strolled about in sparkling gowns sewn of shiny scales that flickered and sparkled in the light. Their skin was a pale green, and there were narrow ridges of flesh that ran along the backs of their arms and legs.

One of Aegir's nine daughters explained that the ridge grew longer when exposed to seawater, giving them soft flowing fins. Tiny slits in the sides of their throats opened when submerged, allowing them to be equally comfortable in water or on land. Otherwise, they looked perfectly normal—

they each had two arms and two legs—and did they know how to have fun. There were constant loud parties where music was played on a combination of blown seashells and drums made of fish skin stretched over coral tubes.

Sam couldn't remember the last time he'd seen Mavery or Perrin and that nagging swan creature that had been hit by the falling rock. Aegir made sure his young protégé didn't lack for anything. Platters of food were passed to him by giggling she-maidens who buzzed around him like bees on pollen.

Whenever Sam asked about his friends, Aegir offered to take him to see them as soon as Sam sampled some more of his delicious sea grapes. With a snap of his fingers, one of his countless daughters would plonk a purple fruit in Sam's mouth, and all Sam's cares would drift away as the delicious sweet flavor made his tongue buzz.

He wanted to rail against it, make Aegir actually do something, but words failed him. It was as though his brain didn't have the energy to pull them out of storage. After all, the sea king was helping him get through this misery of having failed at the one chance he had to save the world from his mistakes.

They had lost Skidbladnir, and Sam hadn't finished reading the map, not to mention that he was having a hard time remembering all the routes he had traced, his mind a jumbled mess.

No. He'd blown it big-time, and everyone would suffer because of it. Keely would be waiting for him to return with Odin. His mom would think he hadn't tried hard enough. The whole world would know it was his fault.

As usual.

But down here, none of that mattered. Everywhere there was color and laughter. Aegir was in the middle of throwing a party for one of his daughters. With nine of them, someone was always celebrating something. One of the girls grabbed Sam's hand and pulled him to his feet, dragging him onto the dance floor, looping her arms around his neck.

He leaned his head on her if only to get the room to stop spinning, and then he forced himself to grin. He had a right to enjoy himself. He had just turned thirteen, and he hadn't had a day of fun since he'd been shot through rock and landed in this blasted realm. Grabbing his partner by the waist, he whirled her around, letting out a whoop as the pace of the music increased.

Boys were idiots, Perrin reasoned as she leaned against a column in the back of the room, glaring across at Sam. For three days they had been stuck down here while Sam was fawned over by a bevy of girls. Nine, to be exact. All daughters of Aegir, and all, apparently, crazy for a new but hardly handsome face.

It was like Sam had forgotten all about their mission. Geela was still recovering from her injuries. Perrin knew that if the Valkyrie had been able, they would have left immediately. But the attack by Jormungand had left wounds that had festered, poisoned by his saliva, and the hit to her head had knocked her out.

She'd tossed and turned in a fever, and it was only now, on the third day, that she'd fallen into a deep and restful sleep. Mavery watched over her. The little imp had been attached since Geela had saved her from drowning in the feeding tube.

A servant offered her a tray with frosted purple grapes, but she waved him away. Those things were potent. She'd tried one and spit it out. Sam couldn't get enough of them. One of Aegir's annoying daughters, a blond thing with skinny legs, looped her arms around Sam's neck. They swayed on the dance floor. She held a slender hand to her throat as she leaned in close, placing a kiss on his cheek.

That was it. Perrin felt a slow burn. It wasn't that she was jealous. It was just that Sam was making a fool of himself, and he didn't seem to realize it.

A hand touched her arm. She whirled, ready to bite someone's head off. Geela stood, looking pale but upright.

"You shouldn't be out of bed," Perrin said, gripping the woman's forearm when she swayed.

"We have to leave," the Valkyrie said. "Now, tonight."

Perrin rolled her eyes. "Not up to me. Sam is falling in love nine ways to Sunday."

Geela gripped her arm so tight it made Perrin wince. The Valkyrie shoved her face close to Perrin's. The yellowed bruising was just beginning to fade. "They're bewitching him with a love tonic. It's in the sea grapes they harvest. There's a reason we're down here. Have you forgotten that?"

Perrin yanked her arm free. "No, I haven't forgotten, but my team is a little off. You're barely on your feet, and Sam, well, just look at him."

They turned and watched as Sam staggered off the dance floor and was pulled into a swarm of girls vying for his attention.

"Sam is busy," she continued, clamping down on the hurt. "And, besides, he didn't get the map. How are we supposed to go on if we don't have the map to Helva's underworld?"

"We have the map," Geela insisted. "Sam saw the markings. He has what he needs; he just has to use it when the time comes."

"Well, you tell him that, then," Perrin said angrily. "He doesn't listen to me."

Sam's head rested on the smooth thigh of Hera, Aegir's third daughter. Or was it his fourth? He couldn't remember the difference between Hera and Hora. The first two, Hestia and Hirana, were easy. Hestia had long black hair and flashing eyes, and Hirana had a short bob that bounced around her shoulders and a nice smile. The rest were sort of a blur.

Sam closed his eyes, a grin plastered on his face as Hera fed him another sea grape. This place was like a permanent vacation. Everywhere he went, he found smiles and laughter. Rego would have frowned at this behavior, but the annoying dwarf wasn't here, he reminded himself.

A tiny furrow etched into his brow.

*Rego. Where is that dratted dwarf?*

*Probably off fighting Surt's men,* his mind replied.

Sam sat up, pushing aside the soft hands of Hera as she pressed him back into his reclining position.

"Rego," Sam whispered aloud. He looked around. The laughter and gaiety went on, but now it was a sick whirling carnival of colors and excess. Bile rose in his throat, and the plate of fruit dropped, spilling purple grapes onto the coral floor. The girls stopped giggling. Around him, the throng of merpeople stared, but he was numb, his fingers tingling.

There were too many people in the room. They stood waiting for him to do something.

Aegir raised his glass in a toast at Sam, but Sam's vision was blurred like he was in a long tunnel. He saw things happening, but he couldn't move. A girl floated toward him dressed in a flowing white gown.

It was Hestia—his mind filled in her name—the eldest of the sea king's daughters. In her hands she clutched a small spray of pink coral flowers. She looked teary-eyed and weepy as she reached his side.

Sam hated weepy girls. He never understood what it was

they wanted. He turned away, but strong hands gripped his arms. Two mermen had him by the biceps and dragged him forward. Sam's feet left the ground, and it was just as well— he could barely stand, barely string two thoughts together. They dropped him at Hestia's side.

"What . . . what's happening?" he finally managed, proud of the way he'd gotten the words out.

Hestia looked at him oddly, putting her slim green-tinged hand on his arm. "We're getting married, silly. Now stand tall. Father is waiting."

It was like someone had dumped a bucket of freezing cold ice water on his head. Sam looked up into the searing blue gaze of Aegir, who was waiting at the end of a long walkway. The mermen and mermaids had drawn back, and suddenly there was this long narrow corridor that led to an altar made of whalebone and decorated with strings of seashells.

He pulled away, but Hestia wasn't letting go of his arm.

"I can't get married," he mumbled. "I'm just thirteen."

"Don't be silly; mermen get married all the time as soon as they're old enough."

"But I'm not a merman," Sam protested, prying at her hand, but the gentle girl had turned into a fierce opponent.

"You're going to marry me because Father says so, and whatever Father says is so," she hurled at him, her face turning an ugly shade of tomato.

Suddenly, Sam knew he was in way over his head. He eyed the room frantically, searching for a friendly face, someone to rescue him, hoping to see someone he recognized—like Perrin, or that imp Mavery. But he hadn't seen them in ages, and he was surrounded by a wall of mermen standing in a semicircle.

Aegir rose from his throne, waving a staff over them. "Joyous day, to see my daughter Hestia wed to this Son of Odin, our two bloodlines joined as the gods intended."

Murmurs and shouts of encouragement greeted his words.

Sam backed away, but strong arms held him fast.

Aegir passed his staff over Sam's head. "I hereby accept this boy into the line of seamen who have come before him. Let our joint blood flow together so that the blood of the sea and the blood of Odin may run together in your children."

Now Sam was really panicking. His knees were wobbly and weak as boiled pasta. This had to be a dream. A really bad dream, like you get when you eat too much pizza past your bedtime and watch a scary movie.

Hestia's face beamed as her father passed his staff over her head and promised her many fruitful years and bountiful amounts of children.

"Let any who object speak now before this marriage is binding," Aegir said.

Sam thought he was going to pass out from nausea. He pinched his arm as hard as he could so he could wake up from this nightmare. Heck, he'd face that sea monster Jormungand again; anything was better than this. He opened his mouth to object, but an elbow caught him in the ribs from the merman next to him, and the air rushed out of him, leaving him gasping and speechless.

Then, behind him, from the corner of the room, a familiar voice boomed.

"I object!" Perrin said loudly.

There were angry whispers, but hope flooded Sam's brain.

The crowd drew back, forming a narrow corridor that revealed Perrin. Under her curtain of jet-black hair, her face had that icy look that told Sam she meant business.

He had never been happier to see someone in his life.

"Who dares object to this union?" the sea king roared, ramming his staff into the ground so that the very walls shook.

"I do," Perrin said, looking left to right, meeting the eye of every merman and mermaid as she slowly made her way forward.

"And what gives you the right to stop these proceedings?"

"Because he belongs to me," she said quietly. "Always has."

There were loud gasps. Even Sam was puzzled. What game was Perrin playing?

"Explain," Aegir said, seating himself back on his throne. Perrin took a stand next to Sam but didn't even glance over at him, though he was desperate for her to look at him and reassure him she was going to fix this.

"Centuries before we were born, our ancestors made a covenant that the first-born son of Catriona would wed the heir to the Tarkana throne to continue the line. He was the first of his kind. I am the heir to mine."

"No," Aegir said, clearly fuming, "he is a Son of Odin."

"Yes, but also a Son of Catriona. A great bloodline that goes back to the earliest days of Orkney. A union between us would assure the purity of the witch bloodline that will never be repeated. The scrolls were signed and sealed eons before our birth. He cannot wed another without violating a sacred covenant, which would make this union unholy."

Hestia collapsed in a faint. Sam found himself grinning even though he wasn't sure if he liked what Perrin was saying.

Aegir scowled, rubbing his hand along his jaw while one of his advisors bent over him, whispering in his ear.

"You have no proof of this!" he shouted, shoving the man aside.

Perrin just shrugged. "Go ahead, don't believe me. I never liked him anyway, but it won't change the facts, and when it is revealed, your daughter will suffer an eternity of shame. It's nothing to me—I won't be the one at fault. I made my claim."

The room fell deathly quiet. Aegir's scowl deepened. Finally, the old sea god growled, "I am calling off the wedding. The boy is not fit for my daughter. Expel these creatures from my realm. See them to the surface, and bid them away. I will not be bothered any longer by the spawn of witches."

Aegir turned to go, but Perrin called out to him. "Hey. You have something that belongs to us."

Aegir froze, turning slowly to pin her to the floor with an icy glare. "You dare challenge the sea king in his domain?"

"I dare, you old goat. Now, hand it over, and we'll leave; otherwise I'm going to cut loose with some magic, and when Sam here snaps out of it, he's going to destroy this place." She sent a bolt of green fire over the king's head, splintering a pretty chandelier of fine bone.

Angrily, the king grabbed his staff and held it up. For a moment, Sam thought they were going to have a full-on battle, but then Aegir lowered his arm. He reached into his robe and withdrew something that made Sam's eyes light up.

Skidbladnir!

The tiny carving was dwarfed in the old sea god's gnarled hands. "Take it, then, and good riddance." He tossed it at them, letting it spin in the air as Sam fumbled his hands up to grab it. But Perrin was there, snatching it and pocketing it before Sam could stumble forward. He really was useless, he thought as the room spun.

"Perrin," he mumbled through a mouth that tasted like sour cotton. She put her arm around him as his knees went out, holding him upright with surprising strength.

"I'm right here, idiot."

"Where have you been?" he grumbled as she led him out.

"Watching you make a fool of yourself. Let's get out of here before another one of these girls decides to marry you."

"I'm going to be sick," he said before the world spun into a black void.

# Chapter 22

Sam opened his eyes. He lay on the hard surface of the deck of a ship. Skidbladnir, he recognized as he took in the tall masts. It was nighttime. The moon was out, sending a blade of white light across the ocean. The warm wind on his face was heavenly, but his head felt too heavy to move.

Last he remembered, Perrin had saved him from being married off to one of Aegir's daughters. Now, he risked sitting up. The world spun, making his stomach heave. He tried to hold it back, but the acid bile choked him. He made it to the railing before spewing his guts into the sea. Sniggers of laughter pricked his skin.

Mavery, that imp.

He dragged in a breath of air and turned around, leaning against the railing. Perrin was at the helm. Mavery was skipping around in a circle, swirling her skirts as she whistled a tune. Geela was nowhere to be seen.

Sam stumbled back to the helm and dropped onto a cushion.

"You're alive," Perrin acknowledged with a snort.

"Fat lot you care," he grumbled back. "You left me with all those girls."

"You didn't seem to mind."

"You were kissy, kissy," Mavery joked, puckering her lips and pushing her cheeks together with her hands and then laughing hysterically.

Sam wanted to pound her, but it would have required too much effort.

"Where are we headed?" he asked instead.

Perrin shrugged. "No idea. The ship has a mind of its own. I figured getting away from that place was the first step. Unless you want to go back? Maybe you left something behind, like your brain?"

Mavery sniggered again, and Sam gave up and grinned with them. "I was kind of an idiot," he said sheepishly. "But what could I do? All those girls found me irresistible."

He ducked as Perrin shot at him with a small zap of witchfire.

Geela came up quietly from down below and sat down across from Sam. She looked pale but steadier on her feet.

"Time is running out. The moon approaches its fullness. We must return to Valhalla with Odin before then." She didn't need to remind them what that meant. Besides their demise at the hands of the gods, Surt would soon reach Skara Brae, and it would be too late to save Orkney.

"How do we find Helva without the map?" Sam asked, seeing his good mood slip away.

He'd failed to get the one thing he needed to finish this. After days under Aegir's spell, he could barely remember the symbols and the pathways he'd tried to memorize.

"That is up to you, witch-boy. Take the wheel and see what happens."

"Fine. But stop calling me that." He gritted his teeth as he looked her in the eye. "My name is Sam. I am a Son of

Odin, and, yes, I am a witch, but I will not be insulted for it. My friends are witches, and they deserve your respect. Without them, you'd be fish bait at the bottom of the sea."

The Valkyrie slowly nodded her head at him. "Sam, would you please take the wheel and see if the ship responds to you?"

Sam stood up, glad his knees weren't too wobbly. Perrin stepped aside. Laying his hands on the wheel, he gripped the smooth wood. The ship stalled, the sails slackening, and it drew to a stop in the center of the ocean. Sam waited, curious. Everyone stood in a circle, looking around to see what would happen.

It was as if the world had gone completely still. Not a sound, not a movement, not a wave lapped at the side of the ship. The moon shimmered, flickering on and off like someone was toggling a switch. Then it changed color, the pale alabaster becoming a sickly green. It cast an eerie glow that peeled across the water until it hit the deck.

When it did, the boat lunged forward across a sea that was suddenly black and cold. In front of them, a huge fog bank loomed, rolling toward them, growing larger and larger until it swallowed them up.

Coldness settled over Sam like ice water dumped on his head. He couldn't see his hands. Feathery trails of mist tickled his face like they were sailing through cobwebs. Mavery crept over and slipped under his arms.

Perrin created a ball of witchfire, but all it did was light up the ghostly gray fog that surrounded them. They couldn't see where they were headed or what was in front of them.

Something solid bumped against the ship, jarring them. Mavery screamed. Geela drew her sword.

The ship bumped again, this time scraping hard against a solid object as it moved past.

"Stop the ship!" Geela called, running to the side and looking over. "We're going to tear a hole in it."

Sam let go of the wheel. The ship slowed to a stop. They sat in the fog, straining to hear or see through the pea soup.

"Do you see anything?" Sam shouted, leaning over the other side, trying to make out shapes in the gray.

"No," Geela answered.

"Nothing here." Perrin's voice came from the front of the ship, though Sam couldn't make her out.

Sam planted his feet, drawing his strength together and centering his mind. They needed to be able to see, or they were going to sink the ship. Running his hands in a circle, Sam braced himself for the sensation of surging energy when he called on his magic.

"*Fein kinter*," he whispered, "*Fein kinter ventimus, ventimus expellia*." He kept circling his hands, murmuring the words, and pushing with his mind. A wind picked up around him, ruffling his hair gently at first and then getting stronger as his magic coiled.

"Hold on to something!" he shouted as the wind raced, swirling around them like a tornado and lifting the seat cushions, sending them spinning through the air.

Geela grabbed on to Mavery and ducked under the helm. Perrin wrapped her arms around the mast as Sam stood his ground. The roar of wind grew, spreading out until, with a loud blast, he released it across the water.

It rippled out, shredding the thick bank of fog to wisps. The girls came out from their hiding places and ran to the rail. The moon still shone a sickly green, but the way was clear.

The bad news was that tall, craggy rocks jutted out of the water like a pinball machine, each large enough to tear a hole in the ship. And, worse, beyond the rock field, a solid cliff rose in front of them, climbing more than a thousand feet straight up.

"Bring us closer," Geela said.

Sam carefully steered the ship, doing his best to avoid the rocks. A sharp bump made him flinch. An underwater rock had scraped the hull.

Mavery scrambled below deck and then shouted, "Sam, we gotta problem down here. Water's coming in fast."

Sam clenched his hands on the wheel. Great, he'd broken the ship of the gods. If the gods didn't hang him for killing Odin, this would surely do it.

Geela studied the solid rock wall and then said, "These are the gates to Helva's underworld."

Sam's eyebrows rose. "Gates? It's a solid wall, Geela."

"Not solid. The entrance is ahead; look."

Sam peered closer at the wall. She was right. As they drifted closer, a pair of dark tunnels just tall enough for the ship to pass through became visible.

"Which way do we go?" he asked.

Geela nodded at him, like she had a bucketful of confidence in him. "The map is in your head. You will guide us from here. I must go help the young one stop the water."

"Great. I'm in charge. Recipe for disaster."

Sam palmed a bolt of lightning at the rock face. There was a splintering sound as the surface of the rock shattered, and then a symbol appeared above each tunnel, glowing with a dim green light, same as the sky. Over the left tunnel, the outline of an eye stared at them. On the right was an outline of an eye that was closed.

"That eye, I recognize it from Helva's map," Sam said excitedly, pointing to the one on the left. "I think I know what to do." The closed eye had led to a dead end. The open eye had led to the next set of tunnels.

Running back to the helm, Sam grabbed the wheel, and the ship lunged forward. Nosing the wheel to the left, he pointed the ship toward the opening under the open eye.

As they entered the tunnel, the ship was swept forward by a strong current, hurtling them through the dark channel. Sam held on to the wheel, blind and unable to see. He imagined a grisly death when the ship ran aground on a sharp rock, but there were no bumps. In moments that felt like a lifetime, they exited the tunnel with a whoosh of cold air and coasted to a stop.

Sam and Perrin made a ball of witchfire to light up their unknown destination. They both gasped. Their wild ride had taken them underground into a large cavern. Overhead rocks glistened and dripped.

A strange green glow lit the water. Behind them, Sam could see the dark hole they had come through. Before them, three dark openings awaited. The ship kept moving forward, pushed along by an invisible current.

Sam folded his hands and sent a blast of energy at the rock over the tunnels. Three different runic symbols appeared:

"X marks the spot?" Perrin joked questioningly.

Sam shook his head. "No, I remember that one. It dead-ended. The other two crisscrossed."

"Which is it?" the witch asked gently, touching his arm in encouragement.

"The three-pronged Y," he said confidently, remembering the path in his head. He nosed Skidbladnir into the center tunnel. Air rushed past as the ship began racing ahead. His stomach dropped as the prow tilted forward, as if they were going over the edge of a waterfall.

"You're doing it," Perrin said in the dark, socking him on the arm.

He grinned like a fool even though she couldn't see him. "Piece of cake. I got this."

The ship slowly straightened out as Geela and Mavery came up from below. They got their first glimpse of the next cavern.

"Cripes," Mavery said with a gulp. "Where are we?"

"This is the second chamber of Helva's underworld," Geela answered, looking around warily. "We must be alert. All sorts of strange creatures exist in this place."

Before them, four tunnels awaited. Sam sent a bolt of witchfire at them, but nothing happened. He did it again, gathering his strength and making it bigger. The rocks stood silent and blank.

"What's wrong?" Geela said, a small frown on her smooth features.

He shrugged. "Maybe we need more juice." He shook out his fingers and didn't object when Perrin took a stance next to him, her hip cocked forward as she drew her hands in a circle. Together they sent out a twin blast of energy. It hit the face of the rocks and bounced off and ricocheted back at them, nearly singeing Geela where she stood at the helm.

"Watch it," she snapped, but it worked. The rocks slowly lit up and revealed their symbols.

Everyone turned to stare at Sam expectantly.

He stared at the glyphs, looking from one to the other. There was a lightning bolt, a radiant sun, a crescent moon, and a star. Which one was the right way?

Mavery put her hand in his, looking up at him with trusting eyes. "You can do it, Sam, I know you can."

He winked at her and cracked his neck, shaking out his hands as he studied the glyphs. He spoke out loud just to reassure himself. "Okay. I'm sure I traced the sun and the lightning bolt to a dead end, so they're out."

Mavery squeezed his hand. Drawing in a deep breath, he looked at the other two glyphs. "The star feels right, but so does the moon. They both went nearly to the next circle, but one of them stopped." He drummed his fingers on the railing.

"So where now, witch-boy, er, Sam?" Geela asked. "Pick one so we can move on. I managed to slow down the leak, but it won't hold forever."

Sam felt drawn to the moon. It glinted at him, like it was calling to him. It reminded him of Keely. Calm and serene. He looked back at the star. It twinkled at him, welcoming him. Which was it? Moon? Star?

Sweat rolled down his back. He had to choose.

"Moon." He nodded to himself. The moon was right.

"Are you sure?" Geela asked.

Doubt clawed at his stomach. He wasn't sure of anything. His hands were slick with sweat as he grabbed on to the railing.

Three pairs of eyes stared at him, and he erupted.

"No, I'm not sure! What do you want from me? I can barely remember my name, let alone the scribbles on a wall in the underwater lair of a serpent that we killed before the map got turned to rubble. I'm doing the best I can, so maybe you can give me a break."

He stalked back to the helm and was about to put his

hands on the wheel when he glanced at the star. It twinkled again. He took the wheel, and the ship jumped forward, heading straight for the star.

Geela looked over her shoulder. "You said moon," she said questioningly.

"I know." Sam tugged on the wheel, but it wouldn't budge, heading straight for the glittering star.

"It's wrong, Sam," Perrin said. "I can feel it."

She tried yanking his hands off the wheel, but it was like they were superglued on.

"Stop the ship," Geela commanded, coming to his side and grabbing his other arm. But not even the great strength of a Valkyrie could pry his hands loose.

# Chapter 23

Skidbladnir lunged forward into the tunnel. As the prow passed the entrance, everything around them went silent and black. There was no rush of movement, no sudden drop; the ship drifted along slowly. Darkness pressed in. Sam couldn't see his hands on the wheel.

"What's happening?" he called. His words sounded muffled, like he was speaking in a world filled with cotton.

"We've gone the wrong way," Geela said from his side.

An eerie yellow glow lit up the water.

"There's something out there," Perrin called. Sam could just make her out in the glow. She stood by the edge of the deck. She backed away as figures flitted up out of the water.

"Stay back," Geela cautioned, drawing her sword.

Mavery squealed and ducked under Geela's arm as the Valkyrie brandished the sword over her head in a shower of golden sparks. Sam lifted his hands off the wheel, relieved he had use of them again.

"What are they?" he whispered as figure after figure rose out of the depths, disembodied, faceless, shapeless but not voiceless.

They sent out high-pitched shrieks that rippled across the water. Sam covered his ears, and the others did the same. Their wailing cries were heartbreaking, filled with a sadness that nearly brought him to his knees with grief.

"They're Helva's wraiths," Geela called. "Everyone hang tight to the ship. They mustn't take hold of you."

She lashed herself to the mast, wrapping the rope around her and Perrin. Sam grabbed Mavery and crouched under the helm, holding her tight in his arms.

The cold fingers of the wraiths passed over him, reminding him of the ones he and Mavery had once encountered in the woods. At least these ones didn't shoot bolts of ice. He caught the fleshless gaze of one. It looked sad, its features drawn back into a wide scream. Tendrils of fog formed and shaped an endless wail in the center of its face.

"Back off," Sam snarled, waving his hand at it and releasing a bolt of energy. It dissipated into wisps of fog. As it did, another wraith came in from behind, wrapping fingers around Mavery, tugging on her.

The filmy fog was surprisingly strong and tensile. He pushed it away, but the wraith had wrapped bony hands around Mavery's waist.

She screamed at Sam, clinging to his arms as her legs left the deck.

"Sam, don't let me go!" she cried.

He held on to her with all his strength, calling on his magic to create a blast of energy, but he couldn't release it unless he let go of her with one hand.

Seeing no other choice, he threw his hand out, palm thrust upward, and sent witchfire that pushed the creature back, dragging Mavery with her. The witchling tumbled back against the side of the ship, then scrambled up, peeling away the wraith's bony grasp as she reached for Sam's hand.

"I've got you," he shouted, grabbing for her, but her

fingers slipped out of his as another wraith swooped down and snatched her away up to the roof of the cavern before plunging straight down toward the water. A dark swirling hole opened, providing an exit. In unison, the other wraiths peeled away from the ship and vanished into the same watery hole.

Sam lunged to the side of the ship, screaming Mavery's name as she disappeared from sight. Determined to follow her down no matter what it took, he climbed on the railing, but Geela tackled him, knocking him to the deck before he could go over.

"Stop, Sam, she's gone."

"Get off me!"

Sam struggled to throw her off, but the Valkyrie pinned him with her elbow across his throat. "You can't help her by going to your own death. If there is any chance of rescuing her, we have to make our way to Helva's mansion."

Sam pounded the deck with his fists, tears burning his eyes. Why did he always let down the people who counted on him? Every time. He couldn't get anything right.

Geela lifted her arm and rolled off him and went to stand by the helm. Perrin came over to Sam and stuck out her hand.

"Come on," she said, pulling him to his feet. "Mavery would want us to keep going. She's a tough little bird. We'll find her."

Sam staggered to the railing, gripping it with all his strength as he kept himself from vaulting over the side. "I'm coming for you, imp," he whispered as tears ran down his cheek.

He swiped at them and then went back to the helm and turned the ship around. It sailed docilely back the way they came in until they popped out in the chamber with four tunnels. The star had burned out. The other three symbols remained glowing.

Sam pointed at the moon without speaking. The ship

lurched forward, making its way silently toward the tunnel. It listed slightly to the left. The steering dragged. They were taking on water. A lot, by the feel of it. Sam looked at Geela, but the Valkyrie just shrugged.

"There's still time," was all she said.

Sam had his doubts. How much time before the ship sank? How long before they sunk to the bottom of this pit of horror? He was tempted to go down below and see how bad it was, and then he decided against it. Geela was right; all they could do was go on.

As they entered the tunnel, Sam clung to the wheel as the ship tilted forward over a steep drop into a free fall. It seemed to defy the laws of gravity, but that was probably his imagination. At last, it evened out until the ship slowed to a crawl.

They exited into another cavern, this one darker and gloomier than the others. Perrin lit up a large green ball of witchfire. Long shadows loomed over the water from rocky spires that hung down from the ceiling. The ship scraped its mast on one of the spires. A tearing sound echoed as the sail ripped in half.

Geela stood by the railing with her hand on her sword. Sam swallowed back the bile and waited for the next set of tunnels to appear.

Five dark openings loomed in front of them. He and Perrin stood side by side and sent out a blast of witchfire. The green ball of energy bounced off and ricocheted around the cavern, but nothing happened.

"We need more power," Perrin said. "We're not strong enough."

Sam stared at his hands glumly, realizing she was right. "We need another witch."

*Mavery.*

The pang hit him again, making him weak, hopeless. And then a stinging voice rang out behind them.

"I knew witches were useless. Useless, powerless, can't even send out a small blast of witchfire to save your friend."

Perrin and Sam turned as one to look at Geela. The Valkyrie stood behind them, arms folded in disgust.

"What did you say?" Sam asked as anger prickled under his skin.

"I'm saying that witches run when it gets hard. Admit it; you can't light them up because you don't care. You have a cold heart. Just like every witch I've ever met."

Anger boiled over in Sam, reminding him of the good old days when rage flowed like water in his veins. "You think I have no feelings? You think I don't care? Mavery is the best person I've ever met. How dare you call me coldhearted!"

He spun around and threw his hands forward, unleashing a tirade. The unfairness, the grief, the loss—all of it overwhelmed him. Beside him, Perrin did the same, matching his blast of energy with her own angry blast. When the air cleared, the symbols glowed over the tunnels.

Geela just smiled and patted them on their shoulders. "That's better. Now, which way do we go?"

Sam glared at her, his chest rising and falling from the exertion. He and Perrin looked at each other, and the truth hit them at the same moment. Geela had just been pushing their buttons.

Not appreciating her methods, Sam turned back to the symbols and took a deep breath, reading them out loud.

"Ox, horse, rabbit, snake, raven."

"Anything?" Geela asked evenly.

Sam bit the inside of his cheek. What did he remember? "Not the rabbit," he said tersely. What if he made another mistake? Who would be lost then? Who would he sacrifice next with his mistakes?

"Don't think about it," Perrin said. "What does your gut tell you?"

Easy, raven. But he had to be sure.

"I don't know."

"Yes, you do. You saw it, you traced the lines, you know which one it is. Just say it."

"What if I'm wrong?" he said, his voice shaky.

Perrin's eyes drilled into his. "You won't be. You know what to do. Just do it."

"I can't."

She gripped his arm, yanking him close. "Yes, you can. Mavery believed in you."

"And look what happened to her!" he shouted. "She's gone, and I'm never going to see her again."

"Why are boys so stupid?" Perrin grumbled. "We're going to come through this."

"What makes you so sure?"

"Because you're Sam Baron, son of Robert Barconian, the last Son of Odin, the first Son of Catriona, the last and first of your kind. You were born to do this, and no one, no one will deny you your role. You are going to win because it's what you do. You just have to believe it, and you can do anything. Anything at all."

He stared at her, his breath heaving in his chest. And then calmness settled over him, a feeling of peace and strength, as if his mother had just given him one of her famous hugs.

"You like me." A grin split his face even though it was the most ridiculous thing to say and feel at this moment; it was all he could think of. "You like, *like* me."

She rolled her eyes, but a hint of color crept into her

cheeks. "You're an idiot," she muttered, but he could tell she was pleased. "Just pick a symbol." She turned her back on him, crossing her arms and tucking her hands in her sleeves.

He smiled again as he made his way back to the wheel.

He would choose. He knew what to do. He was a Son of Odin, and, yes, a Son of Catriona. He was a witch and the son of a god. He would not be defeated. At least not before he'd gotten in there and raised a little chaos of his own.

"Raven," he said, and he put his hands on the wheel of the ship.

# Chapter 24

Keely rested her chin on her knees, arms wrapped around her legs as she warily watched Loki sail the ship. She had cried every tear she had, weeping silently to herself over Leo's senseless death. She hated Loki with every fiber in her body. The heartless god did what he pleased without any thought for the consequences.

That was his problem. He was like a spoiled child. He might not have meant to kill Baldur, but Leo . . . that was on him. She had to get away from him. She had to get back to Sam and the others and help in the fight against Surt. Keely had considered every escape possible, but, so far, jumping overboard into the cold and rough seas and swimming to the distant shoreline was her only option.

Loki perched on the back rail, whistling to himself with his feet propped up on the ship's wheel. He still favored his shoulder, the one she had shot with the mistletoe arrow. It was the only satisfaction she could take from their situation. Based on the direction of the sun, she knew they were heading north, running along the coast of Torf-Einnar.

"Where exactly are we going?" she asked.

Loki rubbed his hands together. "We have an errand to run before we collect our passenger."

Keely sat up straighter. "Passenger? Who?"

"My beloved wife, Angerboda. Queen of the Dokkalfar."

She sifted through her memory but couldn't recall the name. "Who are the Dokkalfar?"

"They're known as the Dark Elves. The opposite of your pretty Eifalians. A race of creatures so deadly they can tie your intestines in knots with a single thought. By the gods, I've missed her."

Loki looked teary-eyed as he reminisced about his evil wife like she was the girl next door. It made Keely want to gag, but she pressed for more information. "Where do the Dokkalfar live?"

"The ice realm of Svartelheim. A long way from Orkney. Angerboda will be missing home, and she'll be furious with me for taking so long. And when Angerboda is furious, well, cities burn to the ground, civilizations end—you get the drift."

"You know where Angerboda is?"

Loki shrugged, his ruddy cheeks crinkling into a nasty grin. "Frey buried her deep in the Gomaran mines of the black dwarves, encased her in ice so far underground it would take a ferret to dig her out. Anyone who knew her location has been dead for a couple thousand years."

"How do you expect to find her?"

Loki tossed a hand in the air. "The black dwarves will have heard I've been released. They know I'll come for her, so they'll be looking for her."

"But how can you be so sure they'll find her? She's been buried for centuries."

Loki tapped his forehead. "Loki leaves nothing to chance. I sent her a wakeup call to get things moving. They'll find her. And try to hide her somewhere new."

"So when they move her, you'll rescue her."

His feet hit the deck as he sent her a searing look. "No, girl, when they move her, she'll kill every one of them and destroy their precious mines in the process. You don't rescue Angerboda. You pray she doesn't leave you alive when she's finished with you."

Loki spun the wheel on the ship to the left, sending it into a sharp turn toward shore.

Land.

Suddenly, Keely couldn't wait to feel solid ground underfoot. She gripped the railing, asking, "Is this the way to the mines?"

"Not quite. I need to pick up a gift for my wife so she forgives me for having her encased in ice. And I know just the little trinket."

Keely's jaw dropped. "You're going shopping for a piece of jewelry?"

Was Loki crazy? With everything he had done to try to destroy Orkney, he was thinking about trinkets? Anger made her snap.

"There's a war going on, you know, one you started. I don't have time for trivial errands. I need to get back and help."

Loki's eyes narrowed. "You need to sit down and be quiet." He snapped his fingers, and a force of magic slammed Keely into the deck.

She fought against the bonds, but Loki's magic was too powerful.

Loki eased the boat into a small cove with a sheltered strip of sand. He beached the hull and leaped over the side, splashing in the water, then turned to give her another one of his broad smiles.

"Well, are you coming, or do I have to carry you?"

Keely struggled to get up, furious at being held in place by magic. "Release me," she said through clenched teeth.

"Say *please*."

She just glared at him, and Loki laughed, snapping his fingers, dissolving the invisible bonds. "Do try to keep up. The black dwarves would love to capture an Eifalian girl and put her to work in the mines."

As Keely leaped onto the sand, she considered her options. She could run, but to where? And Loki could just use that magic of his to tie her up. No. Better to go along, maybe find out what his plan was and stop him. If she couldn't fight in the war, at least maybe she could put an end to Loki once and for all.

They left the shoreline and entered the familiar trees of the Ironwood forest. It reminded Keely of her icy trek with that traitor Rifkin while she was searching for the Moon Pearl. The trees towered over with blackened bark and gnarled branches that created a thick canopy. The sky was gray with clouds, and only a faint outline of the sun was visible. A thin layer of frost covered the ground, crunching underfoot. Birds dipped and flew through the limbs.

"How long are we going to walk?" she asked.

"Not long. It's just ahead," Loki said, and he began whistling a merry tune.

Hours later, Keely was exhausted and her stomach rumbled with hunger. Every time she asked the God of Mischief how much farther, he gave the same answer.

"Quit your whining, I told you, it's just ahead."

Only the scenery didn't change. They hiked up and down along deer trails and animal paths through the eerie forest. Finally, as the sun's gray disc was beginning to slide down in the sky, Keely shouted at him, "I'm tired and I'm hungry! How much farther? And this time don't lie to me!"

Loki didn't slow; he just tossed his usual insult over his shoulder. "Whine, whine, whine." Then he stopped so fast that Keely almost bumped into him. "See, we're here."

Keely raised her eyes. Blue water shimmered through

the trees. They stepped onto a strip of sand before a broad stretch of blue water. It ran as far as Keely could see in both directions. Red sandstone cliffs lined the far side.

"What is this place?" Keely asked.

"This is the Loch of the Lost Princess," Loki said, surveying the water with a glint in his eyes.

Keely looked at him. "Lost princess?"

Loki pursed his lips before answering. "I suppose you want the whole story. Nehalannia was an Eifalian princess. This side of the loch belonged to her people, the other side to the Vanir. It's no secret that they've been sworn enemies since Odin swept these cursed islands into the Ninth Realm."

In spite of herself, Keely felt drawn into the story. "What happened to the princess?"

"Legend has it that Nehalannia was swimming one day and this Vanirian boy out fishing saw her and was so taken by her that he jumped overboard. Only the lad couldn't swim."

Loki went silent. Keely waited for him to go on, but he delighted in tormenting her. With a sigh, she asked, "Okay, so what happened next?"

"What do you think? Nehalannia saved him, and the rest is every girl's fantasy."

"She fell in love with a Vanirian fisherman?" Keely said.

Loki wagged a finger at her. "The boy was no common fisherman. His name was Jeric, and he was a prince, heir to the Vanirian throne. But Nehalannia's father couldn't stand the idea of her taking up with a Vanir. When he found them together, he claimed Jeric had attacked her. The girl denied it, but that didn't stop her family from hauling the lad to the center of the loch and tying a rock round his ankles."

"They killed him?" Keely said, gasping with horror.

Loki nodded. "The next day, Nehalannia ran away to look for him. She took a boat out on the loch and dove in when she thought she saw him. But she never came up. Rumor has it that she haunts the water in the form of a giant loch monster."

Keely turned to stare at the tragic water. It was like something out of a movie. Then she frowned, eyeing Loki. "Why would a heartless creature like you care about a tragic love story?"

The mischievous god tried to look offended, then laughed. "Because when Nehalannia ran off, she was wearing a pendant given to her by her father."

A faint tingle ran up Keely's spine, as if her magic recognized it.

"A pendant? What kind?"

"The kind that's going to get my wife to forgive me. Time to take a little ride." Loki gave a low whistle between two fingers. A lone seabird flew across the loch, diving down to find its breakfast.

Loki whistled again. Keely was beginning to think he had lost his mind when gravel crunched around the bend. She turned to see who was coming.

Her mouth fell open. Loki had to elbow her to get her to shut it.

A solitary dwarf approached them. From the shoulders down he looked as broad in girth as Rego and was dressed just as poorly in burlap and ragged pants. It was the head that had her gaping—or, rather, the *pair of heads* sprouting from a single, thick neck.

One noggin was capped in a sheaf of red hair, the other a sheaf of brown. They were arguing with one another.

"I say we go this way," the brown-haired head said.

"You heard the whistle—we have a customer," the red-haired one snapped back.

"I'm not in the mood for customers."

"Well, I say we need the money."

"And I say they got no money."

They came to a stop in front of Loki.

"I'm Norri," the redhead said cheerfully.

"Don't tell them who we are," the other blustered, swiveling his brown-haired head to glare at his twin.

"Gad sakes, Snorri, they look harmless."

"Oh, now you told them my name, idiot." Snorri reached up and slapped Norri on the cheek.

"You're the idiot."

They began slapping each other across the face.

"Oy!" Loki shouted, interrupting them. "We need a ride across the loch. You lot interested or not?"

They spoke simultaneously.

"No."

"Yes."

The dwarf's right hand came up and covered the mouth of grumpy Snorri.

"Ignore him," Norri said. "We'll take you across just as soon as you pay up."

Loki flipped him a gold coin.

The dwarf caught it with his other hand and nipped it with his teeth.

"We'll take you," they said together. This time they both smiled.

Keely and Loki followed the odd pair around the bend. They were still arguing as they waddled on their shared body toward a rickety dock. A small rowboat was tied up. The two-headed dwarf clambered into the boat and sat down on a bench to grip the oars.

"Ladies first," Loki said, holding out his hand to help her aboard. Keely hesitated, her skin prickling with unease. Something was off; Loki was being too casual. "Get in, or I'll make you," he said softly, but there was steel in his voice.

Keely ignored his hand and stepped onto the boat. Loki

gave the craft a hard shove and leaped on, nearly capsizing them all. When the boat steadied, the dwarf rowed, sending them gliding across the smooth blue water.

For all their bickering, Snorri and Norri rowed in even strokes. Loki sat in the rear, holding the rudder.

Keely looked over the side of the boat at the deep blue surface. The ripples fanning from the rowboat were entrancing. Her senses tingled again, and this urge to touch the water came over her. She trailed her fingers in the cool water.

"Don't touch the water!" the dwarves shouted at once.

She snatched her hand back like she had been burned.

"You were supposed to tell her the rules," Snorri snapped at his twin.

"I thought you told her," Norri said.

"What's wrong? What did I do?" Keely asked.

The dwarves shook their heads in unison. "Eifalian's can't touch the water; everyone knows that."

"Well, nobody told me," Keely said, quickly drying her hand off. "Is it poisonous?"

"It awakens the loch monster," Norri explained, "and she comes a-looking for her Jeric."

"And when she doesn't find him . . ." The dwarves twisted their heads to give each other a look of horror.

The day had been eerily calm, but on cue a wind came out of nowhere. A current swirled the water into an eddy. Waves rose, and the loch turned choppy, tossing their boat. A green fin broke the surface, curling and undulating like a serpent.

Water sloshed over the sides. Loki held the rudder tightly as the twins drew hard on the oars. But the boat was pulled into a swift, spinning current as a massive whirlpool formed.

"It's Nehalannia!" Norri yelled.

Keely held on for dear life as the small boat spun dizzily around the edges. She caught a glimpse of the sea monster slapping the water with a giant tail, sending a massive wave their way.

Suddenly thick hands reached under her arms, lifting her roughly, prying her fingers off the rowboat seat.

"What are you doing!?" she screamed at Loki, wriggling and fighting his hold.

"You want to live, you bring me back Nehalannia's pendant," he shouted. And then he tossed her overboard.

# Chapter 25

Keely hit the loch's surface with a splash. She swallowed a mouthful of water before she caught her breath. As the coldness engulfed her, she was swept into the vortex and sent spinning around the rim.

"Loki!" Keely pleaded, swimming hard to escape the current and reach the receding boat. "Help me!"

But the two-headed twins worked in furious tandem, spurred on by Loki barking in their ear, and the boat quickly reached calm water.

Loki had planned this, planned for her to go overboard, but why bring her all this way just to drown her in the loch?

She desperately paddled for shore. She was a strong swimmer. The water was cold, but if she put everything she had into it, she might— Her pep talk was interrupted when something grabbed her ankle and yanked her under. She kicked hard, but the iron grip of her captor was relentless, dragging her deep underwater before releasing her.

Keely opened her eyes. In place of the green scaly sea monster, a beautiful girl with long white hair floated before her, staring back at her with wide-eyed curiosity.

Her pale blue eyes sparkled in the blackness. She wore a dress made of green algae intricately woven together. Small shells decorated the neckline. Delicate green fins ran across the tops of her arms and the backs of her legs. Along the side of her neck, four pairs of leech-like creatures pulsed, releasing little bubbles of air. Their bodies were yellow, but the tiny tendrils that covered them were tipped in red. Around her neck a pendant hung on a thick silver chain crusted with algae. The stone was blackened with age and tarnish. Something in the pendant called to Keely. An ancient power thrummed in Keely's veins, warming her.

The girl waved her hand, smiling shyly, and beckoned Keely to follow her. Then she swam away, going deeper into the watery darkness.

Could this really be Nehalannia? The Eifalian princess from Loki's story?

Keely didn't know what to think, but something made her want to follow. Ignoring the danger, Keely swam after her. The pressure built up in her ears as she went deeper. She cleared her nose, expelling precious breath. The cold was making her numb. Black spots appeared behind her eyes as she grew lightheaded.

*This was a mistake*, she realized.

Suddenly desperate, she swam hard and grabbed Nehalannia by the hand, pulling the girl around to face her.

"I can't breathe," Keely mouthed.

The girl giggled like she found it funny. "I'm sorry. Here . . ."

Nehalannia peeled off two of the leeches from the side of her neck and placed them on Keely's neck. There was a slight sting, and then bubbles rose up next to her and oxygen flooded Keely's lungs.

"Better?" the girl asked.

Keely nodded. She reached up to touch the two yellow

creatures. They tickled her throat. But she didn't feel light-headed anymore. She tried her voice. "What are they?"

"They're gillybugs," Nehalannia explained. "They'll help you breathe." Then she swam away, the long tendrils of algae from her dress tailing behind. She turned with a smile, beckoning to Keely. "Come, Jeric is just over here, you must meet him."

Surprised, Keely swam as fast as she could, gliding behind the girl.

This was an adventure!

The war between Surt and his terrible red army and Orkney was forgotten as she swam through the silvery blue water. She forgot about the cold as she took in the wonders of this watery underworld.

In the faint light, she made out long-nosed fish and splashes of color when a school of tiny green-and-blue-striped fish swam by. A forest of algae wafted up from the bottom, wrapping slimy tendrils around her legs.

"Wait up," Keely called, stopping to untangle herself.

"Hurry," Nehalannia said, "Jeric's right over here."

Keely swam and swam. Fish and seaweed were all she could see. She tired. Her brain needed more oxygen than the gillybugs were giving her. She remembered Loki's story, how Nehalannia was forever searching for her lost love.

They were going nowhere.

"Stop, Nehalannia. Jeric's not here," Keely called.

That brought the girl to a sudden halt. She whirled on Keely and grabbed Keely's shirt. Her face looked frightening, twisted into an angry mask.

"Don't ever say that." Her necklace glowed with a strange blue light.

But Keely had had enough of this underwater adventure. The cold was starting to seep into her bones. If she stayed much longer, she was worried she might never get out of this place.

"Jeric's gone," Keely stated firmly. "You've been looking for him for hundreds of years. He's not here anymore, and I have to go." She kicked her way up to the surface, determined to leave.

But Nehalannia had other ideas. "That's a lie!" Bubbles sprayed from her mouth as she screamed the words at Keely.

Then the loch princess began to change.

Her algae dress spread across her skin, turning it into green shimmering scales. Her arms flattened as the delicate fins sprouted, growing in size as her entire body thickened and lengthened until she was the size of a small bus. Sharp teeth protruded from each corner of her mouth. A jagged fin ran along her back and ended in a tail.

She was once again the sea monster that had nearly capsized them.

"Jeric is here," she roared at Keely, flicking her tail and swimming forward to butt Keely with her head. Keely cascaded through the water, tumbling head over heels.

She regained her balance, moving her arms back and forth to hold herself steady. "I'm not afraid of you," Keely said, kicking her feet to swim back toward the creature. "You're just angry because you miss him."

"I must find Jeric," the monster growled, snapping at Keely. Her teeth came dangerously close to biting off Keely's hand. If it wanted to, it could swallow her whole.

"He's not here. I miss somebody, too," Keely said, swimming in place in front of the creature. "My friend Leo. It hurts. I hate it, but I have to accept that he's gone to a better place."

At her words, the loch monster stopped. Nehalannia began to shrink back to her normal size. Fangs still protruded, but they slowly receded.

"Where is this better place?" she asked. "I have to go there and tell him I'm sorry. You see, it was all my fault."

"What do you mean?"

"Everyone thinks my father was to blame, but it's not true. I lied to my father about what happened. I told him Jeric attacked me because he was so mad." Her face twisted in pain. "I couldn't bear to see him so angry. But then he wouldn't listen when I tried to stop him." She gripped Keely. "Don't you see? I have to find Jeric so I can apologize. Do you think he'll forgive me?"

"I think if he really loved you, he would forgive anything," Keely said.

At her words, a channel of blinding light cut through the water. Keely squinted her eyes. Nehalannia's face took on a mask of wonder as a ghostly image appeared next to her in the water.

Jeric.

He was handsome, with a square chin, thick brown hair, and golden eyes. His image wavered in the current as he held out his hand. "Nehalannia. I've been waiting forever. Come, it's time to go."

"Jeric. Is it really you?" She held a hand up to his face.

He smiled. "You found me after all this time."

Nehalannia turned to Keely and threw cold arms around her, squeezing her tight. "Thank you," she whispered. "You have been a good friend. Please, let me give you a gift. Where I am going, I will not need this."

She lifted the pendant from around her neck and put it over Keely's head.

"This is the Pendant of Helina. It was gifted to me by my mother. It holds an ancient magic. In your time of greatest need, call on it, and you will find the strength to do what must be done."

Then Nehalannia took Jeric's hand. She flickered and shimmered as her earthly flesh disappeared and she became transparent as he. She smiled at Keely one more time, waving goodbye over her shoulder, and then the light winked out.

Keely floated helplessly in the cold darkness. She had no idea which way was up or down. She wrapped her fingers around the pendant, wishing, hoping with all her might that something might guide her. Energy vibrated under her palm. She could see a light glow from the stone under the algae and age.

And then a hard snout butted into her, pushing her upward. A sleek gray body appeared next to her, its long bottlenose shoving her. It nudged her, giving a playful push. A giant wave swelled, pulling her along with it, sending her rushing through the water.

A pair of hands grabbed her and roughly hauled her onto shore. Keely lay on her back not breathing, just staring at the sun through a haze of clouds. She was alive. Her fingers were still wrapped around the pendant, but it had stopped vibrating.

A two-headed apparition came into view. Something pressed on her chest. Water was forced out of her. She vomited onto the ground. A great tearing breath drew into her lungs.

Keely looked around. They were on the far shore.

"What happened?" she asked, coughing up the rest of the water.

The redhead, Snorri, answered gently, "We thought you were a goner. We saw the giant fins of that monster when she broke the surface."

"I don't think Nehalannia will bother you anymore," Keely said between chattering teeth. "She's gone."

"Gone?"

The pair of dwarf heads looked at each other in horror. "What do you mean, gone?" they said in unison.

"Gone. She's moved on. She found what she was looking for."

Norri groaned. "Ach, that's terrible."

"A fine mess you got us into," Snorri added, as if Keely had just ruined their day.

"What? I thought you'd be happy," she said, cradling the cup of tea they poured her. It kept spilling. Her hands shook like a washing machine on spin cycle.

"That lovely monster was the key to our business," Norri said. "You've put us out of a job."

"We should kill her. Before she tells anyone that Nehalannia's gone," Snorri said.

"That's horrible," Norri answered, slapping his twin in the face. "She's just a girl."

"Fine, we won't kill her. We'll just cut out her tongue."

"I'll cut *your* tongue out," Norri said, grabbing a knife and reaching for his twin's head. They wrestled each other to the ground.

Keely didn't know whether to laugh or cry. She had just faced an underwater sea monster and met a ghost, and now this two-headed dwarf was talking about cutting her tongue out of her head. It was all so absurd.

"Where's Loki?" she asked once she had stopped laughing. She had a few choice words for him.

"Right here, deary."

Keely looked up. Loki sat over her head in the low branches of a tree.

"You threw me overboard," she accused him.

"And you survived." He leapt down lithely and knelt next to her, studying the piece around her neck. "Looks a bit tarnished, but it will have to do."

Keely wrapped a hand around the ancient piece. Every bone in her body warned her not to give it to him. "You can't have it. Nehalannia gave it to me."

He gave a shrug. "Go ahead and wear it if it makes you happy. I'll take it when I'm good and ready. Now up you go; we need to be moving."

"I'm t-t-too cold," she stuttered. "And I have no desire to help you find your wife."

"Too bad. I thought you might want to see your friend again." He glanced down at his nails like they were suddenly interesting.

Keely frowned. "My friend?"

"You know, the dark-haired one that fancies you."

"Leo?" Just saying his name hurt. "But he's dead. You said—"

Loki waved a hand. "I might have exaggerated."

Shock made Keely breathless. "Leo's alive?"

Loki shrugged. "I'm counting on it. I left a very important piece of my knife in his back as a calling card for my beloved wife. With it, she will find him, and everyone will get what they want."

Keely punched him on the arm. "You let me believe he was dead!" she shouted. "That is the most horrible, cruel thing you could do."

He didn't look the slightest bit chagrined. He pointed a finger at her. "And dead he will be if we aren't there in time." Loki turned and began striding off through the trees, whistling that aimless tune.

Joy made Keely want to dance in the air. She closed her eyes in relief as tears pressed against them. Leo was alive. Loki might be lying again, but she had no choice but to follow and find out.

# Chapter 26

Leo was living a nightmare. It was bad enough that Loki had left him for dead. An Umatilla warrior could accept death. But not this.

He was a slave.

After Loki had knifed Leo in the back, Leo had packed his wound with moss before blacking out. Sometime later, he had awoken, feeling weak. The frozen cold of the North had drained what remaining strength he had.

The pain had been a burning prod in his back. Nearby the sound of brush being trampled underfoot had given him the strength to sit up. He had heard someone moving through the trees, the clomping of boots.

He'd lifted his head to shout for help, to draw in the Vanir.

The boots had moved closer. Leo had sighed with relief. And then a trio of bushy black-haired dwarves with grim features and hook noses had entered the clearing, eyeing him like he was a prize.

And now he was their slave. The black dwarves had carried him to a place so deep underground, no errant light traveled down from the surface. He almost missed Sinmara's underworld with its undead chasing him.

It was better than this place.

The layers of rock pressed down, cold and unfeeling. The only warmth was from the sweat generated from swinging a pickax into solid stone ten hours a day.

Lifting his pick, Leo brought it down with all his might. Maybe his destiny as the Sacrifice was unchangeable. He had survived Sinmara's underworld, only to find himself imprisoned again underground. It was cruel of Odin, if this was his will.

Leo kept one eye on the slave master, Altof, as he worked. Altof was a foul-tempered, mean-spirited dwarf with a head full of black hair and a wiry beard he repeatedly stroked as the boys worked in a long row. There were a dozen slave boys in a line swinging their picks for endless hours until Leo's arms ached and his bones were filled with sand.

The other boys were all Vanirian, bigger and stronger than Leo, but young enough to be controlled by the dwarves. One of the boys kept eyeing Leo. His eyes sparkled like the sea on an icy day. He had a square chin, high cheekbones, and a natural confidence. Altof was hardest on this boy, cracking his whip over his head if he so much as paused.

A twinge of pain made Leo gasp. His wound had healed oddly fast, sealing itself closed and leaving only a dull ache. Odin must want him to pay for freeing Loki—that was Leo's only answer for his predicament.

Penance.

At least the work took his mind off the fact that he had failed at every task.

Finally, a low horn sounded.

Leo wearily dropped his pick. The boys shuffled back to the common room they all shared. There were no beds, only rough wool blankets to shield against the chill. The boys slept on the stone floor and huddled together for warmth.

The room smelled of sour sweat, urine, and fear. The boy with the arctic blue eyes sat across from Leo, his back against the wall as he ate his serving of cold rice.

"You work hard for one who is not of this world," he said softly.

Leo's eyes flared in surprise. "How did you know?" He kept his voice pitched low, one eye on the guard outside their cell.

The boy shrugged. "You look Falcory but are not. We have heard stories, rumors of earth children that came to save us all." He looked at Leo, his azure eyes piercing. "Is that true?"

The other boys grew silent, holding their breaths as if the fate of the world rested on Leo's answer.

Leo smiled bitterly, spooning in some tasteless rice. "I was brought here as the Sacrifice. I should be dead, yet here I am, and the mischief-maker is free. I failed at my job."

The boy continued to stare at him. A small smile curved the side of his lips. "Maybe you were brought here for another reason. I'm Eithan," he said, extending his hand. "I want to go home. Do you think you can help us?"

Leo froze, looking at the ring of boys. Who was he to promise them anything? His role had been decided. A sacrifice. Someone to be left behind after his job was done. But something nudged at him, a whisper that asked, *What would your father do?*

Not take this lying down, he answered. Chief Pate-wa would never stand to be another's slave, and a flood of resolve made Leo so weak he almost dropped his bowl of rice. His father would not stand by, and neither would Leo. He set his bowl down and then took Eithan's hand, grasping it firmly. "I'm Leo, and I don't know about you, but I don't plan on staying long."

Another boy pushed through the ring, his face angry and flushed. "This earth boy couldn't save a flea. We follow him, and we'll get a beating and no meals. I say turn him over to Altof and be done with it."

Eithan stood to face the boy. He had a bearing about him, something so familiar to Leo he could swear he had seen the boy before. His golden hair hung in a ragged cut to his shoulders. He had a small scar over his left eyebrow. "Griggs, shut it. Or you'll feel my fists, not Altof's."

After a moment, the boy drew back, folding his arms as he sulked.

They huddled in a circle while one of the boys kept an eye out for the guards. A stubby candle lit up their faces with a tiny flickering light.

Eithan drew on the ground with a stick. "They just moved us to this new shaft last week. They're looking for something. They're not so interested in the ore anymore."

"Is that why they're pushing us so hard?" Leo asked.

Eithan nodded. "They seem in an awful hurry to find it. One of them was talking about how she was worth her weight in gold, enough to set them up for eternity."

"She? Who is it?"

The boy shrugged. "All I know is that she's down here somewhere. But here's the thing. This new shaft's not as secure as the other one. It's too narrow to store the rock we dig out, so they have to haul it away every couple days. They load the rock into these carts"—he drew a long set of tracks—"and take it up to the surface. We can sneak up the rail shaft with the cars."

"And when you get to the top and Altof's waiting to cut our throats?" Griggs sniped.

"Shh!" the lookout hissed. They stubbed out the candle, and everyone dropped to the ground, feigning sleep. A light passed over them before moving on.

After a few moments, Eithan struck a flint and relit the candle.

"Well?" He looked hopefully at Leo.

Leo studied the scratching. "It needs some work. Griggs is right. We need a plan once we get to the surface and enough time for everyone to go up the shaft. Tomorrow we will study their patterns. Everyone, pay attention. We need to know how many of them there are, what time they change shifts, what their weaknesses are."

The next morning, there was a hushed excitement among the boys. Few words were spoken as they shoveled in their rice allotment. Even Griggs looked hopeful, saying nothing as they shuffled along the shaft, taking their picks off the rack under the watchful eye of Altof.

The mine was laid out like a hub with spokes. Their sleeping chamber was at the end of one narrow tunnel. It led to a main room, where all the tunnels met. This hub was where the rail cars were loaded and were run up to the surface by a pulley mechanism that clattered loudly when the handle was being cranked.

As if sensing the unrest, the guards split up the boys into smaller groups. Leo was sent to work in a different shaft, with Eithan, three other boys, and a new guard, Brok.

Brok had broken teeth and bushy eyebrows that grew in a straight line across his forehead. He looked mostly bored as he cradled a whip in his arms.

After a while, he sat down, put his feet up, rested his head back on the rock, and began snoring. The sound of the pick ringing lulled him to sleep, but the moment they stopped swinging, his eyes would open, and he'd give them a nasty glare.

Leo swung his pick down. It bounced back at him. The rock was impenetrable here. He swung again, and there was a clang as the head of his pick broke off.

Brok shuffled over, studying the broken pick like it was Leo's fault.

"Stay here," the ugly dwarf grunted. "No funny business," he added, stubbing his finger in Leo's chest. "You don't want to see what I can do to your pretty face."

Leo didn't answer; he just sat down, glad to have a moment to rest. Eithan sprawled next to him along with the other boys.

"Here." Eithan passed him a small flask of water.

Leo drank it, grateful for the brackish liquid. He closed his eyes and dreamed a cool breeze brushed his forehead. It smelled like pine, like someone had just cut down a Christmas tree. The wound in his back throbbed, like there was a frozen ice chip lodged deep inside.

Strange.

Opening his eyes, Leo sniffed the air. He could make out just the faintest of odors. The other boys had their eyes closed, savoring the rare rest. Leo stood up. That chip of ice in his back pulsed faster.

The tunnel extended on, dark and foreboding. Grabbing the torch off the wall, Leo held it in front of his face.

The shaft tilted downward. He couldn't see more than a dozen feet.

Checking to see that Brok hadn't returned, Leo began walking down the tunnel. The air got even cooler, prickling his skin with the sting of ice. The faint scent of pine led him forward. The ice chip in his back grew even colder. When he put his hand to his skin, he wiped away a crust of ice.

Really strange.

Leo stood perfectly still. A soft breeze feathered his cheeks—coming from a crack in the rock running up to the surface, perhaps.

Holding the torch, he ducked as the ceiling grew shorter. The tunnel thinned out. After a few more steps, he came to the end.

Crouched, he put one knee down and looked around. The draft was still fanning his face. Something was back here, something that promised freedom. Laying the torch on the ground, he ran his hands over the walls, feeling for a crack or an opening.

He pushed on the rocks. One of them moved. Excited, he felt around the edges. The rocks at the end of the tunnel had been stacked here. There was more beyond the end. Prying one of the rocks loose, he was able to create a small opening. Holding up the torch, Leo peered through.

A cavern opened up on the other side. The ceiling was higher than the tunnel Leo was in. In the center was something tall and large, like a large rock maybe. Tossing the torch in through the hole, Leo put his eyes back to the opening. The torch rolled to the center and lit up the object there.

Leo and the woman saw each other at the same moment. She was encased in solid ice. Her eyes were the only things that could move. As their gazes met, a connection zinged across the chamber.

*Who are you?*

Her voice was like a whisper in his skull. She was evil; he could feel it in her spirit.

"I am Leo," he whispered, unable to help himself.

*How did you find me?*

"I don't know. I could smell pine. And when Loki stabbed me, I think he left—"

But at the mention of Loki's name, a piercing pain made him clutch at his head. Blood started to run out of his nose. "Stop!" he cried. "What did I say?"

*My cursed husband's name.*

Leo pushed aside the pain and searched his memory for the day Mavery had told her story of Loki's family. "You're Angerboda."

The pain eased. She looked pleased that he knew her name.

*Queen of the Dokkalfar. I can bring down cities with a mere thought. I will repay you anything you ask if you release me.*

"Anything?" Leo wiped the blood from his nose, imagining freedom for himself and all the boys. He peered through the hole, gathering his courage. She remained frozen in the same place, but her mind reached into his.

*Anything. Now, release me!*

He hovered, trying to think. "If you are so powerful, why can't you break free?"

Instantly, excruciating pain like a nail driven into his temple made Leo's knees crumple and his body bow in half. Slapping his hand to his head, he tried to make it stop.

*How dare you question me? Do it again, and I will blow out your eardrums so that you never hear another sound. I will gouge out your eyes so you never see another creature. Do you hear me?* Her whisper rose to a shriek in his head.

Leo clutched his head, nodding his whole body. "I'm sorry," he whispered. "Please. Don't do that again."

The pain receded enough that he could lower his hands.

*I have many powers I cannot access here. You were sent to release me. Do it, and anything you ask for will be given.*

Before Leo could answer, the sound of Eithan calling to him echoed down the tunnel.

*Quickly, boy, hide the opening! The dwarves cannot know where I am. Come back later when it's clear.*

Carefully putting the rocks back where they were, Leo backed out of the low tunnel on his hands and knees. She sent him a final message.

*We are connected now. If you betray me, I will destroy you.*

He kept backing away until he could stand again. Turning around, he came face-to-face with Brok.

"What were you doing down there, boy?" The dwarf pushed his mean face an inch from Leo, baring his lip to show his broken teeth.

"What do you think?" Leo asked, making motions like he'd just relieved himself.

Brok grunted, fingering his whip. "This tunnel's a dead end. You won't find your mammy waiting down there. Now, get back to work." He gave Leo a shove back to the line.

Leo picked up his ax and started swinging. That spot in his lower back, where Loki had stabbed him, that was the source of the ice that now ran through his veins.

Brok was joined by two more dwarves. They were having a heated discussion. A few words drifted over. Something about running out of time.

"Where'd you take off to?" Eithan asked.

Leo ignored the boy. Eithan stared at him, waiting for him to answer, but Leo's mind was back in that chamber. The pain of Angerboda piercing his head had been worse than any knife wound in the back.

# Chapter 27

The passage down to Helva's underworld had taken a toll on all of them. Since Mavery had been snatched, the hope had been knocked out of Sam. Perrin stood by his side, but she trembled with fatigue. Only Geela remained alert, standing at the edge of the railing, sword in hand, ready to do battle. Every so often a tremor ran through her, and Sam knew that even the mighty Valkyrie grew tired of the endless maze.

It could have been hours or days later when they finally exited the raven tunnel. The ship drifted into a large cavern the size of a football stadium. The water glowed with a sickly green color.

Dark shapes swam underneath, but nothing surfaced, and, after a while, they ignored them. Perrin brought food up from below, some cold stew. They took a short break, eating glumly but needing the sustenance.

The ship listed sharply to the side, tilting the deck. After their short meal, Sam and Perrin went below and used magic to create a small vortex, ejecting the water as best they could. But the water quickly filled back in. The hole in the side of the ship was long and jagged, and they had no materials to repair it.

Geela whistled from the deck.

"Go on," Perrin said. "I'll keep at it."

Sam went back up on deck. It was hopeless. Skidbladnir was going to sink long before they ever got through this never-ending maze. He joined Geela at the railing. Finally, the end of the cavern had come into view. Six tunnels yawned before them.

Sam drew back his hands and released a full measure of magic at them.

Above every opening, a glowing dagger appeared. All identical.

Geela frowned. "Which is it?"

"How do I know?" Sam said as the last flicker of hope died out. They all looked the same, and he hadn't had a chance to finish tracing the right path.

"What do you feel? Trust your instincts," Geela encouraged.

Sam gritted his jaw and swallowed back the frustration. He thought of Mavery's impish grin and the trusting way she would slip her hand into his. He studied the shapes, staring at the glowing symbols. Which one was right? His instincts were telling him nothing. He stared and stared until his eyes blurred. The third one drew his attention. It had a broken tip, like it had been snapped off, or the carving had decayed. Which was it? A fact of nature, or a sign it was the correct path?

Before he could decide, Perrin let out a bloodcurdling

scream from below. Geela flew to the steps as Perrin spilled out onto the deck. Something had a hold of her. A thick black tentacle was wrapped around her leg.

"Let go of me!" Perrin shouted, kicking at the thick arm. Sam shot a blast of witchfire at it, trying not to hit Perrin. The wood next to her splintered, but the creature held on. Geela dove in with her sword, hacking at the grasping arm. The deck under Sam's feet shattered as another tentacle thrust upward, knocking him off his feet. Geela transformed into a swan and flew up, evading its reach. Sam ran, sending another blast of witchfire at it. He stayed just ahead of the thrashing arm. He jumped up and grabbed the rigging and pulled himself higher.

At the front of the ship, a third arm appeared. The creature was everywhere at once.

No, he realized. There was more than one. Out of the water, three black bulbous heads rose, like giant black octopi, each one the size of a tank.

Akkar. The giant squid-like creatures that guarded Balfour Island were even bigger and uglier here in the underworld.

They circled the ship, trying to drag it down with their slithering arms. There were too many akkar to fight.

Perrin clung to the mast as the tentacle wrapped around her waist and tugged her backward.

"Sam, I can't hold on!" she shouted up at him.

"I'm coming down!" He started to clamber down, but she shouted at him.

"No. We're almost there. You have to go on."

"No! Not without you." He couldn't do this without Perrin.

Her eyes were locked on his as she said, "Promise me you'll finish. For Mavery."

Then she let go of the mast. The creature dragged her back over the side of the ship and into the sea.

"Perrin!" Sam shouted, dropping down to the deck. He grabbed for her hand, but he was too late. She hit the water with a splash and then disappeared. The other akkar withdrew, as if they had what they had come for, and sank.

Sam stared at the bubbling dark water. Emptiness opened up in him like a yawning chasm. He felt the clawing of anger that arose when the things he loved were taken away. He tried to take a breath and failed, his chest caught in the chokehold of rage.

Geela settled onto the deck, transforming back to her human form.

"Sam, we need to move quickly. The ship will not last much longer."

"Why didn't you help her?" he turned to shout at Geela. "Why didn't you fight? We could have killed those things."

Geela's face remained impassive. "Ten more would have risen up. This was a test. Helva knows you're coming. She knows you are after something. She is taking away everything you love in order to make you easier to break."

Sam wanted to hit something, pound on someone like he'd pounded Ronnie Polk that terrible day he'd turned twelve.

"Which tunnel, Sam?" she asked.

Sam hated the Valkyrie at that moment, standing with her golden shield and white tunic. He hated her for not breaking down and screaming with him at how unfair it was.

"We can still save them," she continued. "But we have to hurry. The ship is nearly gone."

She was lying about saving his friends. None of them were getting out of this alive.

Sam went back to the wheel and turned the ship toward the tunnel with the broken knife.

The ship wobbled heavily as they entered the next chamber. The cavern was small and circular. There were no visible exit tunnels. Water sloshed side to side below. Sam didn't know how much longer they would stay afloat. Looking behind him, he was surprised to find a blank wall.

"Where's the tunnel we came in?" he asked.

Geela shrugged. "One-way trip. I believe we've arrived."

They sailed into the center of the cavern, and the ship came to a stop. Water rose to the top step of the galley. In moments, the ship would be overcome, and they would end up in the cold water.

"Any ideas?" Sam asked.

"None," she answered. "It seems we have run out of time to play the game."

"You could transform into a swan and fly up, maybe find an exit," Sam offered.

The Valkyrie didn't hesitate. "We go together, no matter what. We don't break up the team, right?" She repeated his words.

The ghost of a smile tugged at his lips. "Some team. We've lost half our squad and busted a ship of the gods."

"We've still got a powerful witch. Can't you conjure us out of here?"

"No, but I can let them know we're here." He rolled his hands and thrust them out, sending a blast of green witchfire, then another and another, lighting up the domed roof and sending splinters of lightning zigzagging around the chamber.

The crackling sound made his ears hurt, but he kept at it, letting his magic sing, zapping every wall, every rock, putting on an incredible shower of lightning for Geela.

Exhausted, he tried to catch his breath, putting his hands on his knees before looking at Geela. She was pointing at the walls.

Sam followed her gaze. His witchfire had done something to the cavern. The entire chamber was lit up with a green glow. He waited for some horrible creature to appear. The water was up to the level of the deck; any moment now, the ship would simply sink.

Then the cavern walls rumbled. A split appeared, and

the two sides opened, drawing apart. The ship lurched forward, tugged by the escaping water.

As water came over the side of the rails, Sam climbed up the mast, pulling Geela up behind him. They stood on the bowsprit, riding their sinking ship into Helva's underworld.

As they passed through the gates, the ship came to rest alongside a stone landing that rose out of the water. On it, a man dressed in a simple black robe waited. He raised his hand, and a gangplank appeared, extending out of the stone to where they clung to the mast. Stepping onto it, Sam followed Geela to the landing.

Behind them, the last sign of Skidbladnir was the top of the mast going under in a flurry of bubbles. Sam waited to see if the ship would change into the small handheld carving, but nothing appeared.

Skidbladnir had been destroyed.

Standing on solid ground felt better than Sam could imagine. The rock was slippery and cold underneath his boots, but it was real.

"Hello," Sam said, raising his hand to the robed man.

The man looked at them with avid curiosity. His redrimmed eyes were a milky gray color.

"You've been expected," he said in a papery voice.

"Well, here we are," Sam said. "Can you take us to Helva?"

He extended one arm, his bony hand sticking out of the sleeve palm up.

"I don't have any money," Sam said.

The man drew back his hand and turned around, walking away from them on a stone path that rose up from the water.

"Wait!" Sam called, "don't leave."

"I've got gold," Geela said. She took off the golden cuffs from her arms and held them out.

The man paused, turning his head slightly to study the cuffs. Still, he hesitated.

She unbuckled her breastplate, holding it out with her other hand.

He inhaled a slow deep breath, as if it pained him to accept her offer, before giving the slightest of nods.

The gold offerings in Geela's hands vanished and reappeared in the man's arms.

He cradled the vest while he waited for them to join him. Black algae clung to the surface of the stones. Each stone was wide enough for one person to step on. Behind them, the path disappeared, sinking under the water as soon as they stepped off the stones.

Sam stepped gingerly, not wanting to slip. It was difficult to see anything. Fog shrouded the area. Rotted plants poked out of the water. It was cold, and the air smelled of sulfur.

Sam hurried to keep up with Geela and the robed man. At one point, he slipped, but the Valkyrie was there with an iron grip on his arm, pulling him back on the path. For a moment, Sam glimpsed something in the water—the ghostly image of a human face staring at him.

The guide stopped at a heavy metal gate that blocked the path. A towering stone wall ran unending in both directions. From the folds of his robe, he drew out a thick ring lined with skeleton keys.

He fingered them slowly until he picked the one he wanted. The key rattled around before he was able to insert it into the hole. The lock turned with a grinding, rusty clank, as if the gate had not been opened in a very long time. As he pushed it open, the hinges howled in protest.

"Enjoy your stay." He acted as if they were checking into a hotel, not heading into the underworld.

Sam took a deep breath as Geela rested her hand on his shoulder.

"Ready?"

Swallowing his fear, Sam nodded and stepped through

the gates. They turned at the sound of the entry slamming shut. The lock creaked as the key turned, sealing them in.

On this side of the gate, everything was different. Helva's realm was shaped like a giant bowl with a flat bottom. They stood on the rim that encircled it. The wall ran along the edges all the way around. Sam couldn't make out any other exits.

A rugged path was cut into the hillside, offering a way down. There was no vegetation, only remnants of trees shriveled with age and dried-up bushes that crumbled when disturbed. The sky overhead was gray, filled with swirling clouds. Bolts of lightning erupted, sporadically shooting out sparks and sending jagged blasts of electricity into the ground. The air was warmer than Sam expected but thick with the dust of ages and trapped air.

Below, in the center, a crumbling mansion was the only sign of civilization. Two columns supported a tall porch with broad steps. Broken pilasters had toppled over where a gazebo had once stood. Lights came from the windows.

"Hurry up, witch-boy, Helva awaits."

Geela had already set off down the path. Sam hurried, not wanting to get left behind. He had that prickly feeling at the back of his neck, like there were eyes watching him everywhere. He could feel the intensity of the gazes.

He looked up as they passed under a mottled black tree. His knees buckled as a figure moved into sight for just a moment. It reminded him of a gargoyle. Its eyes glowed red. Hunched wings arched over gray scaly legs. Its face was scarred and snarling. Then it moved back into the shadows.

"Wait up," Sam called, hurrying after Geela. After that, he didn't look at the trees. Better not to see some things, he reasoned.

The path flattened out and turned into a muddy bog. Geela stepped into it and sank to her knee. She pulled out her foot with a sucking noise. The mud smelled foul and slimy. The Valkyrie trudged on, jerking her head at Sam to follow. By the third step, he'd lost his first boot. He tried to dig it out, but it was useless. By the fifth step, he threw his other boot away.

"What do you know about this place?" Sam asked, hoping to pass the time.

"Not a lot. Helva lives in that mansion. She is tended to by her servants. The door is guarded by her pet, a dog named Garm."

"That's it? Just a dog guarding the entrance?"

Geela shrugged. "A big dog. Helva will invite you to eat with her, but you mustn't agree."

"Why not?" Food sounded wonderful to Sam. His belly had been empty for hours.

"Her dining table is called Hunger. All who sit at it feel only the pain of famine. The knife she carves the meat with is called Starvation."

"Friendly type, huh?" Sam joked.

Geela stopped her trudging to glare at Sam. "This is no time for laughter. Helva will do everything in her power to deny us what we came for. She is even now planning the meal she will make out of our bones and the gown she will knit from our skin."

"Chill out," Sam said. "I get it, okay? She's bad stuff. We're probably going to die. Welcome to my world. But if Odin is here, all we have to do is find him."

"And then what? Do you think she's just going to let him go?"

"No, but he'll be able to help us."

"What if he can't?"

"He's Odin."

"What if we're too late and he's moved on from here?"

"Where else can he go?" Sam cracked, looking around

at the gray skies and smoldering fire pits. "Isn't this as low as you can go?"

Geela shook her head. "There is a place beyond this, but it's not a place. It's a void. When a soul is stripped from its body and destroyed, there is nothing remaining."

"Frigga told me. But that hasn't happened to Odin," Sam said, acting more confident than he felt. "He's here, and we're going to get him out. And Mavery and Perrin, too," he added with less confidence. "If they're here, we'll find them."

The Valkyrie smiled, looking at him with renewed respect. "You are different than I first imagined. You are reckless but also fearless."

Sam laughed. "I've been told that before by a dwarf friend of mine. Must be all that witch blood." He winked at her.

After that, the going got easier, as if the mud gave up on sucking them down. They finally made it to dry ground and began climbing a short hill covered in a thick layer of dead grass.

"It's not far now," Sam said as the walls of the mansion got closer.

"Be careful as we approach. We don't know what traps she has lain." A gravel path cut across a wide lawn that was brittle with dead grass. A wrought-iron fence encircled Helva's home. They could see more choked weeds and dead trees through the bars.

The path ended at a gate.

"Do you think it's locked?" Sam reached for the handle.

Before Geela could answer, a giant mastiff leapt out of the bushes and landed on Sam's shoulders. It knocked him to the ground. Its slobbery breath was hot on his neck. Sam waited for the sharp bite of teeth, but the beast howled in pain.

Rolling over, Sam saw Geela facing off against a dog as large as a horse. It had a broad chest, gray wiry hair, and thick drool hanging down from its jaws. The beast limped toward Geela, its front leg bleeding from the gash of her sword.

"Move behind me," Geela called.

The mastiff leapt at her, fangs outstretched. Sam acted without thinking, thrusting his hand forward and using his magic to push the dog to the side so that it impacted head-first with the wall. It yelped and crumpled to the ground.

Geela raised an eyebrow at him. "Nicely done."

"Being a witch has its benefits." He pushed open the gate the dog had guarded. "Ladies first."

# Chapter 28

Inside the gates of Helva's mansion, the grayness was replaced by vibrant color. Sam wiggled his toes in fresh springy green grass. Flower bushes lined the stone path that led to the front door. Bright bougainvillea vines exploded in reds and purples.

Curious, Sam plucked a blade of grass and stuck it through the bars. As soon as it passed through, it curled up and shriveled into a brown dry wisp. Dropping it, Sam turned to find Geela had moved toward a tree. She stared up at the red globes that hung from it.

Apples.

The most beautiful he had ever seen.

"What are you waiting for?" Sam reached up into the branches to grab one of the ripe fruits. "They look delicious." He tugged one loose, but she slapped his hand, sending the apple rolling away.

"Have you learned nothing?" she hissed at him.

"Yeah, never trust a Valkyrie."

She took her sword and stabbed the apple. It split open, spilling out a swarm of worms that crawled away in every direction. Nausea turned his stomach. He had been about to bite into it.

"I'm sorry." He'd been his usual idiotic self. "I should have known better."

"Come on, let's get this over with."

Geela stalked up the path toward the pair of doors that marked the entrance to Helva's mansion.

They took the steps two at a time. The front door had a large circular knocker hanging from the mouth of a gargoyle. Sam picked it up and knocked firmly three times. Inside, the loud sound of the knocking echoed.

He took a step back from the door. Geela's tension radiated from her, but she kept her sword in its sheath. They waited, but nothing happened. Sam was about to knock again when Geela stayed him.

"Helva, Queen of the Underworld," she called out in a ringing voice, "we have come to seek your audience."

They listened for any sound of approaching footsteps. Maybe Helva was planning on ignoring them in hopes they would go quietly away.

Fat chance.

Sam stepped forward, ready to blast the door off its hinges, when it swung open silently.

They stepped over the threshold into a large entry hall. Overhead, an enormous chandelier made of sparkling glass held hundreds of glowing candles dripping black wax onto the ground. A curving staircase with an ornately carved wooden railing led to a second floor. A set of double doors were open. A drawing room could be seen beyond the doors.

The trailing sound of piano notes drifted from the room. Ready to face whatever was ahead, Sam crossed the marble floor alongside Geela.

They paused in the doorway. The salon was furnished with fine furniture, delicate chairs that barely looked strong enough to hold Sam. A long, low couch took up one wall. A fire burned in a stone fireplace blackened with centuries of soot. A gilded cage with a pair of yellow canaries stood in the corner. Their eyes glittered with a spiteful green at the intruders.

A grand piano took up a prominent position in the center of the room. At the keyboard sat a young woman facing sideways to them, her face partially visible. She was strikingly beautiful, with perfect white skin and lush lips curved in a lovely smile. Her fingers ran over the keys and played haunting music that filled Sam's heart with sadness and longing. Blond hair spilled over her shoulder. Her long white-and-black-striped gown hugged her figure, revealing soft curves.

"Excuse me, we're looking for Helva?" Sam called out.

At his words, her fingers crashed down on the keys, sending out a loud cacophony of sounds. The canaries let out a harsh series of squeaks, fluttering their wings at the noise.

"You dare interrupt me while I am playing?" Her voice was icily angry, but she kept her eyes downcast at her hands.

"Sorry, but we did knock," Sam joked.

Helva, if that's who it was, didn't look amused. "Did you? I didn't hear a thing. Normally, Garm takes care of intruders."

"Sorry about that," Sam said. "But Garm might not be feeling up to it. I'm afraid he ran into the wall at high speed."

Waves of fury rose off her, but she kept herself still. "What do you want?" she asked, folding her hands on her lap, her shoulders hunched in a circle over the keyboard.

"We want our friends back," Sam said, taking a step closer. She wasn't that scary. He could handle this. "And we want Odin."

Helva turned her face to snarl at him, leaping to her feet and slamming the cover on the piano shut. "Never say that name here!" she screamed.

Sam's courage turned to marshmallow because the face

she now showed was only half beautiful—the half he had seen while she had been seated. The other half, the half that had been hidden, was hideous.

Her skull held a hollow eye socket, and her half-decayed lips revealed the roots of teeth long rotted out. Her left hand was skeletal fingers. A red ruby bracelet was draped around the bone, dangling down like a cruel reminder of the flesh it had once adorned.

"What's the matter? Do you not find me so appealing, then?"

Helva, Goddess of Death, sauntered forward. The half of her face that was intact smiled at him with grotesque mockery because underneath it, he could see squirming parasites, like she was decaying before him.

"You look like two-day-old roadkill," Sam said.

The good side of her face tightened. "And you look like a delicious bit of human flesh for me to dine on," she snapped back. She looked at Geela intently. "You there, what are you?" She sniffed the air. "Not entirely human?"

"I am Geela of the Valkyrie," the warrior announced proudly.

"Then you will be mine someday." Helva giggled, like a young girl, putting her good hand over her mouth. "We will have such fun together, just two girls hanging out, picking decaying flesh off the lost souls who end up here. Like those orphans I plucked from the sea," she mentioned idly, running her skeletal hand up Sam's arm. "They are just ripe to be stripped of their flesh," she whispered in his ear.

Her birds sent up another chorus of angry tweets, as if they were serenading along with Helva's mad thoughts.

Sam controlled his urge to strike her, to throttle that half-bony neck so that the rest of her knew what it meant to decay. "I've got an idea," he said. "Let's figure out a way for us to get out of here with what we came for."

"Lovely. We can negotiate, is that it?" She laughed again, tilting her head back so that the sounds echoed in the room. "But first, you must stay for dinner. Chef has prepared a very special meal."

"I'm not sitting at your table," Sam said. "I know your tricks."

"Then this conversation is over," Helva said, turning her back to sit down on the couch. "You can walk out the front gates and return to wherever you came from. I have no interest in you."

Dismissed, and missing his friends, Sam flung his palms forward, sending a large bolt of energy at the piano, shattering it into a pile of black wood and white keys. Broken wire pinged and smoldered in the air.

Helva screamed, coming to her feet, hands drawn into fists. "How dare you?" she screeched. "That was a gift from my father. I will kill you a thousand times a day for the next thousand years for that." She flung out her bony hand, pointing one finger at him.

Paralyzed and unable to move, Sam's heart slowed as his blood cooled. He dropped to his knees, unable to draw a breath. Memories, feelings, thoughts—all drained away as she stepped closer, crooking that finger, drawing his life out of him.

It was Geela who saved him. The Valkyrie drew her sword and moved behind the queen of the underworld, laying it against her throat. "This blade was made by the gods. It can take your head off, as no mortal sword can do. Let him go."

It took a moment, one where another few years peeled off Sam's life, but then Helva dropped her hand and released him.

He hit the floor on all fours, hanging his head as he gasped for air. His fingers tingled as if she'd drained the blood from him.

"Now, you will join me for dinner," Helva said brightly,

as if nothing had happened. "I promise to serve you something delicious."

Geela put Sam's arm over her shoulder, lifting him to his feet, smiling back at Helva. "We'd be delighted."

Helva clapped her hands, and a servant appeared, a stooped woman with a white apron over a black dress.

"Show our guests to the table, Meera. And tell Chef we have company. We must whet their appetite."

"That was pretty stupid," Geela whispered as she helped him walk out of the room.

"I thought it was kind of funny," Sam whispered back, as shooting pain pinged every cell of his body. "It got her attention."

"Next time, I'll let her drain the life out of you," she snapped.

"Then who will you pick on?"

Geela had the grace to laugh. "You don't give up, do you?"

"So far, I'm hanging in there. I am a Son of Odin, you know; they make our kind pretty tough."

Helva's servant, Meera, shuffled along, her back stooped over with age. She reached an ornately carved door and pushed it open. It revealed a long dining table covered with a white cloth. Chandeliers lit up the room. The black candles flickered with yellow light. The table was set for at least twenty people, with place settings and napkins neatly folded, waiting to be laid out on guests' laps.

"Where is everyone else?" Sam asked.

"I'd rather not meet her friends," Geela said with a shudder. "Remember what I told you; eat nothing she offers."

She helped him to a chair and pulled out the one next to him for herself. He sank into the padded seat, grateful for the rest.

The door at the far end of the drawing room flew open. Helva sailed in. She had changed into a long black gown that flowed behind her. The side of her head that had hair was styled into a long braid over her good shoulder.

"Welcome to my home," she said, as if she were seeing them for the first time. She waited for Meera to shuffle over and pull her seat out in a slow *creak* across the floor.

She seated herself like a queen and waited for the maid to take the napkin and lay it across her lap. The old woman moved slow, like her limbs were weighted down with lead.

Helva clapped her hands, and the double doors flew open. A series of servers came through, dressed in white uniforms, each holding a silver domed plate. They had pale gray flesh and eyes that held no life, as if they were the living dead. Still, Sam's stomach rumbled, his mouth salivating at the tempting odors that wafted from the dishes.

Behind the servers, a portly man came out with a tall white cap carrying a platter with a roasted turkey on it, glistening with fat and dripping juices. His cheeks were ruddy and red. He set the platter in front of Sam and waved the smell up to his nose.

"You look like a hungry young man," Chef chortled, eyes twinkling as he gazed at Sam. "How about a juicy leg for you?" He carved the leg off the bird with a long sharp knife.

Turkey legs dancing in his eyes, Sam picked up his plate, holding it out, but Geela the killjoy grabbed his wrist in a vise grip and forced him to put the plate back down.

"He's not hungry," Geela said evenly, looking the chef in the eye.

"He looks hungry to me." Chef held the leg out, offering it to Sam. "What do you say, boy? I can give you a juicy breast if you prefer. Chef has anything you want."

Sam almost cried as the chef set the leg back on the plate. He watched as the man sliced into the crisp brown skin of the breast. Juices drained down the side of it, pooling on the silver platter. Chef speared a thick piece of white meat and put it on Sam's plate without asking.

Sam stared down at the steaming meat. Chef ladled some

thick gravy and poured it over the top. Next to it he scooped a perfect mountain of mashed potatoes, placing a dab of butter in the center. The butter slowly melted along with Sam's insides into a puddle of yellow deliciousness.

"Beware, Son of Odin, or this meal will be your last," Geela hissed.

# Chapter 29

S am heard Geela, but the need to eat was overwhelming him. His stomach was so empty. He hadn't eaten a meal like this in forever. He couldn't take his eyes off the deliciousness in front of him. With a shaky hand, he picked up his fork, holding it over the pile of potatoes. He pressed his fork in, watching as the butter ran down the side and mixed with the gravy. Spearing a piece of meat, he dipped it into the gravy and swirled it into the potatoes and stared at the forkful of heaven.

"Eat that, and you will surely die," Geela said, sounding like a broken record.

"If I don't eat it, I will surely die of hunger," Sam said, and he opened his mouth, pushing in the morsel. As the food met his taste buds, an exquisite feeling ran through him. He'd half-expected something awful, but it was turkey and potatoes and the best gravy he'd ever tasted. He swallowed it, feeling it hit his stomach. As it did, a powerful hunger came over him.

He really was starving, he told himself, forking another mouthful in. With every bite, he grew more and more hungry.

He forked a leg off the platter and put it on his plate, grabbing it with both hands and not caring that he smeared grease on his face as he gnawed it down to the bone. He had to have more. A black hole took the place of his stomach, demanding food, more food.

He reached for another leg. Geela stayed his arm again. "Look at yourself."

He looked down. He was sure his belly would have grown two sizes, but his pants were loose around his waist. Setting down his fork, he ignored the screaming hunger that made him want to dive onto the platter of meat, and lifted his shirt. Rib bones poked out. His stomach was concave, hollowed out.

"What's happening?" he whispered.

"You are starving to death," Geela said tightly. "Do you never listen? I warned you about this."

He tried to remember her words, but things were fuzzy. "The knife, you said it was Starvation," he mumbled.

"Yes, the knife Chef used causes the person eating to slowly starve with every bite. This table is called Hunger. As long as you stay here, you will never be filled."

"But I have to have more." He reached for the platter of meat.

"Then you will die." Geela didn't try to stop him; she just sat back in her chair, arms folded across her chest, her eyes on the woman at the other end of the room.

Sam's hand shook madly as he willed himself from reaching for another drumstick. He thought of all the reasons he wanted it, and then, as his stomach moaned with hunger, he finally drew his hand back to his lap.

Helva laughed, the notes tittering down the table. "Bravo. That was tremendous. I have never seen anyone resist Chef's tableau before. You are one in a million." Clapping her hands sharply, she motioned for the crew of servants to take away the plates and the dishes and the meat platter, making Sam want to cry as they carried it away.

"Come, we will retire to my study," Helva said. "We can conduct our business there."

Geela pushed her chair back, but Sam couldn't move. Every cell of his body cried out for more food. He could have wept as he stared at the empty place where his plate had sat.

Geela forcibly lifted him from his seat and yanked him away from the table. "Come on, then, time to do what we came for."

He looked longingly over his shoulder as she dragged him off. How could something that tasted so delicious be so deadly? Was nothing in Orkney ever good?

Geela dropped him into a chair in front of a roaring fire.

Sam gripped the armrests to stop himself from chasing after Chef and screaming for more turkey. Helva sat down across from him, folding her hands across the glossy fabric of her dress. He'd gotten used to her skeletal half, ignoring the empty eye socket to focus on her good side.

"What makes you think Odin is here?" Helva began, plucking at the folds of her skirt. "The old goat is hardly welcome in my home. He's the one who cursed me here an eternity ago."

"He has to be here," Sam said, struggling to sit up straight. "I killed him."

She arched her single eyebrow. "A mere boy?"

Geela explained for him. "Not just a boy, a Son of Odin. And Catriona."

"I thought that was impossible. So that's how you destroyed my piano." She leaned forward, resting her hideous chin on her hand. "Tell me, how did you kill Odin?"

Sam told the story of Brunin and how he'd plunged his knife into the bear's heart. "But you must know all this. Odin is here somewhere; he has to be."

She drummed the bony tips of her fingers on the wooden arm of her chair. "It would seem you have wasted your time on a fool's journey." She unfolded her legs and stood up. "Which is a pity, because if he had shown up at my gates, I would have welcomed him with open arms." The deadly tone of her voice left no doubt as to her meaning. "I do, however, have your two friends. Perhaps we can negotiate for their lives."

Sam couldn't tell if she was lying about Odin. Short of searching the place high and low, he didn't know what to do. If she really had Perrin and Mavery . . .

"I'll stay," Geela said quietly. "I will serve you the rest of the days of my life. In exchange, you let Sam and his friends leave here."

Interest flared in the underworld queen's eyes, but she shook her head. "Tempting, to be sure, a Valkyrie of my own, but the boy has something of greater value to me."

Sam was puzzled. Unless she wanted the lump of rock that hung around his neck, he had nothing to give.

But Geela had already read Helva's intentions, jumping to her feet and drawing her sword. "No. I will not let him do it."

"Do what?" Sam asked, confused.

"Give me your magic," Helva said, smiling at him with that horrible half grin.

Sam's jaw dropped. His magic for the lives of his friends? He couldn't breathe. His magic was a part of him, like his lungs and his kidneys. It gave him strength and made him special. How could he ever give it up?

Then he thought of Mavery's face, and shame rose up in him. Mavery and Perrin had risked their lives for him over and over again. How could he have hesitated for even a second? "I'll do it," he said, stepping forward. "I'll give it to you."

Geela slumped, her shoulders drooping as she sheathed her sword. "They wouldn't want you to. They would understand."

They might, but he wouldn't be able to live a day knowing he could have saved them and didn't. Sam looked at Helva. "I have your word we can leave, all of us, safely, if I give you my magic?"

She nodded. "Agreed."

He had failed to find Odin, but he could save his friends. He nodded at Helva. "Then do it."

The pair of canaries started shrieking, as if they were jeering at Sam. Helva crooked her finger, muttering some words to herself as the bony digit curled back and forth.

Sam jerked as she clawed his magic out. It felt as if a part of his soul was being ripped from him. His arms spread wide, his chest sucked forward, as his head flung back from the force of her attack. Waves of electric energy rolled off of him, and then a green vapor trailed out of his mouth.

His jaw widened into a silent scream as magic poured out of his veins and formed a snaking trail across the room to her. She inhaled it, sucking it deep inside her. The hazy cloud swirled around her half-open neck. He was frozen in place, unable to move as she crooked that finger over and over. It took an eternity, but the last wisp of magic left him.

She put her hand down, and he dropped to his knees, shattered, broken, as if he were alive but his heart had been removed from his chest.

Her one good eye was closed, and her hands gripped the chair tightly as her chest rose and fell.

"This is amazing," she breathed, and then she laughed, her eyes opening as she leapt to her feet. "Look at me!" she cried, sending a blast of witchfire into the fireplace, disintegrating the logs and turning the orange blaze to a glowing emerald. She sent another blast at the curtains, turning them to piles of crumbling ash. The windows were false, revealing solid block walls cemented over.

Geela kneeled by Sam. "Are you okay?"

He almost laughed. Was he okay? He was nothing without his magic. Not whole. Not even close, but he just gritted his teeth and nodded. "Let's get out of here." He rested his hand on Geela's shoulder. "Time for you to keep your end of the bargain," he said to Helva. "Give us our friends, and send us home."

"Very well, come along. They aren't far." She glided out of the room, her dress trailing behind her. She walked as if she floated above the ground.

"Come on," Geela said, shouldering most of Sam's weight. "I've had enough of this place."

Turning away from the entry, they followed her down a long corridor to a wide set of stone stairs that led down to a dark abyss. She didn't slow down, stepping quickly, expecting them to follow. As she walked, torches lit up on the walls as if they sensed her presence, and they went out after she passed. There wasn't much to see. It was a long narrow hallway lined with crumbling bricks under a curved ceiling. When Sam looked closer, each brick had a name and a date carved into it.

"What are these bricks?" he asked, touching one. As his finger stroked the surface, an eye opened up on it, and he reeled back in horror. Around them, every brick came awake, a single eye in each watching them, following them as they moved along.

"Something's not right," Geela muttered to Sam. "She's making this too easy."

Sam was too busy avoiding looking into any of the creepy eyes.

"A shame about Odin's scar," Geela said loudly to Helva.

The queen of the dead laughed, never breaking stride.

"Losing an eye to that fool, Mimir, and then an ear to a mere boy. What's next, an arm to my pet Garm?"

Geela stopped in her tracks. "We never told you he lost an ear." Her sword appeared in a flash of gold in her hand.

Helva paused, turning slowly so her good side faced them.

"Didn't you? Well, I must have heard it over the grapevine. The dead love to tell me all the dirty gossip."

"No, you're lying. Odin is here." Geela took a step forward, holding the sword before her. "Where is he?"

"I really couldn't say." Her voice remained neutral, but the skin on her jaw tightened, signaling her displeasure.

"Can't or won't? What about our friends?" Sam asked, fear draining his remaining energy. Had he given up his magic for nothing? "Are you taking us to them?"

"Oh, that. Well, to be honest, I lied." She turned with a shrug, revealing that row of rotted teeth. "I could have just taken your magic, but it was more fun to have you give it to me."

"What?" Sam tasted bile as his stomach turned over. "You can't. You gave your word."

"My fingers were crossed." She waggled her bony hand at him. "A little trick my father taught me."

Sam raised his hand to throw a ball of witchfire at her, but nothing happened. Looking down at his palms, the emptiness in his veins hit him. He had grown used to having magic at his fingertips. Without it, he felt hollow.

The goddess of death just laughed and raised her good hand. "Looking for this?" She ran her hand in a circle, drawing a ball of green fire, and sent it at Sam's head. He ducked, and it hit the wall, incinerating several bricks. The ear-piercing screams of the lost souls made his skin crawl.

"This is so much fun." She did it again, sending the blast at Geela. The Valkyrie grabbed Sam's arm and pulled him around a bend in the tunnel. "You can't run from me," Helva called. "This is my playground. I know every inch of it."

Geela ran down the corridor, taking turns and twists, dragging Sam with her. He was numb and getting number. He'd lost his only chance at fighting Helva by giving her his magic, and now there was no way they were ever going to rescue Perrin and Mavery, let alone Odin.

Helva's voice faded away as Geela dragged him on. After a never-ending series of turns, Sam dug his feet in, peeling Geela's hand off his arm.

"Just stop, okay? It's over. She wins."

Geela shook her head. "A Valkyrie never quits."

"Well, I'm not a Valkyrie. I'm not even a witch anymore, and being a Son of Odin isn't getting us any closer to finding him."

She shouted in his face, "How do you know when you haven't even tried? We can't give up now. If we fail, everything will be lost."

"We'll find another way to defeat Surt."

"It will be too late. Frigga is going to destroy Orkney. She won't let Surt get close to Valhalla."

Sam reeled at her words. "What do you mean, destroy Orkney?"

Geela looked shattered as she said, "She will wield Odin's Belt of Destiny and erase every trace of it. Nothing will survive."

Despair and grief tilted Sam's world. "So this was all for nothing? A fool's journey?" He slumped against the wall. "And now I have nothing left, no magic, no way to fight Surt."

Geela shook him roughly. "Snap out of it. Helva was lying. Odin is here. Find him. You alone are connected to him."

Sam's fingers went to the useless lump of rock around his neck. "This is a piece of Odin's Stone. My father gave it to me. Hermodan used it to save Orkney from the witches."

"Then surely it is imbued with Odin's blood. Use it

before that death queen finds us and embalms us into one of these bricks."

Sam lifted the pouch over his head and weighed it in his hand, wondering if he should swing it around. He did that to call on his magic, but he didn't have magic anymore. Remembering how Hermodan had held it up high, Sam decided to give it a shot. Undoing the drawstring, he dumped the small chunk of rock into his palm. It looked like a plain old piece of granite.

Holding the rock up, Sam planted his feet, closed his eyes, and thought about his visit with Odin in the Yggdrasil tree. Odin had been strong and vital then, his legs thick as tree trunks and a blue twinkle in his eye. He'd shaken Sam's hand with great strength. Sam recalled the rough palms and the callused skin. "Mighty Odin," he whispered, "show yourself to me. Guide me with your stone so that I can bring you back."

Sam stood with his eyes closed. Nothing happened. No fireworks. No sudden dizzying drop. Nothing. Geela would have to accept their fate.

He opened his eyes to apologize and almost fell to his knees.

Geela was gone, the dark underworld replaced with a barren landscape of swirling winds that made his skin sting. Fine sand blew into his eyes. He couldn't see a thing, but his heart soared. Odin had done it. Wherever he was, he had brought Sam to him. Heading into the wind, Sam trudged forward, clutching the stone in his hand.

"Odin," he called out, his words taken away by the gusts, "I'm coming."

# Chapter 30

Geela was afraid. She clutched her sword with sweaty palms, taking cautious steps forward. One moment, the boy had been there; the next, gone. He'd been erased, as if she'd imagined him. Maybe she had, her mind reasoned. After all, nothing down here made any sense.

The distant murmur of voices feathered her ears. They were singing her name, chanting it. She prowled forward toward the sounds. Something brushed her face, like a filmy cobweb. Sweeping it aside, she stepped forward into bright light.

The dank tunnels of the underworld were replaced with familiar rolling hills. They spread before her, a verdant green, split by a winding river. The Edris River. She would know it in her sleep. The red roofs of her village were just on the other side.

Geela was home.

Not understanding and not caring how this was, she ran. Jumping lightly over the stones that dotted the river, she crossed it without getting wet and ran the beaten path to her mother's cottage. She recognized the whitewashed walls and patch of garden like she'd left home yesterday, not hundreds of years ago. A thin wisp of smoke trailed from the chimney. Vaulting over the gate, Geela saw her mother in the yard, hanging the wash out to dry. Geela ran as fast as she could, afraid the image would disappear before she could reach it.

"Mother!" she shouted. The words tasted funny on her lips, as if she were underwater. "Mother, I'm home."

Geela reached her side, holding her arms out for a hug, but her mother didn't respond.

"Mother!" she cried again, "It's me, Geela, your daughter returned. How I have missed you." Geela leaned in and wrapped her arms around her mother's ample waist, but it was like she had no substance. Her arms passed right through as the old woman reached for another sheet to pin to the line.

"Mother?" Geela whispered bleakly. She looked ancient, wizened with age. Her lanky hair was a solid sheaf of gray. Her cheeks were thicker, and heavy lines etched her skin, as if she'd known great sorrow.

From the house, a familiar voice called out. It was Geela's brother, Emmet.

"Mother, a storm is coming. Why do you bother with the laundry?"

He leaned in the doorway, resting heavily on a cane. He was old, too, a man of at least sixty. The last time she'd seen him he'd been a boy, only fourteen and bursting with energy. Now he was stooped with age. But his smile was the same, and Geela smiled in response. Some things hadn't changed. That was a gift.

"Come, Mother; it's Saturday. Time for our visit."

Her mother sighed and nodded, putting her hand on his arm. Curious, Geela followed, treading easily as her elderly brother helped her mother along a well-worn path up the hill. Underneath an apple tree, two headstones stood side by side. The name inscribed on the left was her father.

With a rush of tears, Geela sank down in the grass, running her fingers over the date. She'd remembered the day they'd buried him like it was yesterday. Swiping her hand across her face, Geela looked at the next headstone. Choking grief made her swoon when she saw her own name etched simply with just the year of her birth.

"Do you think she'll ever come home?" her mother whispered, laying a wreath of white alpine flowers in front of the stone.

Geela twisted to see her brother kiss their mother on the forehead. "She is a bright star shining in the sky. A warrior princess that looks over us all. At night, I see her riding across the heavens in a blazing gold chariot, her sword held high as she slays the dragons of the dark."

Geela laughed, overjoyed at his words. They were so close to the truth. Her mother drew comfort, letting him tuck her into the crook of his arm as they turned away.

"I only wish I could have told her how much I loved her," her mother said. "I only wished she knew."

Geela couldn't move, couldn't breathe. This was impossible, of course. Her family was long dead. Still, it felt so real—the smell of the grass and the feel of the sun, her mother's wrinkled face, her brother's crooked smile.

Suddenly a dark cloud passed overhead. Geela reeled in horror as a black winged creature formed in the sky, flying down over the heads of her family, breathing a trail of fire and scorching everything in its path. Geela screamed a warning as the flames incinerated the land, but the frail pair barely had time to turn before they were engulfed, incinerating them and turning them to dust.

Geela prepared to run the beast through with her sword, but it tumbled and morphed. A swirling black cloud surrounded them. When the smoke cleared, Helva stood before her, and they were back in her drawing room as if they'd never left.

With the dying screams of her family on her ears, Geela staggered forward, determined to end the life of this half-corpse.

Helva's laughter was brittle. "Oh, come now, it was just a little fun. Surely you didn't think it was real?"

Geela recalled the love in her mother's voice, the pride in her brother's. It had been real. Helva didn't understand it because she'd never received that kind of love before. That was her weakness.

"You're wrong," Geela said. "It was real. Maybe not at this moment, maybe I wasn't there, but they said it. The universe heard it and remembered. I am a Valkyrie warrior, and I have been graced by the gods with gifts of speed, courage, and heart. I can tell when someone is lying, and you, Helva, are lying. I saw a memory. Tell me I'm wrong."

Helva looked bored as she seated herself on her couch. "Oh, believe what you like; the point is that you're never getting out of here."

Geela drew her sword, the flickering fire glinting off her golden blade. "I say I'm leaving, and I'm taking the girls with me."

Helva's eyes were glittering chips of ice. "You have no powers here. And, besides, you don't even know where they are."

"Don't I?" Geela walked toward the rotting creature and then veered left, heading for the birdcage. She raised her sword high over her head and swung at the chain holding the cage, severing the silver links. The cage fell to the ground, shattering and splitting apart. The two birds flew up at Geela, as if they were attacking her.

A flash of doubt pinched her brows. Had she been wrong? Those green eyes had been haunting her. So much like a witch's. But they flew over her head, making a beeline for Helva. They began pecking at the ghastly woman, flying in her hair and clawing at her face.

Geela smiled. No. She had been right. The smaller bird was Mavery, the larger Perrin. Now she just had to get Helva to change them back.

"Get them off of me!" Helva screamed, and then she sent a blast of witchfire as the birds flew up to the ceiling.

The green light exploded the birds in a puff of yellow feathers, and then Perrin and Mavery tumbled to the floor, gasping for air.

"Took you long enough," Perrin said, spitting out a yellow feather.

The imp Mavery just grinned at her. The three of them faced off against Helva. The queen of the underworld's face was scratched and bleeding along her human side.

Geela held her sword in front of her. "We can make a deal, Helva. You wish to see the light of day more than anything, but you can't leave because Odin cursed you to stay here. If you could, you would have left the moment Odin arrived. Even the magic you stole from Sam isn't enough to get you out of here, or you would have left."

Geela could see her words were hitting their mark by the glittering hatred in Helva's eyes.

"Great, let's incinerate her," Perrin said, drawing up a ball of witchfire. Mavery followed. Geela raised a hand as Helva matched theirs with twin balls of green fire.

"What if I had something that could make you whole? A potion given to me by Freya, Goddess of Life. All you have to do is tell us what happened to Odin."

Helva sat with her arms crossed, refusing to speak.

Perrin blasted her witchfire at the chandelier overhead, destroying it in shards of glass. "You should tell her," the witch said calmly, "before I destroy this place."

Helva looked frightened, and she flung her hands in the air. "Okay. Odin was here, for a moment, lurking about. He was looking for something. I barely caught a glimpse of him, and then he was gone. But he took something with him. Now give me what you promised."

She leaned forward greedily as Geela reached around her neck and pulled out a vial held on a long, thin cord.

"If I am ever wounded, I am to drink Freya's potion, and it will revive me. Every Valkyrie carries one. If you drink it, you will be restored to your natural self."

"And end this curse?" Helva said, looking at her skeletal half.

"It will make you whole," Geela said, holding it out to her.

"Then I will be human, and I will be able to leave." Helva danced with glee, holding up the vial. She twisted the lid off and drank the contents down in one gulp, smacking her lips in satisfaction. Almost at once, flesh began rippling along her skeletal arm, making her face pinken and round out. "It's working," she cried, admiring the new flesh. Then, as suddenly as it grew, the flesh began shrinking back and turned gray. The fleshy human side of her face sunk in, the skin peeling and falling away.

"What is happening?" she screamed.

Geela watched in horror, holding Mavery close, as Helva's flesh disintegrated off her, falling off in big patches. In moments, her entire body became a hollowed skeleton with only a thatch of blond hair left attached to her skull. The fabric of her dress hung limply over the bony structure. Green vapor began lifting from her skin, forming a trickle that snaked up to the ceiling, whirling in a circle as it grew, as Sam's magic was drawn out of her, and then, as the last drop left her, the cloud vanished, as if it had never been.

"What have you done?" Helva hissed in a crackling voice as her remaining lung shriveled into a black lump. "You said I could be beautiful!"

Geela stepped back. "I said you could become whole. Just like you asked."

"No, this wasn't what I wanted," the skeletal creature

cried pitifully. She collapsed to the floor, dragging herself forward with her bony fingers.

"But it is who you are. Come"—Geela turned to the girls—"it's time to leave."

They left through the front door.

At the gates of Helva's mansion, Geela held the others back. The guard dog, Garm, stood waiting, paws planted as it lowered its head to growl at them. Wearily drawing her sword, Geela prepared to fight the canine when a blast of green witchfire incinerated it into a pile of ash.

Geela gaped at Perrin. "How did you—"

But Perrin snarled at her. "How could you let him do it? Sam can't survive without his magic; he won't be able to protect himself. You should have stopped him."

Guilt sliced through Geela. The girl was right. "I'm sorry. It happened so fast. Sam would do anything for you two. How could I stop him from saving you?"

Perrin's face twisted with grief. "I don't know. But you should have," she said in a husky voice. "Where is he, anyway?"

"He went after Odin."

Mavery nudged the older witch. "Sam will be fine. He's not just a witch, he's a Son of Odin. We need to find Skidbladnir and get back to Skara Brae. Sam's gonna need our help when he gets there."

"Uh, about Skidbladnir," Geela began.

An hour later they were back at the stone pier where Skidbladnir had sunk. It had taken some negotiation at the gate with the gatekeeper that had ended with Perrin promising not to incinerate him if he returned Geela's golden cuffs and breastplate.

The scarred walls of the cavern displayed the black streaks of Sam's rage.

"So it's really gone?" Perrin said, nudging a pebble into the black water.

"Yes, we couldn't save it," Geela said.

Neither of them noticed Mavery peeling off her boots until the little witch stood on the edge in her bare feet and dove in.

"Mavery!" Perrin cried.

The little witch disappeared into the murky pool. Geela flashed on the underwater creatures that lived there. She and Perrin exchanged a quick nod, and then they were shedding their boots, but before they could jump in, Mavery's head bobbed up. She looked like a seal with her black hair slicked back. Perrin hauled her up onto the stone pier.

"What kind of crazy stunt was that?" the witch shouted. "Do you remember those horrible creatures that snatched you up?"

"I had to get Skidbladnir." She held up her fist. Wrapped around her hand was the end of a rope. It snaked down under the water.

"And what are we supposed to do with this? Haul the ship up?" Perrin asked snarkily.

Mavery stomped her foot. "Stop treating me like I'm a child! I am a witch, and I have magic. Magic is you needing something and believing it can happen. Didn't you ever pay attention to your lessons? We need Skidbladnir to rise, so, by the gods, I'm going to make it rise. Now step back if you're not gonna help."

Geela's eyes met Perrin's. The older witch shrugged. "Okay, imp. You're right. We have nothing to lose. I'm in. Geela, you take the rope. When we say pull, start to pull it up."

Geela took the rope, wrapping the wet twine around her hands until she had a firm grip. She had no idea if this was going to work, but something about Mavery's bravery made her want it to. Bracing her feet, she nodded at the girls.

They dropped into a stance and began moving their hands through the air.

"Go ahead, Mavery. This was your idea," Perrin said.

Mavery began chanting. "Mighty Skidbladnir, ship of the gods, rise and sail again."

She repeated it as they moved their hands. The third time she said it, she raised her foot and brought it down in a sharp stomp. A loud rumble sent ripples across the water. At the same time, Perrin released the ball of energy that had gathered over her head, throwing it at the surface.

"Pull!" Perrin shouted to Geela.

The water boiled and bubbled furiously. Geela put all her Valkyrie strength into tugging. At first, nothing happened. Perrin kept up an onslaught of crackling energy at the water as Mavery kept up her chant. Something budged. The rope slackened, and she pulled it in.

"Keep it up, it's working!" Geela shouted.

Slowly but surely, the ship rose out of the water. The mast broke through first, and then the railings of the ship followed, and then the hull with the gaping hole in the side appeared.

Perrin drew her hands up, drawing water from inside the boat like a fountain spraying through the air until the little ship bobbed on the surface.

Mavery pointed a finger at the hole, sending a small blast of witchfire to dance around its edges as she shouted, "Mighty Skidbladnir, you were built to carry the gods. One little hole cannot destroy you!"

The ship vibrated, rattling its timbers. They stopped to watch as light began to glow around the edges, lighting up every timber in the ship. Then the hole began to fill in, inch by inch, until it was sealed up. The ragged tears in the sail stitched themselves up, and the grime and holes in the deck from the giant squids repaired themselves until the ship was shiny and new again.

Mavery clapped her hands, squealing with glee. Geela

dropped the rope, panting with exhaustion. "You did it!" She hugged the little witchling. Perrin just grinned, nodding as she folded her arms. "Mavery did it," she said, giving her a wink.

A long plank extended from the boat to their stone pier. Mavery skipped on board. Geela strode to the wheel, grasping it with both hands. "Take us to Skara Brae!" she shouted. A crack opened up in the ceiling. Rocks fell until a small hole opened up. Stars twinkled through the opening. The ship launched itself in the air, and they sailed out of Helva's underworld into the night sky.

# Chapter 31

After his encounter with Loki's ice queen, Leo did his best to shield himself from the connection he shared with the evil creature. He crouched in the corner of their cell, not speaking, not looking at anyone. He ignored the offers from the boys to eat. He repeated the prayers, the chants of his forefathers, to drive out the ice prickles in his head.

It was bad enough that he had released Loki. He wasn't about to double his bad choices by releasing Loki's evil wife. Even if it meant she shredded his brain.

*Be still, child, I know you are listening*, she whispered in the middle of his thanksgiving prayer.

Leo dragged in a deep breath, refusing to be drawn in.

*I can make you feel me. I will not be ignored.*

Chanting, keeping his lips moving, Leo armored himself, but a shadow fell over him. Like a living thing, it chilled him to the bone. His jaw froze in place. He couldn't move. Couldn't breathe. The shadow entered his body, and then the pain began, radiating from his fingers up his arm, down his chest and torso to his legs, even down to his toes, until every cell pricked with needles. He was immobilized, unable to speak or even scream.

*I can have you anytime I want. You belong to me now. I must be released. Tonight. Get out of that cell and bring a pick with you.*

Icy sweat beaded his brow. He resisted, but the words were torn from him. "I can't get out; I'm locked in," he whispered.

The pain increased, making his back arch.

*Find a way.*

Rising to his feet, Leo shook his head to clear the fog.

Eithan stood in front of him, looking worried. "Are you okay? You were talking to yourself."

Leo grabbed his arm. "I have to get out of here."

"Now? Tonight? But we agreed we'd wait until we had a plan, or are you leaving without us?" The boy looked betrayed.

"No, there's something I have to do. Can you help or not?"

Eithan's eyes speared into his. "You swear you'll come back?"

"I swear on my father's life."

The boy fished into his pocket and pulled out a wooden key. "It's fragile, so be careful. We pinched the real key off the guard and put it back after we made a carving of it."

"I'll be careful," Leo vowed, grasping it in his palm.

After he opened the door, he moved silently down the corridor.

The guards were arguing among themselves. They seemed to disagree about what to do with Angerboda when they found her. Some wanted to kill her on the spot; the others wanted to move her deeper into the mines.

Leo made his way back to the tunnel he'd been in earlier, bringing a pickax and a torch from the rack. The tunnels were deserted.

At the opening to Angerboda's chamber, he knelt and

started taking down the rocks until he could crawl through. He stepped into the space. The walls had been chiseled out of stone. She was encased in a block of ice that stood on some kind of pedestal.

He held the pick, hesitating, wavering.

She pulled him forward with that mental tether, but he resisted even as she sent shards of pain through him.

"What do you want?" he asked, unwilling to be part of something that would make the situation worse.

*Freedom from this prison.*

"And then what? When you're free, what will you do?"

*That is my business*, she hissed.

He stepped back. "No. I won't help you unless I know." Pain lanced through him. Gritting his teeth, he held his ground. "Tell me, or turn my brain to mush, I don't care. I already made one big mistake to save my own hide. I'm not going to make another."

When she didn't answer, he took another step back. Agony shot through him. He dragged his foot back, and the pain increased in his skull until he thought it was going to explode with the pressure.

Another foot. Although she was immobile in the ice, she was not unaware. Her screaming echoed in his head.

*Another step, and I will kill you.*

"Then we will both die here. The dwarves will find you and kill you."

The pain ratcheted up another notch, and then stopped. Leo's nerves ran out of him, turning to Jell-O as he sank to his knees, grateful the pain was gone.

*I want to see my children one last time*, she whispered in a sad voice. *To kiss my husband goodbye.*

Leo raised his head. "Goodbye? Where are you going?"

*Home. A journey I cannot take trapped here.*

"That's it? You just want to say goodbye?"

*Yes. It is all I can do. My time here is done.*

Leo got to his feet and stepped closer, studying her face in the ice. He could swear a tear ran down her cheek.

Gripping the pick, he steadied himself. It might be the wrong choice, but, somehow, it felt right.

"Here goes." Leo raised the pick and swung it.

Before it could hit the ice, a whip cracked through the air, and the handle was whisked out of his hands and flicked aside. Staggering with the effort, Leo turned, finding Altof the dwarf.

"Step away from her," Altof called, raising the whip and flicking it again at Leo.

Leo was faster and dove to the side in a tuck and roll.

*Stop them!* Angerboda screamed in his head.

More dwarves spilled into the chamber. Leo was backed into a corner. He had no weapon, and this ice queen had no power over the dwarves. They circled him menacingly, each holding a dagger in their grimy, meaty hands.

"Come on, boy, make it easy for yourself," Altof said. "You got no hope of getting out of here."

"Oh yeah? What about us?" came a familiar voice.

Leo looked up. Behind the dwarves, the cavern filled with the slave boys, led by Eithan. Some held pickaxes; others wielded rocks. They looked ready for battle. Leo couldn't stop the grin that creased his face.

"You all right, Leo?" Eithan called.

Leo nodded. Leaping forward, he grabbed the pick from the floor and swung it at the ice queen. The solid block shattered with a loud explosion, spraying the room with shards of stinging ice and a gray mist.

As the fog cleared, a woman stood before them with long iron-black hair and a face that looked like it had been chiseled from granite. Her skin was pale, her cheekbones high and angular. Her chin jutted out as she stared at the dwarves.

Black fire danced in her eyes as if there were a furnace of hatred burning inside her. She raised her finger and pointed at Altof. A bolt of ice shot from her hand and hit the dwarf dead center in one of his eyes, killing him instantly as he fell backward.

She swept her arms across the cavern, and bolts of ice shot out of her hands, sending the dwarves screaming and running.

She stopped as the surviving dwarves cowered in the corner, and she turned to Leo. "We need to leave now."

"What about them?" he asked, nodding at the boys.

"Oh, they know what to do," she said, and she sailed forward.

She was right. Eithan flashed him a thumbs-up as the boys began exacting revenge on their former captors, pounding on them with fists.

Leo followed her up the dark tunnel. Every so often they would run into a pair of dwarves. Angerboda would simply raise her hand, and a shard of ice would fly from her palm, usually landing in some vital organ. The dwarf would barely have time to scream before he was impaled.

They climbed the steep path toward a sliver of light that was the sweetest Leo had ever seen. As they broke out into the open, tears clouded his eyes.

"Why do you cry?" she asked, pausing to look at him. Her eyes were like black crystal, glittering hard but curious.

"Because I didn't think I would ever see the sun again."

"Nor did I," she answered, tilting back her head to take in the warm rays. "But here I am. Husband, where are you?" she shouted.

"Here, my queen."

Out of the shrubs, a bushy head popped up.

Angerboda strode over to him, slapping him once hard across the face before pulling him into a strong embrace. "What took you so long?"

"I was delayed. But I'm here now, and I brought you a gift."

Behind him, Leo spied a flash of color, and then someone hurtled herself at him.

"Keely!"

Feeling like it was Christmas and her birthday at once, Keely swept Leo into a hug. "I thought you were dead," she whispered.

Leo hugged her back, his voice thick as he said, "I thought I would never see you again."

"Break it up," Loki said, prying them apart. He bowed to his wife. "I present you with your gift." He beckoned Keely forward.

The woman before her was tall, with long black hair and skin like ice. She held a haunting beauty, with a thin nose and high cheekbones. Her lips were tinted blue, and her eyes held no trace of emotion.

Angerboda wrinkled her nose. "What use have I of a mere girl?"

"Not the girl, darling; look again." Loki waved his hand at her neck.

Angerboda crooked her finger, and Keely felt herself drawn forward. She wanted to run, but her feet were dragged forward by a merciless force. The pendant began to glow brightly. Its magic made her veins sing with its power.

Angerboda's eyes glowed in the light of the magic. "The Pendant of Helina. Where did you find this?"

"I swam with a ghost," Keely said with just a dash of pride.

"Nehalannia. Her father was a fool, gifting her with this much power. It did her no good in the end. She perished for love." Angerboda let the pendant drop. "Do you know what this trinket does?"

Keely shrugged. "She said in my time of greatest need, it would show itself to me. I know it's powerful. I can feel it. It whispers to me in my sleep."

"You are pleased, wife?" Loki looked anxious.

Angerboda ignored Loki as her gaze bore into Keely's eyes. "The Pendant of Helina is powerful. Too powerful for a young girl to carry." She held her hand out. "Give it to me, and I will safeguard it."

Keely's fingers went to it, wrapping tightly around it. Every bone in her body refused to give it up. It was important. She didn't yet know why, just that it was. "I can't give it to you."

Angerboda's eyes flared in surprise. "You would defy me?"

Keely swallowed her fear, concentrating on the strength coming from the pendant vibrating under her hand. "I know you can kill me with just your thoughts," she said. "But if it's as powerful as you say, we will need it to defeat Surt."

"Surt?" Angerboda grew still. Her eyes went to Loki's. "What is that red devil up to? He's never dared challenge Odin before."

Loki patted her hand. "Much has happened, wife. Odin is dead. Killed by the son of a witch."

One of Angerboda's eyebrows rose. "There hasn't been a witch-boy since Rubicus lost his head. Why would Surt waste his time pursuing humans?" Her eyes narrowed. "Let me guess; you had something to do with it."

Loki shrugged. "I might have passed the word along."

"So instead of coming straight to me, you wasted time stirring things up." Her lip curled in anger. "You haven't changed one bit. I thought eons in the underworld would make you grow up, but, I can see, it was for naught."

She turned back to Keely. "Where I am going, this necklace would be of no use. For that reason, and the life debt I owe this one"—she nodded at Leo—"you may keep the pendant. But, I warn you, power like that can be tempting. Be careful it doesn't devour you." She turned to Loki. "You have made me wait long enough. Let us gather our children."

Loki stepped away from his wife. His body started shifting, growing. First, his legs furred with a light coating of hair, and his feet became hooves. His torso stretched out and lengthened, growing thicker. Then his arms turned into the front legs of a horse, and his head grew until a white stallion stood before them, pawing the ground. He shook himself once, and a pair of silvery wings sprouted out of his side.

Keely had seen a lot of things in Orkney, but this was pretty impressive.

Angerboda climbed atop Loki's back.

"Take me to dear Fenrir first."

The horse sprung into the air and began gaining altitude.

Before Keely could ask Leo what the plan was, they were interrupted by a rush of dwarves fleeing the mines. Behind them, a swarm of boys followed, waving picks and shouting.

"I see you started a riot," Keely said to Leo.

A tall boy made his way over to them, grinning triumphantly. "You did it!" he said, giving Leo a high five.

Leo grinned back. "We did it. Eithan, I'd like you to meet my friend, Keely."

Eithan extended his hand. "You are an earth child as well?" he asked, gripping her hand tightly. "You look Eifalian."

Keely had this puzzling feeling, like she knew this boy. She frowned. "You look familiar," she said. She turned to Leo. "Don't you see it? He has Joran's eyes."

Excitement made Keely's pulse race. Her Eifalian senses were tingling like she had touched a light socket.

*What is lost can be found.*

Ymir's words.

This could be him! Joran's long-lost son. But there was no time to puzzle that out.

"We still have a realm to save," she said. "Surt's army will be on our shores by now."

"Let us help," Eithan said. "The boys and I have no home to go to. We will fight with you."

A pack of boys had gathered around them. Their skin was pale and grimy, blackened with mine dust, but their eyes burned with a fire to do something.

Keely felt her heart lighten.

She had her very own frost-giant army. They might be young, but they were as fierce as any of Joran's men.

"We can use the help. I'm not sure how we're going to get there. The boat I came in can only hold a handful—"

Shouts echoed through the trees, and then Galatin burst into the clearing, sword drawn. When he saw her, his face relaxed. "Keely, Leo, you're all right!"

"Galatin!" She hugged the Orkadian soldier tight. "How did you find us?"

"I brought him," Reesa said as she stepped out of the trees, followed by three of her men. Her eyes locked on the throng of grimy boys. "Word reached us that the captain of your ship was thrown overboard. Knowing Loki, I guessed he would bring you here."

She studied the faces of the boys, and her jaw tightened.

"The black dwarves kept our children as slaves." Her voice was low and throaty, as if she could barely choke out the words. "How did we not know?"

"Some have been here for years," Leo said softly.

Guilt and hope chased across her face. "The black dwarves will be dealt with," Reesa said, still searching the boys. Her eyes rested on Eithan's face, but the boy showed no sign of recognizing her. A ripple of pain flashed so fast that Keely almost missed it, and then Reesa's chin firmed. "But first, we are going to war. Come, all of you, back to my ship. There will be time for a homecoming once Surt is defeated." She turned to one of her men. "Find a horse and return to Rakim like the devil is on your tail. Deliver a message to my husband. Tell him to join us in Skara Brae or lose his wife."

# Chapter 32

For endless hours, Sam kept his head down to avoid the stinging grit that threatened to flay off his skin. He couldn't tell if he was getting any closer to Odin, but moving was all he had. His feet sunk into soft sand. He was in the middle of a whiteout, not a shape to be seen on the horizon. Thirst plagued him. How long since he'd had a cool drink? Days? Weeks? He had a vision of Chuggies, the old hamburger joint he and Howie liked so much. A chocolate shake sounded pretty good right about now.

Busy dreaming about the chocolaty goodness sliding down his throat, Sam almost missed the fact that the wind had died down, or maybe it was because his ears were full of sand. Stopping, he shook his head to the side, clearing his ears and wiping the grit out of his eyes.

The terrain was barren landscape. Three dead trees stood in the center of a desert. The color was flat, as if he were trapped in a black-and-white movie. There were no birds flying overhead. Walking toward the saplings, Sam felt a nudge, something familiar. He'd seen the three trees before.

They poked up from the sand, jagged branches sticking out like skinny, bony arms.

He put his hand on the gnarled gray trunk of the first tree. It moved under his touch. The bark was like rubber, pliable and shifting under his fingers, as if it were alive.

"Who is there?" a voice said.

He recognized the voice. These were the Norns, the goddesses of fate that had told him he was going to die just before he had faced Fenrir.

Stepping back, he shook his head. "No, it can't be."

The rubbery tree trunk shifted and formed a gnarled face. "I know that voice. He was here before."

Next to the tree, the other two trunks twisted into faces. "Yes, here before," they whispered in unison. "Born to die, die he will, why has he not?" They murmured among themselves.

"You were wrong," Sam said louder than necessary, fighting the fear that came from remembering his fate. "I didn't die. If you were wrong about that, maybe you're wrong about other things."

A root burst out of the ground and wrapped tightly around Sam's ankle, yanking him off his feet. Kicking the root, he tried to get his ankle loose. "Yeah, you don't like that? Well, tough. I don't like being sent on a wild goose chase. Where is Odin?"

"Odin is lost," whispered the young Norn, Skald.

"No, I can find him!" Sam shouted.

"Find him, yes; bring him back, no," another whispered.

"His fate is his fate; he gave for another," the eldest said.

"I can help him. Please, we're running out of time. Geela says Orkney will be destroyed if I don't stop Surt, and I can't do it without Odin. Help me."

"Show him," the eldest said in a creaky whisper. "Then he will know. Impossible."

Behind the Norns, a spire of rock began pushing out of the ground, rising up into the air until it towered above them.

Sam's breath was ragged gasps as he asked, "You want me to climb it, is that it?"

The Norns were silent. He looked up. He couldn't see the top, but it was his only option. He started climbing, ignoring the jagged edges and sharp stones as he pulled himself up. He scaled the towering rock, finding nooks and crannies, enough to get himself up. Pulling himself over the lip, he came out onto a large flat spot. He stood and spun in a circle. The breeze whipped his hair.

"Odin, where are you?" he shouted, his voice lost in the wind. He looked behind, ahead, in every direction, but the god was nowhere in sight.

A pile of boulders on the far side had been made into a cairn. He kneeled down in front of it. His heart soared as he recognized who was inside. The massive bear lay on its side.

Sam lifted the rocks out of the way, clearing a space to examine the beast more closely. Its shaggy head rested on its paws. The bloody evidence of Sam's treachery, the missing ear, looked raw and festered. He reached out a trembling hand to touch its shoulder.

"Odin, are you all right?"

The bear didn't stir. There was no sign it was alive.

"Odin, please, you have to get up now. You can't let Surt win."

Not even a flicker. The breeze fluttered his fur slightly, but there was no life in the beast. Sam rocked back on his ankles, refusing to believe it. Odin couldn't be gone. Not now. Not after he'd worked so hard to get here.

He paced the small area at the top of the rock. His eyes kept shifting back to the lifeless creature. *Think, Baron, what can you do?* But it was like the life had been drained out of Odin.

Yet he was still here. Sam stopped, looking back at the bear. Brunin was intact, whole, as if it was just waiting to be turned back on.

Was it possible? Helva had taken his magic, but he was still a Son of Odin. Fingering his pouch, Sam closed his eyes and went deep into himself, remembering his father, remembering how much love he had for this place.

He let himself fill up on memories and then opened his eyes. He went to the far end of the rock, as far away from Brunin as he could, and he cracked his neck once. Then he dug in his feet and settled into a crouch, hands forward.

"Here goes nothing."

He began to run, as hard and fast as he could. As he did, he imagined himself going into Odin as he had done with the black-winged Omera long ago, immersing himself in the creature and becoming one with it.

He imagined Odin's great heart beating and the sharp blue eyes that saw everything. Then he dove, hands first at the beast, and when he hit it he disappeared into the bear in a blaze of white light.

Loki flew across the sea, stretching the wings in his horse form. His shoulder ached, but he was strong enough to fly. Anything for his wife. After several hours, they landed on the rock where Fenrir had been imprisoned. But there was no sign of their furred son. His chains lay in pieces. Angerboda dismounted and ran her hands over them.

"Someone has recently released him." Her eyes grew confused as she held the links. "Who could have done that?"

Loki shifted into his human form. "The witch-boy," he said, "the one I told you about. He would have come to see Fenrir."

She pinned him to the spot with a glacial stare. "And why would he do that?"

A small glint made his eyes shine as a smile curved his

lips. "Because Odin wants to come home. I knew that old goat wouldn't stay gone. The boy would need the key from Fenrir to unlock the map to Helva's underworld."

"And where is the map?" Her eyes were glacial chips, like she knew the answer before he said it.

"In Jormungand's chamber."

One eyebrow arched. "He released him as well?"

Loki shrugged.

Angerboda glowered. "You don't know?"

He grinned sheepishly. "I've been busy rescuing you."

Angerboda gave him a look that told him what she thought of his rescue. "Worthless fool. Take me to Jormungand."

They flew across the ocean until they came to the funnel. Loki dove straight down, heading to the bottom of the sea. They entered Jormungand's chamber. Rocks were strewn everywhere. The bars of his prison were bent and twisted.

The sea serpent was nowhere to be seen. Then a moan echoed in the tunnels. Stepping under the shattered ledge, they found Jormungand in the corner, curled up in a ball. Loki could see he was dying. Bubbles of blood came out of his mouth. A large stalactite protruded from his scaly chest.

Angerboda wailed. "Who did this to you, dear child?" She wrapped her arms around the serpent, stroking his snout. Loki sniffed the air. The lingering smell of sulfur teased his nostrils. Witchfire. Angerboda raised her head. "The witch-boy did this, didn't he?" she hissed.

The serpent whimpered once, and then, with a shuddering gasp, he died in her arms. Angerboda stood, trembling. Green blood stained her gown. "Take me to Helva," she hissed.

Loki nodded, wondering if things could get worse.

Outside the gates of Helva's mansion, he knew they could.

The gate hung on its hinges. The guard dog he'd left her, Garm, was nothing more than a pile of ashes.

They entered the foyer. The place was in shambles. A

chandelier lay shattered. Loki cried out at the broken piano in the drawing room. Someone had obliterated it. Weeping, he pressed his face to the lid. He had sent this to her as a gift.

"Where is she?" Angerboda screamed at Loki.

Then from the corner came a mewling call. "Mother?"

They turned as a pitiful creature dragged itself toward them. It was completely skeletal, draped in a tattered silk garment.

"That is not my daughter," Angerboda said, stepping back. "She was beautiful, a living death like no other."

"Mother, please." The bony fingers stretched toward Angerboda. "She did this to me."

"Who?"

"The Valkyrie. The one the witch-boy brought. She tricked me."

"How?"

"She told me I could be whole, the one person I desired."

"Then this is who you are," Angerboda said, turning away. "Nothing more than death. You were my most beautiful creation, someone to bridge the worlds, but you forgot your way."

Helva reached for her. "Wait, don't leave me."

"Children are such a disappointment," she said to Loki as she swept out of the room. "Take me to this boy who destroyed my family. I want to see how he looks when he is strung up by his intestines."

Loki gave his daughter one last pitying look before hurrying after his wife.

So much for a happy reunion.

# Chapter 33

The blackened hulls of Surt's armada cut through the water, riding the winds toward the green shores of Orkney. When at last the fertile lands came into sight, excitement rippled through Surt. He was in the first rowboat to shore. Standing on the firm soil of Odin's precious realm, Surt squatted down and ran his hand over the waving blades of grass.

How many eons had it been since he'd last felt the green velvet of new grass? How many lifetimes had he spent as Odin's prisoner in a world where there was no freedom? All that would end now. Taking his staff, Surt drove it into the earth and looked at the men who crowded around.

"Let it be said that on this day, the army of Musspell made a claim on Orkney."

The men cheered.

"Let it be known that on this day, the army of Musspell said no more: no more tyranny, no more being cast aside, no more being left to rot in the burning chasms of a land we were banished to by our forefathers who did not have the might to withstand Odin and his army. Let it be said that on this day, we take back our life; we take back our right to be of this land and in this place. To the conquerors, let the spoils of this land be divided!"

A chorus of cheers met his speech. The men thrust their spears in the air and joined him in his rallying cry.

With a raised fist, Surt urged his men out of the sea toward the lands of the Orkadian men, who would be crushed like tiny ants under his boots.

Bellac and Lukas began moving their legion of foot soldiers forward, raising a cloud of dust. The boercats were released from their pens, and, one by one, they shot into the sky with their masters on their backs.

Frigga, queen of the gods and wife to Odin, stared down at the stone floor of the gods' chambers and waved her hand, making it transparent.

"Show me the red army."

Immediately the view filled with the ugly giants flying on their snarling boercats. Below, foot soldiers marched forward, burning the woods before them.

Orkney was going to fall.

Her gut told her that, and it was never wrong. Better she should act before it came to that. Better a painless death of disappearing into a void than facing the burning fires of Surt and his army.

In her hands she held Odin's Belt of Destiny. With its power, she could wipe Orkney from existence. It was the right thing, she told herself. Odin would agree if he were here. As she stretched the belt around her waist, Vor came up behind her, putting her hand on the queen's shoulder.

"Everything will turn out fine," Vor said quietly.

Frigga held herself, her hands wavering.

"Why should I believe you?" Frigga demanded, her voice uncertain. She wanted to, if truth be told. Odin dearly loved these creatures that were a mystery to her. But her husband had not returned, and she didn't know what else to do, lest she risk losing everything. In Odin's absence, the gods trusted her to keep Asgard intact, their house with many rooms. She had to keep Valhalla a peaceful place where they could walk freely and oversee their scattered children from afar.

"Odin is not lost, see?" Vor waved her hand, and the scenery changed. Frigga's breath hitched in her chest as a towering bear roared from the top of a spire of rock. "He is simply delayed."

The landscape was gray around him, but he stood proudly on two legs. For a moment, Frigga could swear his roar echoed in her ears.

Frigga unclasped the belt, unwilling to believe in this miracle. "What if he doesn't arrive in time?"

"He will," Vor said. "Trust in the boy."

# Chapter 34

Howie couldn't remember the last time he had had a drink of water. A day? Two? His throat was as dry as the Sahara desert. Why was he even out here? He was having a hard time remembering, what with the sun baking his brains to a crisp.

That's right, it had sounded like a good plan. Send Howie back to Skara Brae while Jey and his father readied the Safyre Omeras for battle.

*Stupid Jey.*

The Falcory boy had assumed Howie was capable of navigating across the desert, but Howie couldn't walk home from school without taking a wrong turn, and, now, he was hopelessly lost.

His horse, Sunny, had her head down. Her tongue hung out, and her sides heaved as she plodded forward. She moved so slow that Howie could probably walk faster, but his legs were too weak to hold him.

Big D loped ahead of him. He had ordered the mangy beast to stay with Jey, but, as usual, it hadn't paid heed to a single word Howie said. His sides were sunken in with hunger, and his tongue lolled out of its mouth, but the wolf never grumbled, flowing across the sand like a black shadow. Lingas flew overhead, shrieking her complaints at him.

"Come on, ole Sunny, girl. You can do it," Howie said through cracked lips. "It's just . . . right ahead, right, Damarius?" He kept repeating the lie in order to get himself to believe it. Sunny's body wavered. A shudder ran through her, and Howie knew she was finished. He pulled up on the reins, but the horse just sank down on her forelegs. Howie managed to get clear before the old girl fell on her side.

"Get up, Sunny. You can't just lie here. We're almost there." Howie stroked her velvety nose. The horse whickered softly and then went still. Damarius growled at him and tugged on Howie's shirt with his teeth.

"All right, just give me a second to say goodbye," Howie said. He closed the horse's funny cockeye and rubbed her ears one last time, and then he got to his feet and started trudging through the sand.

Lingas pecked at his ear, snapping him awake when he fell asleep on his feet.

The sun was a blazing orb. Endless sand stretched before him. At one point, he thought he saw a green line of trees ahead, but then it disappeared behind a sand dune. He must have been delirious because he could swear he passed out, and something began dragging him.

When Howie came to, the sun had set, and there was something different. The air had a coolness to it. Something rough was moving across his face. And the smell was awful, like rotten bologna. Blinking, he looked up into the eyes of Damarius.

"Shove off, dog-breath," he grumbled.

Pushing Damarius away, he sat up. The red sand of the desert was gone, replaced by pine forest.

He had made it.

The sound of a stream nearby got him moving. He put one hand on the Shun Kara's coat to steady himself as the animal led him to the stream. Lingas perched on a branch, her eyes glowing yellow in the twilight as Howie dropped to his knees and buried his face in the water, gulping down the precious liquid.

Finally sated, he sat back, wiping his mouth, and rubbed a hand over the wolf's ears.

"How did I get here?" Howie fingered holes in his shirt. Bite marks. So he hadn't been dreaming. Damarius had dragged him.

The wolf snorted and sat down, as if to say it was obvious. Lingas skreaked, chiming in her own vote.

"Well, I guess I owe you both one."

Something made his nose wrinkle. The smell of smoke. Someone had a campfire going. Maybe they had some food.

Howie followed his nose, winding through the trees. He could see an orange glow ahead. This was bigger than any campfire. It was a wall of flame. As the trees thinned, he saw the source.

A sign at the edge of the trees read: BRIGHTHOOK.

He remembered this place. It was a small little town south of Skara Brae. He had visited once with Teren. And now it had been burned to the ground. Sadness made him grip the bark of the tree he leaned against until his palms hurt.

Then Damarius growled, nudging Howie back as the sound of wings cut through the air and a boercat landed not ten feet from where he was standing. Lingas flew up into the shadows of the tree.

Fear made Howie's knees go weak as a giant of a man stepped down from the back of the beast. More and more boercats began landing until the area was filled with them. Their attention was on the blazing fire, but any moment the giants would turn and see them. Damarius dove in the center of a large bramble bush. Howie followed, crawling deep into the bush, ignoring the pain as thorns scraped his skin until he burrowed next to the wolf.

More and more fire giants landed and began setting up camp. Howie didn't dare so much as hiccup. Damarius lay still as a statue, his eyes the only thing that moved as he stared out through the brambles.

*Holy guacamole, we're in deep doo-doo.*

The largest of the red-skinned giants strode into the center of the clearing. He had massive biceps that could crush a tank. "Arek, give me a report."

"Yes, Lord Surt." The one called Arek bowed. "We've burned every village we've come across. The boercats have done their job well. You see that the horizon is nothing but a wall of orange blaze and the sky is black with smoke."

"Good. Orkney will fall in a matter of days. These pitiful fools have no defenses. How much farther to the capital?" Surt asked.

Arek knelt to draw in the dirt. Howie stared through the opening in the bushes, listening hard.

"We are here, to the south. One more day's ride, and we can be on the outskirts. If we rest tonight—"

Surt snarled. "No. We are close. We keep moving."

Arek shook his head. "The boercats need to feed. We have been raiding for days while Bellac and Lukas march on foot. We must wait for them to catch up. We rest now, and when we are united, we battle."

Surt drew his blade so fast it was a blur as he placed it against Arek's neck. "You dare defy me?" Flame danced along the blade, but his general showed no fear.

Howie put an arm around Damarius. Surt's boots were inches from them. If the fire giant looked down . . .

There was a high-pitched shriek.

Lingas.

It did the trick. Surt spun around, shoving Arek aside as he asked, "What was that?"

"Just a night bird," Arek said, rubbing his throat. "My lord, forgive my insult. I know you are wise enough to see the men are tired and need rest."

Surt spat on the ground. "Fine. We stop here. Tell them we will have a feast. Open those kegs of ale we lifted. Tomorrow we will ride on Skara Brae and sack the city." He stalked away.

Howie felt his blood chill. Time was running out.

The next few hours were the longest in Howie's life as they waited for their chance to slip away. The fire giants had hunkered down for the evening, feasting on roasted beef and laughing long into the night.

A fight broke out between two of the giants. As they wrestled each other to the ground, a crowd swelled around the pair. All their backs were to Howie and Damarius. Lingas let out a low whistle.

"Let's move it," Howie whispered, backing out of the bush.

They crawled on their hands and knees until they were deeper into the shadows of the woods, and then Howie clawed his way to his feet and began running, not caring if the branches whipped him in the face. He ran until he was winded and couldn't drag in another breath.

Damarius nudged him with his broad head. The wolf looked at Howie with that green stare of his.

"Yeah, I was scared too," Howie said, rubbing his ears. "We got a two-day walk unless we find a ride. Lingas," he rubbed the bird's head as she settled on his shoulder. "You saved our life. Now, I need you to use those wings of yours to get back to Skara Brae and warn the captain that Surt's coming."

He threw the bird in the air, and she took off through the trees.

A faint whimper drifted through the night, like an animal in pain. Damarius turned and let out a low growl.

Something was out there.

It could be one of Surt's men out on patrol. Damarius growled louder, taking a step forward, his hackles rising.

"Let's go the other way," Howie whispered, but Damarius took off like a black arrow. "Dumb animal," Howie grumbled, trotting after him.

The moon was his only light. Coming to a clearing, he caught a flash of reflection across the way. Something was hiding in the bushes, something large, and it was growling at him with green slanted eyes.

Damarius had frozen and was shaking, like he was scared. Whatever it was had to be bad to scare a Shun Kara.

"Let's go, Big D," Howie whispered, tugging on his thick fur. They backed away two steps.

"Stay." The word was scratchy, more of a growl than a voice.

Howie froze. "Are you talking to me?"

The massive head tilted in a nod. "I see you are a friend to the wolf."

"Yeah, me and Big D are like brothers," Howie said, hoping this thing couldn't tell how scared he was. Gathering his courage, Howie took a step closer to those green eyes. "Who are you?"

"I am Fenrir, son of Loki, and the greatest wolf to ever live. If you help me, I will be in your debt."

Big D pressed up against his legs, still shaking, hiding behind the boy. Later, Howie would rub the wolf's nose in it, but, for now, he kept his voice steady as he asked, "What's the problem, my man? Why do you need the help of little old me?"

Chains rattled. Howie caught sight of the glint of moonlight on metal. The giant wolf had stepped into a steel trap.

"I see the problem," Howie said. "You're in a pickle. If I leave you here, you might get free, or the fire giants camped nearby might find you." The beast snarled, and Howie nodded.

"And that would be bad. So you need to get out of this trap and hightail it away."

He took the silence as agreement.

"I might help you." As the words left Howie's mouth, a shaggy paw the size of a dump truck landed with a thump in front of him, one long toenail pinning his boot in place. "I mean, of course, I'll help you," he added, tugging futilely on his boot. "The thing is, I know these red jerks, and they're bound to spot you in the morning when they fly overhead, so unless I free you tonight and you get far away, they're going to do what they do best: barbecue your flea-bitten hide."

The razor-sharp claw pressed harder on Howie's foot, making him flinch. "But of course, my man, I'm not going to let that happen, because the How-master always has a plan."

The talon eased up slightly, and Howie drew his throbbing foot back an inch. "Here's what I think."

He explained his plan to the beast. When he was done, the beast growled softly, but he withdrew his paw.

"Do we have a deal?" Howie asked.

There was silence. Determined not to cave in, Howie shrugged, shoving his hands in his pockets. "Your loss, my friend. Those ugly fire giants can eat you for breakfast for all I care. Come on, Damarius, let's get out of here."

Howie turned to go when he was knocked over by a swipe of Fenrir's paw. He looked up into the eyes of a snarling beast, large as a house. His open jaws hovered over Howie. He could devour him in one snap and not even taste him going down his gullet, but Howie refused to flinch.

"Go ahead, eat me!" he shouted. "I don't care. Just do it because unless we have a deal, I've got nothing to live for. My friends are going to die, and I have to get there and warn them even if it means I die with them. So just finish it and be done."

He shut his eyes and waited for the teeth to rend him to

pieces. Damarius trembled next to him. After an eternity, Howie cracked open one eye. The beast towered over him, a long trail of drool hanging from one side of its mouth.

"Agreed," he rumbled.

Relief flooded Howie as he scooted back, getting to his feet and dusting himself off.

"I'm just going to take a look."

He walked slowly around Fenrir. His rear leg was snared in a large bear-claw trap. Blood oozed from the wound, making a sticky mess on the forest floor. The trap was held by a chain wrapped around a thick tree.

"I'm going to have to pry that apart," Howie said. He looked up into the green eyes of the wolf. "This is going to hurt a lot, so don't eat me by mistake."

Howie put his foot on one side of the trap and lifted up with both hands to separate the steel jaws. The teeth were dug deeply into the wolf's leg. Blood had dried around the fur, blackening it. Howie put his back into it, but the trap hardly moved.

The wolf growled at him, warning him to hurry up. He tried again, getting his shoulder under the edge and pushing his boot downward. His face turned bright red, and he was sure he was going to pop a blood vessel, but finally the spring moved and the trap sprung open.

"Now," Howie grunted. The wolf pulled on his leg.

"It's stuck," Fenrir growled, turning his head and raising his lip in a snarl.

Howie pushed harder, using every last bit of strength, and, at last, the wolf's leg sprung free. Howie let the jaws close with a snap, jumping back so he wasn't caught in the trap.

Fenrir licked the fur around the wound, lapping it with his rough tongue. Howie stood uncertainly. He was just as likely to get eaten by the wolf as killed by Surt's men. He held his ground, tightening his hands into fists.

"We had a deal."

The wolf kept licking his wound.

"You're to take me to my friends," Howie said, moving closer.

Fenrir snarled at him. "Silence. I have to feed first. I am weak." He went back to licking his wound. Behind Howie, the brush rustled.

Damarius appeared, holding a limp goat in his teeth. He dropped it at Fenrir's feet and then bowed his head, extending one paw forward to his giant brethren.

Howie grinned. "Dinner's served. Eat up, my wolf brother. We have a long way to go."

# Chapter 35

As dawn broke, the ship carrying Keely, Leo, and the rest of the slave boys entered the harbor of Skara Brae. Keely stood at the rails and heaved a sigh of relief. The red flags still flew. They'd made it in time.

The same could not be said for the eastern seaboard of Garamond. Roiling black clouds of smoke filled the sky, turning it a leaden gray. Orkney was falling under Surt's relentless attack. They had spied boercats from a distance, but none had come near their ship.

"We are not too late then," Reesa said, gripping the rail.

Leo stood at Keely's other side.

"Do you think Sam is back?" he asked.

Keely shook her head. "I don't know. I hope so."

Behind them, the line of slave boys stood silently watching.

Galatin had spent every minute of their journey training them to fight. Keely's arm ached from wielding a sword against the stronger Vanirian boys, but they had thrived under the watchful eye of Reesa. The woman had surprised

Keely by changing out of her royal garb into a tightly belted leather tunic, her hair tied back in a neat braid as she helped Galatin train the boys how to wield a sword.

Reesa's eyes frequently went to study Eithan's face, but the woman asked him nothing about his past, just gently instructed him the same as the others.

Captain Teren waited for them on the dock, looking haggard and worn. Keely searched for any sign of Sam, but Rego just shook his head at her when he caught her eye.

Keely made the introductions. "Captain Teren, I present Queen Reesa of the Vanir."

Teren bowed low. "An honor to meet you, your highness. I apologize we cannot offer you much of a welcome."

"Surt approaches," Reesa said quietly. "His fires are less than a day off."

Teren nodded. "We know. We have prepared the best we can. Your army, does it follow you?"

The queen looked pained, twisting her hands as she said, "I don't know if my husband will come, but I have brought these young Vanir to help." She waved at the line of boys that stood on the deck. Each had a fierce look on his face. "If you can provide them with armor and weapons, they will be as brave as any man."

Teren eyed the boys, then nodded gravely. "Their help will be appreciated." He turned to his pair of men. "Speria, Heppner, see the boys get outfitted, and get them a hot meal. Come, let us discuss matters in the council chambers."

As they walked, Keely asked Teren, "Has Abigail returned?"

"Yes. She arrived yesterday."

"And?"

He winced. "Hestera proved difficult. Eight witches chose to come to our aid."

Keely was disappointed, but eight was better than nothing.

"What of Gael and the Eifalians?" Leo asked.

"It's bad news. Their ships were attacked and burned en route to joining us. The survivors were able to swim to shore. They are in position on the ramparts, but their numbers are few."

"Any sign of Sam?"

He shook his head. "No word." He touched her arm. "You should know, Howie isn't here. His iolar returned this morning, squawking up a storm, but not even Rego can make sense of what the bird is trying to say."

Teren filled her in on what he thought Howie had done, going after Jey's father with the Falcory boy, and he told her about Howie's crazy battle plan.

"We have almost a thousand buckets of armor out there, and my men stand ready to light smoke fires. With any luck, we can hold them off another day."

Teren's voice was tight. He didn't have to say it wasn't much of a plan. It was all they had. Miracles happened. And that's what they needed—a miracle.

Inside the High Council chambers, Abigail and Gael were locked in a fierce discussion with Rego. A group of eight women clad in black dresses huddled in a group—the Tarkana witches. Most were young, barely out of their teens.

Abigail stood, wrapping Keely and Leo into a hug. "Do either of you have any idea where my son is?"

Keely looked at Leo and then said, "Abigail, Sam's gone after Odin."

"Gone after Odin? But how is that—you don't mean in the underworld?"

"It wasn't his idea," Leo said. "Frigga commanded it, or else she would punish him, all of us, for what happened."

Abigail finally noticed the other woman standing behind Keely. "I am Reesa, Queen of the Vanir," Reesa said, extending her hand.

"We welcome your help," Abigail said. "Come, join us."

They sat around the table. The witches remained huddled in the back, quietly talking among themselves.

Teren sat forward. "Howie's tin army is in position along the front walls of Skara Brae. With any luck, it will make Surt think twice before attacking. We have to hold out hope that more help will arrive. If Surt does attack, we draw in Surt's ground troops and pin them between the walls lined with Gael's archers and the soldiers I have positioned on the other side in the forest."

"A few soldiers won't stop them," Reesa said.

"We will do our part," Abigail said, nodding at the line of witches that had gone quiet to stare calmly at them with their sparkling green eyes. "We are Tarkana witches. Our witchfire can take out a legion or two."

Reesa nodded appreciatively. "That will help balance the odds. I will lead the Vanirian boys in battle. I promise you, they will not disappoint."

"What of their boercats?" Keely asked. The pendant around her neck felt heavy. She wished she knew how to make it work. Things were pretty desperate. A little powerful magic would come in handy.

Gael stood abruptly. "What is that you wear?"

Keely instinctively clasped her hands around it. "It's a pendant."

"Where did you get it?"

"You wouldn't believe me. There was an Eifalian princess, a ghost—"

"Nehalannia. You found the lost Pendant of Helina." There was a trace of joy and awe in Gael's voice. He stepped closer, reaching out trembling fingers to touch the stone. It glowed a bright blue, brighter than ever. A ripple of power flowed through the room.

"Gael, what is it?" Abigail asked.

"Long ago, the Eifalians were gifted with a magic so

powerful and dangerous that it had to be contained lest it be released on the world. Our ancestors placed it in this pendant."

"Where did it get its name?" Keely asked.

"Helina is the Goddess of Protection. She gifted us this magic, trusting the Eifalians to use it wisely. Only the queen of the Eifalians was permitted to wear it. When Nehalannia's mother died, the pendant passed to her. When she was lost, we thought the pendant gone forever. May I hold it?"

Keely took it off and handed it to Gael. He gripped it in his hands and closed his eyes.

He frowned. "I feel nothing. Yet when you wear it, I can sense its power."

He put it back around her neck and held it again. "Yes, it responds to you, Keely. Whatever magic it holds, Nehalannia passed it on to you."

She brushed her fingers over it. "What do I do with it?"

"You will know when the time is right."

She looked into his aquamarine eyes, feeling overwhelmed and wishing she could hand the pendant off. "How? How will I know? What if I can't figure it out?"

He patted her shoulder. "You will know. When everything is lost, and there is no hope . . . when there is nothing else that can be done, the pendant will show you what to do."

There was silence in the room, and then the door banged open and a young boy ran in and started shouting, "Your lordship, come see, come see!"

Keely's heart sank. Had Surt come already? They followed the boy outside up to the ramparts. A blur of black fur moved across the charred fields, stirring up clouds of smoke and ash.

"What is it?" Teren asked.

Abigail frowned. "It looks like a giant wolf."

"Fenrir!" Keely gasped, horrified. "Sam must have freed him."

Teren pulled a spyglass from his pocket and studied the horizon.

"What on earth? There's someone on his back. I think—by the gods, I think it's Howie!"

Keely snatched the spyglass from him and peered through it. Teren was right. Clutching the fur on the giant wolf's back was Howie. And there was a black wolf behind him looking miserable. Damarius.

"It is Howie." She passed the glass to Rego.

"Well I'll be a shreek's uncle," the dwarf said. "Leave it to Howie to return in style."

The giant wolf loped hard until he reached the wall of Skara Brae, and then he simply leapt in the air and scaled the walls in one leap, landing with a skidding thud in the center of the marketplace.

# Chapter 36

Howie felt like a conquering hero as he flew over that wall. The look on the ol' captain's face was priceless, a mixture of terror and awe. He flashed Keely and Leo a thumbs-up, as if he rode in on a giant wolf every day. Behind him, Damarius had his paws spread out, holding on for dear life.

"Howdy, everyone. I'm back," he said, sliding down to land on his feet, Damarius following. He turned to the wolf, wagging his finger. "Be good, Fenrir, or no more goats for you." Howie pointed to a spot near the wall. "Go on. Our deal's not done yet." The humongous wolf growled at him softly, but he followed Damarius over and lay down with a loud thump, licking at his wounded paw.

"Is that really Fenrir?" Keely said, giving Howie a hug as Leo slapped him on the back. "And why is he so—tame?"

"Aw, he's just doing me a favor because I saved his life and all," Howie bragged. A flash of feathers made him flinch as Lingas greeted him, nearly biting his ear off. "Back off, bird-face," Howie said, and then he relented as the bird perched on his shoulder, rubbing her face up against Howie's cheek.

Captain Teren strode over, his face tight as a drum. Howie had been dreading this.

"Did you really bring that bloodthirsty creature inside the sanctuary of our walls?" Teren blasted. "He could devour half my men for his morning snack."

Howie flushed, turning red. "Er, Captain, I—"

"Not to mention you deserted your post." Teren folded his arms.

"I know." Guilt made Howie squirm in his boots.

"A squire never leaves his post," Teren said sternly.

Howie cleared his throat and nodded. "You're right. But I couldn't let Jey go after his father alone. I'm sorry. You can fire me."

Lingas flared her wings, cawing at Teren like he could fire her, too.

Teren glared another moment, and then he snorted, "Fire you? I was thinking of extending your time as my squire. My shirts have been a mess since you've been gone. No one irons them like you." He clasped a hand on Howie's shoulder. "Tell us, did you find Beo?"

Howie nodded, diving into his story. "We found him, all right, and a nest of Safyre Omeras. I came back to let you know they're coming as soon as they can raise the rest of the Falcory."

Bells began ringing, clanging loudly from the far sentry post.

"What is the alarm?" Teren shouted up to the sentry.

"Smoke, Captain, on the horizon. They're coming."

Howie's knees went weak. They had run out of time.

War had come to Orkney once more.

Teren ordered the horses brought up. "The vanguard will leave immediately on my command. Time to see if Howie's plan is going to work."

"I'm coming along," Howie said.

Teren nodded. "I figured you'd want to see it through. Rego, get the boy some fresh armor and be sure to keep him from harm."

Rego snorted loudly. "Those red devils are not going to get the best of us. They'll be hightailing it back to that lump of lava before they can spit in the wind."

A line of witches trailed silently behind Abigail up unto the ramparts and took position. Howie counted nine, with Abigail. They could have used a hundred or two. He marked the clusters of white-haired Eifalian archers along the posts. Not as many as Howie would have liked to see.

Gael stood impatiently as Keely came over to say goodbye. Leo hovered behind her.

"Don't get fried to a crisp by one of those fire giants," she said, hugging Howie tightly.

"I won't. You be safe. Are you on the wall with the archers?"

Keely shook her head, her hand going to a strange pendant. "I'm to stay clear until I'm needed. Howie, we really need Sam to come back with Odin."

"Fingers crossed," Howie said, raising both hands and crossing all his digits.

Gael called to her, and she left them.

Leo hovered, looking uncertain. Howie could tell he wanted to fight along his side, but he was more worried about Keely. He gave the boy a shove. "Stay with her and keep her alive. She needs you more than I do. Besides, you're a better shot with a bow than any of those elves."

Leo smiled slightly. "When did you get so brave?"

Howie snorted. "You mean, when did I get so dumb? I'm heading into what's looking like certain death." A wave of emotion choked his throat. He looked at Leo, his eyes blurred with tears. "Look, if something, you know, happens to me, when you get back to Pilot Rock, you tell my mom, well," he swallowed the lump lodged in his throat, "you tell her I loved her. Promise?"

Leo grasped his shoulder. "You'll tell her yourself when we all go home." He squeezed Howie's shoulder and then hurried after Keely.

A stable boy brought them horses. Rego slipped a set of chain mail and a breastplate over Howie's shoulders and clamped a helmet on his head. Howie mounted amid a flurry of activity as the front line assembled, prepared to face Surt in the first wave.

The frost-giant queen had assembled a small group of oversized boys. Even Howie was in awe of their muscled arms and broad shoulders. Each had a sword strapped to his back and a fierce look of determination on his face as he followed his queen.

Surveying the men on their horses, Howie wondered how many of them would make it back. But not one hesitated or looked doubtful. They were ready to die. If it meant saving this realm, they would lay down their lives.

Immensely proud, Howie held up the flag of Orkney, and they let out a resounding cheer. From the ramparts, the sounds echoed as every soldier raised his or her voice in support.

To Gael, Teren said, "Wait for our signal to attack. If it doesn't come, then the gods be with you."

Howie waved goodbye to Keely as he followed Teren out.

Outside the walls, Howie felt exposed, like at any second Surt could fire a flaming arrow from the sky and burn him to a crisp.

The smoke-pots had been lit. Speria and Heppner had their men hidden in the forest along the opposite side of the battalion of dummy soldiers. A light winked at them from a mirror. The Orkadian forces were in place.

Their job was to mingle among the fake soldiers to add movement and make it look real. A dangerous job. They would be in the line of fire when the battle started.

"Now don't go being a hero," Rego said. "The moment the battle begins, you hightail it to the rear and get to safety."

"Sure, you bet," Howie said, not meaning it. He wasn't going to turn and run. Not a chance.

A scowl crossed the dwarf's face. "You're a worse liar

than Sam," he muttered. He drew one of the swords lashed to his back and handed it to Howie. "Whatever you do, take some of those ugly fire giants with you."

Howie grinned, tapping the sword to his forehead. "Ten at least."

"Only ten?" Rego kicked his horse forward. "I plan on taking twenty-five before they roast my innards."

# Chapter 37

urt sat on the back of his boercat on top of a hill overlooking the valley leading to the walled city of Skara
Brae. The valley was bordered by woods and lined
with fields that crisscrossed the flat plain in front of the city.
Arek sat on his own beast next to him and passed him a
spyglass. He held it up to his eye.

A troop of men on horseback rode in front of a legion of
troops. One of them carried a red banner with a white heron.

Surt looked closer. The fields were smoky, as if fog clung
to the ground, but the battalions of men were clear enough.
There were at least a thousand men lined up in the fields. A
tiny sliver of doubt grew. Surt dropped the spyglass.

"Sire, there are more than we expected—" Arek said.

"Fool, you didn't warn me of this."

"I didn't know—I have never seen this many men. They
must have been scattered to hide their true numbers."

Surt cut him off with a chop of his hand. "We will wait
until Lukas and Bellac arrive. They are only a few hours
behind us. Lukas will take his legions in first. They will draw
them into battle. When they have tired, we will launch an
aerial attack on their city while Bellac finishes them off."

The waiting was the hardest part. Howie could see the line of boercats on the hills above Orkney, poised to attack. Why weren't they already burning them to the ground?

"It's working, Howie," Teren said, wheeling in his horse in front of Howie. "They're holding off."

"Aye, waiting for their ground troops so they can skewer and barbecue us," Rego said.

"Take Reesa's boys, and keep your fake army moving," Teren ordered Howie. "We mustn't let them suspect it's not real."

Howie and the other boys moved among the ranks, picking soldiers up and moving them about. It was hot and sweaty work, but between the men on horseback riding and kicking up dust and the smoke-pots they kept burning, it was impossible to make much out, not from the distance Surt sat.

Howie kept staring at the sky. Jey was going to show up with his army of Safyre Omeras anytime now, but the sky remained clear. And where was Sam? If his bud didn't get here soon, his mission to bring Odin back wouldn't matter. There wouldn't be anything left to save.

Wiping the sweat from his brow, Howie caught sight of something moving across the valley, a small cloud of dust that rolled impossibly fast toward them, as if it were a speeding car.

Howie dodged through the buckets of armor to stand by Teren. "What is that?"

The soldier stared grimly at the approaching cloud. "Don't know." His voice was tense, as if he expected the worst.

"Is it Surt? A trap?"

"I don't know, Howie. Let's go find out."

They rode forward to meet whatever bad news was flying toward them.

One second it was a blur of motion, and then it stopped

suddenly ten feet from them. A swirl of smoke and dust surrounded it. When the dust cleared, Howie's eyes grew wide.

A giant bear stood in front of them. It roared, beating its chest with two hands. Then, before either of them could say a word, a blinding light exploded from it, and the bear shrank down into a familiar figure.

"Sam!"

His buddy Sam was back! Howie ran forward ready to give him a hug, but some instinct made him stop.

Sam was not Sam. Well, not exactly. His skin had an unearthly glow to it, like he was filled with light. His eyes blazed with a sheen of power, but his smile was the same.

"Hello, Howie."

"About time," Howie choked out, holding back all the emotion and relief that he felt. "The party was about to start without you."

"I was kind of busy," Sam said, and then he looked at Teren. "Fill me in." His voice sounded like Sam's, but it was oddly commanding.

"Surt is up on that ridge with his boercats," Teren said. "We think he's waiting for his foot soldiers to arrive before he strikes. We have an army of fake soldiers, just piles of armor. Howie's idea, but it's holding Surt off."

A horn sounded, sending a blaring echo across the valley. The distant roar of thousands of voices raised in a deep battle cry made the hair on the back of Howie's neck stand up.

"It sounds like he's done waiting," the glowing Sam said.

A line of red armor-clad warriors moved down the hillside like a tide of crimson blood. Line after line of fearsome fire giant marched. There were so many.

"I'm afraid we are going to lose," this new Sam said calmly. "There are far too many of them."

Howie knew that. They had all known that. But hearing Sam say it was crushing.

"Let's even things up, shall we?" Sam rubbed his hands and then clapped them together. A loud boom echoed across the valley. There was a ripple of energy that made Howie's hair lift, and then the fake soldiers began to vibrate and rattle. Their armor moved jerkily, and then something miraculous happened.

They began to move like soldiers, drawing their swords from their sides. It was the freakiest thing Howie had ever seen. One of them had its mask open, and there was nothing in it, but Howie could swear he could hear them breathing, and they were definitely preparing to fight.

"Captain, your army awaits you," Sam said.

Teren drew his sword, looking hopeful for the first time in days. "For every one of us they take, let us take ten of them!" The men, both real and fake, cheered. Teren raised his sword. "For Orkney!"

The men shouted in return, raising their swords before marching forward.

The frost-giant queen also raised her sword, turning to face her boys. She wore a golden crown unadorned with jewels. Her face was shining as she called, "For the freedom of all!" They joined her, rattling their swords together.

A trickle of hope made Howie's spirits lift.

They had their miracle.

Sam was exhausted and yet filled with power. Sharing a body with Odin was electrifying. They had journeyed day and night to get here without stopping. Only the great power of the god had enabled them to make it in time to stop the destruction of Odin's beloved Orkney. It had involved loping across the seas between whatever island they had been on and Garamond. Sam would never forget racing over white-capped waves, as if he were weightless and immense at the same time.

Sam had apologized a hundred times, but Odin had never answered. Never acknowledged Sam's presence. No. Odin had been a silent companion, one with quiet power he allowed Sam to wield.

It was nothing like his time in the Omera. Then he had been in control. With Brunin, Sam was like a passenger allowed to put his hands on the wheel to steer the car, but he was never in control.

Exhaustion made him sway on his feet, but now was not the time for rest. Not with the wall of red flesh that was running toward them. Sam had never seen such fearsome men in all his life—thick red skin, angry snarls, black hair tied in ponytails on the tops of their heads, yellow eyes that glowed with an inner fire. The roar of their battle cries made Sam's shirt vibrate with the thumping of their boots on the ground.

*Courage*, a voice in his head said.

Sam shuddered with relief. Odin was still there. Now, ensconced in Sam's body, the god hovered, not taking control, but Sam could feel him pressing on the edges of his consciousness.

Teren and the others had taken position toward the center of Howie's army, the enchanted one that now stood with swords drawn, ready to protect Orkney.

It was a wacky idea—one only Howie could have come up with—wacky but brilliant. Better that inanimate objects bear the brunt than flesh and blood. It would slow and confuse Surt's men when no blood was spilled.

Sam itched to blast the field with witchfire, but not even sharing a body with Odin had restored his magic. It was gone forever. The thought left him sad.

"Hold steady," Rego said. He had Howie and Sam on either side. Farther on, Reesa waited with her army of boys. Speria and Heppner had almost a hundred men in the trees waiting for Surt's army to attack. Another dozen soldiers were on Teren's side. It wasn't much, but it would have to do.

Then there was the clashing of metal on metal as Surt's men reached the first line.

There were shouts and yells, screams of pain from Surt's men as they were run through by the very real swords of the dummy soldiers.

"Hey, Rego, I don't suppose you have an extra sword," Sam said calmly.

Rego drew the second sword from his back and passed the hilt to him. "No witchfire?" he asked.

"Not today. By the way, you're still the most annoying dwarf I've ever met."

Rego snorted. "And you still don't listen a lick."

Sam laughed. "Touché. Good luck, dwarf."

Rego took up a position with his sword over his head. "I don't need luck; I've got you watching my back."

They held their positions, waiting as, one by one, the lines of inanimate soldiers moved off and engaged until finally they were on the edges of the battle.

A fire giant shoved a soldier aside, sending parts of him flying.

"Finally, flesh and blood!" he roared, a sword over his head. He swung it down hard at Rego, but before the dwarf could defend himself, Sam was there. He rammed his sword into the red giant's side, and Howie did the same from the other. The two boys grinned at each other over the still form of the red giant.

"See? Nothing to worry about," Rego quipped.

Sam turned his head, catching sight of the Vanirian queen taking out two red giants. She had eight boys around her, fighting furiously.

Sam marked the line of fire giants pouring down the hill. Even with Howie's army come to life, they needed an advantage. Something to help turn the tide.

*Cut off the head, and the body will be lost.*

Sam knew what to do.

"Stay with Rego," he shouted to Howie.

Then he ducked into the mix of fire giants and fake soldiers. The chaos was dizzying. Sam focused on finding their leader. Someone was in charge.

He dodged under red flesh and avoided a wall of flame, racing through the lines until he spied an oversized fire giant barking orders. He was ugly, with a face like a red bull. The fire giant swung his broad sword, taking off the heads of ten of Howie's fake soldiers, dropping them to the ground in a rattle of armor. His yellow eyes flickered toward Sam and locked in. The giant roared as he began lumbering forward, raising his sword over his head.

Sam held his ground, blocking out everything around him. He couldn't flinch from this. He couldn't hide.

*Be still*, the voice in his head whispered. *I am here.*

So Sam was still, waiting, watching, listening as the bull man ran toward him with his sword held high. His heart pounded out of control, leaving him breathless and weak, but he clutched his sword with everything he had.

The fire giant leapt the last five feet, soaring through the air toward him, bringing the sword down in a killing blow that would cleave Sam's head from his body.

Sam's arm was up, holding a sword that suddenly felt far too flimsy. He shut his eyes as blade on blade clashed with a clang that was loud enough to make his ears ring.

But his blade held.

An immense strength flowed into his arm, into the blade, and, in spite of the superior size and strength of the fire giant, Sam held his ground.

*Again*, the voice in his head whispered.

Sam raised his arm again as the bull man swung at him with another powerful blow.

The fire giant circled him warily now, looking for an opening.

"I am General Lukas, second in command of Surt's great army, and you will beg for your life, little boy."

With a roar, the general charged, this time swinging low to take out Sam's legs.

*Jump.*

Sam jumped, leaping over the blade, and then he brought the hilt of his blade down on the back of the fire giant's head.

There was a sickening thwack and a flow of blood. The general sagged to his knees, shaking his head to clear the stars.

*Finish it*, the voice urged.

Sam hesitated.

*Finish it, or I will*, the voice commanded.

Sam raised the sword. Still, his arm wavered even as he willed it to obey. From a distance, he heard a loud whistle. He turned his head toward it, and the wounded fire giant's hand shot out and grabbed his ankle, yanking him to the ground. In a second, the general was on top of him, a dagger to his throat.

"Die now, human scum."

The fire giant raised his knife to deliver the killing blow, but a loud thumping sound made him pause. He looked up in time to see Fenrir's gaping jaws, and then the giant wolf bit down on the general's head and shoulders, tossing his body through the air.

The wolf barreled through the lines, knocking down the fire giants like bowling pins, sending their bodies hurtling through the air with a snarl and snap of his jaws. Surt's army began to scatter and run for the hills to evade those deadly teeth.

Breathing heavily, Sam let Howie haul him to his feet. Damarius jumped up, putting his paws on Howie's chest and lapping at his face.

"I think we won this round," Howie said, rubbing the wolf's ears.

"Should I ask where Fenrir came from?"

"Nope. And let's hope he keeps going. He eats more than he weighs."

Sam probed around inside his head. Odin had gone silent. He felt cold, like a warm blanket had been removed. He had disobeyed the god, hesitating over taking the life of that fire giant. Was this his punishment?

Men began streaming from the trees. They started racing past Sam and Howie as if the devil himself were after them. They turned to see what the problem was.

A wall of red flesh began to march out of the trees.

A second army. This one bigger and fiercer than the one they had just defeated.

# Chapter 38

While the battle raged on outside the walls, Keely clung to the rampart, willing Sam and Howie to be okay. She had seen Sam arrive, and she cheered with the others, hugging Leo with joy. Even from a distance, she could see he was glowing with some kind of inner power.

Odin. It had to be.

"It's going to be okay," Leo said, his eyes bright. "Sam is back. Look how he glows."

Keely clasped his hand, raising it high. Sam would do something amazing, and Surt would run off.

But that's not how things went. Once the battle began, Sam was nearly killed by a fire giant. Odin wasn't all-powerful, at least not here.

It had taken everything to keep Abigail from rushing to her son, but Gael kept her busy with her team of witches, sending blasts of witchfire at the fire giants that got too close to the wall.

Fenrir had turned the battle—that is until Surt's second, even bigger army had emerged from hiding.

Along the ramparts, the Eifalian archers began firing their bows, but the arrows bounced off the shields and armor of the red giants. Teren and Galatin did their best to rally the men for the oncoming horde. They gathered at the gates, shouting orders at the men as they waited for the signal to rush out to battle.

Leo drew arrow after arrow, letting them loose while Keely gripped the rail. Only the iron bolts of the crossbows could penetrate the giants' thick armor, and they had few of those weapons.

Feeling helpless, Keely's hand went around the pendant at her neck. The power in the amulet made her blood sing. It was like the Eifalian ghost was whispering in her ear.

*You will know when the time is right*, Gael had said. Was that time now?

The gates were flung open as the Orkadians poured back into the safety behind the walls. Surt's army marched relentlessly closer. They would reach the walls in minutes, and then they would tear it apart with their bare hands. Teren's men would be mincemeat.

"Not today," she whispered. "We're not going to lose."

"Keely, what are you doing?" Leo was there at her side, gripping her elbow.

"Trust me," she said. "But don't let go of me."

Keely wrapped her hand around the pendant. Instantly, she felt a powerful magic move in her, like a live current charged with energy. They needed to take out this army, but they had no weapon that could do that.

"Nehalannia," she whispered. "Show me. Show me how to use this."

She felt the stone begin to vibrate under her fingers. It grew cold, colder than ice until it burned. She felt Nehalannia's spirit guide her. Water. Nehalannia loved the water. Water was powerful.

Keely turned toward the seas, letting the pendant fall to her chest as she raised her hands. "Spirit of the water, I command you to rise and obey my command."

"Keely, are you sure?"

She blocked out Leo's voice as the magic surged in her blood and a connection with the sea engaged like a lock and a key.

"Rise," she repeated, lifting her hands up again and again. A cold wind whipped across the seas, carrying the scent of brine and something else, electricity. Waves began lapping at the rocks. The water rose higher as the seas swelled, building up a giant wave.

Leo guessed her plan, and he shook her by the arm. "Stop! Sam and Howie are still out there."

But it was too late. Keely couldn't stop the spiral of power that had taken hold of her, a siren song calling up the water. She raised her hands in the sky as power poured from her. A bright light shot out of the amulet around her neck, and the giant wave swelled, casting a dark shadow over the battlefield.

At the sight of Surt's fresh army, Sam wanted to hightail it back inside the walls of the city, but Howie was running from pile of armor to pile of armor.

"Howie, we have to go!"

"Not without Rego; he's here somewhere. He was battling ten fire giants keeping them off me while I called Fenrir. Damarius, find Rego," Howie snapped at the wolf. The Shun Kara ran around, sniffing the piles of armor, and then he tilted his snout to the air and howled, sitting back on his haunches.

There was a large pile of fire giants, limp and unmoving. At the bottom, a familiar pair of boots stuck out.

"Help me get him out of there," Sam said, pushing off the top giant.

They pulled and pushed the pile of flesh until they got to the dwarf. His eyes were closed. Blood soaked his clothes.

"Rego, speak to me," Sam said. "Come on, you annoying dwarf, don't tell me you let a few nasty giants beat you. I've seen you survive worse."

But this time, Rego didn't move. After a moment, Sam laid him back down. "I guess that's it, then." His voice broke with emotion.

"That's what?" the dwarf said, opening one eye to look up at him. "I was just waiting to see if you were going to cry like a baby."

"Rego, you're alive!" Sam said, crushing him in a hug.

"Don't get all weepy on me. Takes more than a dozen fire giants to wipe me out."

They helped Rego up. That's when they realized the battlefield was deserted.

Surt's army bore down on them.

"Give me my sword," the dwarf slurred. "I can take them."

Sam looked at Howie. This was bad. They could never make the walls in time.

"Friends to the end," Howie said as Sam tossed him a sword. Rego clutched his own, swaying on his feet. Damarius planted wide paws, lowering his head to snarl at the oncoming horde.

"Till the end," Sam said. "Defend Rego as long as you can."

The red giants didn't attack; instead they swarmed around them, forming a circle and marching in tighter and tighter until they formed a solid ring.

One pushed through, a horrible-looking female in studded armor. She had an ugly twisted scar on one cheek, and her yellow eyes flashed with rage. "I am General Bellac," she sneered, her teeth a mouth of polished metal. "I have always wanted to taste Orkadian flesh. I hear it is sweet as young lamb."

The fire giants laughed.

"Then fight me, unless you're scared," Sam said, beckoning her into the tight ring.

A snarl of laughter ripped from her. "Scared of a little boy?"

Bellac stepped into the circle holding a meaty hand up to her men. "If any one of you interfere, I will personally cut your head off. This one is mine."

The she-warrior raised a heavy broadsword over her head. Bellac towered over Sam; she was nearly seven feet tall. She spun in a circle, moving lithely for her size. Her twin braids flew out, spinning like a helicopter blade before she brought her sword down at him.

Sam barely had time to get his arm up. The thrust of her sword against his blade made his whole body go numb, but his arm held.

The thrumming power in him gave him the answer why. Odin was back.

"About time," Sam muttered, moving sideways as Bellac advanced on him. "I could use a little god magic right now."

*You don't listen*, Odin chided.

"Yeah, that's teenagers for you. I'm listening now," Sam whispered. "What do I do?"

Bellac charged him, and Sam's body started to glow, as if lit by an inner fire. She was like a two-ton freight train coming at him. He wanted to run, but the voice in his head commanded him to hold his ground.

The light around him burned brighter until it was almost blinding. Bellac didn't slow down or show fear; she thrust forward with her blade into Sam's middle, only to see it incinerate like it had been thrust into the fires of a forge. She was left with the stub of a hilt in her hand.

*Now!* the voice said.

Sam didn't hesitate; he thrust forward with his sword, but she parried left, ducking into a roll, and he missed. He was about to go after her again when the roar of the ocean brought his head up. The rest of the warriors in the circle all turned as one to stare at the freaky giant wave that loomed over them.

There was no time to scream. The wave hovered over them, and then, with a crashing roar, it broke, and the space in front of Skara Brae filled with the onrush of the sea. The wave came rolling in like a tsunami, knocking men off their feet and roiling them in the water.

"Run!" Sam shouted.

Sam and Howie each got an arm under Rego, but in seconds they were swept off their feet by the flood of water. Sam grabbed on to Howie's arm, and he held Rego's as they were tossed and tumbled. They managed to stay afloat as the water level rose.

"When it goes back out, we're going with it," Sam said.

They would surely drown.

Lingas circled over their heads, letting out a harsh caw.

"Go away, Lingas!" Howie shouted.

Damarius splashed next to them, dog paddling.

The iolar dove, grabbing at Howie's shirt with its claws, as if the bird could tug him to safety.

It was pointless. A single iolar couldn't save Howie, let alone all of them.

But then a ladder splashed into the water next to him. Sam looked up to see Perrin grinning down at him. "Need a ride?"

Skidbladnir!

Sam grabbed on to the ladder, hauling Howie up behind him. Geela lifted Rego by his armpits, Perrin grabbed Damarius, and then Skidbladnir lifted them over the water.

Magic roared in Keely's veins. Power surged through her as she held her hands up to the sky. The seas rose higher and higher. It was thrilling and terrifying at the same time. She couldn't stop it. She didn't want to stop it. The power was like a living torch inside her. Someone was by her side, shaking her arm, shouting words at her, but she couldn't hear them.

Fire giants were bobbing and screaming in the water. Some sank as their heavy armor weighted them down.

A faint voice got through.

"Keely, stop. You're going to flood the city. Everyone is going to drown."

*Stop. I have to stop.* Keely tried to tamp down on the power, but it roared at her, like it wanted to consume the world.

Then a hand gripped hers tightly. The touch was warm and familiar.

Leo. It was her friend Leo.

"I'm right here, Keely. You can do this. Fight it."

Slowly she put a lid on the power, reeling it in, tightening her grip on it. The Pendant of Helina belonged to her. The power belonged to her. She could control it. She would.

The water stopped rising. She pushed harder, releasing her hold on the sea. With a sucking noise, the ocean called the water back, and it receded as fast as it came in, taking every scrap of living thing with it.

In moments, the battlefield was empty, wiped clean, with only a puddle of seawater left.

The pendant in her hand went cold and still. Keely shuddered, then collapsed, but Leo caught her.

Perrin landed the ship in the center square, and Skidbladnir bobbed in the air over the paving stones.

"What happened out there?" Sam asked, jumping down to shout at Teren. "Where did that water come from?"

Leo appeared at the top of the rampart, carrying a limp Keely in his arms. He laid her down on the ground as Gael rushed to her side. "Keely used the magic from Nehalannia's pendant. She called up the water to save us."

Gael knelt over her, passing his hand over her head and chest. "She is resting. The magic has drained her. If she had continued, she would have perished."

Abigail appeared, crushing Sam in her arms, and then she held him at arm's length. "I will lecture you later. The danger isn't over yet. Surt still has his army of boercats. He could burn the city to the ground."

On cue, dark spots dotted the sky as tongues of flame began shooting out, catching rooftops on fire.

"Protection spell now!" Abigail shouted to the witches. They thrust their fists in the sky in unison. Perrin and Mavery joined in, sending up a blast of blue and green flame that flickered and joined with the others, creating a shimmering dome over the city. As the first boercat drew near, it belched out a blast of fire that bounced off the shield.

"Sam, help us," his mother commanded.

He grimaced. "I can't. Helva took my magic."

The sky darkened above them as more and more boercats flew over. There were at least fifty of them flying in formation, drawing tighter and tighter in a circle. Two broke off and flew left, two to the right. They kept veering off until they covered every inch of the sky, crisscrossing fluidly. Then they began to lay down a wall of fire.

Perrin's arm was trembling, and the other witches quickly grew tired. Some of the buildings caught fire as the shield sputtered and wavered. The witches weren't strong enough. Sam clenched his fists, wishing he could join in. People screamed and dove for cover.

They made another pass, coming so close that Sam could see the look of triumph on Surt's face. It had to be Surt. He rode the largest boercat and wielded a flaming sword. With a mighty swing, he lopped off the top of the clock tower and sent it crumbling to the ground in a crash of stone.

More buildings caught fire as smoke filled the air. Sam had never felt so helpless and frustrated.

If only he had wings.

He grabbed Perrin. "We have to call the Omeras."

Her eyes widened, and then she put her fingers to her lips and let out a piercing whistle, passing the word. The other young witches did the same.

They withstood another round of attacks that set the blacksmith shop and the apothecary on fire. The men and women of Skara Brae ran with buckets to douse the flames.

"Come on, come on," Sam whispered. The Omeras would be nearby. His mother and the witches had ridden them back from Balfour Island.

Then a familiar whisper of wings reached Sam's ears. Black Omeras landed in the square. Nine of them. His mother grabbed his arm. "No, Sam, you don't have your magic."

"I have my father's magic," he said, gripping the pouch. "I'll ride with Perrin. You and Mavery stay here and help Teren defend the city. We've got this."

The rest of the witches climbed on their Omeras, and Sam got up behind Perrin.

She urged the Omera into the air. The witches fell into formation behind them. He swung the pouch over his head as they prepared balls of witchfire. They headed straight for Surt. He was laying a blazing trail down over a row of buildings in the lower town.

"Come on, Odin, where are you?" Sam whispered, hanging on as Perrin banked the Omera.

A blast of fire knocked one of the witches out of the air. She fell, spinning through the sky, but Abigail caught her in a spell before she hit the ground.

They needed to take Surt out. Sam had an idea. It was crazy, but his ideas usually were.

"Bring me close to Surt!" he shouted in Perrin's ear.

"You're not going to do something stupid, are you?"

"Probably. Just do it."

She wheeled the Omera in the sky above Surt. Two other witches engaged him with witchfire. One of them fell, and Surt turned his attention to the other.

That's when Sam leapt off the back of his Omera, falling through the air and landing on Surt. He wrapped his arms around the fire giant's neck and held on for dear life.

Perrin and two other witches began blasting Surt's boercat with witchfire. The animal screamed and bellowed in pain as its wings folded and it plummeted to the ground. Sam held on as the beast hit face-first, digging a channel in the paving stones as it slid twenty feet before coming to a stop.

Sam had the wind knocked out of him, but the boercat had taken the brunt of the fall. A pair of meaty red hands grabbed Sam by the scruff of his neck. Surt towered over him, and then the red-skinned giant threw him off, sending him tumbling painfully across the paving stones.

Overhead, the witches continued to battle the boercats. Teren had put together some grappling hooks, and they used them to bring down the flying beasts, but there were still too many of them.

Howie was there, helping him to his feet. "We got a problem. The rest of Surt's army is back, the ones who ran. And they're mighty pissed." Outside the walls of the gates, Sam could hear the marching boots.

Surt was getting to his feet. In his hands he held his famous flaming sword. Bal.

"Surrender now, before we burn this city to the ground!"

he shouted, pounding his fist on his chest. "Or don't surrender. I'm in the mood to tear this place apart. My next stop will be Valhalla. We will take the city of the gods and rule the Nine Realms of Odin."

"Not so fast," Sam said. "I'm afraid Odin has something to say about that."

"Odin is dead," Surt said.

"Naw, he was just taking a vacation in the underworld. He's back," Sam said.

"You lie. Where?"

"Right here." Sam tapped his chest. He took the pouch holding Odin's stone and dropped the stone in his hand, clenching it tight and preparing himself for what he hoped was going to come next.

It happened so fast, it took his breath away.

A crack of lightning split the air, striking the center of the square, sending up shards of stinging granite. A glowing electrical feeling spread through Sam as he transformed into that giant bear. Brunin's mighty shield appeared in his hands. His arms stretched out, and his legs grew thick and sturdy. His eyes grew larger and rounded, and his sense of smell grew so keen he could detect Howie sweating next to him.

This was different. The first time he had been inside Brunin, Odin had been in charge. Now, the god was letting Sam be in control. It was exhilarating.

Surt staggered back.

"What is this?" he said, laughing. "Some kind of trick?"

Sam raised his head and let out a roar so loud the walls of the city shook, knocking stones loose.

Surt flinched. "Who are you?"

Sam prowled forward, pawing at the ground, turning his head to snarl.

"It cannot be," Surt whispered. Taking another step back, he shook his head. "You're dead. You're dead and gone."

Then Sam leapt, his paws outstretched, jaws open. Glistening white teeth reached for Surt's neck, knocking him into the ground. The bear tore at the red giant, but Surt rolled to his side and scrambled away, drawing his flaming sword.

He held it in front of him, sending a bolt of searing flame at Sam, aiming square at his chest. Sam held up his shield, and the flame bounced off. The shield grew hot, but he held it up until Surt ran out of energy, staggering as his sword died out.

Surt dropped his arm, but his eyes stayed fixated on the bear. Sam roared again, this time even louder And then he ran straight for Surt.

The fire-giant lord jumped on the back of his boercat, but the beast was injured and couldn't take off. And then Sam was there, sinking his massive canine teeth into Surt's thigh and pulling him back to the ground. Surt's sword clattered on the paving stones as the fire giant clutched at his leg.

Sam grasped Surt's sword in his mighty paws and raised it. A tongue of fire shot into the sky. He was prepared to bring it down into the red giant's heart when a voice rang, "Let him go, or the girl dies."

Sam froze, swinging his shaggy head around. He blinked, his vision zeroing in on the scene across the square. Bellac stepped out from behind Skidbladnir. Surt's general must have clung to the ship when they were rescued. She had an arm around Mavery's neck with a knife pressed to it.

What should he do? Odin's voice was silent, as if the god was letting him decide.

Sam slowly lowered the blade. The flame went out.

He felt the weight of the decision. If he let Surt go, more people would die. He was sure of it. But Mavery . . . he couldn't bear the thought of her being hurt.

An impossible choice. Sam felt it then, the crushing weight that Odin bore every day—trying to know the right thing to do when no choice was the right one.

Before Sam could choose, a swan launched out of the sky, coming like a missile for Bellac. The impact knocked the general off her feet and sent Mavery sprawling. In a flash of gold, Geela stood before the red giant, her golden sword drawn.

"No one harms the witchling," she said.

Bellac snarled, leaping to her feet, and she brought her sword down at Geela.

A flash of witchfire made the giant stumble and miss.

Mavery had blasted her a good one.

Perrin and the rest of the witches added their own magic, roasting the giant in a bath of green fire until there was nothing left but a pile of ash.

A sudden stabbing pain made Sam roar.

Surt had used the distraction to draw a smaller blade. It stuck out of Sam's back. With a whirl, Sam held the Sword of Bal up as flames shot out. He spun in a circle so fast that Surt didn't have time to react. The flaming sword went through his armor and into his chest so hard that the point came out the other side of his massive body.

Sam staggered back. Pain made him dizzy. His hold over Brunin slipped as he grew light-headed.

A blinding light exploded in the center of the square, shooting up into the sky. It burned brightly for a moment, and then, in a wink, it was gone. In the place of the bear, Sam lay on the ground, grasping his wounded shoulder as he sat up.

Surt was dead, but the massive onslaught of boercats continued. Sam had to help fight them. Grasping Surt's flaming sword, Sam struggled to his feet. He would burn them from the sky, ride an Omera and take them out one by one.

Before he could signal to Perrin, a horn blast sounded from overhead. All eyes turned to see a giant winged creature bearing down on them. Flames roared from its mouth as it aimed for the boercats that seemed tiny next to it. Surt's men screamed as they became engulfed in flame.

The Safyre Omera had come.

Its leathery hide glistened black as tar. Purple streaks marked its wings, and a sharpened talon protruded at the tip of each wing bone.

On its back, Sam could make out Jey and, behind him, his father, Beo. They were grinning and whooping as they guided the giant Safyre in a broad sweep, taking out as many boercats as they could. Behind them, three other Safyres each bore a rider. They were smaller, but their belches of fire were enough to send the boercats winging away in pain.

They flew overhead, sending dark shadows across the square. The boercats and their riders put up a fight, but without Surt or his generals to lead them, they soon turned and headed across the seas, racing back to their fiery island of Musspell. Teren and Galatin led the men outside the gates with rousing cheers to chase off the remaining fire giants.

Jey landed the large female Safyre in the square, and the three smaller ones followed. He had a smirk as big as a barn as he bragged to Howie and Leo about how he had tamed the fire-breathing beast.

Keely looked pale, but she brought her healing crystal over and knelt by Sam.

"You know, I've seen you do some dumb things, but jumping off the back of an Omera, that might take the cake."

"I second that," his mother said, appearing over Keely's shoulder to scan him head to toe.

Sam winced as Keely pressed the edges of his wound together, amazed at her healing power as the two sides stitched together. "Yeah, well, it worked. At least I didn't almost drown everyone." He winked at her.

She smiled. "Yeah, magic can make you do crazy things."

Geela knelt by Sam. "Sam, we cannot delay our return to the city of the gods. They await your arrival. All is not yet settled."

Sam nodded. "Geela of the Valkyrie, meet Keely and my mom, Abigail."

Geela nodded at them. "Your friends may come along. The gods will wish to thank them."

Sam looked at his mom for permission. She rolled her eyes, shaking her head. "You will be the death of me. Go ahead. I have a city to piece back together."

Before they could board Skidbladnir, the loud rumble of many horses thundering toward them made everyone stop, fearing another invasion of Surt's men. But it was Joran's army of frost giants that burst into the square, swords drawn as they pulled their horses up.

Joran searched for his wife. When he spied her, he swept down from his horse and wrapped her in his arms.

"I am sorry I am late, wife."

The queen held back and then embraced him. "You came."

"I am stubborn, but I know when I'm wrong."

"Joran, there are some people I want you to meet. Boys," she called as she waved the boys over. They were limping and battered, but defiant. "These boys were prisoners of the black dwarves. They kept them as slaves in the mines."

Rage darkened Joran's face. "The black dwarves will be dealt with."

One of Joran's men shoved forward. "Malik? Is that you?"

One of the slave boys blinked rapidly. "Papa?"

"Malik!"

The frost giant was blubbering like a baby as he swept the boy up in his arms. "I thought I had lost you forever."

Reesa introduced Joran to the other boys. She seemed to hesitate over the last one.

"Joran, this is Eithan. He can't remember who he was before he was lost. He hit his head in a fall. The dwarves found him at the bottom of a steep slope." Her voice was tense, and Joran's eyes went from the boy to her and then back to the boy.

"You don't think—"

She put a warning hand on his arm. "I think Eithan should come home with us, see if he remembers anything."

Joran shuddered and then nodded. "Yes. Being back in Galas will help him remember who he is." He put a hand on the boy's shoulder. "Welcome home, Eithan."

# Chapter 39

Geela guided Skidbladnir to Valhalla, her hands sure and confident on the wheel. They flew through puffy white clouds, emerging into blue sky and an unfamiliar range of mountains rimmed with snow. A rainbow arched high in the sky, ending in a glittering gold city built on top of a cloud.

The Bifrost bridge.

The ship settled down to glide over the rainbow surface until it reached a set of golden gates that blocked their way. A man stood in front of the gate dressed in leather leggings and a heavy golden vest. On his head he wore a helmet that came down over his face, leaving only a slit for his eyes. In his hand he held a sharp pointed lance.

Geela shouted, "Hemidall, in the name of Frigga, open the gates!"

When the guard didn't move fast enough, Geela drew her sword in a blaze of golden light. "I am Geela of the Valkyrie, and I will not be ignored. Open the gates, or face my blade!"

That got Hemidall moving. He turned and slid the lever to the side, pushing the gate slowly open.

Inside, the city lay before them at the bottom of a gentle green hill. Valhalla was a golden city. Every building was gilded with the precious metal, the spired tops glittering in the sunlight. Even the streets were paved in the golden color.

Skidbladnir floated to a stop in front of the largest edifice. They descended onto the pavement. As Mavery hopped down, Skidbladnir shimmered and groaned, and then, in a twinkle of light, it shrunk down to its pocket size, landing at Sam's feet.

He swept it into his pocket. An imposing set of double doors made of golden metal and inlaid with silver panels opened on silent hinges as Geela led them up the steps. They entered into a large circular room lined with thrones around the edge. The seats were filled with men and women of all ages and sizes.

Odin sat on the highest throne. He was laughing at something the woman on his left said. Sam recognized Frigga from the day she had threatened him with death if he didn't bring Odin back. She looked at him disapprovingly and then softened her face into a smile as she gave him a nod.

They were led into the center of the room by Geela. They stood in a line facing the gods. Howie was on the end, then Leo, Keely, Sam, Perrin, and, of course, the little imp, Mavery.

Odin clapped his hands, and the room grew silent.

"Thank you all for coming today. Things have been a little . . . chaotic recently. I suppose it's time I explain what I did."

Before he could go on, Loki walked in, followed by a tall, black-haired woman with pale skin the color of ice. There were gasps of outrage. But Sam had a bigger problem. He'd gotten one look from the ice queen, and he had lost the ability to breathe. His hand went to his throat as invisible fingers locked around it.

"I have come to punish the boy," Angerboda announced. "He killed my son Jormungand, and his meddling ruined my daughter's beauty."

"How dare you come into my home," Frigga hissed, rising.

Sam tried to drag in a breath, but he had no will over his own body.

"Give me the boy, or not even the strength of the gods will stop my wrath," Angerboda said.

"Please, Angerboda," Odin said, "It was not the boy's fault, but mine. Let me explain. And then, if you still wish revenge, I will pay the price. Just hear me out."

Angerboda hesitated. For that moment, another ten years were peeled from Sam's life before she sat down and released her grip on him. Sam gasped as breath flowed into his lungs again.

Odin spread his hands wide as he began. "A long time ago, a great wrong was done. Arrogance and pride led to tragic events. My dear son, Baldur, was lost forever when Loki found his weakness and tricked him into being pierced by the thorn of the mistletoe bush."

All eyes turned on the God of Mischief. Loki flushed, squirming in his seat. Angerboda elbowed him. Finally, he stood up. "I . . . er . . . I am . . . *ahem*," he cleared his throat before blurting out, "I'm sorry, Frigga. I was not thinking, as I am prone to doing. I thought it would be fun to see Baldur lose. I did not mean to harm him so greatly. I paid a great price for it," he added, with a pointed look at Odin.

"Yes, Loki paid the price," Odin said. "Without giving him a chance to explain himself, I chained him in a hole for a thousand years." He moved to stop in front of Loki. He hesitated and then put a hand on the mischief-maker's shoulder. "My brother. It is long past time things between us were settled. You acted rashly, and I punished you greatly. I am sorry."

Loki scowled, wiping his chin with his hand, even as tears

brightened his eyes. Finally he sniffed and nodded. "You, too, brother. I'm sorry I took your son. I have missed you."

Odin grasped him by the back of his neck and kissed his forehead before he moved on. "But for all the time that passed, I never got over the loss of Baldur, and, I feared, neither did you." He looked at Frigga. His queen wiped away a tear, nodding her head in agreement.

"When circumstances arose to provide me with an opportunity to fix matters, forgive an old goat for trying to surprise you."

Frigga lowered her handkerchief, looking perplexed. "Of what do you speak?"

"From the moment I met Sam, my last offspring, I knew I had one final chance to make things right. I brought these children here because each had a role to play. One only I could see."

The god stopped in front of Howie. "Howie, the great Protector. How many laughed at you when I gave you this title?"

Howie had the grace to shrug. "A couple dozen or so." He grinned. "Okay, maybe everyone."

"You were so full of fear when I first saw you." Odin tapped Howie on the chest. "But I knew you had great things in you. You haven't disappointed me yet. You wielded the Sword of Tyrfing bravely against those Balfin monsters, and you saved Skara Brae once again with nothing but piles of rusted armor. Well done."

Howie's face beamed with pride. "Thanks, Big O. If you ever have another mission for me, just call." Howie saluted the god.

Odin smiled and moved on to Keely. Her white hair fell to her shoulders. She looked at Odin with shining eyes.

"Young Keely. When I first saw you, your heart was locked in grief and guilt over the loss of your mother. I wanted you to be able to feel magic, to believe in the goodness of life.

You, young lady, have made me very proud. That trick with the water?" Odin bent forward and winked. "Very cool, as you kids say."

Keely smiled. "Thanks, Odin." She flung her arms around his waist and hugged the god tightly before stepping back.

Odin moved on to Leo. Leo's jaw was locked, and he avoided Odin's gaze. Odin's eyes narrowed as he studied him. "Young Leo, you still think you failed me, don't you?"

Leo gave a shrug. Pain was etched into his brow. "I was chosen as the Sacrifice. And yet I lived. I let Loki out, and then I freed Angerboda, all to save my own skin."

Odin clasped his shoulder. "My boy, your task was the hardest of them all. I trusted you alone to see it through. You were willing to give everything to save your friends, even if it meant losing your life."

Leo's face brightened. "So I didn't fail you?"

"No. In fact, I had a feeling you would run into Loki down in Sinmara's underworld, and, knowing Loki, I guessed he would trick you into releasing him. Of course, I did not realize he would use his newfound freedom to start a war."

Odin turned to give Loki a pointed glance.

The God of Mischief shrugged guilty. "Brother, you should have known me better than that. I act first, think second. But it's all behind us now; Surt is dead and gone forever. Those beastly fire giants will never threaten Orkney again."

Odin glared at him a moment longer and then relented. "Yes, the fire giants were always in the wings as a threat. Perhaps it was time they were dealt with. And having my heroes here to oversee it was provident."

Odin turned back to Leo, gripping his arm. "You have done well, Leo Pate-Wa. Your father would be proud, as you should be."

Odin smiled at a glowing Leo and then moved on to Sam. Sam was humming with a hundred different questions about why Odin had done what he had done, but he kept silent as Odin looked intently into his eyes. "And you, the last Son of Odin. When we first met, you were bursting with so much anger, I thought you might explode with it. I knew if you continued down that path, it would consume you. You were being pulled in two directions by your own bloodlines. I had to do something to make you face who you were, to decide once and for all what path you would take."

Sam blurted out, "You pushed me into killing you!"

Odin nodded gravely. "I didn't force your hand, but I certainly gave you reason to. I hoped that by doing so, you would learn from it, that it would purge that anger from you. You would either learn to forgive yourself, or forever hate yourself." A smile lightened his features as he tapped Sam on the chest. "You chose forgiveness."

But Sam wasn't ready to forgive himself so easily. "How could you know I wouldn't go to the witches' side?" he asked, his voice thick with emotion. "I was so lost."

Odin put a hand on his shoulder. "I didn't know, Samuel, but I hoped. I had faith. Though I didn't expect you to slice off my ear," he added wryly, rubbing at the gnarled scar on the side of his head. "But look where you are now." His eyes twinkled at Sam. "The best of both bloodlines. A Son of Catriona who fights for good. Besides, your wrong path gave me a chance to pay a visit to Helheim, where I hoped to find my son Baldur."

Frigga rose shakily from her throne. "You did all this just to bring back our son? You are a dear old goat for trying, but it was a fool's journey. Baldur has been gone too long. I have accepted that he is lost to us."

Odin pulled a small pouch from the folds of his robe and held it out, and then he opened it and dumped the contents onto his palm. A large thorn rested there.

"I didn't say I failed. The mistletoe thorn enabled Helva to keep him there. I stole it back." Then he blew on the thorn.

It caught fire, there was a flash of orange light, and then it disintegrated into a small pile of ash.

Behind them, through the archway, a young man appeared, dressed in battle regalia and standing tall. His rugged blond features broke into a smile at the sight of his mother.

"Baldur, is it really you?" Frigga cried, running to him and throwing her arms around him.

Odin moved on and stopped before the ice maiden. "And so, Angerboda, will you forgive me?" he said.

She rose to her feet, surveying all of them before her. Slowly she nodded her head. "It is time to put the past where it belongs. I wish to go home. To my people."

Odin's eyes flared. "You're sure?"

"I am old. Inside this body, I am dying. I need to be with my own kind to be at peace."

"But, my love, leaving so soon?" Loki quipped. The God of Mischief's lips wobbled like he wanted to cry.

Angerboda looked down at him with fond eyes. "Come with me, mischief-maker. You amuse me like no other. You will find a place at my side for as long as I have left. It could be another century or two."

Loki hesitated, then nodded, patting her hand. "Where you go, I go, my love. Besides, no one here is going to miss me."

"Where is she going?" Sam whispered to Geela.

"She is from a world of ice. Her people are the Dokkalfar, the Dark Elves. They live in an ice realm far from here."

Odin grasped Loki by the shoulder. "Be well, brother. We will meet again someday."

Loki clasped him back. "Don't die on me before I get back to kill you myself."

Then Loki stepped back and took Angerboda's hand. Odin passed his hand over them, and they both shimmered brightly and then burst into a shower of ice crystals before they vanished.

Keely tugged on Sam's arm. "What about us?" she whispered. "I really need to go home!"

"Um, Odin?" Sam asked, stepping forward. "We need a favor."

The god smiled down at him. "Anything you want; you've earned it."

"It's not for me. My friends, they want to go home."

Odin looked at the trio behind him. "Back to Midgard? Oregon, you call it?"

"Yes."

Odin nodded. "It will be done. What about you?"

Sam cast a look at Perrin and Mavery. "Oh, I think I'll stay awhile. See how things work out."

"Say your goodbyes, then."

Sam gulped, looking at Keely, Howie, and Leo. They made a small circle, putting their arms around each other's shoulders.

"I'm going to miss you guys."

"You sure you don't want to come back?" Howie said. "Eighth grade's going to be a blast."

"Hey, at least you don't have any more algebra tests," Keely added.

Tears blurred Sam's eyes. "I'm not going to say goodbye. Someday you'll be back."

Leo nodded at him and then threw his arms around Sam and hugged him tightly. "Be well, Samuel. When you look at the stars, know that we see the same sky."

"Say goodbye to the captain, and Rego, and your mom, and Speria and Heppner." Howie rambled on down the list. "Oh, and take care of Lingas for me. She loves to eat fresh squirrels." He turned to Perrin. "And give Damarius a rub behind his ears." His eyes began watering as he realized he wasn't going to see his pets anymore.

Keely pulled off Nehalannia's pendant and put it in Sam's

hands. "This belongs to the Eifalians. Give it to Gael. Tell him to give it to his queen."

The trio stood in the center of the room. Sam stood to the side, next to Perrin. Mavery leaned into him, wrapping her arms around his waist as Odin raised his staff and rammed it into the floor.

"See ya when I see ya," Howie said, and then Sam's friends were gone.

Sam looked at the spot where his friends had stood, missing them already.

"Time to go home, witch-boy," Geela said with a wink. She prepared to lead them out when Odin called out to Sam.

"I think you have something that belongs to Frey," he said.

"Of course." Sam pulled out the little wooden carving. "Frey's probably missing it."

The god pocketed it and then rested his hand on Sam's shoulder. "You didn't ask for anything in return for all your help, but I got you something."

Odin opened his palm, revealing a green emerald the size and shape of a walnut.

"What is it?" Sam asked.

"Take it and see what happens."

Sam picked up the emerald. As he gripped it in his palm, the stone turned into dust.

Odin blew on it, sending the green dust into Sam's face. For a moment, he couldn't breathe. His skin tingled as blood zinged to his fingertips. Energy bubbled up inside of him, and then everything felt alive.

"I've got my magic back," he whispered, looking at Odin with awe as he stretched out his fingers, feeling it course through his veins. "I have my magic!" He spun around and thrust out his palms, unleashing a blast of green witchfire at the ceiling and earning a glare from Frigga. "I'm a witch again." He hugged Perrin and whirled her around as Mavery squealed with joy.

Odin pointed a finger at him. "Don't forget that you are also my son. There will always be two parts of you." He left to join Frigga and Baldur, embracing the son who had been lost to him forever.

Vor came over, patting Sam on the arm. "So, Samuel, your path has been chosen, I see."

Impulsively, Sam hugged the Goddess of Wisdom. "Thank you for all your help, Vor. You have no idea how many times I've remembered your words."

She nodded gracefully. "There will always be more challenges ahead, but I'm sure you will be ready to face them."

Sam smiled confidently. "I'll be just fine."

# Chapter 40

Keely tumbled onto the ground, feeling cold stone on her face. She looked around. The scenery was familiar. They were back on top of Pilot Rock. She could see the city lights in the distance. Keely smiled, helping Howie up. "We're home."

"I wonder if Chuggies is open," Howie said, rubbing his stomach.

Keely's smile grew bigger.

A man rose from the shadows, an Umatilla.

"Father!" Leo cried, leaping to his feet and throwing himself into the arms of the man. "But how did you know we were coming?"

Chief Pate-Wa's eyes glistened with tears of joy as he gathered them all in for a hug. "Tonight, there was green lightning over the rock. We hoped it would bring good news. Come, we have a truck waiting."

They took Howie home first. Even though Leo's father had assured the large Vogelstein family the boy was okay, it was heart-wrenching to watch them hug him and hold him. Mr. Vogelstein kept patting Howie on the back while his mom squeezed him so tight his face turned red. Even his siblings were whooping with joy. Keely had a feeling they would never take their overlooked son for granted again.

Then they were outside her familiar brick house. She could see her father through the window reading the paper in the den in front of the fireplace. Her legs were stuck in place. She couldn't walk up the steps.

"Do you want me to go with you?" Leo asked, touching her arm.

She shook her head. "No. It will be okay."

Keely gave him a quick hug and walked to the porch. She could hear the TV on inside. The door was unlocked. She slipped inside, shutting the door behind her. On the table in the entry was a glass case, something she didn't recognize. She picked it up, looking at it curiously. It held a small object, shiny and white. She looked closer. It was the Moon Pearl!

Ymir had kept his promise. He had let her father know she was okay.

"Dad, I'm home," she called out.

# Epilogue

Eithan stood on a hill overlooking the city of Galas. The lost boys of Rakim all had homes. He had waited and made sure of it before he had left. The queen was a kind and caring woman. She had tried to speak to him, but he had kept his eyes averted, shying away, claiming his real name was Eithan when he knew it wasn't. The dwarves had given him that name.

The truth was that he couldn't remember anything about his past. The fall he had taken before the black dwarves had found him had wiped his memory. The only thing he knew for sure was that he didn't belong here. One look from Reesa's son, Kaleb, had told him that. The look of jealousy had burned in the young boy's eyes. If he stayed, Eithan would tear a family apart, and he couldn't do that, not when he couldn't even remember his own name.

With a heavy heart, he turned away and began walking through the forest. Next to him loped the giant wolf that had swam ashore and now hunted with him. Together they would find another home in another land, somewhere where the sun shone brightly and the wind was at their back.

*The End*

# From the Author

$\mathcal{D}$ear Reader:

I hope you enjoyed *The Raven God*! It has been an incredible journey creating the Legends Orkney™ series. I think off all the books in this series, this one was the most fun to write! My characters finally came into their own and they're ready to save Orkney from the clutches of a fearsome red giant named Surt.

As an author, I love to get feedback from my fans letting me know what you liked about the book, what you loved about the book, and even what you didn't like. You can write me at PO Box 1475, Orange, CA 92856, or e-mail me at author@alaneadams.com. Visit me on the web at www.alaneadams.com and learn about the interactive digital game app you can download on your smartphone.

I want to thank my son Alex for inspiring me to write these stories, and his faith in me that I would see them through. A big thanks to my team at SparkPress for their unfailing marketing support. Go Sparkies!

The adventures of Sam and his friends are over for now. It's time to go back to the drawing board and consider what's next for our heroes!

To Orkney! Long may her legends grow!

—Alane Adams

# About the Author

A lane Adams is an author, professor, and literacy advocate. She is the author of the Legends of Orkney fantasy mythology series for tweens and *The Coal Thief*, *The Egg Thief*, and *The Santa Thief*, picture books for early-grade readers. She lives in Southern California.

*Author photo © Melissa Coulier/Bring Media*

# SELECTED TITLES FROM SPARKPRESS

SparkPress is an independent boutique publisher delivering high-quality, entertaining, and engaging content that enhances readers' lives, with a special focus on female-driven work. Visit us at www.gosparkpress.com

*Red Sun,* by Alane Adams. $17, 978-1-940716-24-4. Drawing on Norse mythology, *The Red Sun* follows a boy's journey to uncover the truth about his past in a magical realm called Orkney—a journey during which he has to overcome the simmering anger inside of him, learn to channel his growing magical powers, and find a way to forgive the father who left him behind.

*Kalifus Rising,* by Alane Adams, $16.95, 978-1940716848. Sam Baron just freed Orkney from the ravages of the Red SunÐbut now, imprisoned by Catriona, leader of the Volgrim Witches, Sam finds the darker side of his half-god, half-witch heritage released, and he fears he might destroy what he saved. As Sam's friends rush to save him, other forces are at work in Orkney's shadowsÐforces that could help free Sam, or condemn him to the darkness forever.

*Blonde Eskimo,* by Kristen Hunt. $17, 978-1-940716-62-6. In Spirit, Alaska on the night of her seventeenth birthday, the Eskimos rite of passage, Neiva is thrown into another world full of mystical creatures, old traditions, and a masked stranger. When Eskimo traditions and legends become real as two worlds merge together, she must fight a force so ancient and evil it could destroy not only Spirit, but the rest of humanity.

*The Alienation of Courtney Hoffman,* by Brady Stefani. $17, 978-1-940716-34-3. Fifteen-year-old Courtney Hoffman is determined not to go insane like her grandfather did—right before he tried to drown her when she was seven. But now she's being visited by aliens who claim to have shared an alliance with her now-dead grandfather. Now Courtney must put her fears aside, embrace her true identity, and risk everything in order to save herself—and the world.

*The Revealed,* by Jessica Hickam. $15, 978-1-94071-600-8. Lily Atwood lives in what used to be Washington, D.C. Her father is one of the most powerful men in the world, having been a vital part of rebuilding and reuniting humanity after the war that killed over five billion people. Now he's running to be one of its leaders.

# About SparkPress

SparkPress is an independent, hybrid imprint focused on merging the best of the traditional publishing model with new and innovative strategies. We deliver high-quality, entertaining, and engaging content that enhances readers' lives. We are proud to bring to market a list of *New York Times* best-selling, award-winning, and debut authors who represent a wide array of genres, as well as our established, industry-wide reputation for creative, results-driven success in working with authors. SparkPress, a BookSparks imprint, is a division of SparkPoint Studio LLC.

Learn more at GoSparkPress.com